Anywhere
and
Everywhere

—for Ann Smith, in memoriam

Anywhere
and
Everywhere

SJ

ISBN: 978-1-943661-59-6

Sij Books
booksbysij@gmail.com

Printed in the USA

Reece's screams unlocked Sara Myers from the ten o'clock news. Looked to be the same old thing. Some rat-hole daycare closed on account of whores. Then a Colley boy killed in Vietnam. She knew some Colleys from back at the homeplace. A lance corporal, the newsman said he was. Died outright is what he said. Flat out killed somewhere in South Vietnam. That poor Colley boy was sucking dirt, and maybe her husband Jim would be next, flopping like a fish, yellow people going through his pockets. Maybe get his head cut off, likely as not. A blanket of goosebumps swallowed her arms, her stomach.

The tornado watch was still in effect. She'd felt some thunder earlier, had thought maybe it was the washing machine, then remembered it was broken. Reece was crying again, taking on like he was being killed. She tossed the dishrag she'd been gripping into the sink and went to check on him, spitting image of nobody she knew. "Kinda looks like you, Sara," her mama had said, holding a pink mirror, pulling stiff black hairs off her upper lip with her fingers.

*

Darkness? Maybe ask the postman. Darkness? Dahlia wants to know. The music runs right by her. Might as well be shit in a sewer pipe. She has one thing, is one thing. That one thing is time, and since that is what she is, that is what she is. There is no darkness, no light. No hamsters, nothing falls, no lettuce, nothing rises. There is no silence, no history. Darkness? Darkness. She wants to say that time is a snowball getting bigger and bigger, but there's no space for it to get bigger in, and there is no Dahlia to say it, and there is no snow. Just the blue light of Dogtown and the infernal Pinch. Nothing but time, lots of it, and not from the beginning, but before, after, and all around it.

*

Scrawny Reece, standing bandy-legged in the crib, wailed his heart out. Sara slowed in front of the TV, a commercial for shampoo, real thick and green and gooey.

In his rickety white crib, too big for it really, Reece clenched his twenty teeth and seethed a wail between the gaps, jetting spit, balling his tater-tot fists to his head. Something was on it, in it. He was only two but had known that face, knew that face like he knew any other face. A pleasant shape is what he knew. Her music, though, every time, set him off, made his eyes screw up, and then he'd pee his diaper, sometimes clean through to his pajama bottom. Now she'd done something to him, hurt him for real. He screamed, felt his screams stuck in his hair, pushed at it with his tater-tot fists, fell back on his bottom, screamed louder, red as a fire truck.

Sara hurried down the short hall, still wearing her tight white assistant dress. She was in training. "Hold up! Hold up!" She shook her head sympathetic, picked him up, and held him out at arm's length, his face a knot of red, salt, and wet. She pulled him close and fell into her baby-don't-cry dance. "Shh, shh, shh, shh." The phone jangled.

/a poodle/red birthday cake/
/a poodle/red birthday cake/
/a poodle/red birthday cake/

"Yeah, the little fucker's down now. I got to love him, though, better than what I ever got. But, hell yeah, if you've got some. I'll just say, hell yeah, come on over and let's fuck like dogs." She popped gum, grinning into the black phone. She was gonna fuck a doctor and smoke his weed.

*

Imagine nothing getting bigger and bigger and bigger.

*

First comes love, then comes marriage, here comes baby in the baby carriage!

Not necessarily in that order, though, or using those words, or those letters.

*

Horton hears a Who hears a Who hears a Who hears a Who hears what? And while hearing Who's the Who hears it is being heard. [ditto]

Not necessarily in that order, though.

*

a all and and and anointest art before beside comfort cup days death down dwell enemies ever evil fear follow for for for goodness green He he He he head his house I I I I in in in in is leadeth leadeth lie life Lord Lord maketh me me me me me me mercy mine my my my my my name's no not of of of of of of oil over pastures paths preparest presence restoreth righteousness rod runneth sake shadow shall shall shepherd soul staff still Surely table The the the the the the the the the they thou Thou thou though through thy thy to valley walk want waters will will with with Yea [ditto]

*

Private Jim Myers, a beanpole of a soldier, slouched on a

cot inside a tent. He was eating an American candy bar, probably a Payday, and drinking a can of American beer, probably Carling Black Label. He twiddled his wedding band. He'd had his boots on for ten days straight, and the thought of standing on his naked yellow feet with worm eggs between his toes made him sick. The long hairs on his big toes hurt. He smelled diesel. He heard goddamn folk music. Somebody called his name from outside, and he took another drink of beer, probably Carling Black Label, and hocked a big one.

*

Little Reece lay still. The light from the end of the hall threw a yellow trapezoid into the far corner of his room. He lay very still. He knew it was two in the morning. His mother said the devil came at two in the morning. That he should always be sure to be asleep by then. At first, only footsteps, small wooden shoes clopping down that long dark tunnel. One, two, three, four, never getting closer, the tunnel zooming longer and longer. The information careening from his brain gradually focused on Dahlia. He was five, and it was two in the morning, and he lay very still on his stomach, with the sheet over his head clutched to his ears, with a trapezoid of light in the far corner of the room. She stood there, Dahlia, feeding on him. He felt her. Reece's eyes shut tight, lines and swirls of light, tiny silent explosions.

*

Kristin and her daughter Mia pulled into the driveway of 47 Asterion Lane. Kristin's husband, Reece, had seen the house once and, pressing the gas, declared it too cute, too small. He knew Dahlia would be nearby, but it was something like a game now. Back for a closer look, and without Reece, Kristin and Mia walked around the house several times. A decent back yard that abutted a fenced pasture. The sun would set just there, Kristin noted, pointing over a storage shed in a neighbor's yard.

Within a week of moving in, boxes lined hallways, frantic hunts ensued for colanders, blank checks, salt, Mia's nightlight. The internet connection, Reece needed PDQ. And, of course, the doorbell rang and kept ringing.

Mia ran and tugged on the handle.

"Always let me open the door, honey," said Kristin. Atma, the poodle, Mia's birthday present, barked, scratching her thick, clear nails on the hardwood. "Well, hello, little girl. Mia, look."

The little girl on the small uncovered cement porch stood with hands on hips, head cocked sideways, her clean blondy hair shimmery bouncing. "You guys moved in yet?" and she walked in, crowding Kristin. Mia, with eyes wide and happy at the prospect of a new friend, backed up slowly.

"Hello," said Kristin, laughing, "And who are you?"

"Charlotte. I live on your street. What's your name?" She squatted, and Atma retreated, barking.

"I'm Kristin, and this is Mia. Mia, say hi."

Mia pushed into the back of Kristin's thigh, staring.

"Mia, say hello. This little girl is Charlotte. She must live on our street."

Charlotte moved past them into the large front room. "Wanna play hide and seek?"

Mia wanted to, and off they frolicked among the boxes, zipping upstairs and down, Charlotte finding Mia every time, Mia never finding Charlotte. And it ended in tears, Charlotte hiding under the kitchen sink with a box of vanilla wafers, Mia's box of vanilla wafers. But then it was good again, and outside they ran back and forth, picking dandelions, shouting to look at the airplane, to look at the snail. Kristin darted glances out the windows, trying to unpack and keep up with them, going from front to back, finally giving up and settling on the low deck with a cup of warm coffee, thinking how like Betsy this little girl Charlotte was, that Betsy Nichols who seemed so grownup, who had bedeviled Mia until Reece broke it off, an "encounter" with her one day in the garage. Was it really Betsy who tried to kill the goldfish?

*

As he grew, Reece resisted the idea of being watched, of being observed. He suspected his mother was behind the whole thing, that she blamed him for his father's absence and allowed Dahlia access as punishment. Reece had always been afraid of the dark and grew to fear twilight and then the promise of twilight. The footsteps...Dahlia came each night, bringing that same charge to his spine, his history scattering like light to all parts and beyond. And he resisted, cringing on his stomach, hearing that tune he taught himself, not so much to fight Dahlia but to disappear.

*

It was a matter of time, Reece knew, and when he came home from the university and there was Charlotte, he knew who she was. He pretended to ignore her but listened intently to what she said and stayed close, following her and Mia onto the deck, watching them cavort on the trampoline left by the previous owners. And that had been a relief, knowing the madness of putting one together by himself, stretching the impossible springs to meet the round frame. Charlotte was strong, singular, and he watched her, knowing his first duty. The visit ended without event, the Earth turning outward toward darkness.

"Daddy, Charlotte told me she has five boyfriends," said Mia in pajamas, getting ready for bed.

Reece held her in his lap, reading *Sammy the Seal,* the impossible seal that leaves his cage and crosses streets and learns to spell. "She told you that? She's too old, don't you think, to play with?" He turned the page.

"She's ten." Mia ran her finger across Sammy's face.

"Ten?" How could she be ten? She should only be seven. "Is she in fifth grade? Did she say that?" Reece heard the front door open and close.

"Uh huh. Is that mommy?"

"Hello!" Kristin called from downstairs.

"Mommy!" and Reece loosed little Mia, reaching out quickly to tuck in the tag on her collar. Atma, the eager little scamp, jumped into his lap, and Reece wondered what they would call the next one, but he already knew.

Reece put on his headphones and logged into the private communication server. There were three others in the live chat room. Jack's avatar was green. Reece double-clicked in with a *bloop.* Jack continued to tell the story of how Dahlia had poisoned his son Nate's hamster, most likely rehashing it for Caroline's benefit.

"I went downstairs and asked that little bitch what she had put in the cage. I held this brown wafer thing, and she looked at it and lied as usual." A pause. "I sent her home, of course."

"Well, mine showed up today right on schedule," said Reece.

"You're kidding. How long did it take her?" asked Pauline. Her nemesis was a little girl named Claire.

"It only took her about a week to show up. Same old thing. Mia's fascinated with this one, too. Endless." Reece could hear Mia singing in the bathtub upstairs.

Caroline remained quiet. Jack had discovered Caroline and her daughter, Mickey, and had overheard her discussing co-sleeping in the waiting room at the pediatrician's office. He'd noticed the rings her daughter held and the way she looked into things, how she repeated the bar of a simple melody, lost in a world of her own. Caroline was the newest member of the group, a few weeks into it and getting over the initial outbursts and rage. Reece knew that sensation of empty disinterest following the fascination and horror, but at least he'd been prepared.

"Double up her Cheerios," said Pauline. An old joke, and no one laughed.

"Mia has a much better chance than I did," said Reece, holding down his press-to-talk button. He heard the pattern of the bubbles emerging from his diet soda and worked it out into the image of a leaf.

*

The footsteps were nothing more than the beating of his heart, but still, it terrified little Reece. His mind fled in the opposite direction, moving silently through the dark Cylinder pinched in the middle at a great speed that never increased the distance of his flight. And now she was here, in his room, standing at the foot of his bed, cloaked in a black something, gazing steadily like an eyeless Aphrodite. He felt the penetration of those empty sockets, searching his empty places, as if they were lost yet sure of their final destination. Only she could see his skull glowing, pulsing. In the next room, his mother snored. His eyes squeezed tight, what seemed to be hair, a redness.

*

Just as the pasta settled into the pot, the doorbell rang. Reece closed his eyes and listened for the frantic feet of Mia to come bursting down the stairs, and they did. The bells on the door jingled as Mia struggled to open it. Murmuring of little girls.

"Daddy, can Charlotte eat with us?" asked Mia, hands on hips.

Charlotte pushed past Mia into the kitchen and grabbed the refrigerator door.

"Charlotte, you need to ask first," said Reece. He clanged a pot into the sink. "What is it you want?"

"We're gonna have a picnic," said Charlotte. Her arms drooped by her side.

"A picnic?" asked Mia. "Yay, a picnic!"

And Charlotte opened the refrigerator. "We need lots of juice," she said. "And a radio. We'll eat on the trampoline and bring Atma with us."

"Mia," said Reece, "we eat dinner in fifteen minutes. No picnics. Charlotte, I'll pour you a glass of juice." Reece looked Charlotte in the eyes, saw two cold suns, and pulled the plastic bottle from her hands.

Charlotte stepped back. Her face was nearly perfect, just a little flat. Her skin unblemished. "Can I have dinner?

My grandparents said it was just fine."

The last thing Reece wanted was to share a meal with Charlotte, but there was Mia, and it was good to have Charlotte in his sights. He heard the sedan in the driveway, the door opening. Kristin came through the front.

"Mommy! Mia's going to eat dinner with us."

"I guess that's okay. Reece, is that okay, honey?" Kristin knelt and hugged Mia, and Charlotte squeezed in for a hug as well.

"Only if you call your grandparents and ask them," said Reece, holding a wooden spoon like a knife.

*

Following a career in nursing, Reece taught philosophy, a fortunate outcome considering his unfortunate circumstances. His parents had never known, had suspected nothing. The music of church, twice on Sunday and at least once during the week, had initially dulled his gifts but then sharpened his awareness that something was incomplete.

After dropping Mia at school, a gray, quiet morning without wind, he drove to campus, still new to him after these few weeks. Each move became more difficult, the coming hardships firm realities. He parked and, after an hour in his office checking email, checking to see if Cynthia Spurlock had dropped his Intro to Schopenhauer, and perusing various news headlines, he gathered his notes and walked to class.

On entering, the din petered out, punctuated by the squeak of a chair, the fall of a pen. He no longer felt obligated to break the tension of his arrival, just a gaze about the room as he erased stray comments on the board and walked the wooden lectern to the side of the room. A glance out the window onto a vast parking lot below. *Who knew, who knew?*

With Reece giving an afternoon lecture, Kristin left the admissions office, picked up Mia, and listened as she carefully recounted the day.

"On the playground, Charlotte told me I wasn't her friend." In her booster seat, Mia snuffled, her eyes losing tears. "She was playing with boys, and they made fun of me."

"Why would she say that?" Kristin was accustomed to Mia's dramas, the perils of playing with older kids.

"I don't think she hears the music." Mia folded her hands in her lap. The seat belt slanted across her neck so that she had to lean sideways.

Kristin paused. "Tell me what you mean, honey. The music she can't hear." Reece always pretended to understand, and it seemed like a game between him and Mia.

"She listens inside me, but she can't hear the music," said Mia. "She wants to, but she can't. Can she come over to play?" Mia listened to the whir of the wheels on the road, noted when the wheels passed over stripes of paint, a piece of gravel. She hummed.

"And you can hear the music? What is that you're humming?" She thought about Reece emailing her for personal info on a student of his.

Mia wanted to tell her, but the words wouldn't come. She wanted to say that the music wasn't always pretty, that to hear the music, you have to hear everything, but to know when to leave something out. "Just something I learned." She heard liquid circulating around the engine, belts running across pulleys, hot air forced through a pipe, the wind, and when she forced it to stop, an image of glass.

Reece wrote a word on the eraser board in orange. He snapped on the cap and turned toward the class of seventeen juniors and seniors. "So, what is it?"

The usual silence ensued, but he sensed pockets of energy developing, answers bubbling to lips. Cynthia Spurlock had not dropped the class, and a steady bass line drummed from her, always within an octave of the general melody, so close that any harmony was lost. She was an architecture major. He pointed again at the word on the board.

Someone said, "Music."

Reece lifted his eyebrows, pursed his lips, and tilted his head. "Yes. And what would that have to do with our assigned reading?"

Cynthia raised her hand. "The most powerful of the arts."

"Of all the arts?" asked Reece, scattering his look about the room.

Someone mumbled a yeah. Someone cleared a throat. Cynthia stared at Reece. Her bass line squelched.

"What does that mean for the other arts, according to Schopenhauer? Are they less important?" Reece searched the room.

Cynthia made brackets with her fingers. "Music." She dropped her hands. "Attains its ends entirely from its own resources." An exact quote from Volume II, which was not yet assigned. A banal consonance ran from Cynthia, sounding like bored fingers tapping a jingle for spearmint paste. A multiplicity of chords filled the room, exclusively in major keys.

Reece assumed Cynthia heard nothing but her own voice. "That's correct. And if music attains its own ends entirely from itself, what does that say about us?" The question always made his heart pick up.

A voice other than Cynthia. "Do you mean that music doesn't need us? I mean, that's what I'm thinking." The stream from this young woman worked into a noticeable rhythm, something fuzzy and numbing like a video game MIDI. Cynthia looked uncomfortable, puzzled.

"That's an excellent question. You're playing directly into what we've been discussing this past week." He imagined Mia and was glad she knew these things.

*

Little Reece surpassed the bed-wetting and lingered beyond and deeper into all things possible. He was able to discern both ends of the Cylinder and see himself flashing instantly from one end to the other, looping but without the barrier of a complete circuit. Indeed, the Cylinder was merely a figment of time, aided in symmetry by the illusion of a particular path. A soft refrain echoing, piercing, at what he came to know as supra-light speed, everything else a vacuum of silence, and when he passed through, even faster. But Dahlia was stubborn, spoke less in rhyme over the ages, and now talked openly of rhythm, although like a child, which was a two-edged sword.

*

The online group met Sunday mornings as well. Reece logged in and slipped on his headphones. Mia called them his talking ears. Only Caroline had arrived.

"Caroline?"

"Here," she said. "Just killing time. Mickey's belly's full, so she's good for an hour or so." Her husband would be over at noon to visit for four hours. The strain of what she now knew to be an abduction had been too much. Neither she nor her husband had had a clue. They were anomalies, what the group called a spontaneous node. But abductions happened even to those who should know better, the established lines. Reece knew that all too well.

"How's it going?" asked Reece. He knew Mickey was too young to have friends over, but the girl next door, Traci, as she called herself, took every opportunity to drop by.

"Traci brought over a CD yesterday for Mickey." Caroline sounded resigned but angry. "I threw it away. Clever, huh? Why would she give Mickey a CD, you think? It was kid music."

"Well, she knows about her gifts for sure." Since Caroline wasn't gifted, he couldn't ask her about the music from this Dahlia.

"Why isn't Mickey afraid of her? I mean, I'm not afraid of her for some reason, although I hate the sight of her, but it seems like Mickey should be." She sat in a hard, white wooden chair at a kitchenette table. Mickey's head leaned left in the swing as she slept, a yellow bubble of snot expanding and contracting in her nose. She jerked, and her eyes quivered.

"Mickey's not afraid, but this Dahlia's afraid of her," said Reece. "Not terrified, but afraid of what Mickey knows, what Mickey can do. What Dahlia can't."

"And so what is it exactly that Dahlia can't do? I have a

headache all the time thinking about it." Caroline sat with elbows on the table, her forehead in her hands.

"She can't fully understand is the fundamental issue. There's too much we still don't know." Reece felt the complexities swirl in his head. "The new nodes always throw her. There's no history, like a snake forming from thin air, is how I imagine it. Or in a more practical sense, like a finite line of her jailers getting longer and longer." He got Dahlia's inability to understand. He felt he orbited the primary dilemma, but could only imagine the boundless mysteries. A chord from Caroline in A major flashed across the connection.

"God, and my little Mickey swinging here in the kitchen has been there, those, those other places." She covered her face. She knew Mickey was there, in those other places, and in the kiddie swing at the same time, but could not bring herself to say it.

"The Cylinder, there and here at the same time. The only clue being the music." Reece felt bad that Caroline couldn't hear the music, but it strengthened her illusion that Mickey was always there. The shifts lasted only nanoseconds. Occasionally, if he could stand it, he focused on his own transitions, which he slowed in his mind, the blunt staccato of the music like the noise of pins being withdrawn from an endless array of cheese, stone, velvet, oranges.

"Damn." Caroline resisted the urge to lay her head on the table.

Reece laughed, knowing he wasn't being helpful. Dahlia had gotten him, but she would never get Mia. Caroline would never have the luxury of truly understanding. "I'm sorry," he said.

"Well, don't be sorry," said Caroline. And Jack popped into the chat room, followed by Pauline.

*

To facilitate Reece's initiation, Dahlia considered the moon and the sun, the clouds, lightning, and so on. This was an old line with many nodes, uncomplicated, a fractal instant gripped in the dizziness of a variety of spells, which Dahlia understood very well. She walked into the small trailer and simply hid under the narrow crib jammed against the wall. Reece's mom, Sara, had found Cory a "funny little girl, real pretty, a real handful. Always welcome anytime, just tell your grandma," she'd say. Sara had put Reece down at seven. He awoke at eight, crying like he was being barbecued. She propped a bottle for him, and by nine, Cory, this Dahlia, emerged, not really taking care to be quiet with the TV blaring up front.

Dahlia slipped an impossibly thin mask over little Reece's sweaty head, a detailed wiring diagram embedded into the nearly invisible fabric. When he began to splutter, she placed the soft magnets quickly over his temples, and they gripped one another tightly through the matter of his skull. The lines in the mask pulsed, casting shadows and light on the walls. The toddler Reece, his gifts now mapped, lapsed into a dream. The mask sank into the flesh. No sound but the notion of foam.

*

Kristin glanced at Cynthia Spurlock's transcripts, the letters of recommendation from the principal and debate team coach, date of birth, parents' names, and so on. Kristin had nixed Reece's request to copy the records.

"So what does this mean to you?" asked Kristin. "I could get fired, you know." On Tuesdays, she and Reece came home for lunch, a bowl of soup, a sandwich, sometimes leftovers.

"Well, to make it easy, it makes me better able to teach her. She's just one of those students who disturbs the general rhythm of the class. It's hard to put a finger on." Kristin had no idea about Reece's mapping or the nature of his or Mia's gifts. During a vacation to Florida, she had asked about the ghostlike tracing on his head after swimming in the ocean. He had joked that he'd been abducted as a child and his mind mapped by aliens. She had laughed and then gotten sand in her eye. So many divorced if it was handled openly.

"I can't do these favors every day, you know," said Kristin.

A slice of sun caught the side of her face through the window, causing her ear to glow red. Reece reached over and touched her cheek, overcome by a deep rhythm, a chord that resonated with love and grief. "I would never hurt you," he said, and to him, his voice seemed off by an octave. A tear welled in the corner of his eye.

"Honey, are you sad about something?" Kristin reached for his hand next to her face and squeezed.

Reece collected himself, drew in a deep breath, and blew it out. He noted the grain in the table, how it wavered, the symmetry trapped within.

Mia lay still, the padding in the Cylinder steady and loud. Plasmas of red against the black, piercing blue light, and she turned toward the sound. She burst from her bed, a deep whine like death.

"Mia!" Kristin froze. The plea of Mia paralyzed her. Reece leaped up.

Into the hallway, Mia ran hard into the bathroom door. "Oh my God, Oh my God, Oh my God, Oh my God," she said.

Reece caught her and held her close as she struggled, eyes open and searching. "Mia, Mia, it's okay, it's okay." His heart pounded slow and hard. He felt cold.

"Stop it," she mewled. "She!" and she buried her head into Reece as he stood and moved her away from the stairs.

"Mia baby, it's Mommy, it's Mommy." Kristin brushed back Mia's hair, her hands trembling, the veins bluer at night.

"Mia's eyes grew wide," said Mia. "They seemed larger than normal." And Mia screamed and pounded Reece's chest.

"Let's get her in the bathroom," said Kristin, breathless. She took Mia from Reece, cradled her upright from behind, and doll-walked her. "Let's go potty, baby, okay? Here we go, here we go, going potty."

"Uh huh," said Mia, trembling, jerking. She squatted to the hall floor, and Kristin told her not yet, not yet. "I told you so. I fucking told you so," said Mia through her teeth, one newly missing.

Reece felt helpless, furious. "It's okay, Mia. I'm here with Mommy. Go potty." And he seemed to be talking to the walls as Mia lapsed into concentration, mulling something critical, something that should be said carefully and clearly. Mia wept and gazed around the bathroom, overflowing with sorrow.

"Good girl," said Kristin. She helped Mia to stand. "Let's put her in bed with us." And it was understood and necessary because she was their little girl, and she would wake up the next morning and ask, "Mommy, why am I in your bed? Where's Daddy?"

"Mother, why am I in your bed?" Mia stretched the length of her small body. Her face vanished beneath the covers. She twiddled the tips of her fingers, brushing them against the headboard. "Where's Father?"

The alarm sounded, a grating like a hacksaw sawing through aluminum, and Kristin silenced the racket. "You don't remember? Father?"

"Did I sleepwalk again?"

"Yes, you did."

"Where's Father? In my bed? He likes my bed."

Awake in Mia's bedroom, Reece lay on a diagonal to give his feet room. He stared at the glow-in-the-dark stars on the ceiling, the palest green in daylight.

Kristin sat up and stroked Mia's sleep-tangled hair. "I'm sure he likes your bed. School day, so let's get going. Few more minutes, okay? Don't go back to sleep." Kristin opened the curtain, opened the closet door, and screeched hangers back and forth, looking for the blue dress. She wondered if they should film the episodes, maybe take Mia to a counselor. Reece was against it, wouldn't consider it.

Reece walked into the bedroom and stared at the bed. He stared at Mia on the bed.

"Honey, what's wrong?" asked Kristin. She had pulled out her green dress by mistake.

His face was pale. His underwear sagged. The house was chilly. It was early morning. Time to get ready for school and work. He looked around the room, into the corners.

"Mia?" asked Reece, his arms folded across his hairy stomach.

Mia made funny eyes. "Father?" she said, pinching her lips, kicking at the covers.

Her music was tinny, looping, scratchy like a recording. A see-through centipede skittled across the white wall above the headboard. Reece closed his eyes.

"Reece! No!" Kristin screamed. But there was nothing she could do.

/tick\tock/

In room seven of the secure medical unit, Reece Myers lay propped on his side. A blue pad spanned the mattress. After only a week, a persistent heat and redness had developed over his hips and tailbone. A pillow separated his knees. A thin, pliable feeding tube curled from his nose, taped there. His chin bent toward his chest, and his spine curved, craving a fetal position. The room smelled of sweet benzoin. An open can of strawberry Ensure and a plastic emesis tray sat on the overbed table. It was neither dim nor bright, shadows clinging to his still body, the railed bed, and a mini bureau bolted to the floor. An egg-shaped security camera in the far right corner of the room, near the ceiling, trained its eye on the bed.

Inside the nursing station, walled with steel doors and wire-laced, bulletproof glass, the monitor tech Claire, a plain woman with straight black hair, scanned a bank of twelve video screens, each room occupied. The station smelled of manila folders and Pine-Sol. Claire flipped to room seven's observation sheet and checked off "sleeping," "in bed," and "four-point restraints intact." She did this every fifteen minutes for each of the occupied rooms.

The two 7a-to-7p guards, Shark and Gumbo, wearing neat gray uniforms and equipped with pistol-gripped batons, paced the halls, changing places at either end of the U every thirty minutes. Shark was tall and fat around the middle with narrow shoulders. Shaped like a chalkboard eraser, Gumbo looked his fifty years and more. They had a habit of looking away from one another and muttering as they passed. "Fuck your mother"—"I already did." Their service guns, handsome Smith & Wesson 5946 9-millimeters, were kept under lock and key inside the nursing station with fifteen-round clips stored in a separate safe. "Sit on your sister's face"—"Bend over and shit in your mouth."

Claire watched Debbie wash her hands, emerge from room five, and enter seven. Debbie was five-eight with short blonde hair, wearing blue scrubs stamped with the Organon logo, the symbol for infinity, an 8 lying on its side. Suddenly, Reece squealed on exhalation and straightened, rocking the bed. Arching backward, his fingers curled under with arms stiff. The bed trembled with his shaking. Hellacious moans tore from his throat. In the nursing station, Claire leaned forward, watching Debbie as she adjusted the bite stick in Reece's mouth and turned on the paper recorder for the EEG connected to his head. The spasms regulated into rhythmic tremors as if a current was swelling and dissipating through his body. His face shone oily, a gauntness of agony.

"Mr. Myers, you're seizing," said Debbie. There was really nothing else to say. She made sure the restraints around his wrists, padded with lambskin, were not too tight. Beneath his eyelids, she could see his eyes darting, like he was watching a handful of ball bearings scatter.

"Debbie? Want me to notify Dr. Markush?" asked Claire over the room speaker.

"No need." She adjusted the folded white towel beside his mouth. The clozapine caused excessive drooling, wet pillow syndrome. The seizure passed with a series of jerky spasms in his arms and feet. His eyes stilled, rolling downward. Debbie checked his blood pressure and temperature, counted his respirations—within normal limits—heart rate slightly elevated at ninety-six beats per minute. She charted her observations, washed her hands, and moved to room five to check on Peters, a barrel-chested failed-suicide, a schizophrenic who hallucinated demons and dragons around the clock. Peters lay with eyes half open, tongue squirming.

An hour later, Debbie lubed a feeding tube. "Mr. Myers, you pulled out your tube, and I'm putting another one in." She snaked it into his left nostril past his deviated septum. Reece gagged and made primitive swallowing motions with his jaw, like a goldfish gasping for air. Debbie took a 60-cc syringe and, while listening with a stethoscope, injected air into the tube. She heard the confirming dull tinkling echo in his stomach and taped the tube to his nose and then his forehead.

Claire buzzed Debbie into the nursing station. The magnetic lock clicked behind her. Debbie had been recruited, as had the other Organon nurses, six in all. She made as much as doctors on the outside.

Debbie put her hands to her lower back and stretched, pushing out her ample breasts. Like the other patients, Reece Myers was one of "them." He'd been marked and subsumed as a child, the mesh beneath his scalp. Reece was traveling, perhaps to another universe. "Did you bring lunch?"

"Yeah," said Claire. "Peanut butter and honey on a wheat bagel."

"Oh, baby," said Debbie.

"You still skipping lunch?"

"Well, sort of. I have a granola bar. Crunchy." Just thinking about it made her hungry. She looked at the monitors and saw Jim in room three, giving the patient a bed bath.

"So, do you think Myers is really traveling?" asked Claire. "He seizes most of the day."

Debbie grabbed a chart and sat in a swivel chair. She looked at the recent orders. "Most likely. Who really knows? Dr. Markush is convinced that he killed his daughter for a good reason."

"Freaky," said Claire. She loved working on base at Fort Knox but wished that she had more contact with the soldiers. Organon was a lonely place at times. She looked at the analog clock, 14:30. She'd joined a church in nearby Muldraugh, but everyone was married.

The door buzzer buzzed. Debbie looked at the monitor. It was Markush. She hit the door release and went to the secure nursing station door and waited. She opened the door. "Hey, Doc."

"Yo, hey yourself," said Markush. "Anything ripe on the vine?"

Debbie raised her eyebrows. Markush was quite the character, with his long, gray hair and peculiar sense of humor.

"Myers is still seizing."

Markush gazed at the bank of monitors. He shook his head. It was like working on a neurological ICU, but the brains were alive and well, communicating with other dimensions of reality. He grabbed a rolling chair and sat at the long desk that ran the length of the room. "The EEG?" Debbie laid it on the long desk, and he looked it over. Epileptiform seizures with polyspikes, attempts to break through. "He's struggling to cross over, it seems. I hope he's successful."

"If you say so," said Debbie. She took another chart and entered vital signs.

Claire focused on the monitors. Markush intimidated her. He smelled like menthol. He was uber-smart and just a little bit crazy. She wondered if he was one of *them,* the fox minding the hen house.

Markush flipped through a few charts, took a pair of smooth ceramic magnets shaped to the inside of a hand, and went onto the unit. He nodded at Gumbo. Gumbo raised his eyebrows. He looked like he was thinking about a big glass of Old Grand-Dad on ice. Markush entered Reece's room.

Reece was trembling. He looked like a science experiment with the twenty-one electrodes on his shaved head. Markush looked at the EEG, which was now normal—slow alpha waves, deep sleep. Markush knew Reece must be exhausted from seizing.

Markush held a magnet in each hand. He placed one on each side of Reece's skull, just above his ears. There was a spike and interruption of the alpha waves. "Come on." He wanted to see gamma waves, eighty to one hundred per minute, which indicated conscious perception, that he was alive and well somewhere else. Nothing happened. He stood there, as if he were holding a cell phone to his ear after the call had ended. He leaned a bit farther over the bed, feeling a twinge in his lower back. Polyspikes, fifty per minute, chaos. He drew back the magnets, and the EEG nearly went flat. He tried one more time. Gamma waves. *Yes!* Reece's heart rate jumped from 82 to 130, and his blood pressure dropped 20 points diastolic. There was no seizing but rather a relaxing. He could see it in Reece's face. Where was he? What was he doing? Maybe Reece would talk when he emerged from his fugue state, but usually he just moaned and raved. Markush withdrew the magnets, and the gamma waves continued.

Nothing. Reece had nothing. He walked from one green-starred buster café to the next, asking about a little girl named Mia. She looked like him, he said. She was a ginger, seven years old. His skin was dry and hot. The high altitude kept him from sweating. He'd developed a chronic cough, a tickling in his throat. Was he the only visitor in Gadam? Everyone knew his status as an outsider. He was tall at six feet and strangely white compared to the creamy brown locals.

Every other identical steel building seemed to be a buster café. It was midnight, but the light was intense, the sun the size of a dime. It was always daylight in Gadam. He walked through the mist door into the dim room, empty save a couple of playing checkers in the far corner. There was a bulletin board, and he perused the various thought postings. It was the usual mix of ads for data fur mining. Where was Mia?

He ran his hand through his thinning mahogany hair. At the bar, he ordered buster. He had no money, no credit, but it didn't matter since everything was free, except for information and sex. He watched the brown, milky bartender. She looked like everyone else with a few minor distinctions. Her hair was in a bun. A button nose, ears high on the side of her head, dark green eyes. A fog of information enveloped her and assaulted his senses. When she moved, a smoke trail of data lingered.

The bartender, Shia, put the cup of buster on the tin-plated counter. "Anything else?"

Reece wasn't sure what he was supposed to say next and just smiled. He lifted his drink and took a sip. The buster slid down easily, and he felt healthy. Tasted like cardamom, with the texture of pulpy orange juice, the same as everywhere else, unless flavored. Chocolate. Mint. Hotdog. He remembered a drug store. The timid cashier had always said, "Be well," at the end of each transaction. He felt well, physically, especially after buster.

He waited for Shia to check on the couple in the corner before asking any questions. Shia returned. Briefly, Reece imagined her as a crocodile, and she turned into a crocodile, eighteen feet in length, crowding the space behind the bar. He bit his tongue. *Jesus,* he had to concentrate. He could only think of yellow daisies, and yellow daisies appeared.

"Nice," said Shia. She'd never seen yellow daisies. "Where are you from?" She already knew, but she was a bartender after all.

"Birmingham...Alabama," he said. "But, I was living somewhere else..."

"On the dark side?"

"It was half dark and half light, a cycle. The earth rotated once per day..."

"That's crazy," said Shia. "So, what brings you to Gadam, although she knew."

"My daughter Mia is here, somewhere. I have to find her and bring her home."

"Daughter?" No one had children anymore. That was legend.

"I'm her father."

"Father?"

Reece pinched his thigh. What was the point? "She's seven, looks like me."

Shia imagined a girl of seven who looked like this guy. She shook her head no. "Not in the data fur."

"Yeah, data fur." He had no idea what she was talking about, that data was stored on the dark side of the planet, that it covered the ground like fur, miles deep. Occasionally, fires were lit to "challenge" reality and "disrupt" the routine. Losing one's data was a nightmare.

"How's the buster?"

He remembered that she had put her finger in it. "Um, really good," and it was, very nourishing. Vaguely, he understood that his time in Gadam was compromised, that it could end at any moment. He wasn't sure how or why, but he needed to hurry regardless.

"What year is it?" he said.

"Say what?" asked Shia. She was shining the buster nozzles with a lint-free rag.

"Never mind," said Reece. Did it matter? Mia was here, and he had to find her. Only then could he return.

"Good night, dick face," said Shia.

Reece paused at the mist door. The sun outside was bright, just a dime, never-ending. He didn't feel tired. He turned back. "Good night."

He stepped onto the wide, smooth lane. There were no vehicles. Dressed in blue shorts and a black t-shirt, he walked in tennis shoes. No one was out. Maybe it was time to sleep. All the square metal buildings looked the same. Colored stars marked the buildings. An old man approached. He held his hands behind his back and looked at the ground.

Reece normally didn't ask for help, but it was now or never. "Excuse me, sir?"

The man looked up. He was perhaps seventy, with crazy wads of white hair on either side of a bald forehead, and wore a high-collared white shirt and baggy trousers. He gazed at Reece for a moment, as if he would vaporize. "Yes, lad?"

Lad? "Is there a hotel nearby?"

The man reached out his hand. He took Reece's in his own, covered with brown age spots. Here was another traveler.

"Uh, hotel?" asked Reece.

"Where have you come from?" He gripped Reece's hand.

"Alabama," said Reece.

"Oh, you have slaves?"

"Uh, no." He retrieved his hand from the elderly man's grip. "Two thousand three. No slaves, just worker bees."

"My name is Arthur," said the old man. "Eighteen-sixty. Do you know the year?"

Reece searched for words. "Nice to meet you. I'm Reece. What year is it? Like right now?"

"Rice? I've been told it's 3981. Do you believe?"

Reece felt dizzy. "What? No. I thought maybe I was a hundred years off, not two thousand." He looked up at the pale blue sky. In the distance were brown, flat-topped mountains. The air was dry, and the sun burned his skin. "How long have you been here?"

"I've no idea. I was sitting on my divan with the cat. I felt a pounding in my heart, and then I am here. I'm worried about my dog, little Atma." He wrung his hands as if applying lotion. "Where...you are fading?"

Reece caught himself. He nearly fell. *What the hell? Shit on toast.* Was it true? His wrists ached. He was suddenly hungry for more buster. "Buster?"

"Yes, that is all there is. Nothing more. Come with me." Arthur turned and walked into a circular opening among the buildings with an ancient fig tree, the largest tree that Reece had ever seen.

"Do you think it's night?" asked Reece.

"I would like to know how one tells the difference between day and night. Come inside."

Reece stooped for the low doorway marked with a green star. The interior was brightly lit. The bar made of wood and metal circled in the middle of the room. He could smell the buster, and his stomach growled. There was no one there.

"We must help ourselves," said Arthur. He went behind the counter. He took a bowl, placed it beneath the buster nozzle, and the liquid flowed.

Reece took the cool bowl and sat on a high chair. A sweater was hanging on a peg behind the bar. Who did it belong to? Arthur joined him, blinking his dry eyes. Reece's grandfather had to use eyedrops for his dry eyes. Reece took a big drink. "Damn, that's weird good."

"Tasty, but my bowels have not moved for many days, and I drink several times per day." He took the chair beside Reece. He held the cool white bowl with both hands and sipped.

"What do you do?" asked Reece, and then he was out, seizing at the bar.

"Scheisse!" said Arthur.

Reece tried to sit up in bed, his wrists and ankles secured with restraints. He pushed out his chest. There was a taste in his mouth—*cardamom? Where am I?* There was a tube in his nose, tape on his face. Things on his shaved head. He looked around the small room, like a hotel room with a hospital bed. There was some kind of crinkly blue pad beneath him. *Fuck, I'm wearing a diaper.* It hit him. He had killed "Mia." "Mia" was dead. He fell back on the bed. He raised his head and slammed it into the pillow. He yelled, "No!" long and hard until he was overcome with coughing. Someone was in the room, a woman.

"Mr. Myers!" said Debbie. "You're safe. It's okay." She put her hand on his chest and rubbed.

"No, no, no..." He closed his eyes. He held his breath.

"Hey, don't hold your breath," said Debbie. "It's okay."

Reece tried to lift his legs. Just a few inches, then he slammed his heel on the footboard and yelled. "Fuck! Goddamn!"

"Hey, hey, it's okay. Open your eyes. Look at me." She moved to the foot of the bed and looked at his foot. There was blood. He'd sliced off a layer of skin. "That must have hurt. You've got to settle down."

The shock of the pain eased into a heavy throb. He wanted to open his eyes. He wanted to understand. He blinked and moaned. He felt that he was needed somewhere far away. How could he find Mia?

"I'll be right back, Mr. Myers." Debbie left to get a tube of antibiotic ointment and a bandage.

The words to "Pinball Wizard." The kid was blind. Reece opened his eyes. The overhead light was off, but there was a bright light on the wall behind the bed. The TV was on, muted. He took a deep breath, trying to smell something unique, a clue. *Buster.* Where was his wife, Kristin? Had she visited him here? He tried to say something. "Hey."

"Hey, yourself," said Debbie. "I'm Debbie, your nurse. You cut your heel." She stood back, hoping for a response that wasn't violent. She touched his foot. "This foot. I'm going to dress it. No kicking, okay?"

He shook his head. The images of Mia. He opened his eyes and focused on Debbie. Short blonde hair, blue scrubs, big chest. She seemed tall standing at the foot of the bed. His heel throbbed. "Okay." He lay back his head and let Debbie bandage his foot. Her hands felt good on his skin.

"You're on a special medical unit, Fort Knox, Kentucky." She tore strips of tape and hung them from the bed rail.

"The hell? Fort Knox?" He'd lived there as a kid, fifth grade. His dad was retired Army.

Debbie wanted to tell him that they knew about his mapping status, that they needed information from him, but it was too early. "You used to play on the tanks at the Patton Museum."

Fuck. How did she know that? "The Patton Museum. Tanks. Thanks." The doors were all welded shut, the turrets frozen. Death traps in battle. He remembered dumpster diving at the Officers' quarters, fishing for *Playboy* and *Oui,* and stealing school supplies from the PX.

"There, done. If we can keep you here for a while, I can

get you some ice cream. What do you say?" She moved to his left side.

"What the hell is on my head?"

"Electrodes. The EEG. You've been having seizures." She glanced at the monitor, low-amplitude squiggles. Awake. Normal.

Reece thought about his classes. He taught philosophy. Was it summer, spring, fall? "What's the date?" He kept his eyes open.

"April the twenty-first. Two thousand and three. Would you like me to wash your face?"

His classes were fucked. Hopefully, they'd found volunteers to finish the semester for him. It had all happened so fast. "Yeah, that would feel nice."

Debbie turned on the hot water and waited, letting the water run over her hand. She soaked a white washcloth and squeezed.

"God, that feels nice," said Reece. He tested his wrists. "Can we get these restraints off?"

"Not yet," said Debbie. "Need to get a doctor's order for that." There was only one patient who was up and moving around, watching TV in the day room, Freddie Mentone.

"Why?"

"You've been here for three weeks. This is the first time you've spoken to anyone. You've had a rough ride."

"A rough ride," said Reece. That seemed right.

"Where have you been?"

This Debbie knew something. "What do you mean?" He had his eyes closed again, feeling the warmth of the washcloth.

"Dr. Markush will talk with you. Have you been dreaming of other places?"

That struck a nerve. Other places. *Buster. Cardamom. Mia,* the real Mia, was alive somewhere, another time and place, another universe. The thought paralyzed him. What had he been thinking? How could he possibly find Mia?

"Not sure about dreams," said Reece. "Something, though. Vague. Mia is alive."

Debbie looked at her watch to make sure she documented his words at the exact time, 10:34 a.m. "Mia is alive. That's good news. Where is she?"

Reece opened his eyes. "I don't know." He quivered. It sounded impossible. "Shit." He tried to sit up. The wrist restraints pulled, and he fell back. "I need a hamburger, a Big Mac, anything."

"You haven't eaten in over three weeks. I can get you some ice cream to start, maybe some juice?" asked Debbie.

His stomach rumbled. "Anything, crackers."

"Hmm, crackers. The orders are for liquids only, but we can try it."

Reece watched her leave the room. *Buster.* What the hell was buster? He thought about his job at the university. He was an assistant professor of philosophy. No tenure yet. The intro class to Schopenhauer. *The World as Will and Representation.* Close your eyes, and nothing is real. Sylvia Plath hated to wash her hair because she would just have to wash it again. Just do it once and be done! *Fuck.*

Debbie returned with a pack of saltine crackers and a pink, plastic pitcher of ice water. "Got'cha dinner."

Reece opened his mouth, watering. He took the entire cracker into his mouth and chewed.

"Have a sip of water," said Debbie. She put the straw to his lips. She mimicked his chewing and swallowing.

"Another," said Reece. The cracker was delicious.

Debbie gave him another and opened another pack. "Any more thoughts about Mia?"

Reece let the cracker bits melt in his mouth before he swallowed. Mia, a sacred subject, his only child. He loved her beyond all logic. She was alive. He'd strangled an impostor. "She's far away. Buster."

"Buster?" asked Debbie. Another patient had mentioned buster. She was looking forward to Sunday, her day off. There was a vegetarian place in Radcliff that served brunch with mimosas.

"Just buster," said Reece. "I can find her, but I need help."

"What kind of help?"

"I don't know," said Reece. "I just need help."

"Dr. Markush can help. He'll be back soon."

"What the hell is on my head?" His head itched.

"We shaved your head. Electrodes for the EEG."

"The EGG?"

"EEG. Recording your brain waves. You've been seizing."

"Shit." That explained nothing. "But why?"

"Markush will explain. He should be back this afternoon around two." She didn't want to mention that he would induce more seizures for the sake of information.

"Markush," said Reece. He felt he was wasting time, that something at hand was more urgent, but what? *Mia.* How could he forget? "Can he help?"

"Yes," said Debbie. What else could she say?

Reece saw yellow, then red. He slumped, his eyes rolling back, his eyelids twitching.

Reece sat in the lane. A man approached with a curious look.

"Hello," said the man. "You're a visitor."

Reece looked at his own tennis shoes, his shorts, and his t-shirt. He looked at his hands. Were they shaking? Where was he from if he was a visitor? "I don't know," said Reece. "I'm looking for a little girl, seven years old. Her name is Mia. She looks like me, in the face."

The man paused.

Reece stood and moved on.

"Buster." He saw a metal building with a green star and walked through the mist door. There was a giant fishhook behind the bar, bronze, ten feet high. *Huh.* Two café-au-lait women sat at the counter. Reece picked the seat a barstool away from them. The bartender, an old man with a shaved head, drafted out a mug of buster and placed it in front of him. Reece was supposed to say something. What was it? "The hyena sleeps with the snake."

The bartender laughed and buffed a glass with his towel. He knew Reece was there to find his daughter. Everyone who met him knew. His daughter could be in Gadam or not. It was all in the data fur.

Hungry and thirsty, Reece drank his buster in three gulps. He felt his head, and there was hair. He scratched his scalp. There was a clock on the wall that read 0400. *Military time? Four in the morning?* It was bright outside. He'd been here before. There was a dark side of the earth and a sunny side. The planet did not rotate. Where the hell was he from? He looked over at the woman nearest him. She had long black hair. He had to start somewhere. There was a kind of light music playing, like a Gypsy wind chime.

"Excuse me," said Reece. The woman ignored him. "Hello, I need some information."

The other woman poked her and pointed at Reece.

"You want to know where your daughter is?" asked the woman. She looked bored.

Reece stood. He moved closer. "What do you know?" What would he do when he found her? Didn't he need to take her somewhere? He imagined her dead and shook his head. A translucent centipede. He grimaced and belched. "Sorry."

"It should be in the data fur, but it's not."

"Data fur?"

The woman laughed. "Sometimes there are fires. Is she from this universe?"

Reece didn't know. "I don't know." He shrank back to his chair. "She's here. I just know. I have to find her." He put his thumbs in his pockets. He was wearing the same blue shorts and the black t-shirt with a word on it. *Exxon. What the hell?*

"Maybe you think you know," said the woman. For a traveler, this guy seemed washed up. He bored her. "Have another one."

Reece tried to understand. "What the hell does that mean?"

"Hey," said the bartender.

"Fucking hey, yourself," said Reece. He stared at the woman. He intuited that her name was Carlotta. How he knew, he had no idea. "Carlotta."

"You know my name, data fur, wowie. You need to leave, Reece," said Carlotta.

Reece collected himself. The woman looked nervous. He felt bad. "I'm sorry. I just need to find her."

"Yeah," said the woman. "Why don't you take a walk. Maybe you'll find her." She turned back to her friend and laughed.

"Yeah," said the bartender. "Hit the road. You're trouble. We don't like your kind around here."

Reece had never been accused of being trouble. He walked outside and looked at the blue sky. He wanted to punch something, somebody. He felt like a freshman at college studying in a third language. A dog was walking toward him, wagging its tail. Reece squatted and called it. "Here, buddy." The dog with head down slowed and approached. "It's okay. Good boy. He held out his hand. The dog lunged and bit him on the wrist. "Shit!" Reece fell over backward and rolled to his feet. The dog slunk away, growling. "What the hell?" That wasn't supposed to happen.

Reece's wrist was red, streaks flashing up his forearm from the dog bite. He needed a doctor. A thought came to him. He followed the thought, wandering for a few blocks through the twisting lanes of Gadam. The data fur. A large steel building without windows. He walked through the mist door. There was no information desk. The waiting room of green padded chairs could hold perhaps fifty souls, but there were only ten. He sat in an empty chair. A spherical object, silent, approached him. He raised his swelling arm into the air. The object hummed. Reece was sure that it was recording him. It moved in close to his arm, scanning it. The sphere rose to a height of nine feet and zipped away.

Reece watched as one of the patients and then another stood and walked through a double door that opened automatically. He waited, remembering Mia. Maybe Mia would be his doctor when he walked through the double door. But what would he do? How would they return to 2003?

Exactly ten minutes passed. Reece heard a distinct voice calling him. He stood and followed it through the double doors, which opened for him. He could only think of onion rings. He loved onion rings. There was a barbecue place in Birmingham that served the best rings.

An illuminated line appeared on the floor, and he followed it, turning right then left. He walked for twenty feet, looking down.

"Reece Myers?"

Reece's head snapped up. There was a woman in a blue jumpsuit in front of him. "Yes."

"Come inside."

Reece walked into a small cubicle with only one chair. As if commanded, he held out his wrist.

"I'm Renee. Looks like you've been bitten. Would you like the cure?"

Reece stared at the bloody fang marks on his arm. He could feel the infection, an evangelical revival of bacterial unction. He'd only wanted to scratch the dog's ears.

"Scratch your own ears from now on," said Renee. "Here, I'll make it easy on you." She pulled a gadget from her pocket. It resembled an otoscope, but with a narrow needle tip encased in a protective cover.

Reece held out his injured arm. Renee scrubbed a patch of skin with a small dry cloth. Reece could hear the play-by-play of what was happening. He also knew that Renee was twenty-eight, creamy coffee like everyone else. She was single. Everyone was single.

Renee said, "Hold on," and slipped the needle into a convenient vein, showcasing through Reece's pale skin. The cure coursed through his system. The redness dissipated, and a sense of well-being drew down.

"We're done."

Reece looked at his arm. The puncture wounds were still there, but the redness and streaking were gone. "What?"

"Good to go," said Renee, drawing on data fur responses from Earth 2003.

Reece said, "Do I owe you anything?"

"No way, are you kidding?" asked Renee. "Just maximize your potential. Are you really determined to find your daughter? Mia?"

The sound of Mia's name jolted Reece. "Yeah. What should I do? Is she in the data fur, where she is? I mean, where is she?"

Renee had other patients to see. "If she's there, you'll know it. I only have time to process work-related fur. But you can pay someone."

"I thought everything was free," said Reece.

Renee laughed. She brushed back her blonde bangs. "Maybe buster and healthcare. Information, though, will cost you. People specialize."

"Is there someone I should see next? That you know of

who could help me?" Reece flexed his arm, no soreness. The fang marks looked clean, like innocent punctures. He needed a drink, alcohol.

"You want alcohol?" asked Renee. "Just look for the red star."

Well, that was good news. "Look for the red star? Is it free, the alcohol?"

"Of course," said Renee. "Just information from the data fur, and sex, will cost you."

"Information, sex," said Reece. "Thanks." He left the way he had come, through an empty hallway with a ten-foot ceiling. Everything was dim. He walked through the waiting area and through the mist door. The brightness was intense, and he felt dizzy.

He focused on seeking out the first red star he could find. He'd once been to London and been determined to find an authentic fish-n-chips shop. He'd wandered around Piccadilly Circus for what seemed hours before he saw in bright red letters his desire, Fish n' Chips. He'd opted to sit versus stand and paid a premium for the chair. The fried fish portion had been at least two feet long and an inch thick. Jesus, it had been good with the fried chips and sweet Coca-Cola.

He passed half a dozen workers, heading home for the day, and wondered what they did, where they were going, and a blizzard of information hit his brain. He briefly fantasized that he would never die in this universe. *Who knows?* The buildings all seemed low from the outside. He spotted a red star and picked up his pace.

The mist door parted as he passed through. Before he could visualize the inside, an arm looped inside his own.

He looked to his right and saw a smooth bicep. His escort was very tall. He was somewhat afraid to look up, and so he looked down.

He found himself at a bar that hit his knees and ascended the round stool. He felt exposed, like a heroin addict in a room full of black lights. He leaned back, grabbing his knees.

"It will be what?" growled a voice.

Reece focused. There were no bottles on display. The bar was made of metal. "Alcohol?" He was thinking of whiskey, Kentucky bourbon, a double on the rocks. He already felt drunk. At least he didn't have to pee.

"Makers be fine?" asked the bartender. He'd never had a request for bourbon before.

Reece stared at the bartender's chest, a reddish shirt, kind of tight. Someone else he knew wore tight shirts. He feared looking any higher lest the spell break. The bartender took a glass and placed it into a metal sleeve. Liquid dribbled into the glass. "Need a lime with that?"

"Uh, no. You're thinking of tequila."

"Tequila. Yeah. You're right. In the fur."

Reece let the bourbon chill with the ice. He wanted to inject it into his veins. *The bartender's name is Henry.* He flinched. There was a hand on his shoulder.

"Rice, my lad." It was a white hand with age spots.

He recognized the old man. "It's Reece." He had been here before. It was 2003, somewhere, and something ungodly here. What had this Arthur called him, *a traveler?*

"Sherry, if you please, Henry." Arthur turned to Reece. "Reece? Shall we take a table? These bar chairs are uncomfortable," and they were.

"Okay. Did you find a hotel?" asked Reece.

"Yes, and *poof,* you were seizing, then gone. Nothing surprises me anymore. This time and place make even the le petit caporal seem like a petty thief."

Reece waited for Arthur to sit on the cushioned black chair. "Who?"

"Napoleon Bonaparte," said Arthur. "Yes, before your time."

"I've heard of him, know of him," said Reece. "And what is your last name?"

"My last name? My family name is Schopenhauer." Henry brought the sherry to the table.

A bell was trying to go off in Reece's head. Why was Henry just standing there?

"Word on the street is that you're trouble, gringo, corn mold." Henry was mining the data fur. "Word up and maybe just get the snap out of here when you're through."

"Dear God," said Arthur.

"Jesus Christ," said Reece. His inclination was to punch Henry in the face.

"You do that and you're toast, big honcho," said Henry. He balled his fists and squeezed his fingers with his thumbs.

Mia. He had to focus. He had to find Mia. What would it take to find her? Henry might be the key. Reece relaxed his tense lower back and shoulders. He thought about a plane skywriting "Mia" above this place. Why was he wasting time with Arthur in a place where he was not welcome?

"I have to find my daughter." Reece drank his whiskey in long swallows.

"Yes, her name is Mia," said Arthur. He wondered if he

could help. Something said that he could, but he wasn't sure how.

Reece glanced to his side, and Henry was still there.

Henry data-furred a film from Reece's 1991, *Zandalee.* "Why don't you put cocaine on his ass and fuck like animals?"

"My my," said Arthur.

Reece had seen the movie. He knew the exact scene Henry was referring to. His glass was empty. "I need to leave," said Reece.

"Douchebag," said Henry.

Reece pressed his lips together and stood. "Fuck you, asshole." He faced Henry, who seemed nonchalant, as if all was well.

"Trisomy 21, faggot," said Henry. He smiled and walked away.

Arthur looked concerned. The energy was bad, and the words were new. "Maybe we should leave."

Mia's favorite treat had been coconut cream milkshakes. Reece felt weak in the knees and walked through the mist door into the dreary heat beneath an enormous jacaranda tree.

"Lad, let's walk. Have you been to the edge of this town?"

"It has an edge?"

"Yes, it just stops as if someone long ago drew a sacred line. Very odd if you ask me. This way."

Reece followed Arthur. He was hated back in 2003 for killing an alien posing as his daughter. And he was hated here for an unknown reason. Did they know that he had strangled the impostor? Was that the reason?

"Look, chickens," said Reece.

A fussy hen led six little chicks across the lane.

There was the sound of a plane. Reece looked up to see the plane releasing smoke, writing in the sky. It towered, arced, and fell. The smoke stopped, and the plane regained height and crossed over. "A," he said.

"Dear God, what is it?" asked Arthur. "A machine?"

The plane continued. "S...S. ASS." Reece felt deflated. It was meant for him, no doubt. Why weren't there others out and about to see it?

"Hmm, dear me," said Arthur. "More riddles, from machines flying in the sky?"

Reece checked his wrists, which ached. The puncture wounds had closed, and there was no infection. His heart pounded as if he had taken speed, not fast, just pounding.

"Dear God—" said Arthur.

Reece bucked up straight, then rebounded onto his back. He threw his fists into the air, but they stayed put. His eyes were squeezed *shit/shut*. He could open them, but what would he see? Where would he be? Would Arthur be standing over him? Maybe it would be Mia's impostor, torturing him in hell. He let one eye open and then the other.

"Hey," said Debbie. "You've been gone for a while. Welcome back."

He sat up and fell back. *Damn!* He let loose a guttural cry. He was at his wits' end. He coughed from the ripping sensation in his throat, like taking several shots of tequila in a row without beer. He needed a cold beer. *Fuck,* his mother had locked him out of the trailer when he was a little kid. Just when she took a bath, though, but sometimes it was after dark. *The fuck!*

"Reece, relax. I'm getting Dr. Markush." She hit the call button. "Claire, Dr. Markush there? Myers is back."

"Hey, coming," said Markush. He'd been charting and not watching the monitors. He swiped at his flailing gray hair. He liked the way it felt on his face and the way it blew in the wind when he drove his ancient Volvo with the windows down, just like the one in *Winter Light.*

Reece opened his eyes and saw Debbie. An older man came through the door. In the corner of the room was the camera. The TV was off. He felt something in his dick, a catheter, no doubt. *Hell.* His ass and tailbone hurt. He glanced from one wrist to the other, lambskin restraints.

"Arthur," said Reece.

"Hey, Mr. Myers. It's Dr. Markush." He wore green scrubs with the Organon logo. He glanced at the EEG and ECG monitors, heart rate elevated at 116, but everything else was okay.

"Who is Arthur?" asked Debbie.

"I don't know." Reece tried to remember. He closed his eyes. "Ass."

"Mr. Myers, you've been seizing and likely to think that you have been dreaming," said Markush. He gripped the bed rail. He could see the trauma in Reece's face, the infinite light-years traveled.

"Creaming?" asked Reece. He looked at Markush. His eyes were dark and twinkling.

Markush laughed. "Dreaming."

Reece saw Markush's hand gripping the rail. "You're missing a fingernail." Where had he heard that before?

Markush looked at his own hand. He'd forgotten about hitting his index finger with a hammer. "Oh, yeah. Very observant."

"What do you remember?" asked Debbie.

Markush knew what the answer would be.

"I don't know. I need to find Mia. She's alive."

"Yes," said Markush. "You killed an alien impostor, right?"

"I did," said Reece.

"I believe you," said Markush.

Debbie tried to keep a straight face. Maybe he really did. The one person on the outside who knew exactly what her job entailed had asked her how she could work with a child killer. She wasn't really sure. Reece didn't look like a child killer. He had a rusty-colored receding hairline, accompanied by a serious, yet innocent, look on his face. He wasn't a brute but rather thin and lean, average height.

"What is the last thing you remember?"

"Arthur," said Reece.

"Who is Arthur?" asked Markush.

"He's an old man. He wants to help me find Mia."

"Where does Arthur live?"

"I don't know." Reece felt a welling in his chest. He felt everyone hated him. He moaned.

"What does he look like?" asked Debbie. She was getting into Markush's groove. She saw the guards changing positions through the door. They glanced in at the child killer.

Reece thought. He twisted his wrists. "Can you cut these damn cuffs off my wrists?"

"Can you tell us what Arthur looks like? We're just trying to keep you safe. You're not yourself quite yet," said Markush.

"Oh hell," said Reece.

"We have your best interest at heart," said Debbie. She needed to check on the other patients.

"Bullshit," said Reece. He realized his ankles were restrained as well, and a flash of anger shot from head to toe. What the hell could he lose? "Untie my feet."

Markush said, "Okay. Debbie?"

Debbie loosened the bow knot on the left side and went around to the other side. She left the loose restraints around his ankles.

Reece drew his knees to his chest and then stretched his legs beneath the sheet. Felt good.

"What did this fellow Arthur look like?"

Did Arthur say that his last name was Schopenhauer? *Holy fuck.* "He looked like a nineteenth-century German philosopher."

Markush nodded. He knew that Reece taught philosophy. Was he actually traveling or just dreaming up bits from his experiences? "What else can you remember?"

"Untie my hands," said Reece. "Otherwise, no deal." He was hungry. A damn feeding tube dangled from his nose.

"As soon as you stop seizing," said Markush. "You get pretty crazy, if you know what I mean. Just trying to keep you safe."

"What is this place?" asked Reece.

Debbie looked at Markush. She pointed at her watch and left the room. Her twelve-hour shift would end within the hour, and she had lots to do.

"It's a special place, a place for folks like you. You know more than I'll never know, but just try to imagine that there are those of us who are trying to protect you."

"To study me," said Reece.

"Well, if you have to put it that way, that's partially true. You are one in a million, perhaps a billion. It's hard to say."

"I sure feel special. Can you at least raise the head of the bed so I can sit up? I feel like I'm going to suffocate."

Markush reached for the bed rail and pushed the head-up button. The bed hummed. "How's that?"

"Better," said Reece. His gut gurgled. "I need the bedpan. I'm about to shit myself."

"Oh," said Markush. He hit the nurse call button.

"Yes," said Claire.

"Can you send Debbie or Jim in here? Hold on, Mr. Myers."

"Why can't you just put the bedpan under me? That's what they're going to do."

Markush had no answer. That was out of his league. "Just hold on, okay." He looked around the neat room, the water pitcher on the bedside table. His wife had died a few years back in a car accident. He couldn't remember how many years it had been. Her skull had been crushed. The casket was closed for the service. He tried to remember what she looked like.

"And hell, I'm wearing a diaper," said Reece. "Once a man, twice a baby."

"Hold it if you can."

Debbie hurried in. Without asking, she grabbed the bedpan from beneath the sink and sprayed the rim with baby powder. "Here we go." She undid his diaper and pulled it off. "Lift your hips." She slid the diaper out and pushed the slick bedpan under his hips. "Good to go. We'll give you a few minutes."

Markush was already out the door into the hall, gripping the magnets in his pocket. Reece arched and his bowels released.

Having returned in a daze, Reece followed Arthur to the "edge" of town. Arthur walked with his hands behind his back. He wore his loose black breeches and a white shirt with a bit of ruffle in the sleeve. His face seemed as if he had lost weight rapidly, a newly minted, concerned look.

They passed more steel buildings, with green-starred buster cafés, which all had the same kind of mist door.

"This way," said Arthur. He turned a corner through the wide lane and headed uphill. The buildings were just tall enough to block most of the distant scenery.

"The paths are very steep, up and down," said Reece. Sweating, he could feel his heart beating in his head. He wondered what the altitude was, and it came to him in feet, 7,343. No wonder he was short of breath. "How long have you been here?"

"It's hard to say since there is only daytime. It seems like quite a while, perhaps seventy Earth days. I just wander from one buster establishment to another. I'm looking forward to a bath later. You are the only other traveler I've met."

"Earth days," said Reece. Maybe this wasn't Earth.

"Ferenj!" came a cry from behind a barred window.

"See," said Arthur. "That's what they call us. Because we are not of this place. I live in Berlin, Germany. You've heard of it, no doubt."

Reece thought, breathing hard, a slight headache in his eyes. "Where am I from then? It seems that my father was in the Army, and we lived in Germany when I was young. I remember going to a dairy shop and smelling milk."

"You said you were from Alabama, the American South, no?"

"I did, didn't I? Yeah." His past came rushing in. "What is this place called?"

"Gadam. We are, my friend, in what appears to be Ethiopia, the Land of Punt, the land of Prester John. Look now, how we are approaching the end of this town." He pointed ahead.

Reece gazed at the round building, crudely made of stones with a tin roof and a cupola with a cross of short poles. A gravel path circled the building. Through the door, not a mist door, a thin aromatic smoke seemed to be pulling itself hand over hand outside into the air.

"It is a church, a Christian church. They are burning incense inside, but we are not allowed. I've tried."

Reece walked around the building, thinking. He had seen this building before. But it had been standing alone on a rocky hillside. Inside was the maq'das, the Holy of Holies, where was kept a replica of the tablets handed to Moses from God.

"Shit."

"What is it?" asked Arthur. A bead of perspiration lined his upper lip.

"This is called Gadam, but it's a weird version of Godo to me, Ethiopia. What year is it again?"

"Three thousand nine hundred and eighty-one," said Arthur.

"Holy shit. Mia is here somewhere. How will I find her?" He wanted to rush inside the church. Perhaps she was inside, perhaps in the maq'das.

In the distance were hills, *like white elephants.* The land dropped away quickly to the east. In the distance to the south were towering flat-topped mountains.

"Ambas, the flat mountains," said Reece. "There's another town that way, about forty kilometers, called Alem Ketema. Why was I in Godo?"

"I can honestly say that I've never been here," said Arthur. "This could very well be my final destination. You, though, come and go. I am expecting you to pop away without warning."

Reece sat on a low stone. The dust was a vivid brown and stained his tennis shoes. Here, there was wind, blowing briskly. The fluffs of white hair on either side of Arthur's head bobbed in the breeze. He looked old and wise.

"Something about canned cheese," said Reece. His mind flooded with images of round cans of cheddar-like cheese manufactured in Australia. There was a phone number and fax for the manufacturing facility in his head. He could see it. The flood of images made him wince. "Stop!"

"Too much information, no? It's been explained as the data fur, but I have no idea what it means, just that I am easily overwhelmed with information at times." Arthur turned in a circle, looking out at the panorama. "Beautiful, rugged. Perhaps we can take a long walk away from this place?"

"I think I need to be here, though. I need to explore. It all seems like a puzzle. The pieces are scattered and mixed." Reece stood and took a deep breath, a vague hint of smoke. "The Hyena lived here." *Or was it the Snake?*

"Holy cow."

Arthur laughed. "I like that saying. Wunderbar, no?" The wind made his eyes water, which felt good in the dry air.

"Where are the flies?" asked Reece. "There were lots of flies." He looked up at the tiny bright sun.

Arthur moved back toward the line of buildings. "Yes, no flies. The thing about buster is that I always need more. Shall we? Do you feel like sleeping?"

"Sure, some buster and then sleep. Maybe I'll have dreams."

"Ah, yes, dreams."

They strolled back downhill and entered the first buster place they saw. Reece primarily needed just water, but buster was mostly water, or was it? "These places are like Starbucks."

The buster places all looked the same from the outside, but each had a unique feature inside. This one had a large vulture in a cage suspended from the ceiling. Reece couldn't tell if it was real or not.

"What'll it be, gentlemen?" asked the bartender. "Flavor of the day is turmeric."

"The plain is fine with me," said Arthur. "I wonder if you have it chilled?"

"Not a prob, doctor."

"I'll have the same," said Reece. He felt strangely subdued, as if chemically restrained in some manner.

"Smart ass," said the waiter. His name was Robert.

"God, here we go," said Reece.

"Are you going to write my name down? Report me to Central?" asked Robert.

"What if I kick your ass instead?" asked Reece. Irritated, he tried to play it cool.

The waiter didn't seem to be deterred and handed Reece his chilled buster in a yellow ceramic bowl. He drew down a bowl for Arthur and placed it in front of him. "Why don't you kiss it instead and lick my rim?"

Reece laughed. He imagined telling this story to a friend. Did he have friends? "Why don't you fuck yourself with a shotgun and pull the trigger?" Reece's eyes glazed for a moment, lost in the data fur.

"Eat my shit and..."

Arthur sipped his buster, ignoring Robert. "You are from another place. I imagine, dear Reece, you are there now instead of here, as you can see, or cannot see. You only need to close your eyes to understand."

"What kind of flaky bullshit is that?" asked Reece, smiling.

"Lick your mother's tit," said Arthur.

Reece processed that. "High five, old man."

Arthur thought, then held up his hand and slapped palms with Reece.

As Dr. Markush removed the magnets from Reece's head, the EEG went from the cognitive gamma waves to motor beta waves. Reece's tremors had stopped an hour ago, but the magnets kept Reece in his traveling state. If only he could remember where and what he'd been doing. Markush stood at the bedside, his back aching. Laura, the 7p-to-7a nurse, had relieved him for a while, but she had six patients to attend to.

Laura peeked in. "Doing okay? Is he back?"

"Yeah, just coming around. I'm going to stay for a few minutes, but give him the travel quiz when you have time. I kept him going with the magnets for over an hour."

"Impressive. We need a doohickey to hold the magnets in place," said Laura. She was tall and thin with long legs and soft red hair. Markush looked like an old hippy to her.

"Yeah, working on that. Seems the DoD would make it a priority. Ha." He liked the personal contact, thinking that maybe his own vibes were interacting with the magnets. Not very scientific, but who knew?

"Yeah, right," said Laura. She moved on to room six, a woman, twenty-three, named Emma. She'd been shot, also in Ethiopia. In fact, all of the Organon patients had some sort of tie to that country. Markush was fascinated and had already traveled there once on a kind of scientific pilgrimage. He only regretted that he could not publish his findings, which were astounding.

Reece's eyes opened. He did not scream or moan, which was new. It was as if he was getting used to the routine. He coughed. The bed was raised to its max so that he looked directly into Markush's eyes. "The doctor with long hair," he said. He tried to scratch his face, but his wrists were restrained. "Untie me."

"Mr. Myers, Reece. We'll get you untied soon. You seem to be doing a lot better. We may release you to walk about if things keep improving. You can play pool, smoke if you like."

Reece smoked cigars, and the very idea sounded glorious. "What about alcohol? Bourbon."

"On the rocks?"

"Yeah, on the rocks," said Reece. "Jesus Christ, untie me!"

Markush pushed a button to lower the bed so that he towered over Reece, a subtle gesture to let Reece know who was in charge. "In due time. I promise. Drinks totally on me. Four Roses?"

"That would be fine, or maybe some Knob Creek." He could taste the coconut flair on the end of his tongue. He relaxed a bit. "At least turn me so I can get off my damn back."

"Sure, not a problem." He pushed the nurse call button, and Lars, the monitor tech, answered. "Send Laura in here, please."

"Right," said Lars. He scanned the monitors. Laura was still in room six, doing mouth care on Emma. "Laura, Markush in six needs you."

"Okay." Laura walked to the sink and washed her hands with pink Hibiclens. The stuff chapped her hands, but killed everything imaginable. She entered seven.

"Can you help turn Mr. Myers?" asked Markush.

"Left side or right side?" asked Laura.

"Right," said Reece. His butt cheeks ached.

Laura started by putting a clean pillowcase on the blue foam wedge. "Going to untie your left arm. She did it slowly. "Okay?"

Markush braced for the worst, Reece leaping from bed and smashing his glasses.

"See, I'm not an animal," said Reece. "Damn, I could get up and sit in a chair." Thoughts of Mia quieted him.

"Just protocol, Mr. Myers," said Laura. "Roll onto your side and I'll put this wedge behind your back. You can lean back against it. The military pays two hundred bucks for these things."

"Hot damn," said Reece. "Probably costs a nickel to make."

Laura rubbed his red back.

"Dear God, that feels good."

"Oh yeah, hold on." She squirted some white lotion onto her hands. She pushed Reece over a bit and rubbed the lotion deep into his skin, running her thumbs up and down his spine and lingering on the reddened area over his sacrum and lower back.

Reece had closed his eyes, blissful. He didn't even notice that his arm had been very loosely retied to the bed.

"Nice work, Laura," said Markush. He walked around to the other side of the bed and sat on the recliner there. Laura washed her hands and left.

Reece wallowed in the luxury of being on his side. He felt like a million dollars, except he was tied to a bed in Fort Knox, Kentucky. Why Fort Knox? He looked into Markush's eyes through the raised bed rail. "Where the hell am I?"

"Organon. We're in Kentucky, Fort Knox. You used to live here when you were in fifth grade. Remember?"

Reece remembered all right. He'd hated Fort Knox, the tiny apartment with only one heating vent. He used to stand on the back of the couch to get close to the vent. *"Welcome Back, Kotter.* On TV."

Markush laughed. "Yeah."

"But, what is this place? Why am I not in prison with all of the other child killers?"

"Because you didn't kill your daughter, Mia. Right? Who did you strangle?" Markush felt a rush of adrenaline. This was real.

Reece hesitated. Even to him, it sounded ridiculous. "She was an impostor, sent by Dahlia. Mia is still alive. I need to find her."

The mention of Dahlia sent a thrill up Markush's spine. "Tell me about Dahlia."

Reece hesitated. He only knew what he knew. He wanted ice cream. "I need some chocolate ice cream."

"No worries, it's yours. I promise."

"When?"

Markush hit the call button again. "Hey, we need some chocolate ice cream for room seven, please."

"Will do," said Lars. In his off hours, he was a male stripper. He dressed in a bear costume.

"Good enough?" asked Markush.

"I suppose," said Reece.

"Dahlia."

"Yeah. Dahlia. She's trying to get back to the beginning. Like she's looking for an orgasm before it happens."

Markush could barely contain himself. "Why?"

"Because, what was there before there was everything?"

"What?"

"I don't know, but Dahlia wants to know. It has something to do with music."

Markush was silent. Did that make sense? Did anything make sense?

Reece went stiff, and the bed trembled.

Reece and Arthur worked their way back to the room they had secured for two weeks. They had been asked not to invite prostitutes.

Inside the tiny room with two cots, a red velvet birthday cake sat on a platter between their beds. It seemed to be fresh. There were two small plates, a butter knife, and two forks.

"Cake?" asked Arthur. He wanted to sit in an overstuffed leather chair and felt strange on the tiny bed.

"Not really." Reece took a fork, though, and tasted the icing, salty. "Yuck."

"Is it a cake?" asked Arthur. He lay flat on his back. Had it been days since he had slept?

"Yeah, cake," said Reece. Arthur was already snoring. Reece brought his head to the pillow and lifted his feet onto the cot. There were no blankets or sheets. Arthur was sleeping the sleep of the dead.

He turned toward Arthur. The cake was gone. *What the hell?* He decided he was indeed thirsty, but just for water or maybe a beer. There were bars. He stood and opened the door. A man sat in the hall.

"Hello," said Reece.

"Where do you think you're going?" asked the man. His face looked burned, his eyes leaking water onto his nose.

"For a drink, to a bar?" asked Reece.

"You signed up for two weeks, motherfucker," said the man. "Hi, I'm Glen." He held out his hand.

"Glen, well may I pass?" Reece was confused.

"No, you may not. Go back to your room and suck your dick."

Reece stood up straight, and his head brushed the ceiling. He tried something new. "Your mother's pussy tastes like my cock."

Glen laughed. "Yeah, just don't be gone long. Melissa will kick my ass, if you know what I mean. Is the old man asleep?"

"Yeah." Reece moved into the hallway and toward what looked to be a door to the outside, and it was. Strange all around, no, queer was the better word.

The sun outside reminded him of how dim it was inside. He looked back at the metal building with the blue star. There was nothing to distinguish it from the other buildings. He spit into the dirt and drew a brown X beside the door. A path ran straight in front of the building, and he couldn't decide if he should go left or right. He shook his head and went left, downhill.

He chose the first bar that appeared, a red star. The mist door was rounded at the top. He entered and felt the chill. The room was larger than it seemed from the outside. On the back wall was painted a rainbow. Twinkly lights outlined the different colors. There was a sign: Suit Yourself. He nodded and sat at a small round table with three chairs. Adjusting to the dimness, he could see perhaps a dozen people scattered throughout the joint. A woman, topless, approached. Reece stared at her full breasts.

"What exactly do you mean by joint?" asked the woman. Her name was Amber, and she was beautiful.

Reece looked at his hands folded on the table. The areolas around her stiff nipples sagged just a bit. She was thirty or so. He looked up again. "Uh, joint, place," said Reece. "Data fur, you know?" That seemed to be a good answer.

"Right. What'll it be? Our special today is fermented cow piss."

Reece laughed. "What about some bourbon, you whore from outer space?"

Amber nodded. "I sat on your father's face and he said hello. Bourbon coming up."

Reece felt a bit relieved, thinking he was getting the hang of this place. He looked one table over. A couple was sipping what appeared to be beer from heavy glass mugs.

Amber returned with his bourbon. "Don't serve this often."

"Thanks," said Reece, or was it Bobby? He wondered who he was. How did he get here? He was rooming with a German philosopher who said that Reece "came and went." What did that mean? He sipped his bourbon, a double on ice, just enough that the lowest piece of ice hovered above the bottom of the glass. *Perfect.* He could sip every sixty seconds. He noticed his heart beating in his neck and tried to count the beats. Did they have cigars here?

Amber returned. Reece looked at her knees.

"Need a cigar?" asked Amber. "Organic or not? Flavored or not? Ligero or not? Shade-grown or not?"

"How about a Nicaraguan puro?" asked Reece.

"Not a problem," said Amber. She slipped away into a back room. There was a man behind the bar, also topless and with a hairy chest.

I'm here to look for Mia. Reece sipped his bourbon and struggled to put the pieces together. He had killed an impostor posing as his daughter. He taught philosophy at a college. Which college, though? He was married to a thoughtful woman, right? And she must have freaked out when he strangled the girl who looked like Mia, the fake sent by Dahlia. Mia was in Gadam, Ethiopia, 3981, and so was he. He took a big sip of his cold bourbon. His thoughts wandered back to Arthur, and it suddenly hit him. *Schopenhauer. Arthur nonetheless!* Reece taught *The World as Will and Representation.* He strained to bring the elements together but could not.

Amber swished through the tables, holding a lit cigar, already cut and smoking. She wore the bottom half of a black cocktail dress and white tennis shoes. "Here you go, fucker."

Reece took the cigar and looked at the label. Oliva. "Thanks. Smells great." He took a puff and blew the smoke away from Amber. She stood there expectant. "Strumpet," he said.

"Canker," and she walked off to wait on the other tables.

"What am I doing?" He was drinking and smoking when he should be looking for Mia. It was all so convenient and distracting. Did he wear glasses? He felt his face. *No.* There was the music to think of. He would know Mia's music. *Yes.* And did Dahlia live here? That little bitch with a thousand faces, like that girl Charlotte back at, what was it? *47 Asterion Lane.* His street address. A college town in Kentucky. He lived there with Mia and his wife. What was her name? *Emma? No.* He dipped the head of his cigar in the bourbon and looked around. He listened for Mia's music, a pure sound. A spider skittered across the table. "Ah!" He swiped it onto the floor. Almost as bad as a cockroach. A sizzle...

It was midnight when Reece opened his eyes. The room was empty. He had been somewhere, but where? He struggled to fix on a solid detail. An old man with white hair. *Alcohol. Bourbon?*

He lay on his side, a foam something behind his back. There was a pillow between his knees. A tube in his nose, in his penis too. "Shit," he mumbled. One hand was tied to the left side of the bed, the other to the right. He tested his feet, untied. *A doctor with gray hair had been speaking with him. There was a woman, too, maybe a nurse.*

"Hey!" he said to the empty room. He pulled on his wrists, and there was definite pain, a wearing away of skin, muscle fatigue. Was it day or night?

Shark, with his overlapping middle, happened to be passing by when Reece yelled. He poked in his head. "What's up?" He was bored out of his mind.

"Hey," said Reece. "Where am I?" He could see that the voice belonged to something akin to a guard. He was wearing a uniform. Images fleeted, coalesced, retreated.

Shark waved at the camera. His belly was in the room, but he was still in the hall. He was talking with a child killer, no doubt about it. A chill curled on his arms. "Organon, Fort Knox, Kentucky." He didn't volunteer any more than that.

Gumbo walked up. "What's the monkey business?" Anything to break the monotony.

"Myers here is talking," said Shark.

"Why am I here?" asked Reece.

"You strangled your daughter, right?" Shark nodded to Gumbo, who was peeking into the room. They had vague ideas of what Dr. Markush was up to, but nothing made much sense from their point of view.

"Mia, my daughter. She was taken and replaced with a fake, a trick of Dahlia's. She wants to experience...pure time, I think." He felt he had to talk fast, to get it out.

Gumbo was as round as he was tall. He tried to follow what Reece was saying. "Sounds like a bunch of malarkey to me." He wasn't supposed to be chatting with the patients. "Next time, pick on someone your own size."

Shark shook his head. Jesus, what about the animal in room three? He had drowned his infant daughter and thrown the body out of a fifth-floor window. The only one they liked was Peters in room five. He was just straight-up batshit crazy. Markush spent hours with him, taking notes.

Reece stared at the pair blocking the doorway. "Untie my hands. Please?"

"No way," said Shark. "Doctor's orders."

Reece stared at Shark. There was something malleable in there. Gumbo was another story. "If we don't do something, Dahlia will reduce us to, to, to..." He wanted to say fluff, but that was the wrong word. "To nothing."

This crazy talk was nothing new to Shark. "Markush is cool with you. That's all I know. He's sorting it out." He looked at Gumbo half apologetically. "In the meantime, happy holidays. George Washington's birthday."

Reece had been to D.C. with Mia. He laughed. They'd ridden a chartered bus, a school trip from Birmingham. He'd started on a new antipsychotic before the trip, and he'd bought dark shades. *Geodon, yeah, Geodon.* He'd worn the shades the entire trip and slept not a wink in ninety-six hours. His wife had suggested that he might qualify for disability. Maybe so, but that had seemed like the cheap way out.

"Is this a hospital?" asked Reece.

Gumbo felt empowered. He sort of knew what Organon was. He'd been through two weeks of orientation, no less. "You are part of an experiment," he said.

"No," said Shark. That was the wrong approach. "We are part of an experiment, get it?"

Reece got as much as he could. "What's the research question? What's the hypothesis? How do I reach Mia?" He let his head thud onto the pillow.

"Tomorrow's a better day," said Gumbo.

Reece had heard that somewhere before. Perhaps it was true.

Arthur awoke. His mouth tasted like a rotten apple. He looked for cake, but there was none, and then there was. It tasted of salt, and he frowned. He was sharing the room. The young man, Reece. Reece was a traveler. His bed was empty.

After finishing his cigar and bourbon, Reece searched his way back to the room. He took a left and, by checking every door along the way, he finally found the X in the dirt. *Arthur Schopenhauer. The German philosopher.* He felt he had drunk a six-pack of beer. A cheap buzz, dwindling fast, he walked inside. The same guy was sitting in the hall. He walked by him.

"Hey, sack licker!" said Glen. "Pay some dues, deadbeat." He held up his hand for a high five.

Reece high-fived him.

"Don't just stand there like a stick of butter is melting in your asshole," said Glen.

"Right," said Reece. He thought. "Why don't you kayak through hell...in a kayak."

Glen smirked. "Lame ass."

Reece knocked on the door and entered. "Hey," he said.

Arthur looked frazzled, not at all rested. He sat on the edge of the bed with his head in his hands.

"I know who you are," said Reece. "The world is my will and representation." There was a brief crackle of light and space. He felt as if he was everywhere at once. "Whoa..."

"And I am getting to know you," said Arthur. "I am here

for a reason, no? My old world has passed away, and I am here."

"I'm a professor of philosophy. I teach your works to undergraduate philosophy majors."

"I'm flattered. Is it a world like this one?" He lifted his head. "I'm not one to piddle with academia. Perhaps you know that."

"I do. Students didn't sign up for your lectures, and you left teaching behind. Right?"

"Only to teach myself, and that was enough," said Arthur. "We are sharing a room. We must also share something deeper. What is it?"

"I need you to help me find my daughter, Mia. She's here somewhere, as well as Dahlia."

Arthur shrugged his shoulders. "I never had children. If you think I can help you find your daughter, I would be pleased to do so. I think that is my desire, something we can share. What of this Dahlia, though?"

Reece thought. *How best to explain?* "Remember the woman you pushed down, Caroline Marquet?"

"Dear God? Is that in the history books as well?"

"Yes, you were forced to pay her damages for the rest of her life. When she died, you wrote on her obituary—"

"Yes," said Arthur. "The bitch is dead."

"Well, Dahlia, to me, is like that. She's a parasite, always interfering. She's trying to make it back to the beginning, when there was no space or mass, not even darkness or light, or so I believe."

"I see, a theory of beginning. I don't quite understand Dahlia, other than she is a 'pain in your arse.' But a missing child is universal, no doubt. Is that cold air coming through that square in the ceiling?"

Reece stood and put his hand there. "Yeah, air conditioning, a machine that makes it cool or warm inside buildings."

"Fascinating. How does it operate?"

"It's complicated. But about Mia. I would love to have your help. I'm a fan of idealism. Perhaps you can 'see' reality where I can't."

Arthur shrugged. "I doubt that, but what I see differs from what you see."

"What is your inclination? Do you think she's in Gadam?"

"I don't know. Perhaps she is far away, but we must start here, correct?"

"Right," said Reece. "I would say let's start tomorrow, but there isn't one."

"It overwhelms me, this place. Perhaps the best place to start is with a drink, no? Some cherry schnapps?"

Reece thought about more bourbon. "Sure, why not? Let's do it."

"Agreed then." Arthur put his hand on Reece's shoulder and squeezed. "Do you know Goethe? He was a friend of mine."

Reece nodded. He did know that, and he opened the door. Glen was there.

"Did you take out his glass eye and fuck him in the head?" asked Glen. He was reading something.

Reece looked at Arthur. "Perhaps soon a schooner filled with shit will tack its way from your arse to your mouth," said Arthur.

Everyone had a good laugh.

Dr. Markush slowed on Bullion Boulevard and pulled into the line of cars entering Fort Knox through Chaffee Gate. His Volvo wagon puttered. He had an unlimited clearance sticker on his windshield, but kept his Organon pass handy just in case. The Organon complex was within walking distance of Tobacco Leaf Lake.

He pulled into a lengthy lane that led to a parking lot beside the secure facility. Reece Myers was on his mind. He was one of the newer patients, but was the most active traveler, the most open about his thoughts, especially regarding Dahlia. He wanted to do an MRI while Myers was seizing, but that had never been done except accidentally.

Markush swiped his badge and entered through the main entrance. It was always so quiet and cold inside. How did the receptionist manage to stay warm?

He nodded. She nodded. He swiped his badge again to enter the secure lock-up, which had twelve beds. He needed to pee first thing and did so before swiping his card a third time to enter the unit. He knocked on the nursing station door, reinforced with bulletproof glass. Claire buzzed him in.

He nodded to Claire, sitting in front of the bank of EEG and ECG monitors. "Any craziness today?"

"Myers has been seizing for over an hour."

"We need to bump his caloric intake if he's seizing like that." He looked at the camera feeds. Richard was in room twelve. Debbie was in the hall talking to the guard. He picked up Reece's chart and read the nurse's notes. The mundane: "Patient with petit mal seizures…" He flipped to the latest travel questionnaire. Reece was still visiting Gadam in 3981. *Why 3981?* The exceptional: "Patient reports meeting a German philosopher, sharing a room with him. This person will 'help me find Mia.'"

Markush examined the screens for room seven. Reece was on his back. His eyes seemed to be closed. "How's the bottled water business going?"

Claire shook her head. Her father was selling carbonated water in the area, a new gig of his with a company based in Clearwater, Florida. "Going broke giving away samples with no orders."

"Can you buy it anywhere around here?"

"Not yet," said Claire. She scanned the monitors, right to left, top to bottom. "Who the hell wants to drink Cat-fresh carbonated water?"

"Catfresh? Isn't it flavored?"

"Oh yeah, but so what?"

Markush laughed. "Why is Debbie still talking with the guard?"

"I think he's sweet on her. He reminds her of her father," said Claire. There was a brief run of V-tach in four. "V-tach in four," she said. She hit the record button, and an ECG strip printed and dropped into a wire basket.

"He's liable to leave us that way," said Markush. The patient in question was seventy-eight. He'd married an Ethiopian woman back in the late sixties when Haile Selassie was at his peak. He'd murdered one of his grandchildren, a two-year-old girl named Mandy. His traveling now was infrequent, and he suffered from organic brain syndrome, which made the interviews nearly impossible.

Markush left the station and entered the U-shaped unit. He said hello to Gumbo, sitting stiff in his office chair, reading a novel by Richard Adams. Gumbo made the motion of tipping an invisible hat. Markush turned the corner and met Shark and Debbie in the hallway. They were arguing.

Debbie cut her tirade short. "Hey, Doc." She folded her arms.

"What's going on?" asked Markush.

Debbie didn't want to say that Shark was joking about her jerking off Myers.

"He's lucky, is all I can say," said Shark. He glanced at his watch. "Fuck. Where's Dumbo?" He hitched his gray trousers with a black stripe and moved on.

Debbie held her tongue. "So, you want to know about Myers?"

Markush looked in seven. He couldn't see Myers' eyes. "Sure. Is the guard okay? Any problems?"

She rolled her eyes. "Just a dumbass is all. So, Myers has teamed up with this German guy to find Mia. He sounded hopeful."

Markush nodded. This was progress. He wanted Reece to find his daughter. He wanted to have done an autopsy on the "girl" Reece had strangled, but that was out of the question.

"Let's see if he can talk now," said Markush.

Debbie led the way. The room smelled fresh, an artificial *uh huh* from a wick'd jar of freshener. "Mr. Myers? Reece?" She squeezed his restrained hand.

Markush was thinking about how Haile Selassie died. No one really seemed to know what had happened after he was taken away in a blue Volkswagen in 1975.

Reece opened his eyes. He looked at the ceiling. Someone had said his name. "I..."

Outside, the sky was clear with a yellow cast. There was no breeze, and it was very quiet as usual. Reece led the way to the bar with the rainbow and the topless wait staff. Inside was cool and dim. Amber stood behind the bar.

"Hmm," said Arthur. "Shall we sit here?" He stopped at a booth along the wall. "The young woman is showing her breasts. Quite lovely."

"Topless bar," said Reece.

"Yes, I suppose so. What is that noise?"

Sounds of an AM station yawning and popping. "I think it's music," said Reece.

"Very odd," said Arthur.

A shirtless guy, Ray, came to their booth. "What'll it be? Oh, let me guess, cherry schnapps?"

Arthur nodded. Reece nodded.

"Coming right up, faggots."

Reece wanted to laugh.

"Reece, you were explaining to me this Dahlia and her relationship to your daughter's disappearance. She is a trickster, no? That much I understand."

"She's always in the form of a little girl, which makes it hard to confront or challenge her. She is one entity but is everywhere as different little girls, seeking some truth and wreaking havoc."

"I say, that is very strange. You've met this Dahlia?"

"Many times. She used to visit me when I was young. For some reason, I wasn't replaced, as was my daughter Mia. I knew it wasn't Mia from the impostor's music. Maybe only girls are replaced. I'm not exactly sure. I've been marked, though, studied. In what manner, I'm also not sure."

Ray approached with a decanter of cherry schnapps and two shot glasses. "Here you go, greasy slit lickers. Anything else?"

Arthur cleared his throat, but was pleased with the schnapps. "Do you know the maker of this?"

"Yeah, Fiddlesticks," said Ray. He flexed his pectorals and did a pose, bulging his biceps.

"I think not," said Arthur. "I do like this establishment, though."

"Yeah, well twist my nipples," said Ray. "I'll be back to check on you."

"Go stroke yourself," said Reece. He watched as Arthur poured them both a shot.

Arthur waved the scent to his nose. He tasted just a sip and then down the hatch, letting it coat and burn his throat. He paused, breathing in the sharp aroma of the liquor and enjoying the warmth in his stomach.

Reece downed his shot and coughed. Tasted like medicine. "Ish," he said. The afterglow was immediate. "Whoa."

"About this music. Music is the perfect art, the one that is purest, no?" asked Arthur.

"Yeah, the music. Dahlia can't understand it. She can only hear it. But the music is the key, I think, to work one's way back to when nothing became everything." Reece poured the next round of schnapps.

"Is Dahlia here? In 3981, Gadam, Ethiopia?" Arthur thrummed his fingers on the table. There was a bit of flush to his face from the schnapps.

"She must be," said Reece. "Especially if Mia and perhaps others like her are here."

"But why would Dahlia replace your daughter Mia with a lookalike and then ship Mia off to the future, perhaps another universe? For God's sake, why was I shipped here?"

"I'm not exactly sure. There are infinite universes with infinite possibilities. Dahlia is trying to narrow the field somehow. There was a point when there was absolutely nothing or perhaps an infinity of absolutely nothings. But it's as if everything is out of control, a chaos of choices. Dahlia has to work her way backward through an infinity of possibilities. Maybe only one, maybe Mia, holds the secret, or it could result from a joining of many, the infinity."

"Perhaps it's the combination of me and Mia in this place at this time?" asked Arthur. He sipped his drink and then took it in.

Reece followed suit and made a face. He really wanted bourbon. "I hadn't thought about it quite like that, but nothing is really impossible."

"What of this impostor who replaced your daughter?" asked Arthur.

"I killed her, strangled her. I killed her. I had to."

"You killed her? Dear God. But why?"

"Because otherwise, I would not have the drive to search for the real Mia. I would just be stuck, and Mia would be stuck, perhaps in a place where she was not loved or safe."

Arthur frowned. "But why would this Dahlia want to simply replace your daughter if it was her music that she was interested in?"

"Yeah, right. You would think," said Reece. "But, I'm

convinced that Dahlia seeks the circumstances that make the music. She's blind to the possibility that Mia or anyone else is simply just gifted. By inserting an impostor, that impostor is trying to figure out what it is about the environment and events surrounding the music. There must be a secret that she wants to discover."

"It's like looking for a lost coin beside a street lamp because the light there is better." Arthur was feeling the schnapps and enjoying it.

"Hmm," said Reece. "That makes sense, sort of."

"The implications are enormous. This tracking back in time, following musical clues, kidnapping, and replacing young girls. I'm not quite sure what to make of it. I would like to know what Dahlia thinks about consciousness, its origins, its place in interpreting the world."

Rachel was making the rounds of guests in the bar, jawing with the regulars. She recognized Reece. Her breasts were quite large and hung to her navel.

"Is this your grandpa?" asked Rachel.

"No, he's my friend—"

Arthur cleared his throat. "May I compliment you on your physical beauty?" He ogled her without blushing.

"Hey, anybody in there?" asked Rachel. She pretended to knock on her skull. "He's *olllld.*"

"I beg your pardon?" asked Arthur.

"More schnapps?" asked Rachel. "In a few?"

"Uh, yes, in a few," said Reece. He poured two more shots and smiled at Rachel. "Can I lick your cow tits?"

"Yeah, sure. Just as soon as you quit looking like a pile of dog shit. I'll send Ray back with the horse spit." She smiled.

"This charade of insults seems to be the status quo, no?" asked Arthur. He sipped his schnapps, raised his glass, and swallowed. "I don't think I can get used to it."

"I kind of like it," said Reece. "It's very disarming. I wonder how you actually insult someone?"

"Perhaps with physical violence?" asked Arthur. "I wonder what the response would be, say, if I were to slap that young lady after she insulted me?"

"Don't forget Caroline Marquet. You don't want to be a one-trick pony in the history books."

"Very funny, but, yes, I should not repeat that mistake at all costs. Tell me more about this impostor you dispatched. You know that I find it repulsive, not completely understanding the situation. I'm actually reconsidering sharing a room with you, out of concern for my own safety. Do you feel remorse?"

Reece laughed. "Dahlia is not human. She took away my daughter, the child that my wife created with a little help from me."

Arthur poured the last two shots. "An eye for an eye? How is it that this Dahlia can live and die but is not human? Surely the undertaker would be puzzled, no? Was there a funeral for this impostor? Ein prosit." He took down his schnapps.

"Cheers," said Reece. He felt a bit drunk and wanted more. "Yes, there must have been a funeral. But I was locked away, am locked away, I think. I'm traveling here somehow from a place in Kentucky. Like you are from Berlin."

"Was this impostor an exact copy of your daughter, Mia? If so, how did you know the difference?"

Reece felt a little thrill. "Yes, an exact copy, except for the music. She did not have Mia's music. It was close, but an octave too low."

"But real flesh and bone, but not human?"

"Yes," said Reece. "An impostor!" He pounded his schnapps and clanked his glass on the small round table. His vision blurred...

Reece opened his eyes, exhausted. His eyelashes brushed against gauze. He tried to bring his hand to his face, but his hand was restrained. He struggled. One leg was restrained as well.

"Mr. Myers!" A woman's voice. "You're back. You're safe. Relax."

The pads came off his eyes. The room was bright, and he squinted. He recognized the woman. He tasted alcohol on his tongue. He was back. He was safe.

"Hey," said Reece. He had killed a young girl, but why?

"It's me, Debbie." She smoothed back his thinning hair, damp with sweat. "You've been seizing, traveling."

"Yeah," said Reece. "I was in Gadam with Arthur. Untie my hands. Please."

Debbie hesitated. Markush had left. Maybe he would be okay untied. What was the worst that could happen? Shark and Gumbo were on duty.

"I need to sit up, hang my legs over the side. I feel like I'm suffocating. We were drinking schnapps."

"Schnapps?" asked Debbie. She untied his left wrist and waited a moment.

Reece's left hand went to his nose. "Thank you."

Debbie circled the foot of the bed and untied his right wrist. He was cute, this Reece, and overwhelmed was the expression on his face. She was his age, around thirty.

"My foot."

Debbie released the knot on his ankle. She watched him sit up. He fell back.

"Shit," said Reece.

Claire buzzed in from the nursing station. "Room ten, Scocpol needs something. She hit her button."

"Okay, see if Richard can check on her. Let me know."

"Will do."

"Is this a hospital or a prison?" asked Reece.

"Kind of both," said Debbie. "Let me help you sit up. Have to do it slow." She raised the head of his bed with the button until he was at a forty-five-degree angle. "Sit like that for a minute, and then I'll swing your legs over. Need to get you walking and get that catheter out."

"Yeah," said Reece. He felt giddy, as if two and two equaled four.

"Tell me about your trip." She reached and smoothed the tape on his nose. "Don't pull out your feeding tube."

Reece focused. "I'm weak as fuck."

"Do you think you could drink some Sprite?" Markush had left a standing order for liquids when ready.

"How about a Pepsi?"

Debbie laughed. "Coke?"

"Damn, water will be fine. Shots of schnapps."

"Yeah, that's what you said earlier. With Arthur? Tell me more," said Debbie. She felt plain in her blue Organon scrubs, her curves subdued.

"Yeah, with Arthur. How did you know? It was a topless bar. The drinks are free."

"It's my job. You're traveling to Gadam, Ethiopia. Thirty-nine eighty-one, right? You've met a German philosopher."

"Schopenhauer. Arthur. I can't believe it. I teach his stuff, or used to."

"Okay, let's try to sit up. I'll help you. We'll let your legs dangle. I'll hold you." She put her hand behind his back, and then Reece was vertical. "Okay?"

"Yeah, so far."

Debbie held him up with one arm and scooted her other arm beneath his legs. "Here we go."

"Can I suck your pussy?"

Debbie let him fall back. "What?"

"You're supposed to say, 'Eat my dung,' or something like that."

Debbie was confused. "Eat my dung." She pulled his legs over the side of the bed.

Reece laughed. He bent over laughing, nearly falling out of bed.

"Whoa. Hold on," said Debbie. She kept her hand on his back and one on his chest. Humor was good. Sometimes it was violence, like with the guy in number three.

He laughed and felt like puking, gradually regaining control. "Jesus. I want to hike the Appalachian Trail with Mia." A wave of nausea. *Where the hell is Mia?*

"Yeah, your daughter." She removed her hand from his back, and he hunched over as if his spine was rubber. "Have you found her, seen her?"

Reece struggled. "Not yet, just drinking with Arthur."

"Schnapps?"

"Yeah, cherry schnapps. He's going to help me find her. Idealism. Transcendental." He felt drained. He felt sick. Was his Mia even real to begin with? He opened his eyes. He saw his hospital gown. Below was a tiled floor.

"You teach philosophy," said Debbie. "This is a kind of friend of yours from the past. He's helping you understand."

Reece felt like he was smoking cigars and drinking bourbon, a deadly combo. It always made him high and in the end sick, chilled and nauseous. "Yeah."

"Let's lay back for a minute, rest," said Debbie. "I need to check on my other patients."

Reece had imagined he was the only one. "Others?"

"I have six patients, all kind of like you, travelers. Dahlia..."

"Shit, Dahlia," said Reece. "You know about Dahlia?"

"A little. Dr. Markush is the one who knows about Dahlia. He wants to talk with you about her."

"Oh," said Reece. "Others, like me? Child killers?"

"If you want to put it that way."

"Dahlia is an alien force. She wants to take everything back to the Garden, back to nothing."

"To when there was nothing?" asked Debbie. She turned on his TV. "What channel, news, sports?"

Reece sensed that she had work to do. He looked up at the TV. It was *COPS*. "Just there is fine." He relaxed his body and let his arms rest by his side.

"Okay, you're unrestrained, but you have to stay in your bed. There are guards in the hall. The call button is here." She laid the large white button on his chest. "Deal?"

"Deal," said Reece.

Reece and Arthur sat in the bar, drinking a second, third, fourth, and fifth round of schnapps.

"Whoa," said Reece.

Arthur craved tobacco, but no one was smoking. There was nothing left to say about this Dahlia. She seemed to be God, wrenching the forward progress of time to stop it and return to the origins of everything beyond, behind.

"Mierde," said Arthur. "Shall we...go?" He wasn't sure that he could stand.

Reece tapped his fingers on the table. Arthur's music, on and then off. He was like Reece, tapped but not consumed. *Damn.* He had to piss like an umbrella...like an anaconda. He laughed. A voice. He looked up.

Rachel stood there, hands on hips. "You guys about parched your peanuts? Looks like you're ready to spoon and make an ugly baby."

Reece had to focus on his hands. His head was trying to spin. "Shit."

Arthur looked up. "Quite finished. Thank you."

"Less go," said Reece. "Mia." He felt that she had passed within his reach, but that he had missed her because of the alcohol. "Fuck a dilly, damn."

Rachel took the empty shot glasses. "Come back when you can't stay so long."

"What?" asked Reece.

"I think you need rest," said Arthur.

"Shut your pie hole," said Reece. "Your wig looks ridiculous." He laughed.

Arthur considered his options. "Sit upon a large nail. Shall we go? You need perhaps to lie down."

"If this is 3992, 86, 23, then I should be able to drink as much as I want without fucking feeling the world is ending. Your dick...is a tapeworm. Less drink until we die and see what happens." He turned and raised his hand. Rachel was behind the bar, and then she was at their table. A flash. Arthur recoiled. Reece's head hung over his lap.

"Trying to work up a case of alcohol poisoning?" asked Rachel. She cupped her breast and licked her expansive nipple. "The cemetery is near, so no problem."

"Fucking bourbon," said Reece. "Fuck goddamn schnapps."

"Good for you, old man?" asked Rachel.

"If it suits Master Reece. Yes. Let's try it."

"Hey, Master Bates. Knob Creek on the rocks, doubles?" asked Rachel.

Reece lifted his head. He tried to focus, *to fuck us.* "Yes."

"Right on, you gonorrhea hippies," said Rachel. "Suck each other, and I'll be right back."

"We can stop if you need to," said Arthur.

"Stop what?" asked Reece. "I have to find Mia. Where she is? Is she where?"

"You said she was here," said Arthur. "We will find her." He felt a massive hangover in his future. But this was the future. Maybe some magic was forthcoming. *Katzenjammer!*

Reece looked at his hand. He imagined he was a nurse and that he was familiar with the signs and symptoms of dehydration. He examined his left hand. He could see veins there. That was good. He pinched the skin below his knuckles. The skin tented for a second and then returned to its original shape. Mild dehydration. He could drink some more.

"Do you have an illustration of Mia? A likeness," said Arthur.

Holy hell. Reece felt his back pockets. There was something there. He pulled out the tiny leather wallet from his left pocket. His heart raced. Why hadn't he thought of this? Inside, a driver's license from Kentucky. *Kentucky?* Insurance cards. A credit card. Something thin. He slid it out with his thumb, and there she was, Mia, three years old, the photo aged.

Arthur examined the picture. "Is this a drawing? Ah, lovely. Very lifelike. She seems to have a strong will. Beautiful." He marveled at the detail.

"Exactly," said Reece. Mia was like two daughters in one, strong yet vulnerable, pretty yet unassuming, a solid human being.

Rachel was back with two tumblers of bourbon on the rocks. "This should shrink your dicks into nothing," she said. "Not that it's anything different." She was tired.

"Amenseganalo," said Reece.

"Yeah, fuck you too," said Rachel.

Reece was blank.

"So, bourbon. I suppose now is the time," said Arthur. He loosened a button on his white shirt and smoothed back his frumpy white hair, balding in the middle.

Reece picked up his cold drink. He drank deeply of the honeyed liquor. He felt he was in a blast freezer, falling head over heels, unable to stop.

Arthur sipped and moved his head from side to side.

"Delightful?"

Reece was skateboarding through a maze of cement half-pipes, running up stairs, plowing through knee-high grass, back into the flooding streets, on a surfboard, with islands everywhere, the waves diminishing. A big plate of sliced bread. A cup of vinegar barbecue sauce. Slaw. He sipped and sipped again. His arms felt like fuzzy TV.

"Mia?" asked Reece. "I need to focus. The buzz."

"I'm listening," said Arthur. "Perhaps we should sleep first?"

Reece imagined running through a forest with a pen and notebook, writing as he plowed through blackberry brambles and holly bushes. *That's how it should be, all or nothing. Fuck. I'm drunk. That chick in ninth grade with the mole on her back.* He'd been in love with her.

"The ice is interesting," said Arthur. "It changes the way one drinks."

"Sips," said Reece. "Just sips. Opens the flower, the bouquet."

Arthur took another sip. "Like a distilled beer."

"Which it is," said Reece.

"Do you like Scotch?" asked Arthur.

Reece sat up. The cold in his extremities had gone away. He took a drink. "Some. Some are too smoky, too rough. Scotch makes me feel...vulnerable, naked. Bourbon is perfect. It waits on you. Scotch rapes you, your wallet."

Arthur laughed. It had been twenty years since he'd had sex with a woman. Schnapps, wine, and beer had been his conjugal visitors.

"Kentucky straight, motherfucker," said Reece. He took

down the rest of his bourbon. His eyes widened. *Type O Negative.* They did a cover of "Cinnamon Girl." *Fucking wig of Jesus.*

After *Judge Judy,* Reece went numb. He felt like he'd drunk a case of Bud Light. Mia was out there. Something whispered to him. *Ethiopia.* Had he been shot in the head in Godo, by the fucking Snake, or was it the Hyena? He wasn't sure. His hands were on Emma's shoulders. *Emma? Goddamn.* He couldn't tell if it was day or night. He opened his eyes, a room, a rectangle. There was a TV playing, a movie, it seemed. He remembered Debbie, the nurse. She'd untied his wrists. He raised his arms. *Nothing.* He was free. She'd kept her promise, but what was his? He grabbed the bed rails and pulled himself upright. His scalp felt queer, itchy.

He fell back onto the bed. He ran his right hand over his head, wires. The EEG. He wanted to rip them off. He concentrated on his chest. Wires there, too. He struggled to sit up again and let out a low whine.

"Hey," said Laura, his night nurse. She waved her hand in front of Reece's face.

It took Reece a while to focus. Mia was close. He could feel it, and then he couldn't. He had strangled an impostor. Maybe the nurse was an impostor. He felt drunk as shit.

Reece opened his eyes. "Hey. Debbie?" He saw a face, puffy red hair

"No, Laura. Debbie is day shift. Tell me what's going on. Tell me about Mia and Arthur."

Reece hesitated. "Is this a trick? How do you know?"

"No, no," said Laura. "You've been talking with Debbie and Dr. Markush."

Reece tried to balance the equation in his head. "Well, Mia is in Gadam."

Laura's jaw dropped, literally. "Oh, wow. How is she?"

Reece tried to put the pieces together. He'd killed Mia's impostor. Mia was in an erstaz Ethiopia, but was she his daughter? "I think she's my daughter, right? Mia?"

"Yes, Mia, your daughter. Go on."

"Three nine eight one. That's the year. People talk in insults."

"What do you mean?"

"Like you walk into a bar and the waitress says, 'Your farts smell like diesel in the afternoon.' And then you say, 'Suck my grandma's face.'"

"Huh." Laura was taking notes. "Weird. Do people get upset?"

"No. Never. Everything is peaceful."

"How do you know that Mia is in Gadam?" asked Laura.

"It seems like I can hear her music there. But, she's hidden. I can't navigate to her. Arthur seems to have some ideas. I need to go back." He threw his legs over the side of the bed.

"Whoa, hold on. Take it easy." She pressed the room call light, which flashed outside the door. Within seconds, the night shift guard was there, Renaldo. He stopped outside the room. He waved off the other guard, Amanda, who was coming around the corner of her end of the unit.

"Fuck, how do I get back?" He wavered on the edge of the bed.

"We can help you. Dr. Markush. He'll be back in the morning."

"I can't wait until morning," said Reece. "I need to go

now. She's in danger."

"It's good. It's all good. You could initiate the travel on your own. It's when you seize that you're gone."

"Seize, motherfucker," he said to himself. His hands gripped his thighs, keeping him from flopping over. He felt so weak and useless.

"What will you do when you find her?" asked Laura. "You need a plan."

Reece thought. What would he do? "I'll bring her back, to here."

"But how?" She was trained to inquire but not to challenge. She was pushing the limit. "This is 2003. You're saying that Mia is in 3981." She stood in front of Reece, ready to catch him if he fell.

"Hey, Laura, looks like room three is vomiting," said Lars over the intercom. "Sorry!"

"I'll watch him until you get back," said Renaldo. His repaired harelip was nearly invisible, but not quite.

"Super. Be back in five minutes, Reece. Okay?" Laura hurried out of the room. Her dad, a cardiologist, had a heated pool. *Oh yeah!*

Reece grabbed the upper bed rail and sort of fell backward. "A little help."

Renaldo entered and scooted his legs back onto the bed. "You need to move up." He moved in.

"Is that your mother's pubic hair in your teeth?" Reece's feet were against the footboard, his knees bent. He laughed.

"What the hell?" asked Renaldo. He put his hands on his hips.

Reece opened his eyes. He looked at Renaldo. "I'm sorry. Inside joke."

Renaldo reminded himself that he was dealing with a child killer. "Yeah. Push with your feet and you'll be up in the bed." He didn't want to touch Reece.

Reece smelled blood. "Are you looking at my dick?"

Renaldo saw red. "What the hell, asshole!"

"Suck it, but don't chew it. I'm not beef jerky." Reece pushed with his feet but was too weak to move more than an inch or two. He was laughing, mainly on the inside. He grinned. "Oh yeah."

"What, you don't like harelips?"

Reece opened his eyes and tried to focus. He was laughing, belly laughing, uncontrollably. He began to gasp and cough. Still laughing. "Fuck."

"Yeah, well fuck you," said Renaldo. He smirked and turned. Along the way, he stopped by room three. "That Myers is a fucking prick."

Laura somewhat guessed what had happened, her gloves covered in vomited Ensure. "It's okay. He's a special case. No worries."

Renaldo felt a little better and sat in his rolling chair at the end of the hall.

Laura stuffed the dirty linen and rags into a rolling cart. She raised number three's head a few more degrees. Grayson freaked her out. He was the serious bitch on the unit. Still bent on killing, no matter the circumstances. Full blanket restraint at all times, the suicide smock. It took two people half an hour to give him a bed bath.

Reece awoke on the floor of the rainbow bar. His neck was stiff. His left arm was asleep. His hip hurt like hell. He wondered where he was. He saw a pair of trousered legs beneath a table. The room was dim. He lifted his head, then hit his head. *Jesus Christ.*

"Hey, loser!"

Reece looked up. A skirt, something like a thong. "What?"

"You and your friend here need to pay some fucking rent or start drinking again."

Reece sat up, crowded under the table. "But the drinks are free. Right?"

"It's a saying, dumbass. But seriously, you're bad for business."

Reece went to his knees and then stood. His vision went black, and he bent over. "Fudge." He smelled yeast, whiskey essence.

The waitress, Michelina, held him steady. She was topless. "Sit."

Reece sat and put his arms on the table. The old man was face down, snoring, ripping it like the temple curtain during the crucifixion. "Ardor. Adam. Arthur," said Reece. He remembered showing Arthur Mia's photo. He checked his pocket and his wallet was still there. He shook Arthur.

Arthur was like a rock. Reece shook him again. "Uh," said Arthur. He raised his head, a deep red crease across his left cheek. He'd been dreaming of Hamburg. "Scheisse."

"We have to find, find Mia," said Reece. He needed to sleep some more.

Arthur's eyes looked like prunes. "Shall we eat?" He was famished.

Michelina clicked gum in her mouth and left them to their miserable lives.

"Yeah," said Reece. "Eggs."

"No, buster," said Arthur.

"I forgot. Buster. I need to piss first."

"I'll go with you," said Arthur.

The two staggered to the bathroom. Inside was a short elf of a man, wearing a pink chiffon robe. "Well, well, look at the gunk between God's toes. Can I wipe the pus from your dicks?"

Reece took the urinal and Arthur took the toilet.

"You guys really guys? You look like coelacanths or sloths." The elf yawned.

Reece flushed. There was no sink. There was the black box that he'd seen before. He stuck his hands inside, and there was a flash of UV light.

"Good job," said the elf. "Count to five and I'll blow you."

Arthur nodded and followed Reece out of the bathroom. "We should really sleep before we begin our search in earnest, correct?" He wiped sweat from his brow.

Reece took a deep breath. What were they up against? *Dahlia.* "Yeah. Wouldn't hurt." He stepped through the mist door into the brightness of perpetual day. *Left or right?* Everything looked the same. Where were the goddamn people? He remembered the tiny brown X he'd marked beside the door. He turned right, and Arthur followed.

The bright light was therapeutic, waking them both. A dog slunk in the path, edging toward them, teeth bared, saliva dripping.

Arthur grabbed Reece from behind. "The dog is mad. No closer. Dear God."

Reece looked for a rock, but there were none. The dog growled low and long and then lunged for Reece, fangs bared. The dog flashed to over ten feet tall. Reece and Arthur fell backward. And then there was only a skinny man, laughing at them. "Cocksuckers," he said.

"What the hell?" asked Reece. Shape shifters. Were-wolves. Snakes. Hyenas. Eating the dead.

"No more schnapps," said Arthur. "There's a blue star." He pointed.

Reece looked beside the door for an X drawn in the dust, but there was none. "Not this one."

"Ach," said Arthur. "We must lie down. I must lie down."

"Agreed," said Reece. "I think we're close. Just here." It was another metal building with a blue star. The X was there. "Here." He opened the door into the main hallway. The same middle-aged man was there in a chair, looking at what appeared to be an electronic tablet.

"Hey, you're a little late. Right?"

"Our room," said Reece. He could already feel the mattress beneath his tired body. He could barely keep his eyes open.

"Yeah, well, we gave your room to a couple of grannies from 1962. They're probably munching carpet right about now. So, in other words, get the fuck lost."

"No," said Arthur.

"Shit," said Reece.

"Can you recommend another room?" asked Arthur.

"Not in this time and place," said the hall monitor. "Now get lost. Scarce."

Reece wanted to strangle the idiot. He remembered the strange little park that had the only trees he'd seen. There was grass there. They could sleep there. "Fuck you."

The hall monitor laughed. "Yeah, you have a good one."

"Come on," said Reece. "I know a place with shade."

"Shade? Is there a bed?" asked Arthur.

"No, but we can sleep there. It's downhill, past the rainbow bar. I think I can find it." He felt like he would roll into a ball.

Outside, the tiny sun was livid.

"What about the data fur?" asked Arthur. "Let me think."

Reece stopped and gazed at Arthur. "Anything?"

Arthur was overcome with a dizzying flood of information. He dropped to his knees and then his hands and knees. Disconnected, unfiltered images from multiple universes. He ran to the bathroom, vomited, and moaned.

"Oh Lord," said Reece. He put his hand on Arthur's back. "Let's just go to the place I have in mind. It's like a small park. The place with the trees."

Arthur stood, embarrassed. "Shall we?" He wiped his mouth.

Reece staggered downhill, his skull splitting. At least he wasn't thinking about suicide. *Two thousand and three. 2003.* He'd strangled that bitch. But before that, there was the depression, the nagging urge just to die and make the world a better place. He couldn't do it because of Mia. She had kept him alive. He'd tried once before he met Kristin, an unsuccessful overdose. *What a puss.* Reece felt useless and dead. He had to find Mia, no compromise. They passed blue and red stars. He looked for the green star of a buster establishment. Maybe that was best. And then there was one. A green star.

Arthur followed him inside. Reece recognized Shia behind the counter, with dark green eyes and a top knot. "Well, well, it's grandpa and his baby goat," said Shia. "Hey!"

"Hello," said Arthur. "We are very hungry."

"Buster fresh?" asked Reece.

"Best buster this side of the Mississippi or the Elbe," said Shia. Her eyes sparkled with youth and something else.

"Vim and vigor," said Reece.

"Ah, the Elbe," said Arthur.

"Straight up?" asked Shia.

"Sure," said Reece.

Shia took a bowl, flipped it, tossed it over her shoulder with her right hand, caught it with her left hand, and filled it at the tap. Less than ten seconds. "Yo and behold, minions of leprous mites," she said.

"Thank you, scabrous locust," said Arthur.

Reece laughed.

"Suds on the beach," said Shia, serving up two bowls of buster. Reece wasn't bad-looking. If only he weren't a traveler.

Reece sipped and then chugged. He was starved. Arthur did the same. Both felt instantly better.

"Hair of the dog," said Reece.

Shia data-furred that one. "Exactly, my friend, with the

tiny dick."

"And your tits are like mosquito bites," said Reece. He smiled. Shia was something else.

"Thanks," said Shia.

Arthur held forth his empty bowl. "What are the flavors? This is nice, but what do you have?"

Shia thought. "How about ox tongue with rosemary?"

"Excellent choice," said Arthur.

"How about you?" asked Shia. She was feeling weak in the knees and needed to pee.

Reece looked surprised. "Turkey pot pie?"

"Not a problem," said Shia. She spun two clean bowls and slammed one and then the other under the spigot. Liquid goodness, nutrition, faith, adenosine triphosphate.

Reece inhaled over his glass. "Damn, Swanson's pot pie. No doubt." He drank the muddy liquid, hot, as if from a microwave oven.

Arthur sipped and groaned. Osso buco. Rosemary. "Thank you..."

"Shia," said Shia.

Arthur and Reece lingered over a third and then a fourth serving of buster before leaving. Arthur stepped through the mist door, a new man but still needing sleep. "You lead the way."

Reece felt like flying to the moon. "Should we start our search now?"

"I'm an old man," said Arthur. "Let's rest, if possible."

"No problem," said Reece. He felt like ice cream, slowly melting in a bowl.

Gumbo smirked each time he passed number seven. What a prick, typical of a child killer. *Asshole.* The rest of the shift was uneventful, with Myers seizing on and off. Myers was definitely traveling.

Today, Wednesday, Richard was Reece's nurse. He swapped out with Debbie every few days. Variety was the spice of life.

Reece felt numb, yet powerful. He remembered his grandparents snapping green beans in their yard in Emerald Valley. *2003? 1993?* Did it matter? He used to run around the lake there, five miles or so, without a shirt, sweat burning his eyes. He was floating within an inch of the ceiling.

"Time to change your diaper," said Richard.

Reece was in a funk post-seizure. He tried to make words with his mouth. "La," was all he could say. He wanted to tell Richard that he and Arthur were on the case, that results were in the making. *Goddamn diaper.*

Reece lay on his side. He felt a cool rag running down his back. "Damn."

"Sorry," said Richard. "Gotta keep you clean." It was the least favorite of his duties, but perhaps the most ennobling. Nobody deserved to soak in their own feces or urine.

"Oh," said Reece.

Richard squirted more liquid soap into the bath pan. Last was Reece's privates. Richard took care, keeping him covered as well as possible. He finished and dumped the filmy water into the sink. He grabbed a towel and dried him top to bottom, adding a bit of scrub to stimulate circulation.

Reece was grateful, but embarrassed. "Yeah," is what he said, on his right side. His clean sheets smelled like heat.

Richard turned him onto his back, shifting Reece's hips with the draw sheet. Reece wasn't quite far enough up in the bed. Richard lowered the head a bit, bent Reece's legs, and then gripped his shoulders and pulled him up. Done.

Shit. Reece was grateful. He felt like a new man. Was he dead or alive? He wasn't sure. *Mia.* Where was she? He opened his eyes and saw Richard. He seemed reasonable, with black hair, a Fu Manchu, clean cut.

"Hey," said Richard. "You still there?" He pulled a clean sheet over Reece and adjusted the pillow.

"Yes."

Richard was surprised. "Two thousand and three here."

That made Reece's head hurt. "Damn. Thirty-nine eighty-one. Mia. Arthur."

"Yeah, you're good. You're bouncing back and forth, no sweat. Don't worry. Tell me about Mia. How is she?"

Reece thought. Something was askew. "In 3981 we're looking for her. In 2003, she's there but...dead, the impostor at least. The real Mia is in 3981? I think. I'm not sure." He felt dizzy.

Dr. Markush would be in the next day, around three p.m. Richard asked the question again. "So, how is Mia?"

"She's fine but tired. She had dinner with us. She's going with us to our compound." Reece didn't quite understand why he had said that. He and Arthur had gotten trashed but had not encountered Mia. She seemed close, in the ether.

Richard was a bit confused. He'd been listening to Limp Bizkit on his iPod. "Did you meet with her?"

Reece thought. He had. "She's okay, eating dabo. We're getting her filtered water. She's strong and lonely."

"How did Mia get there?"

Reece thought hard. "How the hell do I get there? I have no idea." Something to do with Dahlia. Dahlia had kidnapped her. And left the impostor. He had killed her, it. "What about my wife, Kristin? Does she know I'm here?"

"Yeah, she knows, but she doesn't have clearance to visit. Technically, we do not exist. This is a special place. You're special as well."

"I don't feel special," said Reece. "I feel like ass. I'd like not to wear this damn diaper. Don't you have a bedside commode?"

Richard looked at his watch. "Yeah, but when you seize, you lose control. You're improving. Just be patient. At least you're not restrained."

"Can I try to stand? I can't take this bed much longer."

Richard wouldn't let him stand but sat him up and let him dangle his legs for a minute. He had to check on other patients and positioned Reece back in bed. He washed his hands and moved into room six, Emma, the nurse who had been shot in the head in a small village in Ethiopia. She was responsive to pain and light and made feeble gestures with her hands. She was small but looked strong.

Reece pushed the button on the bed rail to raise his head higher. *Mia.* He had to find Mia, but he was watching freaking dog food commercials. She was the only thing that mattered. If he had to seize in order to travel and wear a diaper, so be it. He concentrated on having a seizure. He held his breath. He heard his heart beating, slowing. Dr. Markush, though, could make him seize. He used magnets. He would learn how to travel without seizing. He was sure he could do it, but not sure how. He closed his eyes and thought about Gadam 3981. He saw green plaid, streaks of red. The TV played a commercial for sinus medication. He turned the TV off and concentrated. Gadam was plain, filled with metal buildings that all looked alike. The lanes were very steep in places. He could see this Arthur, an old man with white hair. It came to him again like a bolt. Arthur was Schopenhauer, the German philosopher. He taught Schopenhauer at the university. Did that make sense, though? Arthur was helping him find Mia? There had to be a reason it was him and not someone else. Who knew?

Reece looked around his small square room. He liked the pale mustard color of the walls. "It's 2003," he told himself. "I've been shot in the head. No, that's the lady in room six. Or is it? Dahlia took Mia. Mia is in Gadam 3981. The world is my will and representation." He closed his eyes. The mesh in his scalp hummed.

Reece and Arthur walked from lane to lane, heading always upward, looking for the park, increasingly sleepy. Reece stopped. He could go right, left, or straight. Straight seemed more uphill, which made the most sense. Arthur stumbled along behind. "Soon," said Reece. And there it was, a jacaranda tree in full purple bloom. There was trimmed grass.

Reece ran and fell to the ground, exhausted. He was asleep almost instantly. Arthur was less limber and sat with his back to the tree trunk. His head dipped and snapped, and he was soon asleep, back in Berlin, holding court at the local bar.

Reece awoke. It was high noon as always. His ribs hurt. He felt a kick and opened his eyes. Someone was kicking him. *Hell!* He rolled to his hands and knees and briefly saw a squat bald man coming straight for him.

The thing charged Reece and grabbed his head, pulled, and flipped him over.

"The hell!" said Reece. He swung wild, twisted his torso. He was in the air and slammed on his back. His breath leapt from his lungs. He couldn't think. The bald head was in his face.

"You are human shit," said the face.

Reece relaxed. Maybe the brute would stop. "The fuck you doing?"

The face, a plastic face, twisted into a grin. "The fuck is right. Choke on pussy hair, you freak. Sleeping in the sacred park! Who do you think you are? Fucking...Michael Jackson...You have been equalized. What is your plea?"

Arthur had drowsed awake. At first, he covered his head, but then sat up. An ape of a man was on top of Reece, his hands around his neck. He was bald and muscled, "ripped" from the data fur. "The devil," he said.

Reece's mind raced. "What? Is this a sacred place?"

"Is this a sacred place? Where the hell are you from, 2003?" The squat man backhanded Reece, drawing blood from his upper lip.

Reece recoiled. "I've never met a motherfucker quite like you," said Reece.

"Yeah, Kid Rock. Much appreciated." The goon relaxed his grip and let Reece crawl away. "You and your grandmother here need to get lost. Don't fucking think about sleeping in the sacred place ever again. Got it...retard?"

"Yeah, not a problem, oh Almighty God of...collard greens and hot sauce."

The tough laughed. "You're so good." He smirked, released his grip, and stood. For good measure, he swift-kicked Arthur in the calf.

"Scheisse!"

The equalizer laughed. "Not a problem...amigo. You're cool. Just hang your hat elsewhere. Look for the blue stars."

Reece sat up, wincing. "Yeah, we'll be moving on." He couldn't resist the urge to punch the fucker in the face. He leaned back and threw his weight into it, connecting with a jaw. He felt like he had broken his arm. "Shit!"

The squat executor of divine justice went to his knees. "I see stars," he said. "Fucking..."

"Reece, no more," said Arthur.

Reece was pumped. He swung for the goon's chin and connected. The goon swayed and fell over backward. Reece instantly felt bad. The idiot could know where Mia was. "Let's go," he said.

"We will surely be punished," said Arthur.

"Maybe," said Reece. He looked at the man on the ground. He was thick and short. His jaw looked broken, and it was. "Mia." He drew back to kick him in the ribs, but changed his mind.

Reece's seizure ceased. His knuckles hurt. He sat up in bed, straining his weakened stomach muscles. He covered his face as if shielding blows and grunted.

Claire noticed number seven's activity. He was unrestrained. Not a good idea, she thought. She buzzed Debbie in ten. "Myers is acting strange in seven."

Debbie was running a bedside EEG strip for Scocpol. She stopped the tracer and stepped out to check on Myers. His leg was through the bed rail. "Hey, Reece. Hey." She helped his leg through the rail.

"Damn," said Reece. He opened his eyes, and it was what he feared: a hospital room. He had to find Mia. What the hell was his problem?

"Reece?" asked Debbie. She wore new aqua scrubs with the Organon logo, form-fitting this time.

Reece fathomed the situation. "Can you make me seize? I need to go back."

"Only Dr. Markush can do that," said Debbie. "Sorry. Did you see Mia?"

"She's there. I just have to find her. It's hard to explain."

"What about Arthur? Is he helping you?"

Reece thought. "Not yet. We drink schnapps and buster. Why are we wasting time?"

"Yeah, the buster," said Debbie.

"It's the food, liquid food. It's all there is. Like Ensure."

"Okay," said Debbie. "Are you hungry? I can get you some solid food. We can get that tube out of your nose. What do you think?"

Reece felt his nose. "Yeah, I forgot the tube was in." He lay back. "How about some eggs and grits?"

"I'll see what I can do," said Debbie. "Scrambled, fried?"

"Two eggs, over easy." His mouth watered. "Put some sprinkle cheese on it. Dump some grits to the side."

"Excellent," said Debbie. Markush would be impressed. "Sprinkle cheese?"

"You know. The grated Parmesan cheese in a shaker."

"Yeah, right. I'll see if they have that. They may have to order it." Debbie smoothed back her short blonde hair. "You're unrestrained, because we trust you. You can't leave this room. Got it? We should be able to get you into the day room if you cooperate."

Reece considered his options. At least he was making progress with Mia, but not enough. "Yeah, got it." He sat cross-legged and noted the redness around his wrists and ankles. "Mia is there. I'm sure of it. I just need to go back as soon as possible. When will Markush be back?"

"He's here. He's in the dayroom talking with another patient. His name is Freddie. You two should talk soon. He's in a similar boat. Okay, I'm leaving now, but call if you need anything." She left and returned to number ten, Scocpol's room.

Scocpol had stopped seizing, her sheets wet with sweat. Timera Scocpol was thirty-one years old, about the average age of the Organon patients. Her eyes were fluttering, and her mouth was trying to make words.

"Timera? Hey, it's Debbie. You've been seizing." She adjusted the sheet and walked to the nursing station to order Reece's food. Claire buzzed her in.

"Need to get Myers some food. Looks like he's coming

around," said Debbie.

Claire's straight black hair hung across her eyes. "Yeah, Freddie needs someone to talk to besides Markush." Freddie had a similar story to Reece's. Claire had heard about Dahlia, the impostors, the weird little girls that seemed to be associated with the violence, but she understood little of what the implications were.

Debbie hit the intercom for the day room. "Hey, Doc. Is it okay if we take out Meyer's feeding tube and get him some solid food? He's hungry."

Markush was talking with Freddie Mentone. "Yeah, sounds good. Go ahead." He turned back to Freddie. Freddie was wearing street clothes, jeans and a flannel shirt with disposable hospital slippers. He was thirty-five, short, balding, and had tremendous red ears.

"So, who is this Myers?" asked Freddie

"He's the newest patient. Murdered his daughter, the impostor. So, tell me more." Markush sat in a maroon vinyl chair at an angle to Freddie on the matching couch.

"Will he be out here? I need to see if he can help me." He smirked.

Markush sighed and tossed back his long gray hair. "Maybe tomorrow. We'll see. I've never seen someone come around as quickly as he has."

"Yeah, took me three fucking months," said Freddie.

"You were telling me about Dahlia, the little girl you call Amanda. How do you make the connection between the two?"

Freddie grimaced. "You tell me first just how long I stay locked up in here. I feel like I'm on the moon."

"Would you rather be in prison? You stabbed your

daughter, killed her. You should be locked up in a maximum-security facility. We're giving you a break, right?"

"Break, my ass. How would you like to be tied to a bed for three months?" Freddie clenched his fists.

"Look, I'm sorry about that. But you were a risk to yourself and us. But you have information, things that we're obligated to discover." He jotted in his notebook.

"What if I don't want to talk? Will you strap me back down?"

"Only if you become violent," said Markush. He sat with his hands formed into a steeple, his fingers touching his chin.

"The girl I stabbed was not my daughter. Was not Alicia. I've told you that. She was an impostor. I'm not sure how it happened, but it did. Dahlia visited me at night when I was a kid. My parents didn't have a clue, and maybe that's why I'm sitting here talking to you."

"Could you be an impostor?"

Freddie cringed. "I don't know. Do you think this new guy is an impostor?"

"No." Markush frowned, frustrated by what he didn't know. "I don't think Myers is. He has the shadow membrane, like you, somehow in his scalp. But his family has a history. A great-grandfather of his killed one of his daughters. He has a legacy, and you don't. Besides, it seems that Dahlia only replaces little girls. I'm puzzling it out. It's my job." He wrote as he spoke.

"I know when it happened. I've told you that. It must have been when I was two or three. This thing, Dahlia, attacked me in my room. I remember the blue lights." Freddie put his head into his hands. "Oh, fuck me. Why me of all people?"

"There was something about you that drew her to you. Just like she was drawn to Reece and probably to everyone here. You know the music that you hear? Myers, the new guy, has said similar things, that he can feel the universe vibrating."

Freddie laughed. "Really? Yeah, I need to talk to him."

"I'd like for you two to talk, and I'd like to listen. Would that be okay? I mean, this room is wired for sound, so I wouldn't have actually to be in here."

"What if I say no?" asked Freddie. His ears turned a brighter shade of red.

"Look, you want to figure this out as much as I do. It's in your best interest. In the best interest of us all."

"My wife has left me. As far as I know, no one even knows I'm here. How would that make you feel?"

"There are people who would come after you if you were free. You're safe here. You can learn about yourself. I'm sure some like you are rotting on death row for God's sake. Do you know what happens to child killers in prison? They're targeted, sometimes killed by the other inmates."

Freddie laughed. "That makes me feel better?" He watched Debbie leave the nurse's station and meet someone at the main door. She came back with a tray and walked around to seven.

Reece nodded as Debbie entered. "Damn, I'm hungry. You gonna take this tube out of my nose?"

"Yep, eggs and grits like you wanted. Plus, a cup of coffee. You like coffee?" She put the tray on the overbed table. "I can take the tube out now."

"Yeah, man, coffee. Thank you, thank you." He pulled

the rolling table across his lap. "Eggs are just a bit runny, but they'll do." He unwrapped his silverware.

Debbie untaped the feeding tube. "Here it comes." She slid out the tube and dropped it in the wastebasket.

Reece felt his nose, the sore there from the tube. "God, thank you," and he broke an egg yolk and mixed it with grits. "No sprinkle cheese?"

"Nope," said Debbie. She washed her hands. "Need anything else?"

"No, I'm good," said Reece. "Damn, this is tasty."

"Don't eat so fast. Slow down."

Reece dropped his fork and eased back into the mattress, stiffening. His body trembled, and his eyes rolled back in his head.

Rested, Reece felt better, although his side hurt. He and Arthur had hurried away from the sacred park and entered a buster establishment, a new one, he thought, but they all looked the same from the outside. Inside was dry and cool with odd music playing. It reminded him of Ethiopian music with an accordion. The square room was dim with a huge disco ball hanging from the ceiling. A thin man in a unitard stood behind the bar, wiping the metal counter with a blue washcloth. Arthur and Reece sat on padded stools

"What'll it be, ladies?" The bartender's name was Jacques, and he resembled a fish with his large eyes. There seemed to be too much white and not enough cornea.

"Buster, please," said Arthur.

"Same," said Reece. And then he added, "Twat licker."

"House special?" Jacques turned, grabbed two orange mugs, and dispensed the plain buster. He dropped in a lozenge of fizzing vitamin C. "Keep you from getting a snotty nose. Bumfuckers. You found your daughter yet?"

Reece scrunched his face and took his mug. "No. Do you know anything? She's a ginger, has some freckles on her cheeks, seven years old."

"Yeah, the data fur," said Jacques. "Everyone knows what she looks like. Haven't seen her, though."

"Someone said that I could pay someone to mine this data fur. Maybe it will tell me where she is," said Reece.

"How will you pay?" asked Arthur. "I only have a few Maria Theresa thalers."

Jacques took a clean mug and polished it with a cloth. "Yep, you'll have to pay. Could be a burned section. Could take years."

Reece groaned. "Years?" He swallowed his fortified buster, feeling a cool burst of energy from within.

"You just had a cool burst of energy from within," said Jacques. "Interesting."

"Data fur? That was pretty fast," said Reece. "How does the data get there?"

"Don't ask too many questions, bucko. Get you in trouble." He threw the mug in the air and caught it behind his back.

"It seems to be a brain of sorts," said Arthur. "Is this data fur alive?"

"Alive. Alive," said Jacques. "Nope, not alive, but living. You get my drift? It used to be a country, the United States, whatever that means."

"There are no people there? Just this data fur?" asked Reece. He downed more buster.

"Well, that's the million-dollar question, right?" asked Jacques. "People go there but never come back, just get sucked into the fur, or so the data fur tells us."

"Weird, back in 2003, that's where I live, the United States."

"A land of cowboys and very wealthy bankers and poor immigrants," said Arthur. "I sometimes thought of traveling there."

Reece spun his mug. "I wonder if the data fur includes Alaska and Canada?"

"Could be," said Jacques. "More buster, shitheads?"

Arthur patted his lips and beard with a napkin. "I am

satisfied." He looked at Reece.

"I'll have another. Thanks."

Arthur put his fingers together. "Why do you think it is that I can only access the data fur from within my lifetime? Herr Myers has told me of two world wars, but I cannot seem to access that daten. But of my dear poodles, I am filled with the minutest details. My little Atma, for example, had a beef bone on a particular day."

"Well, there are rules, you know," said Jacques. "If everyone knew everything, then there would be no need for the data fur."

"Hmm, circular logic," said Arthur. He pushed his empty mug forward.

A pair of women, a mother and daughter, entered. Reece and Arthur turned at their voices. The older woman wore a bright red jumpsuit, and the younger a pair of silver pants and a tight blue shirt covered in silver sequins.

"Hold up, you selfish pigs," said Jacques. He went to take the ladies' orders, an old custom, even though he knew what they wanted.

"I wonder why you have to pay someone to mine the data fur," said Reece.

"Yes, very quizzical," said Arthur. "I've asked myself the same question. Perhaps also sex, I've heard?"

Reece laughed. "We need to find someone who will mine the data fur for us."

"But you have no money."

"What do they even use for money? Maybe your coins would do the trick, since they're so old. You said they were silver."

"I would be glad to part with them if it would help,"

said Arthur.

Jacques was back. He pounded his fist on the metal bar as if having a muscle spasm. He laughed.

"Hey," said Reece. "Where can we find someone who will mine the fur for us?"

Jacques shook his head as if talking with mules. "Hold on." He went to the end of the bar and pushed a button. Disco music filled the room, and the disco ball began to turn and cast flashes of light. "So, you want to learn to paint a turtle's back?"

Reece frowned. "No. Find someone to look through the fur, for Mia, my daughter. That's why I'm here, dumbass."

Jacques leaned on the counter and looked both ways as if about to reveal a mighty secret. "Well, there's the old guy who builds rooms into the rock. He's beyond the town, lives alone, eats weeds, is what I hear. Give him a try."

Reece perked up. "How do we get there?"

"How the hell would I know? Just find him. Go to the edge and then keep walking."

"That's a start," said Reece. "Arthur, want to go now?"

"I will accompany you as you wish. Shall we? Why is this man building rooms into the rock?"

"Because he's a fucking nut," said Jacques, and he laughed.

"Okay," said Reece. "Later tater." He stood, and Arthur followed him through the mist door, the strains of "I Feel Love" echoing in the room.

Outside, the bright light blinded them, and they walked uphill, headed toward the edge of town, the spot that Arthur had shown Reece earlier. It took about eight minutes to reach the crude church there. As before, a trail of scented smoke floated from within. Reece went to the door and called out, but there was no answer, and they moved on, stepping into scrub among short, gnarled trees. Reece led the way along the meandering path, his shirt catching on thorns. They came to a small clearing and looked around for clues.

"You know, Arthur—it's strange calling you Arthur—I've been here before. Come to think of it, how could I forget? There was an old monk who was building a church into the rock, back in Godo, 1986. Or was it 1987?" He had visions of an Icelandic medical team. Faces. *Eydis? Svana? Gudmunder?* "There was a large flat field and a path that went down to follow a cliff line."

"But it's been two thousand years since that time," said Arthur. Sweat glistened on his forehead.

"If this is the same world, then why is the sun so tiny and there's no night? It could be that something has changed, but we could also be in another world entirely, a parallel universe. It seems that more than one world can represent us. Does that make sense?"

"As idealists, we are creating this world as we experience it. It cannot exist without us."

"Why is it that I bounce back and forth between two different places, and both places seem to be intact when I return?" Reece found a clear way to the left of the cliff line and followed it down, a sweeping valley below him.

Arthur huffed with the exertion. "My friend, that is a good question. When you lose a coin, does it cease to exist?"

"It might as well. But then you find it, and there it is. I think we're on the right track here. From what I remember, it's about a thirty-minute walk from here." Reece scanned ahead, a chimney of some sort in the distance, but downhill from their destination. A thin line of smoke he could see. "I wonder what that is?" He pointed.

Arthur squinted and held his hand above his eyes. "Perhaps a manufactury." He took in a deep breath.

"You need to rest?"

"No, but perhaps we could walk at a more leisurely pace. I am an old man after all."

"Sure," and Reece forged ahead, pushing past gesho bushes and small trees laden with a yellow grape-like fruit. He spotted a strange object on the ground and stooped to pick it up. "Look, a shark tooth. This land must have been under an ocean at some point."

"Oh my," said Arthur. "I've only heard tales." He wiped sweat from his brow with a handkerchief.

Reece dropped the tooth and moved on, weaving up and down but always following the cliff line, which was forty-five feet above them. Soon, the distance to the top of the cliff began to dwindle, and Reece kept his eyes peeled. When the distance dropped to ten feet, he looked for a place to climb up.

"We have to go up here, I think. There's a wide ledge and then a rock face. Think you can do it?"

"I will certainly make a challenge of it."

Reece scanned the rock and pondered foot and hand-holds. He walked back and forth and then settled on a route. "Okay, here goes." He planted his shoe, pushed up, and grabbed a fissure in the rock. The face leaned in slightly. Up he went until his hand stretched for a hold over the top beyond his sight. He searched and grabbed a groove in the rock with his fingers and pulled as he pushed up. His torso was above the ledge, and he scrambled over. His legs shaking, he looked around, noticing tall scrub where there had been none as he remembered it.

"What do you see?" asked Arthur. "Shall I try?"

"The brush is blocking my view, but I think this is the right place. Come on up." Reece lay on his stomach, ready to lend a hand. He gazed at the prominent bald spot on Arthur's head, red from the hot sun.

Arthur tried to get his foot up to the first protuberance, but he was too stiff. He grabbed the rock to pull himself up, but fell back. He gazed up at Reece. "You may have to go alone from here. I'll wait. Did I mention that I was an old man?"

Reece laughed. "Yeah, okay. Stay there." He stood and pushed his way through the scrub to the rock face and then worked his way to the right. Thorns grabbed his clothes. Within five minutes, he emerged into a clearing, and there it was, just as he had remembered it. A large hole in the rock was framed with a green doorway, and beyond was a primitive hut where the monk had lived, although it had been back to the left before. He listened for the sound of pick on stone, but all was quiet. He approached the open door and looked inside the dark room.

"Abet!" came a voice.

Reece turned and saw the Abba Paulos headed toward him, wearing the same golden skullcap. He felt that he was dreaming.

"Tenesteling!" said Reece.

The Abba walked forward, his hands out in greeting. The Abba was speaking, but Reece did not understand him. Their hands met.

Reece spoke, hoping he would understand. "Do you remember me? Ato Reece."

The Abba nodded and smiled, showing a golden tooth.

"I'm here looking for my daughter, Mia. Do you understand? Set lidj, daughter, Mia? Sebat amet. Seven years old." He noticed a crude ladder placed nearby that mounted the rock wall from below.

The Abba nodded in affirmation, as if he knew, and motioned him toward the hut.

"Hold on," said Reece. "I have a friend. I will bring him. Coy. Wait." Reece climbed down the ladder and soon found Arthur standing with his hands behind his back, as if waiting for a letter. "Arthur, this way. There's a ladder."

"What good luck." He followed Reece, pushing through scrub to the ladder.

"Follow me."

Reece climbed and then watched Arthur make his way up one slow step at a time. The Abba had joined him and peered over the edge with a concerned look. Arthur's head appeared, and Reece helped him to solid ground. Arthur was winded and looked upon the Abba with great surprise.

"This is the Abba Paulos," said Reece.

The two men shook hands.

Reece introduced Arthur. "Ato Arthur Schopenhauer. Philosophia."

The two men gazed into one another's eyes as if establishing a meaningful connection.

"Nah, nah," said the Abba. He led them toward his small square house made of poles and mud.

"Does he speak our language?" asked Arthur.

"No, but I know some Amharic. I think he wants to show us something."

The Abba opened his door made of tin roofing and spoke to someone inside.

Reece's heart jumped into his throat. He felt dizzy, sick...

Reece opened his eyes and stared at the ceiling. The fluorescent light was on, blinding him. He sat up in bed, but his arms were restrained. Where had he been? He racked his brain and remembered the ladder. *The Abba. Arthur.* The rest was murky. Had he found Mia? His bed rails were up. He punched the call button.

"Yes," said Claire. Debbie was charting beside her.

"Can you send a nurse? I want to get out of bed."

Debbie took a notebook and pen. She passed the guard Shark as he passed Gumbo. She paused to hear their exchange.

"Did you dump your diaper?" asked Shark.

"Yeah, for your dinner," said Gumbo.

Debbie entered seven. "You're back, sweetie."

"Yeah. I was there. Arthur and I went to find someone who could help us locate Mia. Can I sit in the chair? I feel like I was on the edge of finding her. I need to go back."

"Give me the details." She was writing on the notepad.

Reece transitioned to the reclining chair with her help and told her all that he could remember. "There was a hut, and I think Mia could have been inside. Does anyone ever find who they're looking for? The people in here? I assume they're all looking for someone."

"Yeah, it seems that way. Looking for the lost child replaced by the impostor."

"Has that guy, what's his name, Freddie? Has he found his child yet? You said he stabbed his daughter, the impostor, I mean."

"You'll have to ask him. He hasn't traveled in over two weeks. You need anything? Lunch should be here in an hour."

"Yeah, can I get these damn electrodes off my skull? They itch." He scratched his head.

"Not as long as you're traveling. Markush would kill me if I took them off. But we'll need to change them out soon, and I'll give your head a good wash. Make you feel better."

Reece frowned. "How about letting me go to the bathroom? Thank God the catheter is out. And you can throw the urinal out. I'm done with that."

Debbie laughed. "Yeah, sure. Can you stand? I'll walk you there." She unplugged the main cord from the EEG.

She held out her hand, and Reece stood. He wavered as his vision blanked black and red. He took short steps, afraid he would fall.

"Damn, I'm weak."

"Lying in bed will do that to you." She walked him into the small bathroom that had a sink, toilet, and shower. The tile was a soothing gray. She flipped on the light. "Just lift your gown and go. I'll stand behind you just in case."

Reece could feel the cool air on his backside. He aimed for the middle of the toilet, a bit shaky, but peed like a racehorse. "God, that feels good."

"Good job. Now back to the chair. Maybe in a day or two, we'll let you into the dayroom. Need to get your strength back." She guided him to the chair, and he fell into it.

"Do you think I'm a child killer? I mean, do you think I'm telling the truth about the impostor? I hope someone does."

Debbie reconnected him to the EEG and put her hands

on her hips. "If I didn't work here, I would have a hard time believing it. That's one reason you're here, to keep you safe."

Reece rubbed his eyes. "Yeah, I guess I can see that. I know of others out there who are fighting off Dahlia. How come Markush hasn't asked me about that, or has he?"

"Let me write that down." She grabbed her notepad. "He's on another unit. How do you know these others?"

"It's been a hobby of sorts, finding them. We meet online and talk. So far, most of the kids haven't been abducted yet, but Dahlia is trying to get them. It's in their music, the way they behave, the night terrors. All of them have a little girl who comes around and creates havoc. Different names, but they're all Dahlia."

"Dahlia. I wish I understood better. And then the connections with Ethiopia. Very strange," said Debbie.

"Connections with Ethiopia?"

"Yeah, there's always that connection. Everyone on this unit has a connection. "

"That's bizarre, bonkers even."

"Markush has been there, just to check the place out. I'm not sure that he discovered anything."

"You know," said Reece, "that's where the Ark of the Covenant is said to be, at a church in Axum. I've sometimes wondered if there's a connection there. The Ark is said to have supernatural powers."

"I know something about it from church, when I was younger. I don't go anymore." She tossed back her blonde hair and smiled. "I bet Markush lets you go to the dayroom tomorrow. I'll vouch for you. So, back to Mia. There's someone new?"

Reece thought. "It must have been the Abba Paulos. Somehow, I met him in Godo when I was there. He was carving a church into the rock with a pick. He was wearing the same yellow cap as back then. Arthur and I found him outside the town called Gadam, which is a weirder version of Godo. I need to get back as soon as possible to stay on the trail. I know it sounds strange to want to have seizures, but I do, to keep looking."

Debbie took notes. "Were you yourself replaced at some point? I mean, are you an impostor? Is the real you lost? That's hard to get my head around."

"I don't think so. Dahlia did find me, though, when I was young. I remember the blue lights, something going into my head. I must have screamed because my mother came. I think if you get the head thing, you're studied somehow from a distance."

"Fascinating," said Debbie. "You're not the first I've heard mention this head thing. Do you mean an implant?"

"Yeah, something like that, but invisible for the most part. I can feel it, like it's just beneath my scalp."

"Did Mia have this implant?"

"Not that I know of. I kept a close eye on her. I think that's why she was abducted, because I was vigilant. I didn't realize she could even be abducted like that, but I instantly knew that it wasn't her." He winced, and his stomach felt tight. "God, I just have to find her and bring her back."

Debbie glanced at her watch.

"They're studying Mia, somewhere, perhaps in this Gadam where Arthur is. I can't figure out why he would be there. I mean, he's a traveler, but he has no children. But his ideas, I think his ideas about transcendental idealism have something to do with it. He knows something."

"Transcendental idealism? Let me step out. I have to check on the other patients. Let's pick up there when I come back. There's a young woman in six, who was shot in the head over there. I have to irrigate her eyes with saline. She doesn't blink."

Reece sat up. "Shot in the head? Why does that seem familiar? What's her name?"

"Her name is Emma, Emma Smith. Kind of short with dark blonde hair."

"You're kidding? I worked with an Emma Smith over there. In a clinic. I was a nurse. But she was never shot, although I was afraid she would be. There was this guy, the town administrator, an evil sort, who was always causing trouble. His nickname was the Hyena. Damn, can I just peek in and see what she looks like? It can't be the same Emma."

"That's not a good idea," said Debbie. "I don't want you to seize and fall. You're still active, very active."

"Come on. I can't help myself. I need to see her."

Debbie looked to see if Markush was back in the nursing station. "Well, okay. But let me get Richard. We'll walk you in, let you have a look, and then come right back. Okay? You can't just wander around for now. Markush will restrain you again."

"Okay."

Debbie pushed the call button, and Claire answered. "Can you have Richard come to seven?"

Claire buzzed into twelve and gave Richard the message. He wore pressed scrubs, which complemented his very white teeth and the neat Fu Manchu. He finished vital signs and walked to seven.

"Hey," said Richard. "What's up? Hey there, Mr. Myers."

"Need you to help me walk Myers into six. He thinks he knows her."

"Is that a good idea?" He washed his hands, keeping his eyes on Reece.

"Probably not, but part of our job is to help put this puzzle together. Just in and out."

"If you say so."

Reece stood by himself, wired to the telemetry unit, which he held in his hand. "I appreciate it."

Debbie unplugged his EEG again. They each took an arm and led Reece into the hall and then into six.

He stumbled forward and came to rest against the bed rail.

"Mr. Myers, hold on," said Richard. "She's comatose, unresponsive."

There were gauze pads over her eyes, making her look dead. Her chest rose and fell with her respirations. Debbie noted that her heart rate had increased from the eighties to nearly one hundred.

Reece gripped the bed rail and stared at her. "What the fuck? It had to be that damn Hyena or one of his cronies." His mind spun. "Get me back to the chair."

They walked him back to seven and placed him in the chair.

"It's her?" asked Debbie. Richard left the room, headed back to twelve to push some Ensure.

Reece stared at the bed. "It's definitely not her. The Emma I knew was never shot. As far as I know, she's still living with her mom back in Hueytown. *How do I know that?* We kind of had a thing, but I was engaged. It was the stress, the loneliness, but we never followed through."

Debbie scribbled as fast as she could, getting the salient details.

Reece pushed up the foot of the recliner and leaned back. He felt a voice calling him, saw a Cylinder of light pinched in the middle, his eyes closed...

Reece opened his eyes and saw Arthur leaning over him. The Abba was behind him, putting magnets into the folds of his robe. The Abba had called Reece back.

"Mia? Is Mia here?" He sat up, feeling the rocks poke his backside.

Arthur held out a hand, and Reece took it and stood, brushing the dirt from his clothes.

"We have not looked, but we shall now that you're back."

The Abba looked a bit frightened, but opened the door to his little house with the tin roof. He stood in the doorway and clapped his hands. Reece peered into the dim room. He could see a small body lying on the bed there, and his heart leapt into his throat.

"Mia!" Reece pushed past the Abba and tripped over a clay pot, spilling water. "Mia!" He fell to his knees beside the bed.

A girl of about seven pulled the old blanket from her face and sat up. "Who are you?" She wore a thin t-shirt that read Varsity and was wearing short pants. She looked pale in the dim light. "Can you take me home?"

Reece's heart sank. He reached and took the girl's hand. "What's your name?"

"My goodness," said Arthur. "Such a little one."

The Abba was speaking in low tones. He reached down and smoothed back the girl's dark hair. "Yezounal, hodian." He rubbed his stomach and made a face.

"Diarrhea, you have diarrhea?" asked Reece. "You've

been drinking the water?"

"Am I not supposed to drink the water?" asked the little girl.

"You need water, but the water needs to be filtered is all. What's your name? How long have you been here?" asked Reece.

"I'm Alicia, and I've been here for a lot of days. Do you know my dad? His name is Freddie."

The name struck Reece. *Freddie.* Who was Freddie? "No, Alicia, I don't think I do. But we'll take care of you. Has this man been taking care of you?" He turned and nodded toward the Abba.

"Yes, he gives me weird food, but it tastes good. My stomach hurts, though, every time I eat it. It's too spicy. I miss my dad and my mom."

"Look," said Reece, "maybe we can help you find them. I'm looking for my daughter, Mia. Have you met any little girls here?"

"No, I haven't seen anyone except for Mr. Abba. Can you take me home now? I don't know how I got here." Her big eyes and dark hair gave her the look of a lamb in the dimness.

"Hello, young girl, my name is Arthur." Arthur bowed a little bow. "Somehow, I imagine we're all here for the same reason, but I haven't the foggiest idea of why. Reece, I think this young lady could use some buster."

"Hello, Arthur." Alicia's voice was sorrowful. "Why are you dressed like that?"

Arthur brought his heels together. "This is the costume one wears in my country. I suppose it looks very different to you." He patted his black breeches with the loose bottom and gatherings about his knees.

"Yeah," said Alicia. "I'm sure glad to see you anyways. Mr. Abba doesn't speak English, but he's real nice." She wiped snot from her nose with the blanket.

"We'll take you into town. There's a town nearby with food." Reece examined the label on the blanket. It was made by Mennonite women from Canada, a relic of the famine. "But first, I need to try and ask the Abba some things, to help me find my daughter. I bet you two would make great friends. She's your age." *But how to ask the Abba?* He stood. "Abba Paulos?"

"Abet?" asked the Abba.

"Um, Mia, my daughter." He pointed at Alicia. "Yeh nay set lidj."

The Abba's eyes sparkled. "Mia." He pronounced the word carefully and nodded as if he understood.

Reece exchanged a hopeful look with Arthur. "To find her. Magnyat."

The Abba patted his mouth as if asking for food. He took from his robe a small leather pouch and opened it. There were coins and bills inside.

"Oh," said Reece. "We have to pay him. Maybe he can mine the data fur for us. Show him your coins."

Arthur retrieved a small pouch from his pocket. He poured five silver thalers into his hand and let the Abba see.

"Ah," said the Abba. His eyes brightened. He picked the coins from Arthur's hand and bade them to sit on the bed with Alicia. "Maqoyat." He motioned for them to stay and walked backward out the door.

Reece couldn't stifle his curiosity and walked to the

door. The Abba walked twenty paces and disappeared through the door in the rock face. Was Mia there? Reece stepped out, walked to the door, and peered inside. The Abba was lighting a candle near a long table with an apparatus of some sort on it. He cleared his throat to let the Abba know that he was there.

"Aiyee, yellum, yellum!" said the Abba. He took Reece by the arm and led him away. In Amharic, he told Reece that he could die if he stood too close, and Reece somehow understood.

"Ishi," said Reece. "I will stay here, just outside the door." He pointed to the ground beneath his feet.

The Abba looked worried but returned to the table, lighting another candle. It was hard for Reece to see, and he strained his eyes. There seemed to be a chest on the table that glinted gold. On top seemed to be wings, golden in color. His heart raced. The Abba was on his knees, praying aloud.

A hand was placed on his shoulder, and Reece jumped.

"Dear boy, may I watch as well?" Arthur shielded his eyes.

Inside, the chest began to glow, and then a bright square of fuzzy light appeared between and above the wings. There was no sound but that of the Abba, who was now chanting in an ancient tongue, Ge'ez. The light grew brighter, and images played across it. Reece stood dumbfounded, watching tanks, loaves of bread, faces he did not recognize, and then a stream of little girls, some playing with dolls, others eating ice cream, and then one of a girl hanging by her neck. Reece looked away, but then returned his gaze. Slowly it dawned on him that he was looking at what appeared to be the Ark of the Covenant, churning out visuals perhaps from the data fur located on the dark side of the planet. The Abba's chants became like squeals and grunts, as if he were in a great deal of pain.

"Could it be?" asked Arthur.

Reece struggled to look on as the images became brighter and brighter, filling the vast rock chamber with light. The speed of the images passing made him dizzy, and he had to look away. The echo of the Abba's voice, conjuring his Mia.

Reece felt himself being braced by Arthur and relaxed, focusing on the fleeting pictures, the faces, the Abba's voice droning. At least half an hour passed, but it seemed like seconds, and the Abba continued to rail as he sank farther to the floor. And then, like a fine stopwatch, the images ceased, and only one floated in the air between the wings of angels, the face of his Mia.

"Mia!" said Reece. Arthur held onto him, preventing him from dashing forward. "Mia! Where are you?"

"Daddy?" The image hushed and shone, broken by bands of nothing, and then went dark, plunging the chamber into complete darkness.

"Damn!" said Reece. "Where? Where?" He began to cry and collapsed onto the ground outside the door.

Debbie washed his face with a cool rag as he came around. Reece felt that he had run a marathon. "Where am I? Where's Mia?"

"You're back," said Debbie. "In the hospital. Organon. You've been seizing, traveling. I've let Markush know. I thought you were going to break this chair. You're okay, though. Right?"

"Fuck." Reece shook his head and examined his trembling hands as if they belonged to someone else. "I saw her. I saw Mia. Debbie, I saw Mia."

"You're kidding. I knew something was going on. So, you've found her? Your heart rate jumped to one-twenty, but it's coming down. Your EEG went insane." She took a washcloth and mopped up spilled water.

"I saw her, but on a screen. You'll think this is crazy, but it was the Ark of the Covenant, inside a rock room. It's the Abba, the same Abba that I met when I worked in Ethiopia, in Godo. He uses the Ark to filter information. Have I told you about the data fur? God, it's all so real. He found her, but where she is, I'm still not sure. But she's alive. She said 'Daddy.'"

"I'm going to page Markush. He'll want to hear this directly from you, okay? But I'm really happy for you, as crazy as it sounds, I mean, what you told me."

"Yeah, sure." Reece pushed the recliner down and put his feet on the tiled floor, buffed to a high shine. He watched Debbie leave and head for the nursing station. He could see her on the phone through the glass of the dayroom. There had been something else important as well, but what was it? He remembered bathing Mia when she was an infant. He and Kristin would bathe her in the kitchen sink, being very careful with her delicate head, the suds gathered around her startled face. He then tried to recall everything that happened while he had been seizing, "traveling" as they said. Soon, from his chair, he could see Markush striding down the hallway toward the bend in the U.

"Mr. Myers? May I come in?"

"I saw Mia." He recounted the images playing between the angel's wings, or were they cherubim? "There was something else, too, a little girl. There was this little girl in the Abba's house. Her name was Alicia, and she wanted to find her parents. I saw Mia."

Markush's eyes went wide. He spoke into a small tape recorder, capturing the essence of the story. "Tell me about this Abba. I assume he's a priest of some sort."

"Yeah, he's a monk, I think, a holy man with the Orthodox church. He lives alone. When I was in Godo, it seems I visited him. His life's work was to build a church into the rock. He used a pick and a long steel bar. But there was no Ark in the room back then. Somehow, the Ark is there now, in Gadam. There's the town, but then there's beyond the town, two different worlds. Funny thing is, he has these magnets, kind of like the magnets you have. Arthur said that he used them to call me back."

"Did he wear a yellow skull cap, almost goldenrod in color?" asked Markush.

"Yeah, how did you know?"

"I've met him. I've been to Ethiopia, into the area where

you worked. That's where I learned about the magnets. He finds them in the rock. I paid him five hundred birr for a pair that he had made that fit the palms of his hands. Incredible."

Reece tried to stand and sat back down, dizzy. He waited for his vision to clear. "Can you send me back? I need to go back."

"It's risky," said Markush. "We lost a patient just a few months ago. It could be that you go and never return. So, tell me more about the little girl."

Reece thought. "She was just a little kid, about Mia's age. She was wearing shorts and a t-shirt. She had black hair and big eyes."

Markush spoke into his recorder. "There's another patient here who needs to hear your story. He's searching for his little girl."

"What's the girl's name?" asked Reece.

"Alicia. That's him in the dayroom. His name is Freddie."

"Holy cow. Yes, Alicia! So, an impostor took his daughter's place?"

"Yep."

"And he killed the impostor?"

"Yep," said Markush, "he stabbed her."

"Can Freddie come in here? He needs to know," said Reece.

"Well, not too fast. She could be gone when you return. Let's not get his hopes up just yet. Promise me that? I predict the Abba will call you back. Meanwhile, you need to eat and drink, in case you're gone for a while. Otherwise, we'll have to put that feeding tube back in." He tossed his long gray hair from his eyes and checked his watch. "Just hang in there for now. I'll send Debbie back. Okay?"

"Yeah," said Reece. "Can I go into the dayroom?"

"Let's hold off on that. If you did tell Freddie, he'd go berserk. Spare him for now. Trust me."

Reece relaxed into the chair. "I hate these gowns and these damn electrodes on my head."

"I get it," said Markush. "Just play along. We're learning from you. Think of it as a way to get Mia back and perhaps help others."

Reece frowned. "Yeah." He watched Markush leave. The guards were changing positions. Reece made eye contact with Shark and nodded. Shark grunted and moved on.

Within a few minutes, Debbie returned with a can of Coke and some crackers. "Markush wants you to tank up, like a camel. What else can I get you? It's three o'clock. A sandwich?"

"Sure," said Reece. "Do they have roast beef, with some mustard? A beer would be nice."

"What, and a cigar too?" Debbie laughed. "The alcohol interferes with the EEG, so ixnay on that one."

"Hell, don't mention cigars. I'm a cigar junkie."

"It's in your chart. Your favorite is a little number that comes wrapped in a sleeve of cedar, shade-grown wrapper, right?"

"Damn, no stone left unturned. Did you get that from my wife, my ex-wife?"

"Not sure, but probably so. She's undergone some serious debriefings."

"God, I know she hates me. Is there a chance that I'll get

to talk with her?"

"If she's up for it. Markush would have to approve. Her name is Kristin, right?"

Reece looked sad. "Yeah, Kristin. She's never had a clue what I know, but I could have never explained it to her. I was afraid too. It just sounds like too much science fiction, and I guess that's what it is or seems to be. The only way to get her back will be to bring Mia back, and that seems impossible."

"But you're on the right track."

"Am I the only one who knows about the Ark?"

Debbie sighed. "No. But you have the best experience with it so far, as far as I can tell. Markush is really the only one who knows everything. Okay, let me get your food ordered, and we'll keep an eye on you."

Reece watched her leave and shifted his butt, which was sore over his tailbone. The blue pad beneath him stuck to his skin. He put his fingers to his carotid artery and checked his pulse. He still had his nurse's instincts from before his days as a philosophy professor. He wondered about his classes, what the students were thinking. There had been one girl in his Intro to Schopenhauer that he was sure was an impostor. What if he were able to teach again, to be able to say that he'd met the famous Arthur in the flesh but in another time and place? He was sure that it had to be something like a parallel universe and not just a matter of time differences. It fit well with Schopenhauer's notion of transcendental idealism. What one perceives is what is real. Arthur was there, in the place called Gadam, for a reason, or was it just by chance? He found himself creating a syllabus for a new class and shook his head, trying to bring back the image of Mia between the angels', no, the cherubims' wings. When Debbie arrived with his sandwich, he was deep in thought.

"Here you go," said Debbie.

"Thanks." He placed the tray on his lap and opened the can of Coke. Debbie was attractive, and he tried to imagine her in street clothes. She understood him, or at least tried to understand.

"I'll leave you with it," and she was off to another patient.

Reece took a bite of the sandwich, and mustard squirted onto his gown. "Well, shit." He chugged his cold Coke and belched and felt a vague tickling in the back of his head...

Reece looked up, and standing around him were Arthur, the Abba Paulos, and the little girl Alicia.

"Excellent," said Arthur. "You're back with us. We, that is the group, were worried about you. You do tremble with such energy."

Reece looked at the Abba. He seemed to have aged twenty years. He turned and tried to stand, but went to his knees. "I saw Mia in the room. Did you see her?"

"I saw many faces, but the one at the end, that was your Mia?"

"Yes, it was her."

"Are you okay, mister?" asked Alicia. She had her hands in her pockets. She was small for seven, had long black hair, and green eyes filled with sadness.

"Yeah, I'm fine. Alicia, right?" Reece sat back on his legs, gathering his strength. His pants didn't seem so tight, as if he was losing weight.

"Yes, I'm Alicia."

"Your dad's name is Freddie, right?"

"Yes." Her wide eyes grew wider.

"I may have found him. He's in a hospital," said Reece. He held his hand out to Arthur and stood.

Alicia frowned. "Is he sick? Is my daddy sick?"

Reece brushed off his shorts. "No, no. He's just in a safe place. He's looking for you, just like I'm looking for my little girl."

The Abba folded his hands in a prayer gesture and walked back to his house.

"Can you take me to my daddy?" Tears welled in her eyes, and she shoved her hands farther into her pockets.

"Poor little darling," said Arthur. "I say she looks hungry. Are you hungry, young one?"

"Yeah, I'm really hungry. The nice man gave me some bread this morning, but that's all."

Reece put his hand on Alicia's shoulder. "I really don't know if I can take you home. But maybe your dad can come here. We'll do everything we can." He turned to Arthur. "I need the Abba to get me to where Mia is. I wonder if he can do that?"

"He may require more money," said Arthur. "I have no more."

"Yeah, that's a possible problem. Maybe there is someone who needs information that we can sell to. That seems to be the only commodity."

"What a strange economy," said Arthur. "It seems there are those who sell their bodies."

Reece laughed. "Would you sell your body?" He turned to peer into the room carved from the rock. He felt a power emanating from the chamber and could see the Ark there in the shadows. There was a smell of burning steel.

"At my age, I think not. But the prostitutes would have money. Perhaps our information would amuse them into parting with a few coins."

"Huh, that sounds crazy, but why not? We'll have to investigate. Let's see if we can get some idea of where Mia is from the Abba. Maybe he'll just tell us."

Reece motioned for Alicia to follow them, and they found the Abba sitting on a three-legged stool at a crude table. On the table was a large and ancient book handwritten in Ge'ez. He was turning through the pages and waved them inside. Using a wooden match, he paused to light a wad of incense in a small can that looked like it used to hold sardines. The incense fizzled and smoked, smelling of perfume.

Arthur was very intrigued by the book and looked over the Abba's shoulder at the drawings there. Reece joined him, and Alicia sat on the floor.

The Abba pointed to the page and spoke in Amharic. It was a sketch of a Cylinder pinched in the middle, surrounded by what looked to be flying angels. Reece searched the image for clues, but came up blank. A black angel hovered at the edge of the image. The Abba turned a few more pages and revealed two circular objects that Reece took to be the Earth. Between them was a plane. The Abba continued to speak in his low guttural voice. He pointed at one of the Earths and then pointed at Reece. He pointed at the other circle and used the word for daughter.

"Huh, so we're here and Mia is there. But how to get there or bring her here or back to my world?" Reece scratched his head.

"Perhaps it's just a matter of will," said Arthur. "Although I've been willing myself to return home, but to no avail."

"Can I look?" asked Alicia. She stood from her crisscross sit.

"Sure," said Reece. He held Alicia's hand as she looked at the browned page.

"It's like in my dreams. I've dreamed about this book, but I never could read it."

"Really?" asked Reece. "And did a little girl sometimes

visit you at night?"

"Oh yeah, and she scared me. I pulled the covers over my head."

"That's what happened to me, too, but I never dreamed about this book. Alicia, we have a lot in common." Reece paused and settled into the music coming from the little girl, chords in A minor. "It just means you're special, is all."

"That's what my daddy said, but it made my mother grumpy."

Reece laughed. "Yeah, it's kind of like a secret that no one can understand. It frustrates other people."

"I miss my mommy. But it seems like I'm still there. Like she doesn't know I'm gone."

Reece decided not to tell her about the impostor her dad had killed. The Abba seemed to be falling asleep. Reece tapped him on the shoulder. "Set lidj? Mia. My daughter?"

The Abba shrugged his shoulders, as if all was lost.

"I think he is suffering from some exhaustion," said Arthur. "Perhaps he needs rest."

Reece nodded. "Let's take Alicia back into town and get her some buster. I need some as well, and perhaps a stiff drink or two."

"An excellent plan, and perhaps we should discover where the ladies of the night congregate, to acquire some money. Come along, little one."

"Ciao," said Reece to the Abba. "Dehna hun."

The Abba stood from his table and took Reece's hand into his. "Xavier meskin," and then he told Reece to be careful, to come and see him again.

They parted ways and headed back to Gadam proper

with Alicia, soon reaching the edge of town populated with its boxlike buildings that all looked the same except for the stars. Blue for dwellings, red for bars, and green for buster.

"We should really find a place to stay," said Reece. "A place for Alicia."

"Yes, but our appetites must be first appeased," said Arthur. His breeches were dusty, his face red in the scorching sun. "The girl is hungry."

They entered the first buster house they encountered, and it was where Shia with the green eyes worked. Reece ushered Alicia to a round table covered in hammered tin. No one else was there.

"The food here is called buster," said Reece. "You drink it."

"It is very nutritious," said Arthur. He took his seat.

"What does it taste like?" asked Alicia. She looked small sitting next to Arthur.

Reece thought. "They have different kinds, but the plain one tastes kind of like cardamom. Maybe like a flowery cinnamon. But you can ask for any flavor you want. What's your favorite food?"

Alicia said, "Pizza with sausage."

"Okay, I'll get you the sausage pizza buster." Reece looked toward the counter. No one was coming to take their orders. "I'll be right back."

Shia was wearing a yellow bikini that highlighted her shapely figure. "Welcome back, stranger. What'll it be? Two plain and one sausage pizza?"

Reece laughed. "Yep, you hit the nail on the head. Light my fire and I'll light yours."

"That's only on the third day of the month," said Shia.

"Oh," said Reece. He watched Shia draw down three bowls. He waited for her to dip her finger in, but she didn't. "Okay, thanks." He picked up the orange tray.

"Fuck you very much," said Shia.

"Uh, yeah, you too," said Reece. Back at the table, he handed down the bowls that read Trinity College.

Alicia stared at her bowl and then smelled it. "Is it hot? I don't like cold pizza."

"Just try it," said Reece.

Arthur took a big drink. "Bravissimo. This quenches my thirst much as water."

Alicia looked at Reece and then at Arthur. She put her head near the bowl and stuck in her tongue. "Yeah, that's good." She smiled, as if aware of some great secret. She raised the bowl with two hands and drank. "Needs more cheese."

"So, we need to find a room," said Reece. "And find some cash."

Arthur puzzled out cash. "Perhaps the young lady could help. I wonder why she is wearing such an outfit?"

"I like it," said Reece. He'd once seen a young mother at the pool where he used to live who reminded him of Shia, homely but with a fantastic figure, nicely brown. He drank his buster in three gulps and felt amazingly better, but he wondered when he would move his bowels again. Did his body just absorb the buster? He couldn't remember when he had last taken a dump, and Arthur had the same problem. He watched Alicia take little sips, puzzling over each one. He closed his eyes and tried to access the data fur for information on Alicia, but all that came up were the events of the afternoon.

Arthur finished his buster and stood. "I shall ask her now." He walked to the bar, a slight hitch in his step from an arthritic hip. "Young lady?"

Shia was polishing a bowl. "What's up, grandpa? Your liver on the blink?"

Arthur cleared his throat. "Yes, I mean no. I would like to inquire of lodgings. Do you know of a room that we could let?"

Shia spat in the bowl and continued to polish it. "Yeah, my ex-boyfriend just died. His place is empty. It's two lanes down and up five. Blue star. Two beds and a big fat chair the girl can sleep on. Unless you plan to kill her." She grinned.

"What?" asked Arthur. "Well, of course not. Yes, that is very helpful." He could see her pubic hair pushing out from the bikini bottom.

"Look, but don't like, old fart. Another round?"

Arthur smiled, said, "Yes, thank you," and returned to the table.

"Any luck?" asked Reece.

"Yes, there is a place, two lanes down and five lanes up, as the young lady relayed to me."

Shia sidled up with three more busters. "The one for the kid is bubblegum. She reminds me of a girl I once saw in a museum."

"There is a museum?" asked Arthur. "May we visit?"

"It's a trip, about twenty-six miles south from here. You have to cross two rivers. But the banditos will catch you if you're not careful. There's a road, and you'll have to walk it, or maybe catch a jeep. Can you handle it, old man?" She leaned down and kissed his fluffy white sideburns.

"I often stroll in the afternoons," said Arthur. He stared into Shia's bosom.

"That sounds of interest," said Reece. "I wonder if we could learn something about Mia there? But first we need to get a room." He glanced at Shia's jiggling bottom as she walked away.

"I don't like museums," said Alicia. "They're boring. But maybe my dad would be there. He likes museums."

Reece smiled. "Let's go check out the room, shall we? I need to ask about finding some cash. I'll be right back." He went to the bar.

Shia was squatting behind the bar, arranging empty bottles, Icelandic IV bottles with red stoppers. Customers used them for carryout buster. She stood and poked Reece in the chest. "You need cash, right? And you think that the whores might have some, and you're right."

"How do we find them?" asked Reece. "Would they..."

"Exchange some coins for some lame information?"

"Yeah, what you said."

"Look for the purple stars, but there's only three. You can try, but I think you're wasting your time, not to mention mine."

"Thanks," said Reece. He turned away.

Alicia was working on her bubblegum buster. "This is yummy."

"We need to find a purple star to find the ladies of the night, although there is no night here." Reece sat and tipped his buster to his lips.

"Indeed," said Arthur. "It's the primary oddity that bothers me. I feel that I have not slept properly since I've been here."

They each finished their second round and walked into the blazing light. They headed downhill, counted three lanes, and then turned up, counting five. On their left was a plain building with a blue star. Inside was a gruff man sitting in a rolling chair. The man looked up, his mind seemingly a million miles away.

"Well, what have we here? A couple of pedophiles and their little butt plug." He needed to shave and had a cowlick, as if he had been wearing a ballcap.

"Ah, yes," said Arthur. "We would like to inquire about a vacant room." Alicia stood behind him.

"You must have met his girlfriend, Shia. Yeah, she tied him to the bed and suffocated him with a plastic bag, cut him up. You're the first to inquire. Just down the hall and on your right. Number six."

"Do we need a key?" asked Reece.

"A key? For what?"

"Never mind," said Reece, and he followed Arthur down the hall, which seemed to be floored with corkboard.

"Shall we?" Arthur opened the door, and a fetid smell emerged. He was the first to enter and stopped in his tracks. "Dear Lord."

Reece looked over his shoulder. "For Christ's sake."

Still tied to the bed was a bloated body with a bag over its head. Reece took Alicia by the arm and led her back to the hall. "Arthur, you stay here with Alicia." He walked back to the hall monitor. "The body is still in the bed."

"What did you expect?" asked the hall monitor. "By the way, I'm Carl." He stuck out his hand for Reece to shake, and he did.

"Can we get rid of the body? I mean, we can't stay in there with a dead body."

"That's your problem entirely," said Carl. "Next, you'll be asking me to paint the room pink." He laughed and folded his hands. "You want the room or not?"

"Okay," said Reece. "So, we just take care of it? No trouble?"

"No, nada, not a problem. Just drag him into the street. That way, the authorities will know he's dead. They'll take him away."

"Okay," said Reece. He looked down the hallway at Arthur and Alicia standing there. "Thanks."

"Thank your mother."

Reece turned away.

"Well?" asked Arthur. He held his hands behind his back.

"Carl, the guy in the chair, said we have to take care of it, to carry him to the street."

"My word," said Arthur. "Then everyone will think we've murdered him."

"Maybe, but that's what we have to do if we want the room." Reece scratched his head and opened the door, holding his breath. "Alicia, there is a man in the room here, and we have to take him outside, okay?" There was another door that was slightly ajar. Reece knocked, and no one answered. He opened the door to the bare room with a bed and a small table. "Just stay in this room, okay? You'll be fine."

"What's wrong with the man?" asked Alicia.

"Uh, he's very sick. The hospital will come to get him, okay?"

Arthur nodded his approval.

"You won't leave me, will you?" asked Alicia. Her big eyes looked sad.

"Of course not," said Reece. "Just sit at that table there."

"Okay," said Alicia.

"Let us do this quickly," said Arthur. He pushed up his laced cuffs.

The man was on his back, stabbed in the chest, his hands tied to the metal frame. He was wearing a mechanic's jumper and no shoes. His feet were gray, as were his hands. They untied him and stared at each other for a few seconds.

"I shall take his feet, and you shall take his hands," said Arthur.

Reece nodded, trying to take shallow breaths. The man was slight but heavy, and they lifted him to the ground for a better grip. Into the hall they went and half-dragged him to the door.

"Carl, can you open the door?" asked Reece.

"Here it comes," said Carl. He stood. "But don't ask me to wash your asshole, asshole." He held the door open.

Reece and Arthur grunted and carried the stiff body into the lane. There was a small stone patio, and they laid the body there.

"Hold on," said Reece. He trotted back to the room and took a sheet from the bloodied bed.

He and Arthur walked back and called Alicia. Together, they entered the bodyless room.

"What's that smell?" asked Alicia. She looked as if she was about to cry.

"The gentleman was very ill," said Arthur.

Reece found more sheets and made the bed, cringing at the odor. He supposed he would sleep there and let Arthur have the clean bed. "Alicia, you'll sleep in this big chair, okay? You've got a pillow there."

"I'm so tired." She crawled onto the chair and fell asleep in a few breaths.

"That was something." Reece surveyed the plain room with its bare walls. There was a desk with a light in the wall. On the desk was a bloody knife. He dropped it in the drawer.

"That drink we were supposing," said Arthur. "I think we could use it while the girl sleeps." He took a thin blanket from the floor and placed it over Alicia.

"Good plan," said Reece.

A very light snow was falling at 47 Asterion Lane. The house was for sale, but there had been no buyers. Everyone knew of the m urder. Kristin had stayed in a motel for two weeks, but having quit her job, had returned to the house, sleeping on the main level and avoiding the upstairs bedrooms.

She had been interrogated by the local police and then by uniformed officers from the base at Fort Knox. There was a Dr. Markush who called regularly, asking if she would come and answer some questions, but thus far she had refused, even though there was a promise of considerable money. Each night as she lay on the blue leather sofa, the murder of Mia by Reece played through her mind, and she had to get up and drink at least three glasses of wine before she could fall asleep. Her parents had begged her to come home to Birmingham, but she wanted to hold onto her last days with Mia, the house providing that. This would be the first Christmas without Mia, just a month away, and the dread she carried was the weight of the world.

It was ten-thirty, and she lay still on the couch, looking at the TV, the slim bookcase that held CDs. Around the TV on the wall, Reece had placed four small paintings to detract from the TV's presence. She turned, facing the couch, and wondered what would become of her life. The insurance policy on Mia had left her only ten thousand dollars. Never in a million years had she imagined that she would outlive her precious Mia. Cold tears wet her eyes and trickled to the feather pillow. Her cell phone rang, and she let it go. A few minutes passed, and the phone rang again. She assumed it was either her mother or Dr. Markush, and it was Markush.

"Hello, please don't call. I've asked you not to." She was slightly drunk.

"Mrs. Myers, I know it's difficult, but we need to talk. There are new developments that you could help us with."

"You're protecting him, and I don't know why," said Kristin. "He should be in prison. I suppose you're going to tell me again that Mia is alive."

"This is far more complicated than you could ever imagine, Mrs. Myers. And, yes, Mia is possibly alive. I know it sounds absurd to you, but you have to let us show you. You could even hold the key to her safe return. This is not simply madness on your ex-husband's part."

"He's a lunatic," said Kristin. "I never want to see him as long as I live."

"Look, I've said it before. There is a considerable...stipend that we are willing to provide you if you will just talk with us."

Kristin considered the mortgage payment. She would be out of money within three months. "If it's so important, why can't you just pay off the house so I can move?"

"That could be arranged too, as I've explained to you. Your husband is a rare case. You need to consider the greater good here. We need your help, your information. Otherwise, we may lose Mia."

"God! I went to the damn funeral. Mia is gone. Why do I keep answering the phone? If I thought you could bring her back, I would be there in a heartbeat, but it's just plain crazy."

"We'll fly you here in private transport. There's an Army Depot near your house. We'll make it as easy as possible. You'll fly directly to Fort Knox, and I'll pick you up. We have guest accommodations."

Kristin switched the phone from one ear to the other. "Will I have to see him, Reece? I can't bear the thought. He's a murderer."

"Of course not. Only if you wanted to. I'll be very open with you about what we know, although we will swear you to secrecy."

Kristin considered her empty life. She stood and walked from the den, through the kitchen, and into the living room, which they had made into the dining room, still set for three. The fireplace was bricked up, and art that Reece had bought for her hung on the walls. She pulled back the curtain and looked into the small front yard, lightly coated with snow. She put her hand to the glass, and it was very cold.

"Mrs. Myers?"

"I'm here. Look, I suppose I have nothing to lose, right? But if I ask to leave, I need to leave. Okay? Do I need to bring anything?"

"Just bring clothes for a few days, a week at the most, if that sounds reasonable to you."

"A week? How about three days? That seems like plenty of time or even just a day. I really don't have that much to say."

"Okay, three days will work, and if you decide you need to leave, we'll have you out asap."

Kristin ran her hand through her dark brown curls.

"Okay, I have your word and I'm counting on it. How will I know where to go at the Depot?"

"It's all taken care of. We'll send an unmarked car to your house, 47 Asterion Lane, tomorrow at nine. You'll fly out from the Depot on a helicopter. The flight should just take forty-five minutes. That sound doable?"

"A helicopter? Really? Are they safe? I have a fear of flying."

"Yes, completely safe. The Depot doesn't have a runway. So, tomorrow at nine in the morning. I'll make the arrangements right away. I'm so glad that you're willing to talk. This is invaluable."

Kristin sat at the long wooden table. "Okay, Dr. Markush, I'm trusting you. I'll be ready at nine. Goodbye."

She toyed with the red placemat and stood, walking to the front door. She looked out through the diamond-shaped window at the tiny flakes of snow swirling in the wind.

Reece fluttered his eyes, with the night-shift nurse Laura standing beside him. Her red hair was very fine, and he could see through it. He heard his name.

"Mr. Myers, Reece?"

Reece stirred, checking to see if he was restrained, and he wasn't. He looked around the room, realizing where he was. "Damn."

"You're back," said Laura. "You've been seizing for over three hours. You must be exhausted."

"Yeah." Reece tried to sit up and fell back. He had a terrific headache. "I was going to drink bourbon with Arthur. We have to find money to give to the Abba."

"Let me wash your face." She went to the sink and ran cool water over a washcloth.

"I need to go back. Is Markush here? He can send me back." He gripped the bed rail and pulled himself up. "God, I'm stiff."

Debbie washed his face. "Better? Dr. Markush is gone for the day. So, you were with Arthur? Is he still helpful?"

"Uh, yeah, we found a little girl named Alicia. Her dad's name is Freddie."

"You told us about that, and Dr. Markush is very interested. He thinks it could be Mr. Mentone's daughter. You haven't met him yet, Freddie, but you will tomorrow, if you're able." She stepped into the hall and dropped the washcloth into a laundry hamper.

"I need to tell him. Maybe Alicia can find Mia. Who knows? We found a room to stay in, for Alicia to stay in while we look. We think we have to visit the prostitutes there. They take money. The only things you pay for there are sex and information."

"Did you visit the buster bars again?"

"Yeah, we did. That's how we found out about the room, but there was a dead guy in the bed. We had to carry the body into the street. Nobody seemed to care."

"Huh, that's a new twist. How did he die?"

"He was murdered, stabbed. The lady at the buster bar, he was her boyfriend. She did it."

"Jeez," said Laura. "That's heavy."

"Crazy is what it is," said Reece. "Did I miss dinner? I'm starving."

"You did, but I'll have a tray sent up. Spaghetti and meatballs with green beans and banana pudding. That sound good?"

"Damn, that sounds terrific. Maybe double portions." He raised his head with the button on the bed rail. "Thirsty too." He poured himself a cup of water and then another.

"Good job. Stay hydrated for us. Want the TV on?"

"Yeah, I can do it." He pointed the remote at the TV on the wall. "I just need to relax. I feel like I've run a marathon. Huh, *The Simpsons*."

"I hate that show, but watch what you like. Keep you occupied for now. You could leave us at any minute, though." She washed her hands and left, headed into six to check on Emma Smith, the gunshot victim.

Emma lay on her side, still unresponsive, but that didn't mean she wasn't traveling. She seized on occasion, just for a few minutes. "Hey, Ms. Smith. It's me, Laura. It's about seven-fifteen at night. You're in the hospital still." She dripped saline into Emma's wide eyes and massaged the lids. Emma blinked. "Holy cow," said Laura. "That's new. You just blinked. Can you blink again?"

Emma stared straight ahead.

"Can you squeeze my hand, honey?" Laura waited, but there was no squeeze. "Okay, gonna put the gauze back over your eyes. I'll be back to check on you." She left and walked into number five to check on Peters. He still had faint rope burns on his neck.

Peters eyed her as she entered, cringing. He had shot his daughter and his wife, although his wife survived. He was on permanent disability before the killing, having slipped into insanity after visiting Ethiopia.

"Hey, Mr. Peters. It's just me, Laura, your nurse." She walked to the foot of his bed. "You need anything?"

"No," said Peters. He glanced at the ceiling and pointed. "Just there, if you please. Point your gun there and pull the fucking trigger."

"I don't have a gun. What do you see?" She looked where he was looking, just to the right of the TV.

"Right," said Peters. He kept his gaze on the apparition. "If you can't...can't see it...then you're blind as a goddamned bat." He tried to put his hand to his face as if warding off a blast of hot air. "Fuck!" He surged against his full-body restraint. "Why am I tied down, you devil, you sorcerer?" He closed his eyes and sobbed.

Laura moved closer. "It's okay. You're hallucinating. What do you see?"

Clark Peters caught his breath and stopped his emotions like a shut-off faucet. He widened his eyes and whispered. "The son of Satan, the father of the thirteen tribes, the man with two heads." He squeezed his eyes shut. Renaldo and Amanda passed, making their rounds.

"Just keep in mind that they're not real. I'm here to protect you, okay? We're here to help you. I have to go now to check on other patients. I have some medicine to give you in your IV in a few minutes."

Peters growled like a dog.

Laura moved on to her most challenging patient in room three, Helmut Grayson. He was big with big hands and an unruly mop of long brown hair before his head had been shaved. His face seemed etched in pain. The blanket restraint kept him from leaping and strangling whoever entered. The leg and arm restraints were pointless and only bloodied him as he struggled against them. He, too, had killed a child, his stepdaughter, drowned her in the bathtub. He was drowsing and mumbling.

Laura checked the EEG monitor, gamma waves with a spike here and there. The feeding tube was taped in place. She checked his catheter bag, and it held 110 ccs of clear yellow urine. His respirations were shallow, eighteen per minute. She hated to disturb him.

"Mr. Grayson?" She waited for the onslaught.

Helmut opened his eyes and stared at Laura. He tried to sit up. He hocked and spit, but she was at the foot of the bed. "Cunt. I'll cut your head off." He spit again, his eyes rimmed with rage.

"No need for name-calling," said Laura. "I'm just here to help. I'm going to push some Ensure and some water down your feeding tube, okay? That's it, and then I'll—"

"Who are you really? You know who you are. You're Dahlia's fucking mother." He twisted and shook the bed.

"I'm the commander here!"

"No, I do have a daughter, though, but her name's not Dahlia." She moved to his side, ready to step back. "No more spitting, okay?"

He watched her every move, pushing his chest out, kicking his legs. "Don't you put your drugs in my body!"

She opened a can of vanilla Ensure and withdrew 60 ccs into a catheter-tip syringe. "Here it comes. Just food. You need food."

"Food, my ass!" He shook his head.

Laura tried to show no fear, but that was hard. She connected the syringe and pushed the contents. "There, just another push of Ensure and then some water."

"Goddamit!" He thrashed against the full restraint, rattling the bed.

Laura continued, pushing all of the Ensure, and then began the 200 ccs of water. Helmut made swallowing motions. "There, that's it. You've already had your bath today, but you look sweaty. Can I wash your face?"

"Get away, and leave me be." His face was large, and his voice sounded as if it came from a deep canyon.

"Okay, no problem," said Laura. "If you need the bedpan or anything, just yell. We'll hear you." She turned off the lights except for one, dimming the room. The TV was on without volume. "You want the volume up on the TV?"

"Whatever, bitch."

"I think you need to watch *The Simpsons*." She changed the channel and upped the volume. Homer was drinking a beer. "Gotta go," and she stepped into the hall, headed to her next patient. She ran into Sheldon, the other night shift nurse.

"Everything okay?" Sheldon was wiry with a full beard and looked kind of like a pirate with the bandanna.

"The usual. Just the name-calling."

Sheldon laughed and passed her, carrying meds for number one, a cranky older woman named Edith Hallmark who smothered her daughter with a pillow.

Laura's next patient was Timera Scocpol in ten, the only non-white person on the unit. She was usually cooperative, but often wept for her only daughter, whom she had bludgeoned with a swing blade. She was large, suffered from high blood pressure, and Laura had her p.m. dose of insulin and her Procardia ready on the med cart.

"Knock, knock," said Laura. The intercom buzzed as she entered. It was Lars, the monitor tech.

"Hey, she just started seizing," said Lars.

"Okay, thanks." Laura surveyed Scocpol in the bed. The vest restraint was off, her hands and feet loosely restrained. Her eyes were quivering, her toes pointed down. Her seizures were perhaps the most graceful on the unit.

"Mrs. Scocpol? Timera? It's me, Laura. Just checking on you. You're seizing." She touched her shoulder and then squeezed her hand. "Have your insulin here for you. Gonna be a tiny stick."

Laura injected the insulin into the layer of fat over Timera's stomach and dropped the syringe into a dirty needle box. The cuff was still on Timera's arm, and she checked her blood pressure, 160 over 110. Orders were to give the Procardia sublingual for a diastolic greater than 100. She took a large needle and poked a hole in the capsule.

"Got your pressure medicine here." Laura took a bite stick and opened Timera's mouth. She squirted the liquid under her tongue. "All done, sweetie." Timera often wet herself, and Laura checked her diaper, which was wet. She removed it with some effort and placed a new one, rolling her from side to side as Timera trembled. "Now, we're all done." She dimmed the room lights and turned off the TV, a *60 Minutes* rerun.

Timera groaned and seemed to be looking into a dark refrigerator. She had close-cropped hair and dark brown eyes, almost inky. Her college roommate had been from Ethiopia, in the southern part, and she had visited her there one summer while she was pregnant with her daughter. She opened her eyes.

"That was quick," said Laura. "Mrs. Scocpol? It's me, Laura. You've been seizing, traveling. What happened?" She raised the head of the bed.

Timera focused on Laura. "Oh Lord, the dope. I was smoking that dope again. The lady there says it will help me find her."

"Do you buy the dope, the marijuana?"

"No, it's free. Everything free."

"Except for sex and information?" asked Laura. She straightened the sheet.

"Yeah, I suppose that's right. Awful strange, but my girl is there. I know it. Met me a new woman name of Theda. She was white and had my last name."

"That's new. Do you think she's there to help, along with Haile Selassie?"

"Yeah, I reckon so. She gave me the dope. I need me some water."

Laura untied one of her wrists and poured a cup of cold water. "Here you go. Anything else you remember?" She jotted down the new information on a clipboard at the foot of the bed.

Timera thought. "Something about an island in a big lake. I think I'm supposed to go there. Priests live there. They got some religion there, but they use the Bible. Can't read it, though, being in their language." She finished the water and held the cup out for more.

"Yeah, that seems to be the case with the other folks here. You're not alone in this. Just remember that."

"Thank you," said Timera. "I just wish I could go and stay there for a few days, not just for a little while."

"Dr. Markush is working on that. But it's hard on your body when you seize, making your blood pressure go up. While you're awake, let me check your sugar, okay? I should have checked it before I gave you the insulin."

"Okay."

Laura pricked her forefinger and let a drop of blood form on the tip of a glucose strip. She waited thirty seconds and wiped off the blood, comparing the color to a chart. "About one-forty, so that's pretty good."

"Thank you, Laura."

"You're welcome. Can I get you anything else?"

Timera smacked her lips. "A can of that Ensure would be real nice, chocolate. I feel tired in my bones."

"Not a problem, be right back." She could hear Grayson railing in his room. She spoke to Renaldo, who was sitting in his padded rolling chair at the end of the hall, reading *Men's Life,* and entered the nursing station from the west side. "Another crazy night," she said to Lars.

Lars sat at his bank of monitors. "Yeah, nothing new, I suppose. That guy, Myers, in seven is up in the chair. I guess that's okay, right? He got up by himself."

"As long as he stays in his room," said Laura.

"Uh oh," said Lars. "Freddie is on the floor crawling. Renaldo is moving toward him."

"Shit," said Laura, and she headed toward the door.

The next day, a black Continental picked up Kristin and drove her to Bluegrass Army Depot. Two men in plain clothes sat in front. The day was bitter with a brisk wind, patches of snow here and there, the sky gray and swirled. They passed through the gate and drove to a heliport beside a large brick building. The helicopter was there, idling, waiting for her.

As promised, Markush met her at Fort Knox and drove her to a small guest house just a stone's throw from the Organon complex. The apartment was warm, had one bedroom, and the fridge stocked with food. There was even a wine rack. Markush, dressed in gray slacks and a matching tie, seated himself on a floral-patterned couch, and Kristin sat on a matching overstuffed chair. There was a painting of fruit and a TV.

"So, where do we begin?" asked Markush.

Kristin was all business. "What have you been doing with Reece? Studying his brain?"

Markush sat forward. "In a sense. Yes. We're monitoring him. He seizes and travels to another time and place. He gives us information. His whole goal is to find Mia, the real Mia. I know that sounds crazy, but that's where we stand."

"Huh, does he have a Jacuzzi?"

"No, but he can ask for anything he wants, within reason. The seizures take a lot out of him."

Kristin shook her head. "And where is this other place that he supposedly travels to? Mia is supposed to be there?" Her face shifted into a glare at what a joke this all seemed.

"You have to understand. Well, anyway, the place is most likely another version of the village in Ethiopia where he worked as a nurse."

"Oh Lord, you mean Godo. That's all he ever talked about. I think he may have slept with one of the nurses. Her name was Emma. So, answer me this: why in the hell would Mia be in Ethiopia?"

Markush pulled a pack of cigarettes from his pocket. "Mind if I smoke?"

"Yes, I do mind."

"Not a problem."

He then slipped out a small tape recorder and placed it on the coffee table. "Okay if I tape this conversation? We need every detail we can get."

Kristin thought. "As long as I don't end up on the evening news again. Jesus, I think I need a glass of wine."

"That works," said Markush. "I'll have one with you, special occasion. Red okay?" He went to the kitchen and returned with a bottle of red, two stemless glasses, and a corkscrew.

Kristin watched him pour. "Thanks, Doc. By the way, what is your name again?"

"Clyde. Clyde Markush. Feel free to call me Clyde, although it's a jarring name. Not sure what my parents were thinking. Here." He handed her a glass and turned on the recorder.

Kristin took the glass and smelled it, sipped it. "Not bad."

"So," said Markush. "I'd like to know what you know about Reece's childhood, but first, was there ever anything about him that you found odd or strange? Any crazy stories he told you?" He sipped his wine and placed it on the table.

"Not really. Although he would joke that aliens had abducted him."

"Oh," said Markush.

"Something about a dream, and this thing would stand at the foot of his bed watching him. He'd be terrified, too terrified to call his mother. His dad was overseas, in Vietnam. It was just him and his mother. She was a nut job."

"And they were shot. In the restaurant, right? In Killeen, Texas."

"Yeah." She took small but steady sips.

"Tell me more. There are more like Reece, here at Organon, and they sometimes have similar stories."

"We were at the beach one time, and I noticed this shadow on his head beneath the hair. He's prematurely balding, you know. He joked that it was his alien implant."

"Hmm," said Markush. "That's something we've noticed on the CT scans, but it seems to be there and not there at the same time. I do believe that he has some sort of device that's integrated."

"Jesus." Kristin looked cozy and open. "He said it happened when he was a kid, that he had night terrors."

"How young was he?"

"Oh, little. He makes it sound like he remembers. I guess when he was maybe four."

"And his mother didn't seem to notice the change. I mean, she didn't try to kill him. There was no impostor, as we say."

"Huh," said Kristin. "I don't know. He's different somehow?"

"All of the killings happen later, though, always at seven years of age. Mia was seven."

Kristin shivered. "Please don't talk about Mia like she was a science project. She was my daughter." A burning tear formed in her eye, and she wiped it away.

Markush coughed. "I'm sorry. It's just that she plays a huge role here. Tell me what you know about his childhood."

Kristin laughed. "It sounds like he was a regular Oliver Twist. His parents would just let him wander off and do what he liked. He liked to play with matches and burned his grandparents' barn down, his mother's parents. His dad being in the Army, they moved around frequently. I think it scarred him. He always wanted to be alone, like it was his natural state."

"Hmm," said Markush. "What else? Do you think he was neglected?"

"From what he tells me, his mother was certified crazy. She couldn't hold a job, plus she was pretty promiscuous, from what I hear. His dad was kind of quiet, just let her have her way. It seemed that they were always orbiting one another, as if others didn't exist."

"How did Reece do in school, moving around so often?"

Kristin thought. "He did surprisingly well. He said he always scored well on the verbal parts of standardized tests. He hated the moving, though. The Army wanted him to go to nuclear engineering school. After his parents were killed, he went back to Alabama and lived with his grandparents, which is what he had always longed to do. A pretty unhappy childhood overall, but maybe with a good ending. Of course, there was him getting shot in the head before we married."

"Yes, that is quite a story. He does seem to be very solitary, but he was an only child as well."

"I have to pee," said Kristin, and she excused herself and returned. She sat back on the soft chair.

"Let's talk about the shooting in Texas. How did that affect him?"

Kristin poured herself more wine. "I suppose he was in shock for a while. He always wondered why he lived and they didn't. He definitely had survivor's guilt, but that's to be expected, I guess. Overall, though, I think he was much happier being back in Alabama, as cruel as it sounds. I suppose we would have never met had that not happened."

"I suppose you're right," said Markush. "Did he ever think that the gunman was specifically there for him? That he was the real target?"

Kristin ran her finger around the rim of the glass. "No, and why would he?"

"Just a thought," said Markush.

Kristin crossed her legs and uncrossed them. Markush kept her busy with questions, having to turn the tape over, and finally reaching the death of Mia. Kristin poured herself a third glass.

"Look, can we save talking about that for later. It's after noon, and I'd like to eat something."

"Yes, certainly." He adjusted his tie. "You can eat here, or we can go out. Your preference."

"I saw some nice fruit in the fridge, and I can make myself a sandwich. This wine is going to my head. Can you come back later?"

Markush turned off the tape recorder. "Yeah, sure. Not a problem. I'll just walk next door. Will, say, two be okay?"

"Let's make it three. I might take a nap."

Markush agreed and stood. "This is all extremely helpful. I know it's hard, but it's necessary to bring some sort of happy closure."

Kristin laughed. "If you say so. If you can make me happy again, if you can bring Mia back again, then I'm indebted to you for the rest of my life."

"Great," said Markush. "See you at three," and he left.

Reece had seized at the bar, falling onto the floor, knocking over his bourbon. It was the bar with the giant fishhook. The bartender, the old man with the shaved head, didn't seem alarmed by the quivering body of Reece, and neither did other customers, although they sat in the far corners.

"Up you go," said Arthur. He was behind Reece, pulling him to his feet.

Reece grabbed the edge of the bar and slid onto a stool. "God, I hate this."

"You've been gone for nearly two hours, as I estimate it," said Arthur. "Would you like a drink? You did not finish."

Reece's head pounded. "Just some water, please."

The bartender placed a glass of water on the copper bar top. "Drink up, my twitching friend."

"Twitch my ass," said Reece. He drank the warm water in three gulps. "Jesus, where were we? I feel like I need to sleep a thousand nights."

"Well," said Arthur. "Little Alicia is at the lodging, and we were about to visit a house of carnal knowledge, to find money to pay the Abba."

"Yeah, right," said Reece. "Bartender, anything for a headache?"

The old man smirked. His name was Leo. "Are you saying I gave you a headache, bumfuck?"

"Yes, and do you have anything?"

"In fact, I do." He held a mug under a dispenser and frothy liquid filled it.

"Next time, don't murder your daughter."

Reece shook his head and smelled the mug. It seemed to be seltzer water. He drank it in quick sips, belching, and just like that, his head cleared. "Amazing. You're good."

"Yeah, that's what the old lady says when she swallows my cum." Leo's eyes twinkled.

"Let us proceed," said Arthur. "Alicia may wake soon and be afraid."

They left the bar into the arid glare of the tiny sun.

"God, it must be ninety."

Arthur paused, accessing the data fur. "Yes, exactly, centigrade thirty-two. A good guess. He wobbled a bit, having had three glasses of sherry.

"It's the purple star, right?"

"Yes, the purple star. Shall we go left?"

"Might as well. You know we should probably get some new clothes. I feel filthy." Reece dusted off his shorts.

"Yes," said Arthur, "and a bath as well."

They walked by the nondescript buildings, all the same, looking for a purple star. Some buildings had no stars at all.

"Why are there no children here?" asked Reece. His shoes raised a bit of dust as he walked.

"Yes, that is strange. Except for Alicia."

"And maybe Mia, if we can find her."

"One hopes," said Arthur.

They walked aimlessly, looking for a purple star, working up a light sweat in the dry heat. And then, a building with a purple star.

Reece looked at Arthur. "Shall we?"

Arthur stepped through the door, followed by Reece.

The smell was of eucalyptus, oily and aromatic. The front room reminded him of the clinic where he'd had his dog bite treated, rows of connected yellow chairs, twenty in all. There was a receptionist behind a glass and an old man reading a magazine. A double door seemed to be the portal to the fleshy riches that lay beyond.

"Excuse me, ma'am, is this a place of sex for hire?"

"Yeah," said the lady. Her name was Beatrice. "Just like you hired a hitman to kill your parents." She looked tiny behind the glass, hair tinted blue, smooth brown skin. She looked frumpy in a jumpsuit that was too big.

"What? Is there a way we could speak to one of the ladies, or men?" asked Reece.

"This is not a house of cock, and you'll have to go elsewhere for that. Why do you want to speak to one of the 'hookers', as you say, in your dismal time and place? Do you want to explore the possibility of trading your lousy information for some money to pay the old man who digs in the rock to help you find your daughter?" She popped some gum.

"Yes, precisely," said Arthur. "I think we may prove, though, to have information that would prove either amusing or useful in some practical matter."

The double door opened, and a small spherical object slipped into the room, hovering at nine feet. It glided to the old man in the corner and scanned his face. The man stood and disappeared through the doors.

"The problem here," said Beatrice, "is that you pay first and then get what you need. No exceptions." She popped her gum.

"Well, that's a problem," said Reece.

"Maybe you need a loan?" asked Wanda.

"One can acquire a loan?" asked Arthur. He spoke with hands behind his back.

"Yeah, but only for sex," said Beatrice. "You put your balls up for collateral. You don't repay the loan, then slice and dice, and off to the reproduction unit."

"Jesus," said Reece. He looked at Arthur. "Do you want to borrow money against your family jewels?"

Arthur laughed. "Perhaps I am older and in less need of them."

"I say we both do it and get the maximum amount of cash," said Reece. "What do we do? How much can we borrow?"

"Five hundred per ball," said Beatrice. "Just sit in the chairs and our friendly spherical object will process you."

"Do the funds come in cash, like bills and coins? We're dealing with someone outside the town."

"You're kidding, right?" asked Beatrice.

A middle-aged woman entered, took a seat, and began to comb her hair. A spherical object appeared and scanned her face.

Beatrice smirked. "The value will show in the data fur. Everything is data fur, if you haven't noticed. Look, I could talk all day with you, but as you can fucking see, I'm pretty busy."

Reece and Arthur pondered their options, Reece gliding his hand through his thinning hair.

"Perhaps the Abba will take goods in trade," said Arthur.

"That might work. But what would he want? A new pickaxe?"

"Ah, perhaps we can give him sex. We can bring him here, a treat of sorts," said Arthur.

Beatrice pushed a button and opened an empty drawer. "Yeah, it's the gift that keeps on giving. Look, you want the loan or not? If so, get your tails in the chairs and be done with it."

"Huh, I guess we have no other choice. We'll do it then?" asked Reece. He imagined himself without his testicles.

"Yeah, everybody does it," said Beatrice. "Go, sit. Be gone." She flipped her fingers as if shooing away flies.

Arthur and Reece walked to the middle of a row of chairs and sat. Within seconds, a spherical object arrived and scanned their faces. The object disappeared, and that was that. They looked at one another.

"That's strange," said Reece. "I think I just accessed the data fur and saw that my net value was five hundred units. One ball. Units of what I'm not sure." He looked at his hands to see if anything was different. "You?"

Arthur struggled to replicate Reece's access. "Not quite. I do have an image of a young man reading what appears to be a book, though."

Reece tucked into the data fur and searched for Arthur's net worth and found the five hundred units. "Huh, I just accessed your account. It's there, the five hundred. One ball for you, too." He concentrated on Mia, but could only conjure the final image of her on the Abba's ethereal screen. *Daddy?* He winced and felt thoroughly tired, as if he had walked a long distance.

"Well then, a thousand," said Arthur. "Perhaps that will be enough to provide the old man with a roaring good time." His eyes sparkled.

"One can only hope. But he is a holy man. It may not work. How will we explain it to him?"

"Perhaps the words will come to you through the fur."

"I hadn't thought of that." Reece concentrated, feeling life drain from his body. He saw a string of Amharic characters and heard a pronunciation. "Huh, pretty cool. The word for pussy is ems. The word for having sex is bidi."

Arthur nodded. "Shall we go there, to find the Abba? I suppose he must come here. Perhaps a drink or two with him in a bar would be fruitful ahead of time."

"Yeah, let's do it. One can only hope."

They had to wander and find the edge of town, but soon, within twenty minutes, they found the crude church. They picked their way through the scrub and within ten minutes were following the erstwhile path that ran beneath the rising cliff face. Hot and tired, they arrived at the wooden ladder and climbed up. A distinct sound of metal on rock echoed.

They approached the green door in the rock, which was open.

"Hallo! Tenesteling!" said Reece. He stepped down into the cavernous room. His eyes adjusted to the dimness, and the air was cool. Where was the Ark? Only the rough-hewn table on which it had sat was there. His heart dropped. "The Ark is gone."

The Abba placed his pick against the wall and approached them with a serious smile, his white teeth flashing in the dark. "Salaam," he said. His wiry forearms glinted in the light from the door.

"How to begin?" asked Arthur.

"I think we should get him to a bar and ask him there." Reece turned to the Abba. He pointed at the empty pedestal. "Yeht no?"

The Abba lost his smile and made a motion with his hands as if flying away. The Ark had flown away to another place. It changed places, he said in Amharic. To keep it safe.

"Mia, set lidj, my daughter," said Reece. He pointed to the table. "Uh, how much, sentino?"

The Abba paused and withdrew a pouch from his robe. He opened it and pulled out ten one-hundred-birr bills. "Shih birr."

"A thousand birr," said Reece. "That's a lot of cash. But we have a thousand units of credit."

"Perhaps, our generosity will be sufficient," said Arthur. He dusted off his shirt.

"One would think," said Reece. He held out his hands to the Abba. "Hmm, areke? Katikala?" He named the two liquors he knew from his days in Godo. They were similar, but areke was infused with things such as garlic or cloves.

The Abba pulled his hands away but smiled. His look seemed to ask, "Well, where is the drink?"

"Come with us," said Reece. He pointed to the door. "Nah, come." He hoped the Abba would follow and walked outside into the blistering sun. The top of his head was burned. He remembered Alicia and went to look in the hut. She was asleep on the crude bed.

They all looked at one another, as if deciding who would drive to the mall. Reece noticed a rash on the Abba's neck.

"Nah, come," said Reece. He walked toward the Abba's

house and to the ladder just beyond, and the Abba and Arthur followed. He went down the ladder and pointed toward town. "Godo...Gadam."

The Abba hesitated, and Arthur held out his hand, urging him to go first. The Abba took his time, descending the ladder, wearing his sandals made from old tires. Arthur went to his knees and had some trouble, but soon reached the ground, cursing.

"Nah, come," said Reece. He felt like the Pied Piper herding children. He walked forward and looked back. The Abba was following, babbling at Arthur behind him.

Soon, they walked uphill and approached the town near the old church with incense leaking from within. They gathered there, and the Abba walked forward through what seemed a crack in time, and it was. Reece pulled up short and marveled at what he saw.

Reece stood with his mouth open.

"What has happened?" asked Arthur. "The town is gone."

"Holy fuck," said Reece. "We're in Godo, the way it used to be. This is where I was shot." He explained being shot in the head by the town administrator, known as the Hyena. He looked back up the hill and saw the shelter there, could hear children playing. There was the rocky path leading down into the village. A small boy, his face covered with flies, was pointing at them.

"Ferenj!" and the little boy ran.

The Abba seemed puzzled at Reece's reaction and walked forward with Arthur at his heels.

"Holy moly, I wonder what year it is? If the shelter is here, then the clinic must be here too." His first thought was of Emma. She would be there?

Soon they were in a wide muddy lane with fenced compounds on either side. The Abba was greeting an old man. Reece recognized him. They wound their way through the village and soon came to Afewerki's house. Afewerki was his former assistant in the clinic. There was no one about, and they followed the Abba, who walked through the market square and stopped in front of a bar, one of the huts where home-brewed areke and katikala were served. Reece wanted to run to the clinic or run to the old compound where he had lived. Had he been shot there?

They entered the dim hut that smelled of sour mash, and the men inside took off their ragged hats and mumbled to the Abba. The low stone wall that was the base of the hut seated five men, all with yellow drinking cups. The barmistress, a young girl of sixteen and mother of two, stood from squatting. Fuzzy Amharic music played on a small radio.

The Abba took a seat and motioned for them to follow.

"Reece, how do you explain this?" asked Arthur. "It seems as if we have entered a new reality, very primitive in nature." He took the yellow cup offered to him by the young girl. She returned and filled their cups with smoky katikala.

"I don't know. I don't know," said Reece. "I used to work here as a nurse. I've told you the story, or have I? I was shot. Was I shot? I worked with a nurse named Emma." His mind strained. "Icelanders?"

"Icelanders, you say? Of the Norwegian colony? Such a colorful gathering." Arthur sipped his drink and frowned, nearly spitting it out. "Such a strong drink. I was not ex-pecting it."

Reece sipped. "It's the real thing. Ethiopian vodka." He turned to the Abba, who was smiling, drinking, then back to Arthur. "You know I don't have any money to pay for this." He checked his empty pockets. "I need to go and see who else is here. Can you stay? I'll come back as quickly as possible."

"Yes, lad, I suppose nothing stranger could happen in your absence."

"Okay, great. But you have to drink. To be polite." He sipped his katikala until it was gone. The barmaid asked if he needed more, and he put his hand over his yellow cup and stood. "Okay, be right back."

Reece stooped and stepped into the heavy air. Clouds of white billowed overhead, almost within reach. The sun was not the size of a dime. He trotted down the lane to calls of "Ferenj!" and reached Afewerki's family compound. The gate was open.

He walked to the round hut, thickly thatched with straw. "Hallo!"

"Abet?" came a voice, and there appeared before him Afewerki's kind mother, wiping her hands on her long patched dress.

"Tenesteling. Afewerki?"

Her hands were shaking. "Afewerki, yellum," she said. She pointed to some place beyond the compound with a worried look.

"Ah, ishi, amenseganalo." He glanced around the familiar compound. Afewerki's little square house was there. Inside would be his prize hen, possibly roosting in the rafters.

He left and took the rocky lane, skirting puddles, and soon passed downhill, his heart pounding. He knew that Emma would be there. She had to be. He walked down the rocky path, and there it was, the compound walled with tin sheeting, a line of eight patients sitting beside the fence. By their numbers, he guessed it was the afternoon, the busiest part of the day over. He gazed and nodded to the people squatting there, a young mother with her baby on her back. Before entering, he stopped and took a deep breath.

The guard inside eyed him and ran to the clinic, announcing the arrival of a ferenj. Reece followed him, heart racing. He looked into the clinic and stared. "Oh, my

God!" Emma was staring back at him. She tapped Afewerki on the shoulder, and he turned and stared. "Emma! Afewerki!"

Emma came to the door wearing a half-smile. "Well, where did you come from?" Afewerki peered over her shoulder.

"Emma, it's me, Reece." She didn't recognize him, didn't know who he was.

"Rice? Did you come in a jeep?" She stepped out and down with her arms folded.

"No, Reece, like the peanut butter cup. You don't recognize me."

"No, but I guess I need to." She wore jeans and a white scrub top with hiking boots.

"Oh my," said Afewerki.

"Gee," said Reece. "I don't know how to explain. But I know you and Afewerki. I worked here for a couple of months. I was shot in the head by the Hyena." He could barely catch his breath. "I'm a nurse, from Birmingham." Or was he? Didn't he teach philosophy?

"You're the guy who was shot before I came here? But you died. How can this be?" Emma stared at him.

Afewerki spoke. "How is he knowing our names?" He frowned and adjusted his Exxon ballcap. His mother had just shaved his head.

"You have to believe me. I'm alive, right? I'm sorry to interrupt the clinic, but I had to see if you were here. And you are." He wanted to tell her that he loved her, that she was in danger, that she should never drive up from Addis Ababa without a gun.

"Well, it's nice to meet you," said Emma. "Did you come

from AK, Alem Ketema? When did you get here?"

"No, no, it's all so hard to explain. I've come from the church in the rock, the Abba Paulos. I'm with another man, Arthur. We were drinking at the bar near the market." He was wringing his hands.

"Are you supposed to be with the Icelanders? They're out weighing the kids. Does Dr. Thorsson know you're here?"

"No, but I seem to know them somehow." Reece was piecing the puzzle together. Emma was here. The Icelanders were here. He was not supposed to be here.

Afewerki stepped down. "The missionary who was shot has died. You cannot be him. I knew him. But you are looking like him. He was called Bobby Hartwig. He has promised to bring me to the US, but then he has died."

Reece thought. "I'm not that guy. Do you believe in time travel?" It's all he could think of. "I'm from another time and place. I'm here somehow because of the Abba. He's digging the church into the rock."

"He is sometimes making magic," said Afewerki. "He is tinqway. This is not good."

Emma smiled. "Nothing you're saying makes much sense, but you have to be here for some reason. You're welcome to stay with us tonight. We have an extra room. Are you here for long?"

"I don't know. We, Arthur and I, were trying to make some money. He's in the bar now. We need money to pay. I'm supposed to give him, the Abba, a thousand birr."

Afewerki whistled.

Emma frowned.

"For now, can I borrow a few birr to pay our tab at the

bar?"

"The Icelanders are always drinking, but they have birr," said Afewerki.

Emma dug in her pocket and produced a five-birr note. "This should do it, unless you drink like the Icelanders."

Reece took the bill. "Thanks, Emma. I know you think I'm crazy. Maybe I can explain better later." His eyes wandered to a man approaching them. It was Isaac, wearing his mechanic's jumpsuit and wire-rimmed glasses. "Isaac?"

"Yes," said Isaac. He looked surprised.

"Right," said Reece, seeing the futility. "Hello, I'm Reece." He held out his hand, and Isaac shook it.

"I am happy to see you," said Isaac. He moved along, headed to barter for some poles they needed to expand the clinic.

"Do you need help in the clinic? I'm pretty good with tapeworms and earaches."

Emma laughed. "We have plenty of that, but I don't know you from Adam. You should come to the compound, though, and eat and stay with us. We can talk more. You're the first ferenj to just pop in like this."

"Thank you, thank you," said Reece. "Yeah, I'll come there. I have to go back and see about Arthur."

"He's a nurse, a doctor?" asked Emma.

"He's a philosopher. He's German."

"A German philosopher. Good Lord. Okay, and bring him too. Dr. Thorsson would love to meet you, I'm sure, and the others. What the hell..."

Reece slumped to the ground. His eyes rolled back in his head.

Kristin awoke from her catnap with a headache. She walked to the bathroom and washed down three aspirin with tap water. She checked her watch, a few minutes until three. She brushed her teeth, refreshed her hair, and wondered if she should have another glass of wine. Right on time, there was a knock at the door. She walked that way and stopped to lower the heat.

Markush still had his tie on, although the knot was loosened. He looked tired. "Thank you for letting me come back. I know you don't have to do this, and I am forever grateful." He went straight to the couch and placed the recorder beside him.

"Yeah, it's making me think," said Kristin. "Making me think that you're as crazy as Reece. You want wine?"

"I'm fine. Don't think of this as crazy, just complicated."

"Well, it's that," said Kristin.

"If you're okay with it, we should talk about Mia," said Markush. He turned on the recorder.

Kristin sighed. "I buried my only child, for god's sake. What can I say?"

"That must have been the hardest thing in the world."

"Yeah, it was, and without the support of a husband. She was just such an interesting little girl." Kristin's cheeks were red, her eyes hot. "Reece was always so protective."

"What was it that made her so interesting?"

Kristin reached for the wine bottle. "She was always listening to music in her head, humming tunes. Everything had its music: the rain, an airplane, even a quiet room.

She was just so in tune with her environment. She liked to dress up in all of her princess clothes and loved the *Barbie Princess* movies. And sometimes, though, when she talked to you, she sounded more like an adult than a child." She wiggled the cork out and poured herself a glass.

"What were some other things with this music that she connected with?"

"Pretty much everything. Even music had its own music, as if something was hidden inside. She could hear it and hum it. When she learned about atoms, she said she could hear the atoms singing, that they sounded like sponges soaking up water."

"Did she ever talk about music from dreams or music coming from faraway places, not of the Earth? I've talked with one other little girl like Mia. She can hear the stars, follow the music back to a star's origins. It's pretty incredible."

"She may have with Reece. They seemed to have this secret connection that I wasn't a part of. It made me jealous. I don't recall anything about stars or planets, though. But the music was always very simple, not complicated like you'd think. There were little girls who came around that Reece didn't care for. There seemed to be one everywhere we lived.

"Maybe that should have clued me in to his violent side. He hated those little girls. You know, it's funny. Mia said they couldn't hear her music and that it made them angry. The last little girl was in Richmond. Her name is... Charlotte, a cute and inquisitive little girl. She came the first day we moved in. She lived with her grandparents, she said, although I never met them. And then there was that other little girl in Birmingham. We think she tried to kill Mia's goldfish, or at least Reece did. He threatened to kill her one day, but I thought he was joking."

"Did Reece ever mention Dahlia?"

Kristin paused, took a sip of wine. "He never did with me. But that's what he was screaming after he...killed Mia. I had no idea what or who Dahlia was. Do you?"

"Keep in mind that this is speculative, but Dahlia seems to be a collective name for these strange little girls. The others we have at Organon, who killed their children, talk about Dahlia as if she were an ancient being that is on some unknown quest. She, or it, takes the form of these curious little girls with the nearly perfect faces. Your husband, ex-husband, is convinced that Dahlia abducted Mia, sent her away, and replaced her with an impostor." His hands trembled. A thrill of excitement played on his face.

Kristin parted her brown curls with her hand and sighed. "None of this makes any sense, even though you sound like you know what you're talking about. I suppose I could believe what you're saying, but I have no reference point, nothing to hold onto. Do you think this Dahlia is an alien? But there's no such thing as an alien, as far as I'm concerned."

Markush looked thoughtful. "It is hard to grasp. One does have to believe to make sense of it. That's one reason our conversation today is classified. If the public found out what we were up to, they would revolt. To those on base, Organon is a facility for the criminally insane, a place for child killers. But to the government, something very serious is occurring, something of great consequence is falling into place. I'll admit that I remain baffled and that the information is overwhelming, but we're onto something grand, something beyond what anyone has ever imagined." He seemed out of breath.

"I wish that I weren't a part of this. I just want Mia back, to be back to the way things used to be. If Mia were to return—I can't believe I'm saying that—I suppose I would have to forgive Reece. But no one comes back from the dead."

"This is hard to say, but don't think of Mia as deceased, just think of her as missing. I can't promise anything, but one of my primary objectives is to find Mia and other children like her. Reece took the last bed on our secure unit. It's only a matter of time before we have to add more rooms. The requisition is already in."

"Taxpayers looking for this Dahlia."

"Basically," said Markush.

"Are you one of them?'

"One of who?"

"I mean, like Reece. Or maybe you're an impostor."

Markush's eyes gave him away. "As a matter of fact, I share some commonalities with Reece, although I've never married or had kids. I have vivid memories from when I was four or five of being visited at night by this strange little girl. She would stand at the foot of my bed and stare at me. I would become hysterical, and my parents would hustle me into their bed. It seems that night terrors of this sort are indicative of something larger. And this shadow that shows on Reece's CT scan, I have it too. It happened one night. The little girl attacked me and placed something on my head. I remember eerie blue lights. I think I must have had a babysitter that night, because my parents didn't come even though I was screaming bloody murder. You could say that my interest is personal."

"How long have you known about the others, the killings, the impostors?"

"How to explain? I believe that because of my encounter, because of the device placed into my head, that I developed an acute sense of music, or I had it to begin with. I'm not sure. I played classical violin, beginning when I was five. I was very, very good. And like Mia, I could hear the music in things, everyday things, a candy wrapper. But there was a tragedy in my family. An uncle murdered his daughter and went insane. He was diagnosed as paranoid schizophrenic. This was around the time that Thorazine in the 1950s was introduced. It seemed to work miracles on most, but didn't touch him. He died at the age of forty-seven, as insane as he was after killing my niece. In my gut, I knew there was a connection with what I came to know as Dahlia, and I decided to become a psychiatrist. I never discussed my ideas with colleagues, but was always working on the problem. It wasn't until a pattern of child killings, psychosis, and rantings about Dahlia that I began to come out of the closet, so to speak, and moved my career into the field of forensic psychiatry."

"That's quite a story. How did you get to be the boss here, of Organon?"

"I was approached, let's say. Some things have to remain secret. It's my dream job, and maybe that is the best answer to your question. This is my marriage, my quest." Markush leaned forward, as if about to take flight. "If I had had children, I would perhaps be a patient rather than the doctor. I spared myself that agony, although I did consider having children just to see if it led me to Dahlia, but I ruled that out. That's why Reece and Mia are so important. They hold the key."

Kristin shook her head, crossed her legs. "So, answer me this. What's the connection with Ethiopia? I don't get it. You've told me that everyone here has some connection. Why is that?"

Markush laughed. "That's where it gets exciting. I have hunches, but I don't know. Let's just say that it's a magical place, a place of tremendous suffering at times, but a place that holds many secrets. It's rural, impoverished, and an unlikely hiding place."

"Hiding place? God, I need more wine. Do you mind?" She stood before he could answer. There was a bottle of aromatic white in the fridge.

"By all means." He sank back into the couch, watched her hips in her loose white skirt.

Kristin returned with the open bottle and two fresh glasses, which she placed on the coffee table. "So, Ethiopia." She poured for them both. "You know they eat raw beef there. Ugh."

Markush laughed. "Yes, kitfo, finely chopped meat with a variety of spices. It's actually pretty good. There's a restaurant in Addis Ababa attached to a Shell station that serves it."

"Is it true that they cut the meat from living cows and then sew up the hole?" Kristin made a sour face and sampled the wine.

"Did Reece tell you that? Yes, I think it's true at times, perhaps more so in the countryside than in the city. The muscle just grows back is what I understand. Pretty ingenious if you ask me."

"Yeah, but cruel," said Kristin.

"Perhaps, but necessity is the mother of invention, as they say."

"But why Ethiopia? If Reece hadn't gone there, would none of this have happened?"

"That's a great question, and I'm not sure I have the final answer, but it does seem to play into the pattern. You would have thought the media would have picked up on the connection, but the cases are scattered and few, although growing." He paused. "Are you familiar with the Ark of the Covenant?" He looked a bit deeper into her languid brown eyes.

"Well, there's that movie, *Raiders of the Lost Ark,* and I know a little from the Bible, but not much. Is that part of the magic?"

"Again, I don't fully know. Reece has given me the most solid details so far. I suppose I should tell you—"

"Tell me what?" asked Kristin.

"He had an encounter. He seizes and travels back to Ethiopia. It's a different Ethiopia, perhaps in the future, perhaps in another universe. He encountered what seems to be the Ark and saw Mia. She was alive."

"He saw Mia?" She uncrossed her long legs. "He said that?"

"Yes, the Ark showed him. There is a monk in charge, in a room built into the rock. Reece saw her...and she spoke to him."

Kristin closed her eyes and held her breath, then let it out in a long exhale. Her face flushed. "So, why does he get to see her and not me? God, I miss her so much, and talking to you makes me want to believe she's alive. I don't think I can handle this."

Markush touched her bare knee. "I'm sorry, but it's what he says. He comes and goes, between here and there. It's the best lead I've had so far." The recorder strained and clicked off.

Reece awoke on a narrow plank bed, sweating. Yellow plastic covered the walls, and the roof above was made from tin sheeting. He glanced to his side, and Arthur was looking at the cement floor. He strained to remember what had happened, and a torrent of information flooded his brain.

"Lad?" asked Arthur. He stood.

"Where are we?" Reece propped on an elbow. Three black flies attacked his face.

"It seems to be another time, but this is a primitive place."

Reece looked out through the open door and could see the dining hut. He was in Godo, the bona fide Godo. "We're in Godo," said Reece. "Where are the others?"

"I have met a young man named Afewerki, I believe. He came to the bar and paid for the drinks. They carried you here up the steep hill. There are two women cooking."

"Misrak," said Reece. "And Zenebek, the cooks." He threw his legs over the side of the bed and sat up.

"I'm delighted to see that you are well. Each time I worry that you will not return." He went to the door and looked out.

"Yeah, sorry about that. It just happens, without warning. There is a woman, a nurse, who works in the clinic. Did you meet her? Her name is Emma."

"No, I did not meet her. I was led here by Afewerki. He asked me to stay with you."

"This is the village I worked in back in 1986, where I was shot. They had to fly me back to the States. But she doesn't recognize me. Damn." He wobbled on the edge of the bed, the board cutting into his thighs. He waved the flies from his face.

"Perhaps she will come soon," said Arthur. "You said fly?"

"Where is the Abba?" Reece felt a quick of panic. He couldn't afford to lose him. He held the key to Mia.

"He was drinking in the hut and did not come. Perhaps he has returned to his cave." Arthur paced in the small room, his hands behind his back.

"Damn," said Reece. "We need him. But we can find him, I hope. He's expecting a thousand birr, so maybe he hasn't gone far."

"Yes, the odor of money and priests."

Reece decided it was safe to stand and tried. He fell back and then stood, his vision blanking for a few seconds.

"Let's go to the clinic. I have to make sure I'm not dreaming this." He put his hand against the yellow plastic.

A face appeared in the door, and it was the guard, Irigit, dressed in his shabby clothes held together with patches. He looked frightened and took off his scrappy cap.

"Irigit!" said Reece.

Irigit startled back, and there was a noise at the gate. Reece stepped outside beneath the small overhang of tin and saw them. Dr. Thorsson, Eydis, and Svana. They stopped in their tracks, as if seeing a white man for the first time.

"Who is this?" asked Gudmunder.

Reece struggled to piece it together. Gudmunder was tall, stocky, and had thick red hair. Eydis was short and blonde. Svana was bulky and with jet-black hair that seemed to spike of its own accord. Had he worked with them?

"Hello, I'm Reece. You must be the Icelanders? Dr. Thorsson?" Reece walked forward and held out his hand. Behind them, he could see Misrak and Zenebek peering from the smoke of the cook house.

"And I am Arthur. Herr Schopenhauer." Arthur stood at Reece's side.

"Oh, a boy!" said Svana. "You are American?"

"Yeah, American," said Reece. He shook Gudmunder's hand and then Svana and then Eydis, and Arthur did the same.

"Are you here by jeep?" asked Gudmunder.

"No, we have walked, I suppose," said Reece. *How to explain?*

"Walked? From Alem Ketema? It is a long journey," said Gudmunder.

"We came from the room in the rock. The Abba Paulos brought us," said Arthur. "There seems to be some confusion with time and place. You're a doctor?"

"Yes, a doctor. We are here to weigh the children and provide vaccines."

Arthur looked confused.

"You are visitors here, no?" asked Eydis. "We shall have a feast tonight, to celebrate. Why are you here? To help with the clinic?" She eyed Arthur's black breeches and ruffled shirt.

"I was. I worked here before," said Reece. He wanted to say with Emma, but that was futile for now.

"Come," said Gudmunder. "We have been walking all the day. Let us sit by the tents."

They took chairs around the dead fire. Gudmunder called for Irigit to start it up. "Esat," said Gudmunder, and a long silence ensued as they watched Irigit arrange kindling.

"How are the weighings and vaccines going?" asked Reece.

"It is good," said Gudmunder. "The children are gaining weight, but there is still malnutrition. The vaccine is hard to explain without an interpreter, but the people have had vaccines before. They are very trusting. Ah, but the little ones cry like baby goats."

"We have weighed and measured fifty-two children this day," said Svana. She looked restless.

Zenebek came from the cookhouse, juggling a hot coal, letting it fall into the fire pit. Soon, there was a small fire.

"I think we need some drinks," said Gudmunder, and Svana and Eydis agreed. "Do you like the Ethiopian vodka?"

"It is very smoky," said Arthur. "But a drink would be refreshing."

"Sounds good to me," said Reece.

Gudmunder fished in his pocket for some birr and called out to Irigit, who was bringing more firewood. "Nah, Irigit. Katikala, sost liters."

Irigit tumbled the wood onto the ground, took the

money, and nodded.

"So, are you with the Mission, perchance?" asked Gudmunder. He wore long cotton trousers and a button-up dress shirt.

"Yes, when I was here before," said Reece. "Is there any water? I'm so thirsty."

"Just wait," said Eydis. She wore blue scrubs like Svana with the imprint of an Icelandic hospital. She went to Emma's little house.

"Yes, some water would be very nice," said Arthur.

Reece struggled. He wanted to tell them everything, that he had worked with them in Godo, or was it Gadam? That he'd had many adventures with them, that in another life he had worked with Emma. But, he wasn't sure.

"Now you are only a visitor?" asked Svana. She leaned toward the fire and placed a few more iron-hard sticks.

"Yes, that is a good way to say it," said Arthur. He placed his hands on his small belly. "I am from Germany."

Reece followed the thread. "And I'm from Alabama, in the US. I'm from the same place as Emma."

Svana looked at Gudmunder and then at Eydis, who held a liter of cold water from Emma's propane fridge.

"Hmm, Emma is from Alabama, no? Do I say it correctly?" asked Gudmunder.

"Oh," said Reece. "Yeah, right. Thanks." He took the water from Eydis.

"Yes," said Svana. "Where is this Alabama?"

"It's next to Mississippi. Very close, the next state." He popped the rubber plug from the bottle and then remembered his manners. He offered the bottle to Arthur.

"How long have you been in the country?" asked Gudmunder.

Reece looked at Arthur and took the bottle from him. "I come and go. Arthur has been here, yes, here, but in another time, for some weeks. Right?"

Arthur looked impatient. "What he says is true. Unfortunately, young Reece here travels from place to place as he seizes. I arrived not here but in another place, somewhat similar, perhaps two months ago. It is hard to say because there is no night there, only that damnable sun shining every hour of the day."

Reece laughed at the absurdity of it all. "He's from the past and I'm from the future, but in the past I worked here. The Hyena shot me."

No one spoke for a moment.

"Hmm," said Gudmunder. "I am not understanding. There was a young man shot, many years ago, but he died."

Reece tried his best. "The Abba Paulos, you know him, he is carving the church into the rock. He brought us here from a time in the future. One moment we were there and then we were here. It can't be explained, but we need to go back. I'm looking for my daughter, Mia. Maybe she is here."

"Your daughter?" asked Gudmunder. "Here is the katikala. Perhaps that will help." Irigit set the bottles beside him. "Amenseganalo."

"Yiqirta," said Irigit.

"Have you seen a young white girl, seven years old?" asked Reece. He looked desperate.

"We are the only whites here," said Eydis. "We would notice a young girl like that. We go to all of the places and have not seen such." She looked to Svana for confirmation.

Gudmunder took the corncob stopper from a bottle and took a drink. "Here, my friends, this will illuminate the problem. And you are from Germany? Arthur?"

Arthur took the bottle and drank, wiping his whiskers. He coughed. "Yes, I am living in Berlin. Do you know it? I was there and then suddenly in a new place, and then I met young Reece here. I'm helping, it seems, to find his daughter. That is our hope. Perhaps when we find her, I will be released back to my home."

"I know Munich only," said Gudmunder. "Ah, here comes the rest."

Reece turned and saw Emma followed by Afewerki. His heart leaped in his throat. How could this be? *Emma.* There were no more chairs, and he stood.

"Keep your seat. I'm surprised to see you walking around. You had a seizure at the clinic," said Emma.

"Take it," and Reece sat on the stubbly grass, a cooling wind.

"He has a wild story," said Emma.

Afewerki hung back.

"Yes, we are hearing it," said Gudmunder. The bottle had made the full circuit, and he took it from Eydis. "I am hoping the katikala will help."

Emma laughed and gazed around at the unlikely group.

Reece bucked and shivered, feeling the cool air of the AC. He opened his eyes, and no one was there. The TV was on, *Jeopardy.* He wanted to jump up and run screaming through the halls, but didn't have the energy. The pillow hurt his neck, and he sat up in bed.

"Hey, Reece, it's me, Debbie." She had slipped into the room. She wiped sweat from his face.

"God," said Reece, "I need some water." He fell back. "Plus, I have to pee."

"Man, you've been coming and going. Markush is going to get an earful." She poured him a cup of water. "Here."

Reece sucked the water down. "Just give me the urinal, please." He placed it between his legs and concentrated. "God, almighty. You'd think I would piss myself when I seize." He filled the container with nearly a liter. "Jesus, I feel better."

"So, how is your progress with Mia?"

"If I remember correctly, Arthur and I were trying to acquire money to pay the Abba to filter the data fur. We went back, but the Ark was gone. When we returned to town with the Abba, suddenly it was Godo, the place I worked when I was shot. Emma was there. I told you about her. And the Icelanders were there. It seems that in another life, I worked with them in Godo as well. I know them, but they don't know me."

"You're not in the place called Gadam, but in Godo?"

"Yeah, I think." He gulped another cup of water. "What's got me worried is that the Ark was gone from the room in the cliff. That's how I saw Mia, through the Ark. Who knows when it will return, if we can even get back there."

"I'm getting the gist of what you're saying." She wrote on the clipboard at the foot of the bed. "Your memory is pretty good, better than most here. Some have little to no memory of their travels at all. Right now, you're the star patient."

"I guess I'll take what I can, including some food." He looked at the analog clock, eight-thirty. "I missed break-fast."

"Yep, you do seem to miss your meals. I'll have a tray sent around, probably a sandwich, though, some fruit and chips." Debbie emptied the urinal in the toilet and washed her hands.

"Is Markush around?" asked Reece. "If he wants to send me back with the magnets, I would be up for it. We were sitting around a fire, drinking. I was trying to explain where we came from. Of course, they're thinking that Arthur and I are lunatics just appearing from nowhere."

"He was in early this morning. The young lady in number six has started to blink and move her hands. He was pretty excited about that."

"She was shot in Ethiopia," said Reece.

"Yeah, in the head. It's a miracle she's alive."

"And did you tell me her name?" A tiny thrill shot through him. He wanted to leap from bed and take a look. Had he already seen her?

"Emma, a sweet young lady she seems. She's a nurse. We let you see her a day or so ago."

"Can I see her again? I don't remember seeing her. I need to see her. You know, the nurse I worked with in

Godo was named Emma. It has to be her, except I was shot and not her. Please, just a peek. I won't speak to her unless you say it's okay."

"Well," said Debbie. "I'm really not supposed to let you guys interact."

"I'm begging you, just for a minute."

"Okay, but don't go seizing on me while you're up." She let the bed rail down. "Just take it easy." She unplugged him from the EEG.

Reece swung his legs over and winced. His neck and back hurt. He sat there for a few seconds and then stood, shaking. He let Debbie take him by the elbow and walk him into the bright hall. Freddie, in the dayroom, looked back and made eye contact, a lingering stare. Reece waved and thought he smiled. Freddie turned away.

"Here," said Debbie. She steered him into the adjoining room.

Reece stopped and stared. "Emma? Her face is so bruised. It's not her, though. She would be my age." He stepped into the room and walked to the bedside. He reached and touched the sheet.

Emma's eyes blinked in slow motion, and her mouth made an O. He saw her fingers move, but that was all.

Debbie tugged on his elbow. "Okay, I think that's enough. She's still fragile. Let's go back, okay?"

Reece walked backward out of the room and tripped. Debbie caught him. "Whoa, now. Want to sit in the chair?"

Reece's legs trembled. He felt like a used eraser. "Yeah." He sat down heavy.

"You rest and let me order food, okay? And stay put."

"Sure," said Reece. He leaned back and propped his

feet. He closed his eyes, his brain squirming with notions and images, and he fell asleep from exhaustion.

Half an hour later, he awoke, hearing his name. There was a tray of food. He looked up and saw Dr. Markush.

"Reece? You look bushed. Sorry to bother you. Debbie's filled me in on the latest, but I wanted to talk with you." He sat on the bed.

Reece told him about somehow migrating from Gadam to Godo, about the Icelanders and this other Emma in Godo, about the Ark missing from the cave. He spoke as if telling his story for the first time, breathless.

"Fascinating," said Markush. "I keep getting the feeling that everyone here is part of one big extended family. Listen, I have some news for you. I have permission to tell you."

"What?" Reece reached for the tuna salad sandwich.

"Kristin is here. I've been debriefing her, getting her side of the story."

Reece took a bite of his sandwich and chewed. "You're kidding? She thinks this is all lunacy, right? I mean, you said she divorced me in a heartbeat. What do you mean *here?*"

"She's staying in a guest house we have for family. She arrived yesterday and will leave tomorrow. I asked her if she would be willing to sit down with you and talk, but she said no. That's unfortunate, but at least she came."

Reece inhaled a bite of sandwich and drank a cup of grape juice. "Sorry, I'm famished."

"No problem," said Markush.

"Does she know about the others here?"

"She knows that the others are like you, that they all

have the Ethiopia connection. She's overwhelmed but seems to have let her guard down in relation to Mia. I think she's considering the possibility that Mia is alive. We talked for several hours yesterday and had dinner last night at the Officers Club. I'm on my way to the guest house now to talk with her."

"Wow, I wouldn't have expected that. I could never bring myself to tell her what I knew. Does she know about Dahlia? That I was in a sense abducted by aliens?"

"We covered that. She didn't buy into it, but she was thoughtful nonetheless, as if reevaluating the whole situation. She told me more about Mia's night terrors, about your paranoia with certain little girls. I tried to make the connection with Dahlia as best I could without sounding too crazy. Let's just say that I tried to be objective, to persuade her with facts. She still sees you as insane, but she's willing to talk with me, which was not always the case." Markush crossed his legs, revealing argyle socks. "She's a bright young lady."

"Yeah, she just got tangled up with the wrong guy. I mean, we loved each other, but I always felt that I was compromised, that she deserved better."

"Do you wish you'd tried to explain the situation to her in more depth?"

Reece belched. "Sorry. I often wanted to. I had a group of people that I met with weekly, people whose children had been mapped, you know, had the membrane implanted. That's what I call it anyway."

"I like that term, mapped. I'll have to use it. To be clear, was Mia mapped before her abduction and replacement?"

"That's what I was always on the lookout for. I thought

I had been vigilant, but Dahlia is relentless. In hindsight, I think that Mia was mapped when she was younger. For whatever reason, Dahlia was unsatisfied with the information being gathered and went to the next level, the actual abduction. Maybe it's my fault in some way. I should have just let those little girls come around more often, but they freaked me out."

"This is a big question, Reece. What is Dahlia? I can't categorize her or it. Is she a person, an alien, a collective conscience? What's your opinion?" He stood and paced.

"That's the million-dollar question. I think she is some sort of trans-universal being that exists everywhere at all times. It seems to be the only answer. I don't know how that could be or why, though."

Markush looked bright, cheerful, his eyebrows bushy and neat. He was in his element. "Hmm, that's along the lines that I've considered. One has to make room for the idea of a multiverse. It's almost a given, but with lots of faith involved. What is that Bible verse about faith? The Book of Hebrews."

"Now faith is the substance of things hoped for, the evidence of things not seen," said Reece. "Hebrews 11:1."

Markush lit up. "Exactly. I never thought I'd be relying on scripture to explain."

Reece laughed. "I was a missionary back in the day. Hardcore Southern Baptist. But that all started to fade away with the murder of my parents and then disappeared completely after Ethiopia, like a puddle drying up."

"So," said Markush. "Could there be some notion here of Dahlia as a kind of god? An omniscient being? I did talk with Kristin about your upbringing."

"Maybe I will regret saying this, but Dahlia is the closest reality to God that I've ever come across. Instead of Jesus, we have these awful little girls creating havoc. But why choose little girls to terrorize?"

"Because they're innocent. The perfect cover, right?" said Markush.

"Yeah. But I love Mia with all my heart and soul," said Reece. "I always wanted a little girl. Little boys are hard to handle, but the little girls we're talking about are pure evil, as far as I'm concerned. If I were to say that publicly, people would call me crazy...crazier."

Markush nodded. "In the absence of knowing precisely what Dahlia is, we can still hypothesize about what it is that she wants. What do you think it is she wants? From me, from you, from Mia, and all of the others?"

"I don't really know," said Reece. "But there is some grand secret that some little girls must possess. I would go so far as to say it is genetic. Dahlia is seeking out information to accomplish an unknown task."

"We do have money in our budget for extensive genetic testing, but so far, we haven't been able to follow through. Parents are unwilling. I would die for the chance to examine the DNA of one of these impostors or to examine the DNA of those abducted. I think you're right to speculate in that direction."

"You know, Doc, I think that Dahlia works to protect that information. If Dahlia had wanted the impostor to live, she would have intervened. She let me kill Mia's double, and she's in the ground now, as far as I know. The impostors are disposable in a sense."

"What would she gain from letting them live, though?

It just seems to be a part of the plan. Expendable as you say." Markush rocked on his heels.

"I suppose they would pile up and make a huge mess of things. It's one less thing for Dahlia to worry about. But I think some of these little girls actually live and grow up." He thought about his students. Reece tore open a bag of chips and munched.

The intercom: "Dr. Markush, Freddie is seizing in the dayroom," said Claire. "Debbie is with him, but she could use some help."

"Shit," said Markush, and he bolted.

They laid him out flat on the ground, letting his body tremble, his eyes darting to and fro like tadpoles. Emma was beside him, sitting with her hand behind his head. Arthur stood over them, waiting for a look of presence to emerge on Reece's face.

"Hello? Anybody there?" asked Emma. "He's coming around."

The fire was bright and the light beginning to dim, swallows flitting overhead, zapping bugs. Gudmunder had fished around in the supplies and found some IV phenytoin for Reece's seizures, which he had slowly injected. Eydis and Svana were there, and a bottle of the katikala had been consumed, giving them a cheerful glow, although Emma had declined the drink, watching over Reece. As she gazed at him, she could see that he was of her place back in the American South, his prominent chin, his long eyelashes, his skinny body all seemed familiar to her.

Reece opened his mouth and yawned, his eyes watering. He felt that he was coming from a deep sleep and looked up to see Arthur above him and Emma at his side. He spoke, but his voice croaked. "Some water?" He rolled onto his side and then back again.

"Yeah, water," said Emma. "Be right back." She hurried to her little house, followed by Afewerki. He brought back her wooden chair for Reece.

Dr. Thorsson stood and came over to have a look. He squatted. "You are okay now, no? You have been seizing for two hours. I have never seen anything like it, just a little trembling. Do you know where you are?"

Reece opened his dry mouth. "Godo. I've been traveling, back to the States, to a hospital in Kentucky. There's a doctor there. His name is Markush." He pushed up on an elbow.

"Shall we place him in a chair?" asked Arthur. "I'm glad you're back. The doctor here gave you some powerful medicine into your vein."

Emma held a yellow cup of water. She took Gudmunder's place, kneeling beside Reece. "Here you go."

With the help of Arthur and Gudmunder, Reece stood with his cup and then sat. "Thank you."

"You're welcome," said Gudmunder. "You say you have been traveling. What does it mean?"

"Yes, you make us worry about you even though we've just met," said Eydis. Her pink cheeks gave her a healthy glow in the dimming light.

Reece stared at the fire. "What kind of medicine did you give me?"

Svana spoke. "He gave to you phenytoin for the seizures."

"Oh," said Reece. "That may not be a good idea. I can only travel when I have seizures. I need to travel, to find Mia." He sipped the water, cooling his parched throat. "Thank you, though. I suppose it seemed the right thing to do. I've been back to Kentucky, to a place called Organon." He didn't want to say why he was there, that he had killed a little girl impersonating his Mia.

"You are dreaming you are there, no?" asked Gudmunder.

Arthur chuckled.

"No, I go there. I was there. There and here at the same time," said Reece.

"We are needing more drinks for this," said Svana, laughing. She unstoppered the second bottle of katikala, took a sip, and passed it to Eydis. "Are you married? You have a little girl, you say."

Reece thought. "I was, but she divorced me."

Arthur spoke. "Yes, you see, he had to kill a child, what seemed to be his child, but she was merely a substitute."

Emma sat on one of the stools. "What? That's crazy."

Reece took the bottle and sipped, and then took a swallow, coughing. "It's not what it seems." He then went into detail about Mia, about the impostor, about the murder, about his lapse into insanity, about Organon, about the other place, Gadam 3981, where he was trying to find Mia. "But maybe she is here. I want to go again to the Abba's place in the rock. He's the one who can help. He controls the Ark."

"My, what a story," said Gudmunder. He had perked up when Reece mentioned the Ark. He was interested in seeing one of the local replicas of the holy tablets, but had thus far been unsuccessful. Overhead, the stars spilled over Godo, bats joining the waning swallows.

The group sat in silence, a scratching of unwashed heads, dusty ankles. Dinner would be soon. There was a noise at the gate, words being exchanged.

"Damn," said Emma.

"Fuck," said Gudmunder.

Into the compound staggered the Donkey, the village administrator, his pistol at his side. Two young men dressed in green fatigues followed him. Zenebek and Misrak cringed in the cook house, looking out through the smoke. The Donkey drew near.

"We have some visitors, my ears have told me!" said the Donkey. He was short, dressed in fatigues, and had a neat haircut. His gold tooth flashed.

Svana reached and held Eydis's hand. The Donkey had attacked her as they were walking, had tried to grope her.

"Welcome!" said Gudmunder with a grimace. "Yes, we have two visitors with us. They are just here."

The Donkey moved closer, trying to adjust his vision. "They must register with my office. They do not have permission to be here! I am the authority in this place."

Afewerki translated.

"Come, come," said Gudmunder. He motioned the Donkey toward an empty chair. "Katikala for you, no?"

The Donkey smiled and looked pleased. He managed to sit without falling into the fire. "Bah. Katikala. I want the white man's drink. You must share!" He glared at Reece and Arthur. "Who are these ferenji?" Afewerki translated.

"They are just here to help the people," said Gudmunder. He walked to his tent for a bottle of Reyka vodka and returned with two yellow cups. He handed the bottle to the Donkey.

"Yes, the vodka, am I right? The delicious vodka." He fumbled with the cork and poured and spilled. "Goddamn." He wiped his hand on his blue shirt.

Arthur stood to introduce himself. "Good evening, sir. I am Herr Schopenhauer." He did a slight bow.

The Donkey stared at him, his ruffled sleeves and baggy pants. "Who is this busheti?"

"He says it is nice to meet you," said Afewerki.

"And I as well," said Arthur. He cleared his throat and returned to his seat.

Reece tried not to stare at the Donkey.

"Ah, what a night with the crazy ferenji," said the Donkey.

"He is happy," said Afewerki.

A pall settled over the group, all glancing back at the two armed men. Afewerki knew that Zenebek and Misrak were waiting for the Donkey to leave before they served dinner. He took a deep breath.

The Donkey guzzled his drink, smacking his lips, gazing around as if at a family reunion. "Such a nice group, but I will have to arrest these newcomers. No doubt about it. They are not following the law."

Afewerki translated, biting his lip.

"No, that is a bad plan," said Gudmunder. "Here, have some more drink." He picked up the bottle and poured. "Perhaps he should have dinner with us? To make things smooth?"

Afewerki growled and didn't respond.

"What is it? What you are saying?" asked the Donkey.

"They have asked you to dinner," said Afewerki. He took off his hat and ran his hand across his bald head. He started to turn toward the cook house, and Misrak was beckoning for him. He shouted that they could leave. To cover the dishes.

"I'll be damned," said the Donkey. "Perhaps to poison me! I'll have none of your food. But maybe we should dance? Where is the radio? Why do you not have music for your guests?"

"Dear God," said Svana. She squeezed Eydis's hand.

"Emma, the radio?" asked Gudmunder. "A little music, and he will leave, no?"

Emma sighed and went for the radio.

"They will spend the night in the jail," said the Donkey. "They will not forget this place."

No one spoke, waiting for Emma and the radio. She returned, the radio on, breathing weird squeaks and pops. She handed the radio to Afewerki, and he tuned in a yawning station with Amharic music. The music animated the Donkey even further, and he tried to stand but couldn't. He drained his cup of vodka and tried again. He stood close to the fire, wavering.

"Who is the first to dance!" He rocked back and forth.

Reece wondered if he would fall into the fire and wished that he would.

"Yes, I am dying to dance with a man called the Donkey," said Svana. She had grown up with three older brothers and could beat them all at arm wrestling. She stood and led the Donkey away from the fire. The two guards moved back and grinned.

"This is the life!" The Donkey moved his feet in slow motion to the music, heavy with accordion. He stumbled and fell to his knees.

"Get up, you donkey," said Svana. She hauled him up by his shoulders. "Dance like a man."

The Donkey's eyes crossed and uncrossed. "What she is saying?"

"She is honored to dance with you," said Afewerki.

"Of course! She is a beautiful bitch." He moved his hips and stumbled toward the guards, who caught him. "I am not well." He bent over and vomited the precious vodka. He went to his knees, spitting and cursing.

Svana stepped away, resisting the urge to kick him.

"Arrest them," said the Donkey.

The two guards eyed one another and moved toward Reece and Arthur. With the barrels of their AK-47s, they motioned for them to stand.

Afewerki mumbled an explanation. "You must go with them to the jail."

"My word," said Arthur. "Is this true? We've done nothing."

Gudmunder stood. "Your highness, I beg you not to do this. We will make sure they leave very soon. They will come again with the proper documents. You have my promise."

The Donkey listened, being helped to his feet by the guards. He stared at them, gathered around the dying fire, his eyes dark and receding. "You are a disgrace to God, all of you, meddling in my business. They must be gone by morning. Nah," he told the guards, and they led him away.

"That was close," said Reece. "Thank you."

"Yiqirta," said Gudmunder, holding the empty bottle of his precious drink.

Markush took a rare afternoon shower in preparation for dinner with Kristin. They would dine at the Alpine Haus in nearby Radcliff. He dried his long gray hair and shaved. Wearing black slacks and a paisley shirt, he inspected himself in the mirror. Dinner was at six, and he checked his watch, five-fifteen. He reminded himself that he was gathering information and, at the last minute, put the small tape recorder in his jacket pocket. Before leaving, he downed a shot of Jim Beam.

He knocked and she arrived at the door in a simple blue dress with a belt around the waist and a pair of matching pumps.

"Hello," he said. "You look nice. Ready for some German food?"

"Thanks," said Kristin, blushing, brushing back her brown curls. "I've never been to a German restaurant before. You'll have to help me with the menu."

Markush opened the door to his other car, a silver Jaguar coupe, and helped her in. They made small talk, driving off base toward Radcliff. At the restaurant, they were seated by a thin woman wearing a German dress embroidered in red and green, wearing fishnet stockings. Markush ordered a bottle of Austrian white wine.

"Mmm, this is good," said Kristin. "Fruity."

"Yeah, like me," said Markush. "I guess this is a working dinner, so I have some more questions for you about Reece. Do you mind?" He took out the recorder.

"I suppose not."

The décor was simple, old barn planks painted white with red trim.

The waitress came for their orders, and Markush ordered the schnitzel and roasted potatoes for them both.

"I want to know more about Reece's childhood. What you know. I gather it wasn't happy."

"The way he tells it, he was depressed since he was a kid. He said he thought about killing himself with a razor blade in the fifth grade. He did move around quite a bit, so he was kind of ungrounded."

"Any serious attempts that you know of?"

"Yes, one that I know of, but he's been treated for depression ever since I've known him. We went to counseling, and the therapist kept saying he was bipolar, but Reece brushed that aside. He could act a little crazy at times. One time, he went to the dentist and came home with a new car, a Mercury Cougar. We couldn't afford it, and he had to turn it back in. Ruined his credit for a while."

"That's interesting. That's definitely a manic gesture. What about when he was younger? What did he tell you?" He scooted the recorder to the middle of the table, covered in a white cloth.

"He liked fire and burned his grandpa's barn down when he was eight and set a lady's house on fire when he was only four. For a while, he smoked cigarettes and chewed tobacco, but he says his mom never caught him. He was wild, especially without his dad around." Kristin exhaled, as if confessing on behalf of Reece.

"Typical boy fantasy, fire, although most don't act on it like he did. What else?"

"You probably know this, but his mother was crazy.

She was the last to know it, though. I know that a lot of his problems stem from having lived with her. She had a temper that wouldn't wait. She had a good job as a dental hygienist, but she cussed out the dentist one day and was fired. Just really fragile, unstable. She would have screaming fits, begging God to take her life. He more or less just got used to it but hated it at the same time."

"Yes, the family history. Reece had a great-grandfather on his mother's side who killed a child as well. He was institutionalized, but that's all we know. Maybe his mother was an impostor, one that went unrecognized, but that would be impossible to prove at this point." He poured them each another glass of the Zierfandler.

"Yeah, that was always kind of hush-hush," said Kristin. "But I don't think his mother could have been an impostor. She turned religious when he was a teenager. They had Reece in church every time the door opened. How could an alien be religious?"

"Religion is a learned behavior," said Markush. "It could provide the perfect cover for impostors, a veil of holiness. I'm not convinced that Dahlia is necessarily pure evil, like Reece and others believe, but there seems to be an element of the macabre, especially with the murders she instigates. What else can you tell me?"

The waitress appeared with the two plates and warned them they were hot. "More wine? Can I get you anything else?"

"Yes, another bottle, please," said Markush. "We'll definitely want a dessert menu."

Kristin examined the large, breaded cutlet on her plate and tasted the dark gravy. "Mmm."

"Can't go wrong with schnitzel," said Markush. "So, back to Reece."

"He had those night terrors. He said that he was scared at the thought of the sun going down and dreaded every minute of darkness because of the visits by the little girl. He never called her Dahlia, though. Mia had night terrors as well and would sleepwalk. It was so creepy. She would use words she would never use while awake and fight us when we tried to get her back in bed. Sometimes, Reece had to restrain her and just hold her until it passed. It almost always ended with her going to the bathroom, having to pee." She forked a potato with a bite of the schnitzel.

"Yes, the night terrors. Did he say how old he was when they stopped?"

"Probably not until he was thirteen or fourteen."

"Was he a bed wetter? Do you know?"

"Yeah, he said he wet the bed until he was twelve or thirteen, which I always thought was odd."

"The two often go together, night terrors, bed wetting."

"He said he never once went into his parents' bed. They were like that. Not really negligent, but as if they just didn't know any better."

"That's too bad. I know you let Mia sleep with you, right?"

"Oh yeah, she'd always wind up with me, and Reece would sleep in her bed. He insisted on it."

They ate in silence.

"What's in this gravy? It's tangy?"

"Red wine. That's probably what you're tasting."

"Well, it's good."

"You two met before or after he had been to Ethiopia,

when he was a nurse?"

"It was before. He asked me to marry him about a month before he went over. I was thrilled but devastated too. He was a nurse in the same critical care unit in Birmingham where I worked. I stayed home with Mia until she was five."

"Right," said Markush. "Did that life suit you, being a stay-at-home mom?"

"I loved it, taking care of Mia. It was hard when Reece went to school to pursue his PhD in philosophy. That was a huge shock, moving to Connecticut. We almost split up. He didn't work, and we lived on student loans."

"Why did he leave nursing for philosophy? Did he say?"

Kristin thought. "Well, it had to do with Ethiopia. That changed his life. He was obsessed with the difference between there and here, how one place could be so poor while another place could be so rich. I think it warped him."

"Tell me more about what he's said about the Ark of the Covenant."

"He mentioned it on occasion but never really discussed it. I'm still hazy on what the Ark could have to do with anything." She pushed a piece of schnitzel into the gravy and sipped her wine.

"I think he definitely was transformed by that experience, which is to be expected. I've only been to Ethiopia as a tourist of sorts and found it overwhelming—the smells, the beggars, the poverty, as you say. But the people are friendly and the country ruggedly beautiful."

"What is it about the Ark? The Ark of the Covenant. It's in the Bible, but it seems so far-fetched, even for a believer, that it could hold such great power, that it would kill you if you so much as touched it."

Markush wiped his lips with a red napkin, obviously energized. "I think it plays a role in regard to this Dahlia. It connects her somehow with this place and other places. That's how Reece saw Mia recently, through the Ark."

"My poor Mia." Kristin's eyes misted. "If only it were true that she was still alive. I hope you know that you've gotten my hopes up, despite the craziness of it all. It's a sacred thing to be toying with...Mia."

Markush swallowed and sighed. "I don't mean to be causing any harm here. I'm just on a trail of information, and Reece is a huge part of the puzzle, and Mia."

Kristin focused on not crying, but could only imagine her little Mia coming down the slide into her arms, Reece coming down after Mia, laughing. "We had great times. But...those days are gone. The divorce is almost final. It's been a huge drain on me." She gazed into Markush's eyes, looking for something solid to grasp.

"I'm just trying to help, perhaps to bring joy back to your life in the process. I can't promise anything, though. In a sense, it's up to Reece and the others to show us the way."

They finished their dinner, and Markush ordered the baked apples along with a sweet dessert wine. They talked more, and the conversation drifted to Markush and his journey to become a forensic psychiatrist. Kristin was glad to have the focus taken from her and listened with interest. She guessed that Markush was her father's age, but he seemed younger somehow.

Back in his Jaguar, he asked her if she would like to see

a movie, but she said not really, and he drove her back to the guest house. He came around and opened the door for her and helped her out, both being tipsy. At the door, they stood. Markush tried very hard not to put his hands in his pockets, but he did anyway.

"Well, that was fascinating," said Markush. "You have been very helpful. I suppose you still want to leave tomorrow?"

Kristin put the key in the lock. "I think that's best."

"You sure you don't want to see Reece?"

"No. I think that would be too traumatic at this point. You want to come in? Have another glass of wine?"

Markush brightened. "Sure," and he followed her inside.

Reece slept the entire night without seizing, and he wondered if the medicine that Gudmunder had given him had been the cause. Doves clawed the tin roof, and roosters crowed. A single fly zipped around the room, as if hunting a corpse.

"My God," said Reece. Arthur was sitting in a chair, his head and shoulders slumped. "Arthur?"

Arthur opened his eyes. "You are well? We drank much liquor last night."

"You sat in that chair all night? Here, take my bed, lie down."

"No, no, I am fine. You are one who deserves watching." He stood and stretched his back. "We must leave today, before the Donkey comes. Correct?"

Reece struggled to remember the night before. *The Donkey.* "Yeah, we need to get back to check on Alicia. I'm sure she's upset. We promised not to leave her."

"Yes, but who would have known how far our short walk would bring us? Is it even possible to return?"

Reece stood. "We have to try. We have to retrace our steps and see what happens. We have to find the Abba. We have to get back."

"Perhaps some breakfast is in order before we leave." Arthur's face glistened with oil. He opened the door and looked out toward the tents. Gudmunder was sitting by the fire ring. He waved.

"I suppose."

"The food last night was delicious," said Arthur. "But

my stomach was surprised to have anything but the buster. My bowels moved during the night. Ah, Gudmunder, the good doctor, is coming." He stepped out beneath the overhang. Smoke poured from the cook house.

"Good morning," said Gudmunder. "You are well?"

"Yes, very well," said Arthur. "The lad slept soundly the whole night."

"For the first time in a long while," said Reece. He yawned and stretched. "Thank you for your hospitality and for handling the Donkey last night."

"He is a devil. One must just say what he wants to hear, and that is all." Gudmunder wore gray khaki pants and a colorful light sweater. "He can be a dangerous man. He is the one who shot the young man long ago." He gazed at the scars on Reece's head. "We will have breakfast soon. Come and sit."

They walked to the folding chairs.

Inside the dining hut were voices: Isaac, Barra, and Mariam eating a meal of leftover enjera and wot.

"The girls, they are still sleeping," said Gudmunder. "Wake up, sleepy heads!"

A curse came from the green tent.

Emma walked from her small house, bringing her cup for tea.

Reece stood. "Have a seat."

"You look well. No seizures?"

"He slept the entire night," said Arthur. "He is one to snore."

"My apologies," said Reece.

"You know the Donkey has ordered you to leave this place," said Gudmunder.

"Yes, and we'll go as soon as we have a bite to eat," said Reece. "Arthur is hungry." He had explained the buster bars to them the night before. "I want to say goodbye to Afewerki. Will he come?"

"He'll come soon," said Emma. "Will you catch a jeep? I know you came here by magic, but can you leave that way?"

Reece looked at Arthur. "We'll return the way we came and hope for the best. We have to visit the Abba. He'll help us."

Gudmunder scratched his stubbly beard. "You are an apparition, you two. I am still unclear about your origins, but I wish you the best. If you cannot leave, we have to explain this to the Donkey somehow."

"An unpleasant man," said Arthur.

"Indeed," said Gudmunder. "We have another long day of vaccines and weighing the children. Svana! Eydis! Wake!"

Emma laughed.

"Shut up, you old fool!" came Svana's voice from the tent. She unzipped the fly and poked out her head. "I need some tea."

Just then, Irigit appeared, coming through the gate with two large ancient kettles. He was all smiles and made the rounds, pouring tea for everyone except Eydis, who was still lounging in her sleeping bag. He stepped into the dining hut with the tea to serve Isaac, Barra, and Mariam.

Everyone inside the hut sipped and glanced at one another. Misrak came from the cook house with a tin platter piled with kita smeared with niter-kibbeh. She smiled and hurried away. She had her children to see to, as did

Zenebek. She spoke to a young girl who had entered to pour water into the barrel from a jug on her back.

"Nice and crispy," said Reece. The kita was greasy, and he wiped his fingers on his pants. "Afewerki!"

Afewerki entered, wearing his Exxon ballcap. He looked puzzled at Reece's enthusiasm. "Hallo." He squatted beside the fire ring.

"You know, I'd stay and help you in the clinic, if I could," said Reece. He wanted to say that it would be like the old days. "But we have to go."

Emma nodded. "We could sure use some help."

"Yes," said Arthur. "We must return. The little girl is waiting for us." Again, he went into some detail about Alicia.

"And she just appeared in the Abba's cave?" asked Gudmunder. "Perhaps she was brought by the Ark?"

Reece thought. "Maybe. I travel by having seizures, but she doesn't seem to have that problem. There is definitely some connection, I think."

Svana was shaking her head. "You are a little crazy, no? The two of you."

"What one sees is what one sees," said Arthur. "There is no other logical explanation."

They ate in relevant silence as the team exited from the dining hut, nodding to all in turn. Reece watched them walk away, each headed to their various tasks of running the warehouse and feeding program. Barra sang as he left.

Reece waited for Arthur to finish. "Shall we? I don't want to see the Donkey if possible and wind up in jail. I'm worried about Alicia."

Eydis emerged from the tent, her blonde hair a wreck.

"I must say goodbye." She stumbled out.

Everyone stood, Reece hugging the ladies. He gazed at Emma, her half-smile, and then, with Arthur, left the compound. He began to puzzle over the location of the old church and the point where they had entered Godo. The cave had been that way in Gadam but not in Godo. He voiced his concern to Arthur.

"Well, let us try to leave by the church in the first instance."

"Sounds good," said Reece.

"Ferenj!" came small voices as they passed down the lane and up the hill to the church. Flies circled them. High above, a pair of vultures glided.

"There is the church," said Reece. "Shall we walk side by side, perhaps?"

"Let us proceed."

They walked past the church. Ahead was the shelter, and they walked that way. Nothing happened.

"Huh," said Reece.

"Well," said Arthur. "We must find the Abba, correct?"

"I suppose so," said Reece. He turned to face the other way, and Arthur followed.

They passed back down the steep path and wound their way through the market square. A little boy took their hands and walked with them for a while, grinning from ear to ear. They walked past the airfield and then down to follow the path to the Abba that Reece knew. Within half an hour, they reached the place, but there was no ladder, and they would have to scramble up. Reece listened for the sound of pick on rock but heard nothing. Already the sun was heating the earth, and he wished for a hat.

"Let's try here." Reece scoped out the way up, looking for handholds. "Just here." He planted his shoe and pushed up, grabbing a long root. It took him a minute, but he soon pulled himself over the edge and looked around. They had passed their destination by a hundred feet or so, but he could see the Abba's square hut. He glanced down at Arthur. "Can you do it?" He lay on his stomach and watched.

Arthur tried to place his cumbersome black shoe, but it slipped. He leaped for the root but missed it and fell back. "Scheisse." He tried again with the same result.

"Arthur, wait there. The Abba may have a rope." He trotted down to the house and called out, but there was no answer. Then he heard the telltale noise of steel on rock and walked to the heavy door in the cliff face. He peered in and saw the wooden bier, but without a trace of the Ark. "Abba Paulos?"

"Abet?" The Abba set down his pick.

Reece stepped back out into the hot sun. The Abba appeared in the doorway with a puzzled look on his face. Right away, Reece knew that he didn't recognize him. "Damn."

The Abba stepped out, wearing his yellow robe and matching skullcap. Reece motioned for him to follow, and he did. He led him to the edge of the path and pointed down. The Abba peered and saw Arthur. Reece pantomimed climbing up, and the Abba seemed to understand. He went to his house and returned with a worn rope made of three twisted braids.

It took about ten minutes, but Arthur scrambled up and over, gasping for breath, covered with brown dust.

"Heavens," said Arthur. He sat for a moment before standing. "What a struggle."

The Abba looked pleased and waited for something to happen. Would the ferenji give an offering?

Right away, Reece got down to business. He spoke in English and then said "set lidj," the word for daughter.

At that, the Abba's look changed. He motioned for Reece to come closer, and he examined the skin of his scalp. He touched the two faded bullet wounds and murmured.

Reece felt that an impasse had been crossed. He tried another word. "Dahlia."

The Abba recoiled as if touched by fire. "Yellum, yellum," he said. "Nah."

Reece and Arthur shrugged their shoulders and followed the Abba to his small house. Inside were a simple bed, a stool, and a crude table on which lay a dusty book bound in leather, a Bible. The Abba turned to the Book of Exodus. With a shaking hand, he turned to an illustrated page that showed the Ark of the Covenant.

"Yes, yes," said Reece. "Ow, ow."

The Abba scratched his thinly bearded throat, where there were some pustules. He spoke for a moment and paused.

"Money, we need to give him money," said Reece. "Damn, but we left without bringing any."

"Oh," said Arthur. "The good Gudmunder gave me some birr last night, for our journey." He pulled a wad of bills from his breeches pocket.

The Abba's eyes lit up.

Arthur handed the money to Reece, who counted.

"This is a thousand birr. Wow. That was very generous,"

said Reece. "Sentino?" he asked the Abba, inquiring as to how much was needed.

"Shih birr," said the Abba. He was asking for the full thousand.

"All of it," said Reece. "Ishi, okay. Shih birr." He handed the bills to the Abba, which disappeared into the folds of his robe. He then turned the page of the old Bible to another illustration, which looked to be a vest covered with four rows of jewels.

"The breastplate," said Reece. "The holy raiment that the high priest would wear in the presence of the Ark."

The Abba's look was grave, and he wrung his hands. What he was about to do could possibly kill him, he said in Amharic. There was a small wooden trunk in the corner of the room with a heavy lock. He withdrew a large key from a string around his neck. The lock was noisy and opened. It was nearly too large for the hasp, and he struggled to free it. Reece held his breath, wondering if a mighty cloud of fire would emerge and strike them dead.

The trunk opened, and the Abba pushed back the lid, revealing a vest studded with the four rows of precious jewels.

Arthur's eyes grew wide at the sight, as the Abba withdrew the raiment with great care. The Abba held it up in the light from the open door, muttering in Ge'ez. "Nah," he said, and they followed him to the room carved into the rock, stepping into the cool and shadows.

The Abba proceeded with great care and had them stand in front of the empty wooden platform. He stood on the other side and raised the vest, placing it over his head. For a moment, he was silent, and then began a prayer in the ancient tongue. The air in the chamber seemed to warm. Reece and Arthur remained silent, their eyes glued to the Abba Paulos, who had begun a guttural chant.

Soon, a wind began to swirl in the room, lapping at their clothes. The Abba's voice grew louder. The wind increased and began a dull roar as a ball of light appeared over the table. The sound grew, and the wind rose. Reece wanted to close his eyes, but could not. The room filled with an electric blue light as the noise escalated to deafening. The Abba leaned toward the table, the vest taking on the different colors of the precious stones: carnelian, chrysolite, emerald, turquoise, sapphire, amethyst, jacinth, agate, crystal, beryl, lapis lazuli, and jasper.

Arthur braced himself in the wind, reaching for Reece. Together they planted their feet as the light grew too bright to endure, and they closed their eyes. Reece imagined being sucked into one of the jewels and remaining there in suspended animation. The wind roared, and the blue light became a white-hot torch of flame. The Abba was shouting but could not be heard.

What seemed like hours took only seconds, and just as suddenly, all was quiet. Reece opened his eyes, and there was the Ark of precious wood, the cherubim of gold facing one another, their wings reaching. He'd forgotten about Arthur and looked down to see him on the floor. The Abba was gone.

"Arthur?" Reece dropped to his knees. He knew the Ark was deadly. "Arthur?" The Ark was still, but from it he could feel an eternal power. He grabbed Arthur beneath his arms and pulled him toward the door, which was closed, leaking light into the chamber. He struggled and then pushed the door out and open. The great light of day flooded in. "Arthur!" He dragged him up the single step and out into the hot sun the size of a dime.

Reece pulled Arthur from the cave and felt for a pulse. "Arthur, talk to me!" The Abba's house was there, and the Abba had come outside, walking toward him with his hands in greeting. "Wuha!" said Reece.

The Abba saw Arthur on the ground, disappeared, and then came with a large gourd. Reece spilled the water onto Arthur's face, and Arthur spluttered, his eyes opening one at a time. His eyes roved the blue sky above.

It took a few minutes, but soon Arthur was sitting up, clutching his chest and taking deep breaths. It was as if he'd held his breath for an eternity and then tasted sweet air once again.

"Dear...God," said Arthur. He sipped water from the gourd. "What has happened?"

"We're back, I think, in Gadam. The Ark. It's in the cave." Reece jumped up and motioned for the Abba to see. The Abba peered in. Reece looked over his shoulder and could see the low table but no Ark. It was elsewhere, onward on its secret journey. "Damn."

Arthur sat up. "What a frightful experience, lad."

Reece pondered their next move. "Let's get back to town and see about Alicia. We can worry about paying the Abba for another session later. He may have a holy vest, though, like the Abba in Godo."

"Yes, we were going to pay him with sex, as I recall," said Arthur. "We received some credit, correct?"

"Yeah, we were going to try. Can you walk?"

"Help me, lad."

Reece grabbed his hands and pulled, slipping backward. "Umph!" and Arthur was standing, but bent over, hands on knees, taking deep breaths. "Slowly," said Arthur.

Within a few minutes, Arthur was ready to travel, thoroughly rumpled. They said goodbye to the Abba and began the trek back to the edge of town, and soon reached the old church. They continued, led by Reece as he navigated for the blue star where they had left Alicia. Reece did not know how long they'd been gone or if any time had passed at all. He looked up at the tiny sun and cursed it.

"This way," and they continued a few lanes over and up. "Here," said Reece. He half expected to find the body of the bartender's former boyfriend rotting in the sun, but it was gone. He wondered what happened to those who died. Were they buried, recycled? A flash from the data fur, and he knew. "Gross."

Reece opened the door and held it for Arthur. Inside, Carl was in his chair, reading a magazine that was all pictures.

"Well, well," said Carl. "The baby killer and his little sister. 'Bout time you were back. I had to give that snot-nosed brat a piece of my mind." He rolled up the magazine and tapped it on his knee.

Reece counted the doors on the left. "Alicia?"

"Is she here?" asked Arthur. "Poor lass."

"Hello!" said Reece. He eyed the soiled bed, the bloodied sheets in a ball there.

The bathroom door opened a crack. "Daddy? Mommy?"

"Thank God," said Reece. "It's us, remember? Were you hiding?"

"I was scared. That man in the hall said he was going to cut my head off. He tried to grab me."

"Bastard," said Reece.

"A frightful thing to say to a child," said Arthur. "Are you hungry, dear one?"

Alicia nodded and brushed back her dark brown hair. Her big eyes looked vacant and tired. She'd been crying. "I drank some water."

"Okay, good," said Reece. "Let's get some buster. You remember the buster? You liked it." He kneeled on the floor and hugged her. "I'm sorry we left, but we had to see about some business. We're going to help you find your parents. I promise. This is just a crazy place, right?"

"Thank you, mister. I don't like this place. There's no kids."

"Call me Reece, and this is Arthur. We'll protect you."

"Okay, Reece and Mr. Arthur."

"Shall we?" asked Arthur, and they entered the hall.

Reece looked to see if they could exit without passing Carl, but there was only one door. He picked up Alicia. "Here we go. Just ignore the man." Alicia buried her head into his shoulder.

Carl was ready. "Oh, gonna snuff another one, I see. You bloodthirsty pedophile. Going out for some buster, I see."

Reece and Arthur didn't speak and pushed into the hot and dry air. "Here, you can walk now," said Reece.

"Can I hold your hand?" asked Alicia.

"Sure thing," and both he and Arthur gave her a hand.

There was a buster joint just two buildings down, a

new one, and they passed through the mist door. The place was dead silent. A huge faucet seemed suspended in mid-air, pouring a torrent of water into a barrel. Reece had seen something like it at a Ripley's Believe It or Not in Gatlinburg, Tennessee. No one was at the bar, and they sidled up, taking seats there. There was a bell and Reece rang it. From behind the bar came a brown woman with a flat forehead, wearing gray sweatpants and a yellow halter top that accentuated her curves. A tattoo of a long twisting vine covered her back and shoulders.

"What'll it be, buckos?" asked Leonora. Without waiting, she drew down three bowls of buster. "Got'cha a little one, I see. Makes a tender...roast."

Reece tasted his bowl, pineapple. "She's with us." He urged Alicia to try hers.

"That tastes like peanut butter." Her wide eyes looked glad.

"And mine of cherries," said Arthur. He took a deep drink.

"Yeah, fruits," said Leonora. "Like you." She seemed tired, as if the insults were hard to come by. "Who's got the most matches?"

Arthur pondered that.

Reece said, "*Ulysses,* James Joyce."

"Brilliant," said Leonora. "How much for the little one?"

"She is not for sale, madame," said Arthur, furrowing his brow.

"Yeah," said Reece. "Why would you even ask?"

"For the circus, dumbass," said Leonora. "The circus comes through in a few days. You could use the...cash, right? You want to pay the Abba Paulos to trek you around, to find your daughter…Mia."

"Do you know anything? Where Mia might be?" asked Reece.

"Nope, not in any fur that I can access. That's why you need cash, bucko." She plumped her breasts and coughed. "You could sell the girl here."

"We have credits," said Reece. "A thousand credits."

"When did the mighty Abba start taking credits?"

"Yes, that is a dilemma," said Arthur. "But we have a plan, madame."

"Yeah, yeah, sex him up, give him some booze. Sounds crazy if you ask me." Leonora put her chin in her hands at eye level with Alicia. "Boopy woopy."

"Not cash, though?" asked Reece.

She reached to touch Alicia's cheek, but Alicia pulled away.

"Hey, you're scaring her," said Reece.

"Shut up…Jesus crucified sideways. The circus will suit her."

"Where do you get your credits? Are they loaned?" asked Reece. He drank down his pineapple buster.

"Born with them, dodo."

"Oh," said Reece. "Alicia, you want more, honey?"

"No, this was good. I'm full. I don't like the circus. The clowns scare me and those tigers, too."

Reece laughed. "Don't worry, we'll keep you safe." He rubbed her head. "Does the circus travel around?"

"Yeah, comes here once a year, like I said. Right now, it's in Alem Ketema. They have to cross two rivers to get here, so that has to be factored in. Never know when there might be a flood."

"Does it rain here, ever?" asked Arthur.

"Well, there's a sky. Of course it rains. In fact, it rained about five years ago." She took the bowls one by one and placed them in a sink.

"Five years?" asked Reece. "Jesus."

"Take it or leave it, bucko."

They talked with Leonora for a few more minutes. When it rained, everyone went nuts, running around with their mouths open, sleeping in it naked. Reece asked if there was anything fun for kids to do, and Leonora just laughed. He asked her if there were other little girls in the circus, and she said yes, that it wouldn't be a circus otherwise. They stood to leave, and a group of four men entered, crowding them at the bar.

"Hey, buckos!" said Leonora.

One, a brute with a long beard, reached out to touch Alicia, and Reece slapped his hand away.

"Fuck off," said Reece.

The man swung and Reece ducked, pulling Alicia toward him. The others seemed poised to pounce on them. Arthur stood his ground, straightening his back to appear taller.

"Okay, sorry," said Reece, trying to cut his losses. "Just don't touch the girl, okay?"

"Ass licker," said the brute. "Send you to hell."

Reece backed away with Alicia behind him, and Arthur followed. "Yeah," said Reece. "To you and yours. We're on our way."

They passed through the hum of the mist door.

"That man was bigger than you are," said Alicia. "He scared me."

"Indeed," said Arthur. "I say we must be careful now with the little one."

"Yeah," said Reece. He looked up at the hot sun, imagining rain. "What's next? She said that there were little girls in the circus."

"Yes, perhaps you will find Mia," said Arthur.

"She said the circus was in Alem Ketema, AK. I used to pass through there on my way here."

"Perhaps we should travel there," said Arthur.

"It's twenty-six miles, if I remember correctly. Hell of a walk. Hold on." Reece conjured the image of a jeep, using the data fur. "That's it. A jeep comes here on a regular basis, at the bottom of the hill. It comes in six hours." He broke away from the stream of data, an image of shoes, a swastika.

"What is this jeep? A form of transport?" asked Arthur.

"Yes...a motorized vehicle. It'll take about two hours." Reece smiled, relieved that there was something he could do in his quest. "We need to get out of this crazy place. Hopefully, it will somehow be different there."

"Yes, that would be splendid," said Arthur. "Like a vacation of sorts."

"Is my daddy there? His name is Freddie," said Alicia.

Reece patted her head. "We can only go and see, but I can't promise. We might find my little girl, Mia, and then you'd have a friend."

"That would be nice," said Alicia. "I don't like the adults here. They're mean."

"Well said," said Arthur. "Shall we rest until time to leave?"

"Yes, get some rest," said Reece. "But we can't miss the

jeep. It might be wise to get there an hour or so early, in case of others who want a ride."

They arrived at the blue star and entered. Carl wasn't in his chair, and there was shouting from down the wide hall.

"What's next?" asked Reece. "Let's not get involved." He walked Alicia to their door and pushed inside.

When Reece ascertained that five hours had passed, he prodded Arthur on the clean bed. Arthur awoke from his deep sleep.

"Time to go, okay? For the jeep." Reece went to the big chair and woke Alicia. She looked up at him with sleepy eyes, and his heart melted, yearning for Mia. "We're going for a ride. Come on."

Arthur stood. "I won't be a moment," and he entered the bathroom to tidy up.

When Arthur was ready, and Reece had washed his face, they entered the hallway. Carl was sitting in his chair, chewing gum, and staring at his fingernails.

"Here comes the happy family! Hey, old man, is that cum on your fancy pants?"

Arthur harrumphed and passed him. Reece went first through the door and then doubled back. "Wait! Jesus."

"What is it?" asked Arthur.

"Just stay here with Alicia. Don't go outside, okay?" He ran back to the room and returned with a sheet. He walked outside and glanced at the corpse, its face bloodied, missing its hands. He covered the body with the sheet and opened the door. "Okay, but let's go quickly."

Arthur led Alicia out by her hand and glanced at the

sheet. "Oh my," he said and pulled Alicia to walk with him.

"What happened?" asked Alicia. "Did somebody get hurt?"

"Just sleeping is all," said Reece. He walked at a brisk pace with Arthur and Alicia in tow.

They wound through nondescript buildings and soon took a wide lane that headed downhill. Reece surmised where the clinic would be. Two buildings beyond was the edge of town where everything stopped and the paved lane gave way to dirt. At the turnaround, two people waited. One was a thin woman with a topknot of hair held in place by pins. The other was a short man wearing a tattered hat. Both were very brown, and they seemed to be a couple. Reece kept his distance with Alicia, but Arthur walked over and engaged them.

"You are waiting for the jeep, I believe it is called? And so are we." He motioned toward Reece and Alicia.

"Yeah, you fat fucker," said the man. He was smoking a long cigar.

"Creep," said the lady. She laughed and poked the short man.

"Well," said Arthur, and he gave up on the conversation. He surveyed the barren land strewn with fist-sized rocks. There were no trees, just patches of thorny scrub. In the distance, he could see a flat-topped mountain and guessed that it was far away.

They scuffed in the dirt, toeing it, walking in circles. Alicia sat and made a small house from the rocks. In the distance came a mechanical sound, and down the hill came running four others, intent on a ride.

"Uh oh," said Reece. "We'll have to fight for our seats."

The engine grinding grew louder, and around a bend in the dirt came the jeep. The transmission whined as it climbed the steep hill.

"Come on. We have to be ready," said Reece.

"We were here first," said Arthur. He held Alicia by the hand.

"Doesn't matter. We'll get put on top."

The jeep ground up another thirty feet and stopped. Everyone was there in a wad, waiting for the occupants to emerge.

"The back seat," said Reece, "Behind the driver." He pushed a heavy-set man away from him.

One by one, the passengers climbed out, and Reece was already in, calling for Arthur and Alicia.

"Hey, you trollops," said the short, fat man. He stamped his feet.

Reece hauled in Alicia, passed her over, and then pushed back the skinny woman with her topknot. "Arthur!"

Arthur more or less fell in and found himself beside Reece. "Dear God, what a commotion."

The short, fat man and his skinny friend piled into the front seat. The driver looked bored, but pushed on his horn and screamed for everyone to settle down. The back hatch opened, and three of the latecomers squeezed into the space with the spare tire. The last man put his hands on his hips. "Cocksuckers!" and he climbed on top. The sound of the horn had brought two more running pell-mell down the hill, and the driver put it in low, turned, and headed downhill, soon coasting, looking in his side mirrors, laughing.

They were on their way.

Markush and Kristin drank more wine and succumbed to their passion. Afterward, lying in bed and talking, Kristin agreed to visit Reece the next day, but when she awoke and Markush was gone, she wondered if she had really agreed. With a headache, she took some Tylenol and made an English muffin in the toaster oven. She measured out coffee and turned on the maker. Markush was supposed to come at ten to talk more. She had an hour and took a hot bath, soaking for thirty minutes, thinking, wondering why she had slept with Markush. Had she done it to help with Mia's return? But that was so hokey. She supposed she had done it out of loneliness. And Markush was so sincere, so convincing. She would do whatever it took to resume a life of normalcy, even if it meant considering the impossible.

She was ready at ten, wearing soft blue jeans and a Wildcats t-shirt. She checked her watch and peered through the blinds. She sat on the couch and imagined Markush's first words. Would he acknowledge they had slept together, or would he be all business? She stood and walked into the small kitchen. There was a half-bottle of red on the counter and one of white in the fridge. She resisted the urge to have a drink and heard the knock at the door. She opened it, and he was wearing jeans and a t-shirt too. His gray hair was slicked back in a ponytail.

"Hey," she said.

"Hey," said Markush. He had the tape recorder and stepped inside.

"You look youthful."

Markush laughed. "Saturday, casual day." He moved in for a kiss, but she held him back. "Not right now, okay? We have work to do, right?"

"Yeah, you're right." He sighed. "Thanks for a wonderful time last night. I haven't been on a real date in ages."

"My pleasure, and thank you for dinner. It was scrumptious. Coffee?"

"That would be perfect, thanks. Black." He sat on the couch, stretching his legs.

Kristin returned with two cups and sat. "You seem so far away. Come to this side of the couch."

Markush laughed and scooted down. "You still up to see Reece? You know he's been seizing nonstop for over a day. I'm worried about him. I may have to interrupt him with some meds. Seizing requires an immense amount of energy. Started an IV. He may not actually be awake if you come."

"What would be the point?" asked Kristin. She held her coffee like a souvenir.

"Your presence could bring him back. I'm not sure if it really works that way, but it could. He comes and goes." He sipped his coffee and smacked his lips.

"Maybe. Let's talk some more first."

"You know, I've asked you all the questions I can think of. Just tell me what it was like to be married to him."

Kristin thought. "Well, he was a very loving father, until the...incident. We argued, more so than I thought was healthy. After quitting nursing and staying home with Mia, I took a job at Reece's college, working in student records. I thought maybe it would help me understand his life more. He was always so busy with his classes and his research on Schopenhauer. I guess I should have been more inquisitive, but I really didn't know what questions to ask."

"We only know things as they appear," said Markush. "The world as will and representation. Schopenhauer. I think Reece is onto something, but I'm not sure what. That's still a long conversation that we've yet to have. I'll admit that I have a hard time myself, getting my head around it. So, don't feel badly. What else?"

"No recorder today?"

"Yeah, right," and he turned on the recorder.

"He was always a hard worker. One thing that stands out, though, is his ability to be private. He was always such a private person. I used to joke with him that he'd be perfectly fine living in a cave by himself. He often felt very distant, caught up in his own thoughts. He never had more than one or two friends, and I had to drag him to dinners with other people. More than three or four people and he would clam up, like he couldn't engage more than one or two people at a time."

"He has an antisocial edge, but he was never violent with you or Mia, was he?"

"No. He loved the dog and Mia's hamsters. Sometimes he would use violent language, though, say that certain people should die, that certain people, most often politicians, should be taken out."

"But he never acted on those threats?"

"No. He would just get riled up, usually while watching the news."

"Hmm," said Markush. "Was he engaged politically at any level?"

Kristin laughed. "He hated politics. Said it was the lowest common denominator. That anything reduced to politics was just mush. He didn't vote, never voted as far as I know. He had this whole thing about being able to vote no. He said that you should be able to vote yes or no to everybody and not just yes to one person. Reece was a bit extreme in that realm."

"Hmm, voting no is an interesting idea. If you were a democrat, you could vote yes for the democratic candidate and vote no for the republican."

"That would be one option. Another would be to vote no for both. The winner would have to have a majority vote, with the no votes taking away from the yes votes. It gets complicated, but you see what I mean. And I'll throw this in. He hates parades."

Markush swirled his coffee. Reece was just eccentric, in addition to being prone to depression. "We know he was hospitalized for his depression."

"He was in three or four times, once after we married. He was definitely depressed while he was doing the PhD, but was able to muddle through. Those were some miserable years, trying to raise Mia while we scrimped and got by on student loans. I really thought that if we could endure that, we could endure anything." She was feeling weepy and blinked.

Markush sighed. "We've sequestered his medical records from those hospitalizations, but I haven't seen them yet. I suppose they could shed some light on his current condition. I'm interested to see if Dahlia came up during his hospital stays." He put his hands on his knees.

Kristin was out of things to talk about regarding Reece.

The conversation turned to her, her strict upbringing, her parents' reluctant acceptance of Reece, and the strained relations with them. Markush asked if Reece had ever been unfaithful, and Kristin said that he'd had an affair in graduate school with a woman from the Dominican Republic. She hadn't found out about it until his descent into major depression, a couple of years after the fact. Her parents had wanted her to divorce him, but there had been Mia to consider. When asked if she had ever been unfaithful, Kristin stammered, wondering if the night before counted. She thought about her return home to the big empty house, about how lonely she felt there, and then asked about the money that Markush had promised if she cooperated.

"It's already in the works," said Markush. "We'll take care of your mortgage and living expenses, thirty-five hundred per month. You said that would take care of your needs."

"Wow, you really don't know how much I appreciate that. It's a lifesaver. I suppose you'll want to see me regularly?" She twirled a curl of her shiny brown hair. "I mean, I think that would work."

Markush coughed and gazed at her. "Yeah, I was thinking about that. I might even come to visit you from time to time. I...I have a personal interest. You are critical to the overall work being done." He paused. "Plus, you're damned good looking." He caught her eye.

Kristin blushed. "That makes me happy. Yeah, sure. You could come by anytime. I'll show you Richmond, although there's not much to see. There is a cute little Italian restaurant. I'd like to take you there." She pressed her palms against her jeans.

"That sounds like a plan," said Markush.

They talked for another half hour, making small talk.

"What about lunch, and then we go to check on Reece? You're scheduled to fly out at four." He checked his watch. "It's eleven-thirty."

"You've got me in the palm of your hand. I can't believe I'm agreeing to see him. It might be best if he is out of it, if I don't have to talk to him. I thought you were crazy before I came, but you've got my hopes up that there is some remote chance of bringing Mia back. I can't believe I'm even saying that. You're a smooth talker, Dr. Markush."

Markush laughed. "May I use the restroom?"

"Sure, and then me," said Kristin.

They each tidied up and stood on the front stoop of the guest house.

"There's a nice little hole in the wall in Muldraugh, about fifteen minutes from here. The food is average, but the place has character, as they say. Ready?"

He drove her past the gold repository, down Bullion Boulevard, and exited the base onto 31, heading north. Within ten minutes, they came to Muldraugh, and Markush pulled into a ratty motel parking lot. Next door was a restaurant called The Ritz. Gravel crunched beneath the wheels, and it was a warm day, the season moving into late fall.

She let him come around and open her door and followed him inside. Booths of red vinyl lined the windows. The smell was of fried potatoes. A chunky waitress with a tooth missing up front seated them and handed over laminated menus.

"Special today is liver and onions," said Charlene. Her apron was tattered but clean. "Drinks?"

"Sweet tea," said Markush.

"I'll have the same," said Kristin. Markush seemed so far away on the other side of the booth. She perused the menu and noticed the little jukebox at the end of the table.

Markush flipped through the music selection, dropped in a quarter, and soon it was "Tie a Yellow Ribbon."

Kristin resisted the urge to sing along. "What's good? I'm not a fan of liver."

"I'd play it safe and get the burger. It's decent."

A bell rang, and Charlene was hustling to keep up. Through the order-up window, a man with a paper chef's hat was moving back and forth, minding the grill.

"I stayed at the motel next door for a week before they found me housing on base," said Markush. "My back still hurts from the hard bed."

Kristin laughed. A moth struggled in the window, beating its feathery wings. Charlene took their orders, scribbling on a paper pad, and hurried away. Markush dropped another quarter in, and it was a tune by José Feliciano. The burgers arrived. They talked and laughed, wiping the grease from their fingers with paper napkins that stuck to their hands.

After lunch, Markush took a scenic route back to the base and pulled into his private space outside the Organon complex. The guard let them pass into the cool building where Reece was housed. Markush swiped a card and ushered Kristin into a hallway with a waiting room. The heavy steel door to the unit had no window, and he pressed a buzzer.

"You ready for this? You'll be the second family member to ever visit. Just remember that what you're about to see is classified. You can see but don't tell."

Kristin nodded, her hands shaking. The lock clicked open, and they met Shark with his pen and clipboard. He hunched his narrow shoulders.

"Afternoon, Doc. She have clearance?" asked Shark. His face was drawn into a blank.

"Certified," said Markush. "Family member. We'll be visiting with Mr. Myers in lucky seven."

Markush knocked on the nursing station door. "Let's take a look at the room monitor before we go in. Laura's inside."

Kristin followed him into the station, eying the bank of video monitors and ECG and EEG screens.

"Hey, Doc," said Laura. "What's up?"

"I've got Mrs. Myers here to see Reece. How's he doing? That's him, number seven." He pointed.

Kristin looked and saw a man on a bed that must be Reece. Her stomach felt hollow and heavy. She held her hands together and stared at the screen. The man who had killed her Mia.

"Still seizing," said Laura. "Gamma waves, slow and steady. IV going at a hundred ccs per hour. "You still thinking about oxygen to give him a boost?"

"Not yet. Let's give him two more hours, and then I'll need to interrupt him." He turned to Kristin and explained again that Reece was most likely traveling, burning through calories like a marathoner. "You ready?"

"Not really."

As they passed each room, she glanced into each one,

a body on a bed. In number five, Peters was calling out with a wild look in his eyes. To her right was the empty day room, a TV playing to no one. They turned the corner.

Kristin followed Markush, and there he was, on his back, his body trembling as if he were cold. "My God, Reece? He looks dead."

"But he's alive and well. He's looking for Mia. When he comes around, he'll talk about his progress. It's fascinating. I know it looks scary, but he's fine. You can talk to him if you would like."

Kristin bundled the pangs of panic in her stomach and stepped closer. Here was the man who had killed Mia, or so she thought.

"Reece? It's me, Kristin." She reached and touched his arm, which was cool. His eyes fluttered beneath the lids. "Reece?"

"Whether he can hear you or not, I'm not sure," said Markush.

She had to say it. "Reece, you bastard, where is Mia?"

Markush watched the spikes register on the EEG.

The jeep jounced and rocked with its cargo of human beings. The driver gripped the wheel with both hands, grinning at some private joke. Behind him, with Alicia between them, Reece and Arthur held onto the seat. Arthur seemed composed but uncomfortable, shifting from hip to hip. Reece had to pee and cursed his bad timing. He would just have to hold it until they reached Alem Ketema.

Soon they were headed down the steep hill to the first river crossing, and there was a solitary woman bathing in a pool of brown water. She slipped beneath the water, waiting for them to pass.

There was another climb and then the rocky descent to the second river, which was larger and fuller, foam carpeting its surface, dead limbs floating. The bridge was of metal with heavy planks, and the jeep thudded across. No one spoke, and with the windows up, the inside of the jeep took on the fragrance of its sweating passengers.

The final climb was into Alem Ketema, and the road wound up in switchbacks to the top of a plateau dotted with scrub but no trees.

"Almost there," said Reece.

"I'm thirsty," said Alicia. Her dark hair was oily, her face dirty.

"Dear child," said Arthur.

Soon, there appeared plain buildings of metal and stone, none with windows, much like those in Gadam. Reece noted the stars on the fronts: green, blue, then a red one, which was a bar. A cold beer would be nice. The jeep ground up a slight incline, which flattened, bringing them to a large round stone wall that he recognized as the town center. Something was nagging him, a voice from the distance, calling his name. The jeep stopped.

"Get out, you freaks of nature!" said the driver. He would spend the next few hours in a bar before his return trip to Gadam.

The three piled out, brushing their clothes and stretching from the rough ride. The hot sun bore down on them. The driver was walking away, and Reece caught him.

"The circus. There is a circus in town?" he said.

The driver spat. "Yeah, I know that. But you want to know where it is. You want to see if your daughter Mia is in a cage there."

"In a cage?" asked Arthur.

"Yeah, you deaf, old man?" asked the driver. He was brown, thin, and had muscled forearms.

"So," said Reece. "Where is the circus?"

"Cost you fifty credits," said the driver. "What do I look like, the Abba Paulos? Just keep walking that way. On the other side of town. Good enough for you?"

"Thanks," said Reece. He could see in the fur that fifty credits had been deducted from his five hundred on loan. He turned to Arthur. "Let's get Alicia some buster. We have to find a place to stay as well."

The next building had a green star, and they entered through the mist door. Inside was brightly lit by over a hundred single bulbs hanging from the ceiling. The short, fat man and his skinny companion were already there. The muscular bartender wore a leather vest with bells.

They took a small table, and Reece went to the bar, waiting his turn.

"Well, fuckety fuck, the Lone Ranger with his precious little girl and Grandpa Dickweed. How may I assist you? Three bowls?" He turned away before Reece could answer.

"Three bowls," said Reece to his back. He felt a longing. He felt chemically restrained and remembered the seizure medicine that Gudmunder had given him. He wondered how long before it wore off. Reece took the tray to the table. "Here we go, little one."

"Thank you, Mr. Reece."

"You're welcome. What flavor did you get?"

Alicia tasted her buster. "I don't really know. It just tastes like pudding."

"Yes, pudding fits it well," said Arthur.

"We should be able to find lodging a bit farther into town," said Reece. "When I came here before, I always stayed in the same hotel, the Beselfui. I doubt that it's still there, this being a different universe, a different time. Right?"

"The world is my, um, will and representation," said Arthur. He chuckled. A flash of blue light went from ceiling to floor. "Shite!"

"Whoa. That was strange. So, everything is all at once," said Reece. "Or just one world at a time?"

"From whose perspective?" asked Arthur.

"What if I say Dahlia?"

Arthur drank and wiped his mouth with his sleeve. "This being that is godlike, playing pranks, posing as others. I do not have a firm grasp of what this Dahlia is."

"Neither do I," said Reece. "Still working on that one. I

suppose she's the ringleader."

"Who is Dahlia?" asked Alicia. "Is she my age?"

"She's hard to explain," said Reece. "Do you remember when you lived with your parents, if there was ever a strange little girl that came to visit, that your dad, Freddie, or your mom didn't like?"

Alicia frowned. "That would be that girl, Irma. We would play hide and seek, and I could never find her. Daddy said she was aggressive and said she couldn't come over, but she did anyway. She would bring me presents, though. She came to my birthday party even though she didn't have an invitation and ate a big piece of cake. She pushed my best friend off the couch."

"Well," said Reece. "Irma is most likely a part of Dahlia. Does that make sense? Dahlia is made up of more than one person, even though that sounds strange."

"Yes, extraordinary," said Arthur.

That struck Alicia as funny, and she laughed. "Daddy said she tried to hurt our dog, but I didn't believe him. Why would she do that?"

"Dahlia is a character all right," said Reece. "At our house, she was called Charlotte, at least the last one was. Capable of just about anything. Did Irma try to listen to your music, your inside music?"

Alicia nodded. "How did you know about that? Irma couldn't hear it, and it made her mad."

"The most perfect of the arts," said Arthur. "I wonder if Madame Marquet could be classified with this Dahlia? Foolhardily, I nudged her, and she feigned to fall and be injured. She sued, and I paid her a penalty for the rest of her very long natural life. She was a pain in my arse, but she was a grown woman and not a little girl."

Reece nodded, knowing the story of Caroline Marquet. "And is it true that you pushed her for disturbing the peace?"

"No, indeed, she raised a ruckus in my parlor, but she placed herself at the foot of my stairs and claimed that I had pushed her when I had merely brushed against her in passing. The bitch, pardon my language." Arthur pinched his lips.

"The most perfect of the tarts," said Reece.

Arthur laughed. "Indeed."

"Dahlia's mean," said Alicia.

Reece raised his eyebrows at the remark. "She does seem that way at times. The question is why? That's what I'm trying to figure out. And you could help us figure that out."

"I don't know why," said Alicia. "Can I have some more buster?"

"Sure, honey," said Reece, and he headed to the bar.

The man with bells on his vest looked him in the eye. "Careful what you wish for, butt licker. Three more bowls?"

Reece took the tray back to the table. They took their time with the second bowls, noticing that one by one, the lights hanging from the ceiling were going out, lengthening the crazy shadows they cast. Soon, they were finished, and Reece suggested they be on their way to find lodging and then the circus.

Outside in the hot sun, they walked, looking for a blue star and found one within a few hundred feet. It had three floors and was fronted by a tiny statue of what appeared to be a gnome. They walked inside, and three women wearing yellow dresses stood behind a counter. They looked to be sisters and wore pendants of metal around their necks.

"May, we, help you cunts?" They spoke in stepwise fashion with big silly grins as if the joke was on them.

"We would like to inquire about a room," said Arthur. He placed himself between the counter and Alicia, hoping to shield her from the verbal abuse.

"There's, no, way, in, fucking, hell, that, we, have, a, room, for, the likes, of, you," said the sisters. "Oh, did we say that?" asked one. "Of course, we have a room," said another. "Right this way," said the one on the end, exiting the counter and emerging through a beaded curtain. "Of course, if you don't like it..." "You can eat shit and die," chorused the other two.

"This way, please."

The room was on the second floor, midway down the hall. Reece wondered if there would be a body. In they went with the door closing behind them. The room was square with two round beds and a couch. On the walls were paintings of fruit in science fiction fashion, as if bananas and apples were strange and forbidden objects. A painting of a pineapple with a bloody knife in it. And there was no body to deal with.

"Praise the lord," said Reece. "This isn't half bad. He opened the door to the bathroom and quickly closed it. "Fuck."

"What did you discover?" Arthur opened the door and closed it. "Dear God."

"Is it Dahlia?" asked Alicia, hiding behind Reece.

"No, but we can't use that bathroom, okay? Don't go in

there. We'll find another one to use." Reece's urge to pee was ferocious. "I'm going in, though, okay? You stay here with Arthur."

Reece opened and closed the door. On the toilet was an old woman, her head split open. She was slumped backward, her long throat exposed. Reece touched her, and she felt warm as if freshly killed. He turned the sink water on and peed there. "Jesus." It occurred to him that someone had to die whenever they needed a room. He shivered and looked at the ceiling, finishing his business.

"All done," he said, closing the door. "Alicia, do you need the potty?"

"Yes," said Alicia.

"Okay, when we go out, we'll find one for you. That one is really dirty, okay?" said Reece. He whispered to Arthur that he'd peed in the sink.

"Shall we go?" asked Arthur. "The less time we spend here, the better, I think."

Reece agreed, and they descended the stairs, finding the three sisters with bright smiles.

"Did, you, find, the, room, to your, liking?"

Reece and Arthur nodded and hurried Alicia onto the paved lane.

"I suppose we go this way," said Reece, turning left. He saw a young man approaching, wearing a backpack, and asked about the circus.

The man had a large mustache and pointed at the sky, mumbling to himself.

"That was helpful," said Reece. He recalled the Alem Ketema he had known and roughly imagined where the old jail would have been, where the faucets to the well would have been, but the sameness of the buildings was disorienting. He imagined the former site of the Beselfui Hotel with its bar and diner as being close by, and soon they came to a high wall topped with broken bottles, a single steel door with a knocker.

"What is this?" asked Arthur. "It looks foreboding."

"Huh," said Reece. "Let's check it out." He rapped the heavy knocker and waited.

The door made a noise and opened just a crack. A small dark woman peered out at him, dressed in a tattered green dress with a cotton shawl around her shoulders.

"Lebna?" asked Reece. It was Lebna with her protruding tooth.

She looked frightened and opened the door, hurrying them inside to a courtyard of dirt, the tables outside the bar beneath a small tree, a row of rooms on either side. Reece smelled smoke and milk. It was the Beselfui, just as he remembered it.

Lebna took his hands. "Nah," she said, heading into the dim restaurant. The rickety bar was there, a radio playing Amharic music. Two men in ragged clothes sat playing checkers with beer caps, drinking St. George beer. Reece examined the shelf and saw Johnny Walker Red and bottles of Awash wine. Through a door into the back was smoke rising from a cookfire. Lebna motioned for them to sit.

"Once again, an ancient place amid the new," said Arthur.

"I need to go to the bathroom," said Alicia.

"Yeah, right," said Reece. "We'll be right back." He took Alicia outside and around back to the crude shintabet. He opened the door to reveal the hole in the floor. The stench of urine and feces stifled him. "You have to squat over that hole, okay?"

Alicia shrank back. "Yuck, do I have to?"

"Yep," said Reece. "I'll close this door and stay right outside, okay? Do you need toilet paper?"

"Not now."

"Okay, go on." He closed the rickety door and waited.

"I'm done!"

Back at the bar, Arthur nursed a glass of warm white wine, the bottle on the table.

Lebna came to take their orders.

"Is anyone hungry?" asked Reece. "Birra, and he pointed to himself. Alicia, I think they may have some orange Fanta. Would you like one?" She said yes, and Reece said, "Fanta arancia," and pointed to her.

Lebna returned with the drinks and waited to be paid fifteen birr.

"Hell, we don't have any money," said Reece. "Data fur, credits?"

Lebna frowned and pulled out a folded piece of paper. She wrote the number fifteen and had Reece sign the paper. He would owe the bar.

"Amenseganalo," said Reece. "We'll have to find some birr somehow to pay her before we leave."

"Certainly," said Arthur. "Curious how this is a small oasis of sorts. It seems a relic."

"I get it now," said Reece. "This must be the museum."

"A strange approach, rather realistic. But you know the woman, the maiden who runs the place?"

"Yeah, she's from 1986, or is it 1987? Gwar or Godo? It

seems I came here with the Icelanders when I was working as a nurse with them. So, then it would be Gwar. But I came here too when I was working as a nurse, so Godo. I don't understand how she's here, but she is."

"Perhaps no stranger than our being here," said Arthur.

"True," said Reece. "How's your Fanta?"

"Good," said Alicia. "But it's warm, which is funny."

"Yeah, everything is warm, the way it used to be." Reece sipped his foamy beer.

Lebna brought out plates of shurowot with enjera for the two men playing checkers. She came over and wanted to sit in Reece's lap, which she did.

"Uh oh," said Reece.

Lebna ran her finger around his ear and across his face, laughing.

Reece shifted her from one leg to another. "I wonder if we can take a room here? God forbid we go back to the blue star."

"That would please me very much," said Arthur. "Do the rooms have beds?"

"Yeah, not so comfortable, but at least there are no bodies."

"Well said. I think this maiden is fond of you."

"It seems that way. Oh!" Lebna was grabbing his member through his pants. He stood her up. "Uh, yellum," he said.

Lebna made a pouty face and turned away, dancing to the music on the radio. She turned and shook her finger at him, smiling, as if making a plan for later.

"The little devil," said Arthur. "I suppose I should be jealous, but I am an old man."

"I'm sure we can find you a lady in town, perhaps at a purple star."

"No. I am doing well without that sort of company, but you as a younger man…"

"I think I'm divorced. Yes, my wife has divorced me. I'm not sure if it's official yet. But we have to find Mia." He had the notion that he could hear Kristin's voice. His vision blurred, and he put his head into his hand. "I feel I may…" Sweat broke on his upper lip. He put his head on the table and then…

Kristin froze as Reece coughed and sat up in bed. He fell back. Markush had his hand on her shoulder. Reece opened his eyes and saw Kristin standing there, wearing jeans and a t-shirt. He tried to speak but faltered and cleared his throat.

"Reece?" asked Kristin. "It's me." She stood back, resisting the urge to either strike him or hug him.

"Reece, you're back at Organon," said Markush. "I invited your...wife to visit. She wanted to see you. I hope that's okay."

Reece smiled and held out his hand, but she didn't take it. "We were going to a circus. I met the Icelanders and Emma, but they didn't recognize me. We somehow traveled back to Godo, another one. The Abba had the holy raiment, the Ark, back in Gadam. There were bodies in our rooms—"

"Whoa, hold on," said Markush. "You've been gone for a while, longer than usual. Let me take some notes."

"Reece," said Kristin. "I've been talking to Clarence, Dr. Markush. He's explained some things to me. I...don't know if I believe it yet." She moved a step closer to the bed.

Reece pushed up on his elbows, the wires from the EEG crowding his shaved head. "Kristin, I'm looking for Mia. I've spoken to her. She's alive. Kristin, she's alive, and I will find her." He took a cup of warm water and drank.

"Reece, I want to believe that. But how will you bring her back?"

"I, I don't know, but I will. You have to help. I think you

can help."

"We're here to help any way we can," said Markush. "I'm afraid the job is up to you, but we can be supportive. Right, Kristin?"

"I want to think that I can help. I'll do whatever it takes. Clarence, um, Dr. Markush, says you travel back to Ethiopia. You spoke to Mia? What...did she say?"

Reece winced at the memory. "Just, 'Daddy.' It was through the Ark. I yelled her name, and she said 'Daddy.' It was her."

"Let me sit down." Kristin noticed the TV was on, but muted. "Did she look well?"

"It was just a flash, just her face."

"Dr. Markush told me, but I didn't believe him."

"Tell us more." Markush had his pen ready. "You returned to Godo, and you saw the Icelanders and Emma?"

Reece recounted the story of following the Abba, of suddenly being in Godo and finding the others there. Then the Abba had used the holy vest with the precious stones to return them to Gadam.

"Someone mentioned a circus, that little girls were part of the circus, and Arthur and I took a jeep to Alem Ketema to see." Reece spoke of Alicia, the three sisters in yellow dresses, the body in the bathroom, and then of finding the Beselfui Hotel as it had been when he was working in Godo. "I was drinking a beer and now I'm here."

"You think you might find Mia at the circus?" asked Markush. "And this Alicia could be Freddie's daughter. We have to follow that up for sure. If you hang around long enough, I'll let you speak with Freddie. He had a setback yesterday, seized, but couldn't remember anything."

"That was the plan. But I need to go back. I know I always say that, but I do. And we're taking good care of Alicia. She likes the buster. I hope it's his daughter. It has to be."

"Wow," said Markush. "If we can figure out how to get her home, then we'll have a plan for Mia."

Reece nodded and lay back. He raised the head of the bed and turned to Kristin. "I have to apologize for what I did. I know you don't completely understand, but I had to do it before she established herself, the impostor that is."

Kristin brushed the curls from her face. "I'm still not on board, but I'm learning. I mean, there are others like you here. Either you all have the same delusion, or you're actually telling the truth."

"It's the cold, hard truth," said Reece. "I'm glad you came."

"I was skeptical, but I've been talking with Dr. Markush. He's very convincing, and just seeing this place has given me some hope."

"Are you still in the house? I figured you would burn it down."

Kristin laughed. "I thought about it, but it's my last connection to Mia. I did quit my job at the university, though."

"How will you pay the bills?"

"We've worked out a plan," said Markush. "Do you mind if I tell him?"

"No," said Kristin.

"In exchange for her cooperation, we're placing her on a stipend, enough to pay the mortgage and bills plus some. Talking with her has been very helpful in understanding who you are, what the bigger picture is."

"That's super, and thanks, Doc. That helps me worry less. I need to be able to focus on finding Mia." Reece poured himself another cup of water.

"It's the big picture coming together, one elaborate crime scene if you will," said Markush.

"And I'm guilty until proven innocent," said Reece.

"Well," said Markush. "Guilty in the eyes of the general public. For propriety, we have to maintain that illusion. The return of one of these little girls, like Mia, would change everything. Have you asked Alicia much about Dahlia, what she knows?"

"Huh, maybe. Everything happens so fast, and there's no night there. It's just one long continuous day. She did say that she thinks Dahlia is mean. There was a little girl who was harassing her before she was replaced. Irma, I think."

"Yes, Irma, that's exactly what Freddie says!" said Markush. His face was bright. "That's astonishing, to make the connections between here and those other theres. We definitely have to get you together with Freddie. Wow."

Kristin was frowning. "Why would you find Alicia so easily and not Mia? I don't understand."

"I don't get it either," said Reece. "It seems so random. Can I get some food, Doc? I'm famished. Maybe start with that can of Ensure on the table." Markush handed it to him, checking the expiration date out of habit. Reece popped the lid and drank it in three gulps.

"Hit your call button and Debbie'll order you something. I estimate you burn at least ten thousand calories a day seizing. I can tell you've lost weight."

"Yeah, you look skinny," said Kristin.

Debbie appeared in the doorway. "What's up?" She introduced herself to Kristin.

"Just some food is all, and not a half sandwich. I don't mean to be grumpy."

"No problem," said Debbie. "Glad you're back."

Reece turned to Kristin. "What about my classes? I guess they fired me after what happened."

"They released you from the department. I'm pretty sure that they divided up your classes among the other professors. There was never any official mention or letter."

"They've been dealing with us," said Markush. "They released you, and we requested that no publicity be attached. You can imagine the shock. I know some simply don't believe you committed the murders."

"I could probably tell you who they are," said Reece. "Sometimes academia is so, pardon my language, fucked up. But I guess it was a shock, especially to the students. I can't imagine what they're thinking. Makes me sad. I just want to find Mia, regardless of whether or not I'm vindicated. I can imagine one hell of a class to teach if I find her with the help of Arthur."

"One hell of a revelation for the entire planet," said Markush. He checked his watch. "Kristin, are you still set to leave? We have an hour. We could definitely use you for another day. Not use you, but have your input. The guest house is yours for as long as you like." He looked hopeful.

"Yeah, stick around," said Reece.

"I'll stay one more night," said Kristin.

"Excellent," said Markush.

Reece watched Kristin stand.

"I think maybe I need a break," said Kristin. "This has

been almost too much. I think I need a nap and a glass of wine."

"Don't go so soon," said Reece.

"I need to leave on a positive note. I'm beginning to remember things that I'd rather not think about."

"It's been quite a lot to digest," said Markush. "Reece, I'm going to have Debbie introduce you to Freddie and record the conversation. I'll make sure that Kristin gets dinner and has what she needs, but we'll go for now, okay?"

"Yeah, Doc, but I need to go back. Can you send me back?"

Markush fidgeted. "I think your body needs a rest. Let's let it happen naturally, okay? The circus will be there when you get back."

Reece sighed and hugged his knees to his chest. "If you say so, but I'm going to focus on going back." He wiggled his toes, skin peeling between them.

Markush patted him on the back and left with Kristin, his hand on her elbow.

Debbie entered, carrying a foil tray of lasagna. "Got you some fuel, the family size." She placed it on the overbed table. "Want some soda with that or tea?"

"Yeah, two Cokes would be nice," said Reece. "Damn, that looks good."

"How did your visit with your wife, ex-wife, go?"

"I'm shocked that she came. It went pretty well, considering. Dr. Markush seems to take good care of her."

Debbie lifted her eyebrows. "Indeed, he is." She left for the Cokes and returned.

"Say," said Reece. "Tell me about the Emma in six. Is

she married? Did she kill a little girl?"

"Well, single is my best guess. I need to change out the electrodes on your head. You could get a quick shower with them off. Want to do that?" She alerted Claire that she was going to remove Reece from the EEG and peeled them off, twenty-three electrodes. She'd had her hair cut and was wearing new pink scrubs instead of the Organon issue.

"Damn, that feels so good," said Reece. "When can I get them off for good?"

"If you stop traveling, but you can talk to Markush about it. He might be agreeable to taking you off." She dropped each sticky pad into the garbage. "Do you think you and Kristin will get back together?"

"God, I haven't considered it a possibility until today. I mean, I need to focus on Mia first and then see what happens. Nice haircut."

"You noticed. No one else has said anything." She peeled off the last electrode. "There, all done. Hop up and get a quick shower before we get in trouble."

Reece swung his legs over and walked to the bathroom, his gown blowsing behind him.

"Nice butt," said Debbie, laughing.

Without thinking, Reece said, "Thanks."

Debbie followed him to the door. "Need any help with the hot and cold? Just keep turning it all the way for hot."

"Yeah, okay. I think I got it." Strangely, he felt himself getting an erection and stepped into the stall, removed his gown, and turned on the water, standing back to let it warm. The bar of soap was small and hard, and he lathered a washcloth and scrubbed his body from top to bottom, enjoying the feel of hot water. There was no shampoo, and he used the soap to wash his scalp, making it feel stiff and squeaky. He stood under the water for a few minutes. He dried himself, wondering where Mia was, wondering if she had food to eat, wondering if she had the luxury of a hot shower. Standing there naked, his vision clouded for a moment. He felt he was floating between two worlds, but he forced his mind back into this one. He wondered if he'd stalled a seizure.

"Clean gown!" said Debbie. She'd opened the door and was holding the gown.

"Thanks. I want street clothes, though."

"When you're able to stay up in the dayroom, we'll let you have regular clothes."

"That sounds like luxury." Reece slipped into his gown and crawled back into bed, winded from the exertion.

"Looking good," said Debbie. "Eat your lasagna before it gets any colder," and she got busy putting on the new electrodes.

Reece popped open a Coke and took a deep drink. "Ah, that's good." He dug into the lasagna, finishing half of it in mere minutes, the time it took Debbie to place the sticky leads.

Back at the guest house, Kristin and Markush were drinking a glass of red wine, sitting on the couch together, recounting the conversation with Reece.

"He did say that he saw Mia, which makes me feel some better," said Kristin. "But then there was the circus, which just sounded outlandish to me."

Markush put his hand on her leg. "All of it is outlandish, and I have to fight to stay objective. None of this is in the realm of any known possibility, but I've staked my career and life on it."

Kristin put her hand on top of his. "Without you, none of this would be possible, would it?" Her cheeks flushed.

"Sometimes I feel like a blind man, running my hands over surfaces to make me believe in the substance of things."

"Do you think he'll find Mia?" She moved his hand and crossed her legs, putting his hand back, rubbing his fingers.

Markush swallowed. "Yes, I do think he will. He's determined. He's already located one of the missing girls, or so he says. Freddie's girl, Alicia. I really should have stayed to follow up on that, but..." He leaned close to her.

"But what?" asked Kristin. She was breathing deep and slow.

He leaned in for a kiss, but only got her cheek. "But this."

Kristin took his chin and led his face toward her mouth. "I'm betting on you, you know," she whispered, and let herself go into his arms.

Arthur sat with Alicia as Reece slumped over the table, his head on Lebna's shawl, trembling. Arthur had worked his way through the bottle of wine and was growing tired. Alicia had finished two orange Fantas. Arthur had taken Alicia again to the shintabet, and he'd had to use the disgusting hole as well. The two men playing checkers had left, as if retiring from shift work.

First, Reece's arm moved and then his head. Arthur stood and paced around the table, calling his name.

"He's waking up," said Alicia. She sat at a table to herself, playing with some green yarn that Lebna had brought.

Reece raised his head and looked around, groggy and sweating. He tried to speak, but nothing came. Arthur fussed over him, straightening his shoulders. "Come around, lad."

Reece moved his lips. "I willed myself to return. Mia. The circus." His eyes stared a million-mile hole into the table.

"Here, drink," said Arthur. He put Reece's hands around the warm beer.

Reece gripped the bottle and brought it to his lips, letting the liquid lubricate his mouth and throat. He saw Alicia and smiled at her.

"Hi," said Alicia. "I was worried about you."

"You willed yourself, you say?" asked Arthur. He clicked his heels on the cement floor.

"God, I'm woozy. But I did it. I thought about coming here, and here I am. Maybe I'll gain some control over the seizures.”

“That would be most promising.” Arthur was a bit dizzy from the wine and sat.

“I saw Kristin. She came to visit.”

“Your wife, I presume,” said Arthur. “But she has divorced you.”

“Yeah, but Dr. Markush convinced her somehow.”

“I would like to meet this doctor,” said Arthur.

“He believes it, all of it,” said Reece.

“Can we get some food? I’m hungry,” said Alicia. “I want some buster.”

“Of course, lass. Shall we go to find the circus?”

Reece tested his legs and, feeling them secure, pushed up from the table and stood. Lebna had come from the back and looked surprised but seemed somewhat glad that they appeared to be leaving, even though they owed her twenty birr. She rubbed Reece’s back, speaking rapidly, and walked them outside. Reece looked up and saw a large yellow sun, but as soon as they had passed through the heavy door, the sun was once again dime-sized. The door closed behind them with a clank of the metal bar.

They walked and soon found a buster establishment. Several customers sat at red tables. Behind the bar was a stage on which danced a brown woman with bleached white hair. Weird, tinny music played.

The bartender came over, looking bored out of his mind. “What’ll it be, pilgrims? Got’cha a little one. Does she do head?” He turned and, in a flash, procured three large red bowls of buster.

Reece just nodded, thinking it best not to talk, and led them to a table in the middle of the vaulted room. “Alicia, what flavor did you get?"

"I wanted apple, and this is apple, so it's good."

Reece and Arthur had apple as well, although Arthur called his pear. They drank in silence, watching the people around them. Reece locked eyes with a middle-aged man who seemed familiar. He looked like a respiratory therapist from his nursing days.

"Why don't you take a picture?" said the man. His face was smooth, his hair neat and trim.

"You'll never be the man your mother is," said Reece.

The man laughed and slapped the table, seeming to forget about them in an instant.

"People aren't very nice here," said Alicia.

"Well said," said Arthur. He relished his bowl of buster, taking long drinks, but soon he frowned. "But not so good for the bowels, eh?"

Reece laughed. He hadn't gone since he'd been there. "Just one of the quirks of time travel, I suppose." He pushed back his thinning hair, then finished his bowl of cloudy liquid, which reminded him of miso.

"It's one of life's pleasures, you know," said Arthur. "To move one's bowels."

"Less wear and tear on the system, though. I wonder if people here ever have to go or if there is such a thing as colon cancer. Buster certainly seems healthy."

"Perhaps there is an advantage," said Arthur. "But not one that I enjoy." He finished his bowl.

They talked for a few minutes and then headed out through the mist door into the blazing sun. Reece led the way, aiming for the side of the town opposite to where they had arrived. Blank buildings. Red stars, blue stars, green stars, but no purple.

"Look, a black star," said Alicia.

Reece and Arthur paused.

"A black star," said Reece. "Shall we check it out?"

Arthur hesitated. "Perhaps one of us should look inside to spare the young one of any great surprise."

"Okay," said Reece.

He walked to the front of the building. It seemed like the others, but had a solid door without a window. He knocked and tried the lever. No one came, and he pushed the door. There was a small foyer, dimly lit, with what looked to be a gumball machine. A ruckus was coming from beyond another door. He pulled the door open and saw a vast theater filled with people. He let the door close behind him and watched as a man was led onto the stage. There was a contraption there, and Reece recognized it as a guillotine. The man was led to the machine, and he kneeled of his own accord, placing his head through the stock. A great wave of nausea flowed through Reece as the blade rose to a height of twenty feet and, at the sound of a bell, dropped. He turned away, hearing sounds of light applause.

Back outside, he urged Arthur and Mia along.

"What did you find? You look like a ghost," said Arthur, trying to keep up.

"I'll tell you later," said Reece and nodded toward Alicia.

"Yes, right," said Arthur. "But perhaps slow down for this old man."

"Yeah, we're kind of running," said Alicia.

"Sorry," said Reece, and he slowed.

They walked, staying on the wide and winding lane, the only sound being their shoes on the pavement. Soon, in the distance, they saw the top of what looked to be a large tent of red-and-white stripes. From a pipe in the roof came smoke and a vague, puttering mechanical sound.

"The circus," said Reece.

Within two minutes, they were at the edge of town, where the buildings just stopped. Open before them was a vast arid plain studded with scrub. Perhaps 250 feet out was the tent, as wide as it was tall. They approached, and there was a short line of people waiting at the open flap. To one side were large, old, unmarked wagons, and then a tremendous flatbed of sorts. They stood in line, hearing a hurdy-gurdy playing from inside. The line seemed to be stalled, and the three waited, Reece hoping to avoid conversing with anyone.

After a few minutes, the lady in front of them turned and said, "Shouldn't she be in a cage? I thought the circus was inside." She wore a thick quilted coat and had little ringlets of sweaty hair.

"Is there a charge to go inside?" asked Reece.

"Charge? What for? It's just a whale and some girls in cages and then some animals." She unbuttoned the top button of her coat.

"A whale?" asked Arthur. "I should like to see."

Finally, one person was allowed inside as another exited, carrying a small carving of a whale, a minke whale. The sun beat down on their heads. They waited and waited, Alicia finally sitting on the hard, gravelly ground. The line decreased one by one, with three more coming in behind them.

A man with a sallow face and a narrow mustache poked Arthur in the ribs. "Say fuckface, whaddya know? You from around here?"

"I beg your pardon," said Arthur. "My name is Arthur." He extended his hand in greeting.

The man, his skin an off-yellow, spat on the ground. "Did I ask you your name, ass munch? You chappy chaps been in line long?"

"It's moving slowly," said Reece. The man looked like he had hepatitis, and he did.

"Who's the little cum bucket?" The man pointed at Alicia.

"Come on," said Reece. "Maybe just mind your own business, fartknocker."

That got a grin from the man, a look of appreciation. Another half hour passed, and then it was Reece's turn to enter. He planned on walking through with Alicia, whether they let him or not. A black curtain opened, and a man in a striped suit and top hat motioned him in, eying Alicia. He seemed pleased and said nothing. Inside, the mechanical sound was quite loud, and Reece saw its purpose. On a giant sled, nearly sixty feet long, rested the whale, unmoving, but its sides trembling. A system of showers wet its skin and re-collected the water being pumped through again. A long black tube snaked over the gray-and-white whale's back and descended its blowhole, pumping air into its lungs. A red velvet rope circled the whale. Lining the inside of the tent were cages jammed against one another. The first held a giant frog, as big as a pig. A smell of petrol filled the tent, and Reece coughed.

"Why isn't the whale in the ocean?" asked Alicia. "It

looks so sad."

Reece walked along the length of the whale, mesmerized. He came to the head and noticed the dark eye moving in jerks. "It's cruel, isn't it?" He had failed to notice the cages behind him and turned at the sound of a small voice. It was a young girl, about seven, with brushy brown pigtails and a birthmark on her cheek. There was straw on the bottom of her cage and a bucket of water. The cage was of metal and wood, rickety and weathered. There was no lock, but a contraption that resembled a puzzle.

"Who are you?" asked Alicia. "And why are you in a cage? I don't like this place."

"My name is Hominy," said the little girl. "I want my mommy and daddy."

"Jesus." Reece squatted to get a better look and glanced at either side, cages holding other little girls. "Fucking Christ. Are you okay? How long have you been like this?" He stood and noticed a spherical object hovering nine feet from the ground.

"I don't know," said Hominy. "My parents are trying to find me. Can you help me?"

The girl in the next cage was weeping. The one to the left was holding the bars and calling out, "Daddy! Daddy!"

"We need to help them," said Alicia.

"Yeah," said Reece. He saw Arthur stop and stoop to peer into a cage. He had found a hunger artist, wasting away to skin and bones, a man in his fifties who looked to be a hundred and ten. The man didn't respond to Arthur, just moved his narrow eyes a notch.

"Dear God, what is this place?" asked Arthur. He looked at little Hominy, thin as a rail.

"It's a circus, and this is the freak show, I suppose. We have to check all of these cages for Mia." Forgetting the whale, he walked back to the entrance, looking in each cage. He returned and then began to sweep around the perimeter, calling out for Mia, followed by Arthur. One girl was particularly tiny and frail. "Who are you, little girl? We're going to try and help you."

"My name is Neenee. I'm sick. I feel bad in my tummy."

"Jesus," said Reece. "Just hold on. I need to look for my daughter, Mia. Do you know a Mia?"

"No. They don't let us talk to each other. The man said he would cut me with a knife and hang me in a sack." Neenee's eyes teared. "Please don't leave me."

"I won't," said Reece, and he swept down the line, passing more little girls and then an armadillo that walked blindly inside its cage, bumping into the bars. Two others were peering into the cages, turning to look at the whale and then back again, as if deciding which was more interesting. He made the curve and continued, soon drawing close to the engine that pumped air and water for the whale. It puttered and clanked and was manned by a short man with an engineer's hat and an oil can. Holding his breath, Reece glanced into the three remaining cages, seeing only the strange faces of little girls taken from their parents. He heard a scream and shouting and ran toward the noise.

Two men held Alicia by the arms, her feet kicking. They were putting her into an empty cage. Arthur was protesting.

"Fuck! Hey!"

But it was too late, and the door with its lock contraption closed, Alicia screaming and crying.

"Let her out!" said Reece.

"You brought her here, so what's the problem, sad sack?" The man was old, and his belly hung over his belt. He had bright yellow hair and bad teeth.

Reece shook the cage. "Alicia, it's okay. We'll get you out." He turned to the other man, who had a broad chest and was stooped, as if he read in bed without a pillow. "Open the cage, dildo."

The man with yellow hair grinned. "You brought her here, dumbass. What did you expect?"

Arthur intervened. "I say, unhand her this very moment. I shall break you in half otherwise." He stood with his feet spread, his hands in front of him.

"Open it, now," said Reece.

"You open it," said the man with the broad chest. He laughed. "This is a freak show, right? And she's a freak. Dahlia says so, right?"

Reece rushed him, recalling his high school days as a wrestler. He swept in for the man's leg and spun around behind him, putting him in a full nelson and then tripped him to the ground. The man grunted, his face turning red as Reece choked him from behind.

"I'll fucking kill you," said Reece, and the man with yellow hair escaped and kicked him beneath his chin, knocking him out. Reece went limp, and his captive jumped up, ready to square off with Arthur.

"The world is my will and representation!" said Arthur, and he was standing in the empty field, the circus gone, Reece at his feet, blood trickling from his mouth.

Reece awoke in bed. He had knocked over the pitcher of water, soaking his sheets. He felt the electrodes on his head and ripped them off. "Damn, dammit to hell!" He let out a mighty roar and collapsed, remembering, hoping that it wasn't true. He had led Alicia directly into captivity, back to Dahlia. He felt his head and ripped off the new electrodes.

Laura, hearing his shouts, had run from ten to his room. "Hey, Reece. Hold on. What happened?"

"God. Why?" He opened his eyes. "I was tricked. Alicia's been taken into the circus. I blacked out. I have to talk to Freddie about his daughter. I may have lost her."

"So, this circus..." said Laura. "Do you need something to help you settle down?"

"No, no. The circus. It was just outside of town. There was a whale and cages with little girls. Arthur and I were distracted, looking for Mia, and they grabbed Alicia and put her in a cage. God, what a dumbass I am. I should have known better than to take her there."

"Okay, okay, you're talking it through. Take some deep breaths. You took your electrodes off."

"No more goddamned electrodes. I swear, what's the point? I have to get back, but first I need to talk with Freddie. He deserves to know."

Laura thought. "Markush gave us permission to let you talk with him, but you need to settle down first. How about a soda or some juice? A sandwich?"

"Yeah, sorry, something to drink would be good. Dammit." He pounded his fist on the bed.

"Okay, you relax. I'll get you a Coke or a Sprite, whatever we have cold, okay?"

"I'll be a good boy, if that's what you mean." He shook his head in defeat.

"You're okay, you're good. I understand that you're upset. No need to upset Freddie, though. Be right back."

Reece raised the head of his bed all the way. He remembered fighting the guy with yellow hair, and that was the end. Something had happened, but what? His jaw hurt. Was Arthur okay? He played back the smell of petrol, the clanking, the whale roving its obscenely small eye, the cages with little girls. He determined Mia must be in a cage, maybe in another circus. It was something. Maybe Freddie would have some clues.

Laura came back with a Sprite and a cup of ice. "Here, drink this. Once you've settled down, I'll take you into the dayroom. Freddie's in his room. I'll let him know, okay?"

"Sure," said Reece. He felt exhausted, as if he had been pulling the whale on its perverse sled. *Why a whale? Why little girls in cages?* He poured his soda over the ice and drank.

Fifteen minutes passed, and Laura returned. "Ready?"

Reece stood and wobbled, catching Laura by the shoulder. "I'm so damn weak. I need to exercise when I'm awake." In the hall, he could see Freddie in the dayroom, standing near the TV, which was off.

Laura walked with him around the corner and held the door open. "Hey, Freddie. This is Reece Myers. Markush said it was a good idea for you two to talk."

Freddie didn't smile but took a chair beside a small table with magazines. "Yeah, sure." Blood flushed his large ears. He seemed to be overheated.

Reece pulled out a chair and sat at an angle. Freddie was short, balding, and had a hard look in his eyes. Reece wondered what he looked like to Freddie. "Hey, I'm Reece." He held out his hand.

Freddie stuck out his hand and shook. "Yeah, Freddie Mentone. Let me just start by saying that I don't want to hear any bullshit."

"What would you consider bullshit?"

"I don't need any crazy talk, is all. Just the facts."

"Where you from?" asked Reece.

"Cedar City, Utah, not far from Bryce Canyon. You know it?"

"Yeah, and Zion National Park. I have friends out there, been there once."

"Yeah, better than this hellhole."

"I assume we're in the same boat, right?" asked Reece. "You killed your daughter, or rather, an impostor that looked like your daughter."

Freddie leaned forward and looked at the tile floor. "Yeah, and you?"

"The same," said Reece. "What's your connection to Ethiopia?"

"My father was a missionary, Lutheran. I grew up there until I was ten. You?"

"I was sort of a missionary myself, a nurse. I was there during the big famine, back in the eighties. I have a daughter, Mia. I'm looking for her over there."

"Yeah, so was I, until a couple of weeks ago. I haven't been able to get back, even though I've had a seizure, like a switch was turned off." Freddie drummed his fingers on his palm. He was wearing frayed jeans and a Victory Motorcycles t-shirt.

"That sucks. I've been going back and forth like a ping-pong ball, to a village I worked in, but it's in the future in another world."

"When I travel, it's always to Addis Ababa," said Freddie. "And like you say, another world altogether."

Reece cleared his throat. He still had his cup of ice. "Huh, Addis. Looks like we have a lot in common." He gazed through the glass at Laura and Lars, the monitor tech.

"It seems," said Freddie.

"I think we can help each other. In fact, I have some information that might help you. I met a little girl over there."

Freddie clenched his fists.

"Her name is Alicia." Reece waited.

Freddie's ears grew even brighter. "What does she look like?"

"Kind of pale with dark brown hair, big eyes, seven years old."

Freddie bit his lip. "So, you're telling me that you found Alicia? I find that hard to believe. Are you sure?"

"Pretty sure. A priest, the Abba, found her. I've been taking care of her, along with a friend, Arthur. She's really sad and asks about you and her mom." Reece tipped ice into his mouth.

"Holy fuck, I don't believe it, but I want to. If what you say is true, I'm indebted to you. What year is it there? If you say thirty-nine eighty-one, I'll fall out of my chair."

"Thirty-nine eighty-one. We're traveling to the same world, just different places in Ethiopia."

"Tell me what buster is," said Freddie.

Reece laughed. "The green stars, what you eat, and you never have to shit."

"Wow," said Freddie, but then his eyes narrowed. "How do I know you're not just repeating what Markush tells you?"

Reece thought. "I don't really know. I mean, it's a strange place. Everyone insults you. Red stars are real bars. Green stars are for buster. Blue stars are housing. Purple stars are whore houses."

"What about the black stars?"

Reece flinched. "The guillotine, a place you go to die, although I'm not sure why."

"Damn," said Freddie. "Look, I'm going to go out on a limb and assume you know what you're talking about. If you're lying, though...Is she getting enough to eat? Is she safe? Who is Arthur? Can you trust him?"

"Yeah, she likes the buster. We make sure she gets plenty. She's in shorts and a t-shirt, but it's so damn hot. Arthur is just a guy I met, an older guy. He's as good as they come." Reece wondered if he should bring up the circus.

"This is big. So how do we get her back home? That's something I've been sweating over."

"I don't know," said Reece. "Maybe there's a way to piggyback her when I travel. I think, though, that the Abba would be able to send her back using the Ark. We would have to pay him. Have you encountered the Ark?" Reece explained how the Abba Paulos had conjured up an image of Mia, how he had transferred them back to Gadam from Godo.

"It's only been an idea before. I don't know much about it. It sounds like some kind of magic chest. But, if there's a chance it will bring Alicia home, then I'm all for it."

"Definitely a chance," said Reece. "When I go back, we'll return to Gadam from AK and visit the Abba. We just have to figure out how to pay him. But for now..." He wanted to say that Alicia was in good hands, but couldn't. "Something happened. I have to tell you. You'll get upset, so here goes."

"Something happened to Alicia?" Freddie frowned, his pale face contrasting with his large red ears.

"It starts with a circus that we visited."

"A circus?"

"Yeah, a circus, but a strange one. The main attraction was a whale, but they had little girls in cages as a sideshow. Arthur, Alicia, and I went to see if Mia might be there. I had no idea what would happen. Anyway, they took Alicia and put her in a cage. I couldn't get her out and tackled this guy. I was gonna break his neck. I swear. But then something happened. I blacked out. I may have been hit. So, I need to get back. The circus was supposed to be going to Gadam."

Freddie rubbed his thin fuzz of black hair and his face. "Should I be thanking you or strangling you? How could you let them put her in a cage?"

"I was looking in the other cages for Mia. It happened so fast. In retrospect, it seemed like a setup, like they knew we'd come. I'm sorry, but at least I know where she is."

"I'm appreciative, I think. I want to help. If we're traveling to the same world, we could meet there. I could travel from Addis to this Gadam. We could work together."

Reece thought. "Maybe you're right, if it's the same world. That would be a good test. Just take a bus or jeep from Addis to Alem Ketema and then on to Gadam in a jeep. We have a room in a blue star there, if we can find it again. The more the merrier, I suppose, but we have to travel at the same time. Maybe Markush could arrange something."

Laura peeped in. "You guys okay? Need anything?" Renaldo and Amanda were swapping ends of the hall.

"I'm good," said Reece.

Freddie nodded.

"I guess it's a plan. You know I willed myself to travel earlier. I feel like I'm gaining some control over the process. Have you tried?"

"Oh yeah, I've tried, but maybe not in the right way," said Freddie. "You may have to teach me."

"Sure. I think maybe my friend Arthur has something to do with it. He's a philosopher. He understands the various realities from a unique perspective. Have you heard of Schopenhauer, Arthur, the philosopher?"

"I've heard the name, but have no clue," said Freddie. "I thought he was dead, though."

"Well, surprise, he's alive in that world. He's dead in this one, except for his writings."

"You know, that's curious. I met Che Guevara in Addis, and he should have been dead," said Freddie.

"The apple is not a revolution that falls when it is ripe," said Reece.

"Ha," said Freddie. "You have to make it fall." He held out his hand, and Reece slapped it. "Well, look. When you go back, tell Alicia that I love her so much, that her mom loves her very much, okay? Tell her you talked with me."

"Of course," said Reece. He was feeling a little woozy, a pain in his head. He tried to stand and sat back down. "I think..." His eyes rolled.

Arthur paced in the open field. He had taken a stray grain bag and covered Reece's face, shielding it from the sun. Arthur was sunburned and scratched his itchy skin. He was about to return to the museum for help when Reece stirred.

Reece opened his eyes and saw brown grass and rocks. His jaw and head hurt like a motherfucker. He moved the grain bag from his face and looked up at the worried Arthur.

"Careful now, lad. You took a kick to the head. Take my hand."

Reece went to his knees and pulled up with Arthur's help. He looked around at the empty field, at the blank town just beyond. "What happened? Where's the circus?"

"It seems to have disappeared, and I may be at fault for that."

Reece bent over to clear his head. "How could that be?"

"My thoughts exactly," said Arthur. "I spoke a few choice words, and all was gone."

Reece stood erect and wiped debris from his clothes. "The circus was supposed to be going to Gadam. Maybe... it's there. Alicia is there. We have to find her."

"Let us return to the museum and rest, eat," said Arthur. "We can get solid food there. Perhaps my bowels would be pleased." He walked that way.

"Yeah," said Reece, and he followed, soon reaching the edge of town and the paved lane. They came to the black star and then walked on, coming to the tall walls of the museum.

It took a few minutes of knocking, but the door opened. It was Lebna, her tooth protruding. She looked surprised and ushered them in, babbling a mile a minute. Daylight was waning inside the courtyard, and they stepped into the relatively cool bar. Reece felt like he was home again and took a chair at the first table. He noticed two other ferenji at a table against the wall and guessed they were visitors to the museum. They wore bright clothes and sun visors, as if fresh from a golf course.

Lebna returned to the table, asking them what they would have.

"Some food?" asked Reece. "Before we drink?"

"Oh, that would be most beneficial," said Arthur.

"Enjera b'wot?" asked Reece. He pointed at Arthur and himself. "Hulet Fanta."

Lebna nodded and hurried to the bar and returned right away with the warm Fantas.

"This is the drink liked by Alicia," said Arthur. He took a sip. "Hmm, quite delicious."

Reece downed his soda in four gulps, belching. "I feel like I've been roasting in an oven."

"Yes, I was worried about your lying in the sun, but you are too heavy to carry."

"No doubt," said Reece. "I talked with Alicia's father. I told him that we had found her. He didn't believe me at first. I can't believe I was suckered into bringing Alicia to the circus."

"Do you mean we were tricked?"

"I think so. I think Dahlia was behind it. You'd think that she could just take her versus having a circus kidnap her."

"Yes, you've mentioned this Dahlia. But I do not quite understand," said Arthur. He took a long swallow of his orange Fanta.

"I don't understand Dahlia completely myself. She's the root of this whole problem, of the impostors and so forth. I keep imagining that I'll confront her, or it, at some point, but that she is not a mortal as we are."

"Another puzzle to be solved. Do you imagine she inhabits this world?"

Reece bounced his empty on the table. "I think she inhabits every world, that she is a force, a conscience of sorts that interacts with us, but for what purpose I'm not sure."

"Do you mean that she is like God?"

"I no longer believe in God. God can't be the reason for our experiences, but I do believe that Dahlia represents or attempts to understand all that we know, kind of like the student teaching the teacher. Dahlia strikes me as curious."

"And perhaps evil," said Arthur.

"Perhaps," said Reece.

Lebna emerged from the kitchen in the back with a large platter of enjera and a mound of shurowot in the middle. She smiled, giggled, and brought them two more Fantas.

"Amenseganalo," said Reece. "You've never had this before, have you?"

"I can't say that I have," said Arthur. "Is it a bean?"

"Yeah, lentils in the middle of the bread, which is called enjera. The bread batter is fermented for a day or two and has a unique taste. The lentils are probably spicy, good for your bowels. Here, like this." He tore off a flap of enjera and used it to pinch a wad of mushy lentils. "Only use your right hand."

"Ah, yes, the biblical proscription." He mimicked Reece and chewed. "Yes, very spicy but quite tasty. The bread is spongy and tart."

"It's damn good," said Reece. "And it won't give you gas, which is a plus."

Lebna took two St. George beers to the colorful visitors and then came to check on them. She talked and talked.

Reece and Arthur smiled, nodding in agreement to whatever was being proposed.

"I guess we can spend the night here, since there is a night," said Reece. "I wonder how the sky can be different from one side of a wall to the other."

"That is queer," said Arthur. "I suppose it's what we want to see in this particular world."

Reece flagged down Lebna and asked about rooms. "Hulet kifl?"

"Ow," said Lebna. She looked happy that they would be spending the night. Not many did. She pointed at Reece, "Amist," and then at Arthur, "Sadist."

"Great," said Reece. "You have room six, and I have room five." He asked Lebna what the charge would be. "Sentino?"

"Assir birr," said Lebna. She held up ten fingers.

"A little more expensive than usual," said Reece, "but still cheap. I suppose we have to add it to our bill." He tore some enjera and scooped some wot.

"I do hope that Alicia is okay," said Arthur. "I feel responsible for the disappearance."

"As they say, shit happens. We can't fret about it. We just have to find the circus again. We'll use a gun if we have to, if we can find one. They used to be everywhere here."

They finished eating and ordered beer and shots of Johnnie Walker Red. The other visitors had left after taking a picture of Lebna. They chatted, Arthur telling him about living in Berlin and fleeing during a cholera outbreak. Reece told him about burning down his grandfather's barn.

"Ha, you would have been placed in jail in my country. That is a grave offence," said Arthur.

On their third round of Johnnie Walker, the electricity kicked in, and a single bulb lit up the room. Lebna hurried to turn on the tape player, and it was the plain and soulful Jim Reeves.

"He sounds heartbroken," said Arthur. "Such a sad voice."

"It's called country music," said Reece. "Not my favorite, but it's fun to hear it here."

"I would have called it music of the folk," said Arthur. "I recognize the piano. What are the other instruments?"

Reece listened. "Just an acoustic guitar and some light drums."

"I'm not accustomed to this guitar. Perhaps it is similar to a lute."

"Close enough," said Reece. He toasted Arthur and downed his shot. "Here's to finding Mia, and Alicia."

Arthur nodded and took a sip, grimacing. "The whiskey is good, but rather strong. It has a petrol quality."

"Good for your liver," said Reece.

"I doubt that very much," said Arthur. A smile creased

his face.

Just then, a man entered. He seemed to be in a hurry and announced something to the room. He was saying that someone had stolen the tabot, the replica of the Ten Commandments, from the church. Lebna was saying, "Tsk, tsk, tsk," and the man came and whispered in her ear.

"I wonder what that's about?" asked Reece.

"I wonder as well," said Arthur.

"Maybe it's time to get some rest," said Reece. "Hit the hay."

"Yes, I am weary, and this liquor is causing me to close my eyes."

Reece motioned for Lebna and made a scribbling motion with his hand. She understood and brought the paper over that he had signed earlier, adding twenty birr to the IOU. Reece signed, wondering how they would pay, wondering if they could leave without paying.

"Shall we?" asked Reece, and they stood slowly, saying good night to Lebna.

Lebna looked hurt and put on a pouting face.

Outside, the wall was missing, and a full moon lit the night.

"What's this?" asked Arthur. "A village has appeared."

"Jesus," said Reece. "We're back in the 1980s, I think." He walked, looking down the rocky lane at the maze of leaning buildings. An idea occurred to him. "If this is 1986, then the Baptist compound with the helicopter will be down the road. We can get birr there to pay our bill. He wondered if the pilot, Terry, and his wife, Lisa, would be there.

"An excellent idea, though I'm exhausted, but let's explore and see what we find."

"It's a long walk, perhaps a mile," said Reece. "We have to pass through the town."

Together, they walked along the moonlit path. Dogs fought in the distance, and they met a farmer who tipped his hat to them. They reached the circle that marked the town's eastern edge and walked in the cool breeze that quickened as they left the town. It took them another ten minutes, and a fence made of corrugated tin roofing appeared. All was dark as they descended and approached the wide double gate. Someone was whistling.

"Hallo!" said Reece. He knocked on the gate.

The whistling stopped, and it took a minute, but the creaky gate opened a crack. It was the night guard with an ancient rifle. "Abet?"

"Um, Terry? Lisa?" Reece made eye contact with the guard, urging him to open up.

The guard told them to hold on and closed the gate. Soon, he was back, and the gate opened wider this time. It was Terry, dressed in corduroy pants and a heavy sweater. He looked surprised.

"Terry?" asked Reece.

Terry stepped through the opening. "Who are you guys, for God's sake? Do I know you?" He was swarthy, with thick, windblown brown hair.

"I guess not. I used to work for the Mission. We're staying in town. It's a long story, but we need some cash. We're flat broke. This is my friend Arthur. I'm Reece."

"Nice to make your acquaintance," said Arthur. He was out of breath from the brisk walk.

"Huh, well, come in. How much do you need?" He followed them inside the compound under the wary eye of the guard.

"I think fifty birr will take care of everything. We're leaving tomorrow, but I'll find a way to pay you back. Dr. Guthrie's not here, is he?" Reece wondered if he reeked of alcohol.

"Nope," said Terry.

They walked along the rocky ground past the main dining hall and the warehouse. The helicopter was on the other side of a small house with the guest house across from it. Light leaked from behind the crude door.

"Honey, coming in. We have guests," said Terry. He ushered them in and closed the door to the stiff wind. Lisa was beside the bed in a thick white bathrobe. "Have a seat." Lisa looked puzzled.

Arthur and Reece took chairs from the small table.

Terry took a wallet from a shelf near a tiny propane stove and withdrew some bills. He handed them to Reece. "What are you guys doing in AK?" He gave Arthur a good gaze, pondering his odd clothes.

"There was a circus—"

"Well, we heard there was a circus here," said Reece. *Where to start? Where to end?*

"Honey, this is Reece and Arthur. Reece says he used to work for the Mission. Circus?"

Lisa moved her long black ponytail from her back to her shoulder. "Nice to meet you. Yeah, what are you guys up to? It's late to be walking around here. Not so safe."

"Well," said Reece. He took a chance. "We've been in Gadam, I mean Godo. We saw the Icelanders and Emma there."

"Were you working with them?" asked Terry. "You guys want some tea?"

"Tea would be lovely," said Arthur.

Lisa took down a pot from the rafter and filled it with water.

Reece looked to Arthur. "Well, sort of. It's a crazy story, but I'm looking for my little girl, Mia. She's been...kidnapped."

"That is crazy," said Terry. He glanced at Lisa.

"Yeah, well, that's what we're doing. But never mind that," said Reece. "We know she's not here, and we're headed back to Gadam, I mean Godo, tomorrow. To keep looking."

"How old is she?" asked Lisa, covering the pot with a lid.

"Seven," said Reece. "You haven't seen a little girl, have you? A ginger with bangs, thin, seven years old?"

Terry and Lisa looked at each other. "No," said Terry. "And we would have noticed. You lost her in Ethiopia?"

Arthur crossed his legs and smacked his lips. This was Reece's territory.

"I suppose you could say that. It's complicated."

They spoke for a few minutes more, as if in riddles. When the water came to a near boil, Lisa added the tea and sugar. She let it steep for a minute and poured out two mugs.

"Thank you, lass," said Arthur. He sniffed the steam from the yellow cup.

"Yes, thanks," said Reece, and he took a sip. "Hot."

"A strange story," said Terry. "I don't know what to

make of it. But if you say you're looking for your daughter, I guess that's what you're doing. I'm flying to Godo tomorrow, if you need a ride."

"Thanks," said Reece. "But we have other arrangements. If they fall through, we'll come by. When will you leave?"

"About eight or so," said Terry.

When they had finished their tea, Reece said that it was time for them to go, to get back to the hotel.

"Thanks, Terry, for the money. I owe you a big favor," said Reece.

"And thank you for the delicious tea," said Arthur.

"I'll walk you to the gate," said Terry.

"Good luck with finding your little girl," said Lisa, toying with her ponytail.

They said their goodbyes at the gate, and Reece and Arthur made their way back to the hotel. The lightbulb in the bar was on. It would stay on until ten. A soulful ballad of Ferlin Husky drifted from the bar.

They approached their rooms. "Hopefully, all will be well in the morning," said Reece. "If you use your chamber pot, make sure you empty it in the morning. Lebna gets angry otherwise."

"Yes, one can hope, and perhaps dawn will bring us to the right place again."

They entered their rooms, and soon Reece could hear the loud snore of Arthur.

With Sheldon's help, Laura put Reece back in bed, as he trembled from head to toe. Freddie had gone back to his room, enthused over the information about Alicia but worried that she was in danger. Reece had given him hope, but the strange story about the whale and the cages had unnerved him. All was rather quiet on the unit, except for the occasional bellow from Helmut Grayson in three. He railed about the alien implant in his skull and fought his full-body restraint with diligence.

That evening, Markush picked up Kristin from the guest house. He was freshly showered and smelling of tea-tree oil, his favorite scent. He brought flowers, and the plan was Chinese food at the Forbidden City in Radcliff. Kristin had showered as well and wore a navy pinafore over a long-sleeved white sweater with a simple gold chain.

A bored waiter seated them and took their orders. Kung Pao chicken for her and vegetable lo mein for him.

"I'm so glad you decided to stay another day," said Markush. "You know you could stay the entire week. I'd like that."

Kristin smiled. "Maybe I would like it too, but you need to stay focused on Reece. He needs you."

"Do that face again. You looked so serious." He sipped his ice water and placed the red napkin on his lap. From the ceiling hung Chinese lanterns. A mural of the Great Wall spanned the open room.

"I am serious. What if he needs you?" She ran her

tongue over her teeth.

"You're an important piece of the puzzle, my dear. Perhaps you'll find that you need me as well." Their knees touched under the table.

"Ha," said Kristin. "Good one." She lowered her voice. "You know we're committing adultery. The divorce isn't final. Shouldn't you worry about that?"

"I suppose I should, but I'm not. To make it more businesslike, let's make this a working dinner. Tell me more about yourself. What attracted you to Reece? You say that you grew up in one house, lived there through high school?"

"Maybe that's part of what attracted me to Reece. He moved around constantly, his dad being in the Army. I couldn't imagine changing schools like that. He said they always moved over Christmas, so he was always the new kid in the middle of the year. I think it really warped him, especially being an only child. At least I have a sister that I can confide in."

"When you say warped, what do you mean? I know he has the diagnosis of major depressive disorder and that he's possibly bipolar."

"He can be so withdrawn, withdrawn to the point of blanking out everything around him, as if he wasn't even there. That used to frustrate me to no end. He says he never had friends and that he lived inside his head, especially during high school. That's when he had it the worst. He hated high school. He confessed that he'd had elaborate plans to blow up the school, that all he could think of to relieve his misery was going back to Alabama."

"You mentioned that he ran away from home."

"When he was in tenth grade, not long before his parents were shot. He had a motorcycle, and one day he just took off for Alabama, headed back to his grandparents' house. I think he had forty dollars or something crazy like that." Kristin sipped her water, leaving a bit of bright red lipstick on the glass.

"Why did he run away? Just unhappy?"

"I think he got into a fight. The school expelled him, and his parents didn't take up for him. That really seemed to hurt him. I don't think they realized how miserable he was. He said that he felt like a dog that was just let in and out of the house."

"That's quite a simile," said Markush. "I wish his parents were still alive. They may have known more than they let on. Perhaps they just didn't know what to do with him."

Kristin nodded, looking around at the other patrons. "His dad was slow, as Reece would say. He drooled. He always kept a paper towel in his shirt pocket to wipe away the drool. Something about the way he was born, some sort of brain damage, but not enough to disable him."

"That's bizarre. Reece is pretty bright in his own way. On some level, I feel that he's been chosen to break the mystery. He's onto something. I think he's been puzzling this out through his interest in philosophy."

Another waiter dressed in a black smock brought their orders and checked to see if they would like another glass of wine.

"Please," said Markush. "Go on, about philosophy. I've been doing some preliminary research on Schopenhauer, and I can see the link, an obsession with what's really real."

"You know, he gave up on religion after his experiences in Ethiopia. I think that left a huge void, and he filled it with his studies."

"I think that's an astute observation," said Markush. "I think that probably kept him from going insane."

"That and then this talk of abductions and Dahlia, the strange little girls, the impostors. I don't know where his sanity ends and his insanity begins."

Markush held up a finger. "It's a continuum, one's mental health. To be diagnosed with a mental illness, one has to meet certain criteria, but I think that approach is too rigid. If I were not privy to what I know, I'd say he is bordering on schizoaffective disorder, although he is lucid. He has definite paranoid tendencies, and I think his obsessive nature has emerged with the task of finding Mia. The waiter brought two more glasses of white wine.

"That's pretty heavy. He was hard to live with. I mean, he genuinely loved Mia and me, too. I think he just didn't know how to show it. His parents were very standoffish, he told me. He insists his mom had some mental problems, but that she would never admit it or be treated."

They talked more, finishing their dinner, and decided to get ice cream to dull their wine buzz. After scoops in cups, Markush drove her back to the guest house and opened the door for her.

"Should I invite you in? Don't you need to get back to the unit?"

"No one's paged me, so I think we're good. The nurses are very efficient. They'll page me if they need something. And, yes, I'd love to be invited inside." He slipped in behind her, putting his hand on her back.

Kristin shrugged her shoulders. "A nice neck massage would do the trick, but let me use the restroom first," and she left him standing there. She stepped into the bathroom and gazed at herself in the mirror, feeling guilty. She brushed her teeth and ran a comb through her curls. Markush could be her father, being the same age as her dad. An image of Reece with his hands around Mia's neck stopped her cold, and without thinking, she stamped her foot, feeling again that all was lost. She took her time and entered the tidy living room to see Markush on the couch.

"How about that neck massage? Ready? Maybe sit in a chair in the dining room?" He stood, looking like a little boy at the carnival.

"I don't know. We'll just end up having sex again."

"And what's wrong with that?"

"I'm just feeling weird, is all. But a neck massage would feel really good. Come on." She walked into the tiny dining room and sat in a chair.

"Would you like a glass of wine? I think there's some Scotch as well."

"Maybe not. I've had enough." Kristin leaned forward, letting her curls fall forward.

Markush put his hands on her neck and began to rub. "Feel good?"

"Yeah, feels great." She rocked back and forth with the motion of his hands.

He used his thumbs to apply pressure to her cervical vertebrae, pushing down below her collar. She made noises of approval, losing herself in the experience. She heard a vibrating noise.

"Shit, my pager. It's the unit, dammit. I have to call."

Kristin turned toward him. "Yeah, take it. I understand."

Markush picked up the cordless and dialed. Laura answered. She told him that Grayson was having a grand mal seizure, and he hung up the phone, apologizing to Kristin.

"No problem," said Kristin. "We need to call it a night anyway."

Markush leaned in for a kiss, and she let him brush her lips. He grabbed his keys and was out the door.

Markush pushed onto the unit, said "Hey" to Renaldo, the guard, and stepped into the room of Helmut Grayson, number three.

"Good to see you," said Laura. "He was in full tonic-clonic for over fifteen minutes, but now he just seems to be traveling." Grayson's body trembled. His raw face framed by his bald head pushed against the air. The monitor showed gamma waves with polyspikes.

Markush listened to his heart, looked into his eyes, pupils constricting to light. "I wonder what that was about? Was he traveling before the grand mal, like he is now?"

"Yeah, I had Lars check. He was in travel mode about six minutes before he started in with the reeling and bucking. I thought the blanket restraint would fly apart."

"We'll definitely need to see what he's been up to when he comes around. I know he's a bastard, but see what you can get out of him. If he convulses again, we'll need to do some IV Dilantin."

"Got it," said Laura. She adjusted the sheet and put a cool washcloth on Grayson's head, then washed her hands.

The intercom: "Hey guys, Myers is back in seven, sitting up in bed. Just FYI."

"Thanks, Lars," said Markush. "Shall we?" What would Reece do if he found out he was hot for his wife?

They walked to the end of the hall and bore right into seven. Reece looked woozy, his shaved head shining, sweat in his eyebrows. He looked at them as if stunned by a blow.

"Reece," said Markush. "You're back at Organon." He washed his hands.

Reece fell back on his pillow. "Yeah. I was in a hotel room in Alem Ketema. It was some kind of time portal in the middle of the town, like it was 1986. No one except Lebna knows us. We found the circus."

"Tell me about that. You thought maybe Mia would be there is what I heard." Markush folded his arms. His cashmere sweater was itchy, and he rolled his shoulders.

"There was a whale on a big sled surrounded by cages with little girls and some animals. We were tricked. While we searched the cages, they clapped Alicia into a cage. There was a fight. I can't remember much, and when I woke up, the circus was gone, tent and all, with Alicia." Reece caught his breath. "I told Freddie. I feel sick that we lost Alicia."

"Hmm," said Markush. "Some sort of steampunk anachronism, the whale. I'm not quite sure I understand."

Reece raised the head of his bed. "Yeah, maybe, but then we went back to the museum/time portal to get a room. We just walk through a door, and it's another time. The people go there to see what it was like back in the day, I suppose. Arthur and I had dinner in the bar and had a few drinks. When we walked outside, the wall around the place was gone, and we were back in the old Alem Ketema. We were hoping that it would revert during the night somehow. I have to get back to Gadam. The circus was going there next. Poor Alicia. I bet she's terrified."

"Freddie took it pretty well," said Laura.

"Yeah, but what a fuck up. Dahlia is behind it. She orchestrated the whole thing."

"Maybe to throw you off the track of Mia?" asked Markush.

"Exactly," said Reece. "But if we figure out how to bring Alicia back, we can do the same with Mia. I hope."

"You want some juice or water?" asked Laura.

"Some grape juice, two cups, would be great," said Reece. "I'm exhausted."

"Okay, rest up," said Markush, writing on the clipboard. "I see your EEG leads are off. Will you let us put them back on? The data is useful."

Reece coughed and felt his head. "No way. I say no. Is that okay?"

"We'll leave them off for now, but we may need to replace them if you stay gone for longer stretches of time. I know they itch, or at least that's what I guess."

Reece laughed. "Yeah, they itch like hell. So, did Kristin go back home?"

Markush cleared his throat. "No, she's staying another day. I made sure she had dinner. She's resting at the guest house."

"I guess that's good," said Reece. "Maybe she knows something I don't."

"Her information is invaluable." Markush stepped back to let Laura pass with the juice cups. Reece peeled off the foil lids and drank them back to back.

"That's good. Maybe two more."

"Sure thing," said Laura, and she was off again.

"Glad you're back," said Markush.

"One more thing," said Reece. "Freddie travels to the same version of Ethiopia that I do. We're going to try to meet up, if we can travel at the same time. Could you arrange that?"

Markush regained his animation. "That's incredible. I suspected the possibility based on similarities in your stories, but didn't want to rush things. Let me think about it. We lost a patient just a few months ago, after I induced him with the magnets, so it's risky. Letting it happen naturally is safest."

"What do you mean 'lost him'?"

"He died after traveling, had a flat EEG."

"Yikes," said Reece. "Probably in a cage in some circus."

"Who knows?" asked Markush. "Okay, I'm going, and keep me updated, okay?"

"Yeah," said Reece. He watched Markush leave and Laura come in with more juice. He was reaching for the cups...

Reece awoke to the sounds of a rooster crowing, and dread filled his chest. He gazed at the slanted metal roof over his head and the bright green paint on the walls. Would he be in the museum? He swung his legs over and sat there rubbing his eyes. It was now or never, and he went to the door and looked out. The wall was there, and he breathed a sigh of relief.

He knocked on Arthur's door.

"Hello, lad." Arthur looked rumpled and shabby. "How was your rest?"

"I traveled during the night, back to Organon. But look, the wall is there. We can go back to Gadam today, as long as the other side is as it should be."

"I have some good news," said Arthur.

"What's that?"

"My bowels have moved for the second time in what seems to be months, in the night. The meal last night worked an act of magic."

Reece laughed. "I'm not so lucky, so far. Let's see if there's some breakfast."

They walked to the bar and entered the cool space, illuminated by the light through the door. Lebna was absent, and they took a table, scraping their chairs on the cement floor. Within a few minutes, Lebna appeared, grinning and speaking in Amharic.

"Some food—bread and tea?" asked Reece. "Dabo. Chai?"

"Ishi," said Lebna, taking off for the kitchen.

"Ah, bread and tea will be very nice," said Arthur. He stretched his legs out to the side of the table.

"Maybe good for another poop." Reece started to explain poop, but the data fur beat him to it.

Lebna returned with four wheat buns, the size of small saucers. She left and returned with two orange cups of sweet, spiced tea, steaming. "Amist birr," she said, reminding them of their tab.

"Yiqirta, no problem," said Reece. He took a bite of the brown bun.

"Heavenly," said Arthur, chewing bread and sipping his tea.

"Yeah, good for the soul and body. Let's get out of here, though. No telling when a jeep will arrive."

Eating took longer than he would have liked, the buns being large and hard to chew. He settled up the tab with Lebna and gave her a five-birr tip. She screamed and hugged him, laughing. And they were on their way to the door with Lebna in tow, frowning.

"I think she thought I was offering money for sex," said Reece, and he let Lebna open the door. He gazed out, seeing the uniform buildings, and felt a thrill that all was well. "Ciao," and he and Arthur stepped into Alem Ketema 3981.

"One moment, lad. A rock in my shoe." Arthur struggled to bend over.

"Let me help." Reece squatted, took off the offending shoe, and shook out the rock. "There."

"My foot thanks you."

In their walk down the main lane through town, they met only one person, brown skinned and wearing a wide-brimmed hat. They said hello and hurried on, not waiting to be insulted. Within five minutes, they reached the traffic circle and stood there, waiting for a jeep. Reece remembered the data fur and conjured the information that a jeep would be there within two hours.

"We must wait then," said Arthur. He sat on the low circular wall, the sun blazing down on them. "How was the good Dr. Markush, if I may ask?"

"Fine, I suppose. He's taking care of Kristin while he interviews her. She may be able to help in some way."

"Two mules plow faster than one."

"Exactly."

A woman approached, wearing a long black dress, cut very low in front, with what looked to be a hoop skirt. She made straight for them, shaking her finger.

Arthur paled. "Dear God, it's her! The woman...I pushed. The woman who caused me years of grief. Dear God."

"Really?"

The woman was upon them, berating them, her voice loud and clear.

"Here you are, you old fool," said Caroline Marquet. She cooled herself with a Japanese fan.

"Yes, madame, we are here. What brings you to these distant parts?" Arthur made a sweeping motion with his hand, as if offering the world to her on a plate.

"Thought I was dead, did you? Called me a bitch, did you? Well, I'm as alive as you are." She sniffed and folded her fan. "What say you now, oh great man of ideas?" She stood very close.

"I'm on an adventure here with this lad, Reece. We are

searching for his daughter. You certainly don't look dead, as alive as a peach."

"Well!" said Caroline. She seemed to have lost her steam. "What a horrible old man to be keeping company with." She looked to Reece for affirmation.

"He's a gentleman as far as I'm concerned," said Reece. "Perhaps we should discuss this over a drink. The sun is hot, and we have two hours to wait."

"Those red-star places," said Caroline. "I find them repulsive. The staff are very rude, as are the rest of the uncivilized nation that resides here."

"Yes, dear Caroline, language aside, I think the lad's suggestion of a drink is timely."

"I need a parasol from this frightful sun. My skin will be ruined."

It only took a minute to find a red star, and they passed through the mist door, and it was the one with the hundred light bulbs. The bells on the bartender's vest jingled as he greeted them.

"Welcome back! I see you've brought an old horse with you. Headed to the glue factory?"

Arthur stifled a laugh. "Yes, greetings."

Caroline sneered and stood beside the table as they took their chairs. "A lady is to be seated first." She pinched her face and sat on the small chair, spreading her dress beneath the table. "Such manners."

Within seconds, the bartender was at hand with a tray holding two glasses of schnapps and a bourbon over ice. He did a curlicue with his hand and withdrew. "Let the pigs drink!"

"Sit on your sister's face," said Reece.

The bartender laughed and winked.

"Herr Schopenhauer," said Caroline, "how is it that we find ourselves together once more? Is this some magical mountain that you've created with your words? I say that I'd rather be dead than trapped in this Sodom."

Arthur sipped his schnapps and then downed it. "I say, dear lady, that you may be able to explain better than I." He smacked his wet lips.

"You two are quite the pair," said Reece. "I've only read about you in books, and here you are."

Caroline sneered, then coughed.

They talked, Reece telling Caroline of his search for Mia. She expressed complete disbelief in his story and soon finished her drink, calling for another. As time passed and it grew near the jeep's arrival, Caroline grew quite soft, and her belligerent tone took on the quality of a docile child.

"You found me attractive, didn't you, Herr Schopenhauer, being a younger woman that is. I realize that I am plain to many, but my charms are not wasted on the likes of old codgers like you." She downed her third shot of schnapps.

Arthur, having finished his third, smiled. "Perhaps you should have been less loud in my quarters, and I would not have overlooked your charms."

Reece laughed, absorbing the conversation, thinking about how he would weave the exchange into a lecture.

"My charms, dear boy. You admit it, I am charming. I knew it, you old fool." She giggled like a little girl, her bosom heaving in her bodice.

Reece checked the data fur, and the jeep would be arriving any minute. "My friends, the jeep is coming, so we should head out."

"The jeep?" asked Caroline.

"A mechanical creature that will carry us to another town."

Reece wondered if Caroline was planning to accompany them. He could tell that Arthur was worried about the same.

"What more will I have to endure?" asked Caroline. "And don't think that you will leave me here. I...I am coming with you." She hit the table with her palm.

They stood.

"But you perhaps have business here," said Arthur. "There must be some reason that you are quite forgetting."

"No, as far as I'm concerned, I'm here to punish you further, dear boy. Perhaps this is your hell." She laughed and loud.

"Dear God," said Arthur. He looked to Reece for help.

"The more the merrier, right? What could it hurt? If we find Alicia, Caroline could be of some comfort to her, being a lady that is."

"Yes, well said," said Caroline. "Shall we?"

Arthur looked defeated and followed them through the mist door into the broad lane. In the distance could be heard the jeep, and soon it arrived, but with a crowd of six already waiting.

"Dammit," said Reece. "Hurry, we have to get a seat," and he took the lead, but the crowd pushed him back as the jeep came to an abrupt halt twenty feet in front of them. Before he could fight his way in, the jeep had emptied and filled, leaving only the top. "Come on!"

"What's this?" asked Caroline. "The transport?" She found herself being pushed along by Arthur.

Reece was the first atop the jeep, and he held down his hand. She would have to climb the bumper and then the spare tire. He saw the futility and called for Arthur to climb aboard first.

"Don't you leave me here, you scoundrels!" She watched Arthur clamber up with the help of Reece, her mouth agape.

"Must we?" asked Arthur. His face had reddened, and sweat dripped from his forehead.

"You never know," said Reece. "Help me, before the jeep takes off."

They leaned down, each taking a hand, and dragged her atop the jeep. She lay on her belly, her dress swooning above her. She cursed a thousand kings, and the jeep jerked into motion, eliciting a scream.

There was an empty cargo net atop the jeep, and they held on for dear life as the jeep circled and began its journey to Gadam. It took them a good ten minutes, but soon they had Caroline in the middle, clutching at the ropes, the wind pouring through their hair, the road uneven and rocky as they passed from Alem Ketema toward the descent into the first river valley.

"This is high adventure, don't you think?" said Reece, his left leg hanging over the edge.

"Yes, indeed," said Arthur. A rut dislodged him, and he bounced.

Caroline had her eyes closed, refusing to open them, her legs folded beneath her. "Oh, what a curse!"

Reece laughed, ignoring the hot sun. He could swear that he saw a twinkle in Arthur's tired eye. This was much better than pushing her down some stairs, and the ride was free.

After the perilous two-hour journey, the top-heavy jeep pulled up the hill and stopped at the edge of town. Reece felt like spaghetti from hanging on and had to pry his hands loose from the rope netting. They helped Caroline down, her dress coming over her head, amid laughter from the other occupants.

"Jesus Christ," said Reece.

"Dear God," said Arthur.

"I am ruined," said Caroline.

Reece shook the stiffness from his legs and flexed his fingers, feeling blisters there.

"What a dreadful journey," said Caroline. "I only have this dress, and look."

Reece looked. Her blonde hair, done in tresses, had come undone, hanging in her face. She was plain, but had a fetching figure and smooth skin. "You're alive, right?"

"No, dear boy, I'm near death, I'm afraid." She sounded humble.

"Let us walk," said Arthur. "My legs feel as if they were made of lead."

"Is there not a carriage? A horse? I am utterly tired, I'm afraid. I feel as if I would faint."

Reece took her by the elbow. "No fainting allowed. We'll see if our room is still available. You can rest there."

"Thank you, dear boy. Do you think we might find some of this buster to clear my head?"

"A good idea," said Arthur, and they began the long and steep walk uphill past the self-same buildings. Even Arthur extended his arm as an aid to Caroline, which she gladly took.

At the top of the hill, they soon came to a buster bar with a topless bartender.

"Light my fire," said Reece.

Arthur cheered at the sight of a woman approaching them, her nipples like bullets. "Well, we are in need of nourishment." A mural of a polar bear behind the bar twinkled.

Caroline gasped at the display of bared breasts. "What is this, a joke of some sort?"

"Look, old bitch, you want some calories or what?" asked Lura. She flashed her dark green eyes.

"I will not have you speak in that manner. I am Caroline Marquet, and I am a lady, madame. You should cover yourself as well." She sniffed and said, "Hmmph."

Lura laughed. "I know you came to mob my tits, you old whore. Buster coming right up. Flavor of the day is acacia gum. Any takers? I thought not." She spun away to the bar.

"Haven't you learned yet, Frau Marquet, that the custom is to engage one another in vulgar exchanges. I find it tiring but slightly humorous." Arthur twiddled his thumbs.

"Yeah, like water off a duck's back, just let it slide. It's when they're nice that you have to worry," said Reece.

Lura put the bowls of buster on the table and held her tongue, but gave Caroline a nasty look.

"That woman despises me, and I despise her," said Caroline.

"You should get a job here," said Reece. He grinned just a bit, and Arthur laughed a deep laugh.

"You are *so* sensitive, young man," said Caroline. "What

have I gotten myself into with you two? But you can't leave me. I beg of you. Surely between us, we can discover a way to return home. Oh, how I miss lovely Germany." She produced two tears, one from each eye.

"First, we have to find the circus," said Reece. "We have to find Alicia, liberate her from that damn cage." He downed his buster.

"Yes, a good plan," said Arthur. "Shall we drop Caroline at the room, allow her to rest? You do need rest, my dear."

"No, you'll leave me. I don't trust you, sir. I will accompany you to this circus. Perhaps I may be of some assistance." She sat up a little straighter. "So there."

Reece glanced at Arthur, who was biting his lip. "Maybe she's right. It could be we need a woman's touch, and three are stronger than two."

"Yes," said Caroline, and she leaned over to adjust a buckle on her leather shoe, squashing her dress down, making it flare.

They ordered another round of buster and then stood to leave. Outside in the glaring sun, Reece led the way toward the only area flat enough to pitch the large circus tent, the old Polish airfield. They passed through the center of town, meeting no one, and skirted their way beside one last set of buildings to the edge of town. The tent loomed in the distance like some grand revival.

"Aha!" said Reece. "I was right." He turned and smiled at Arthur. "So, what is our plan?"

"Perhaps the Fräulein and I will distract the operators while you extricate the young one."

"Okay," said Reece. "And when we have her, I say we go straight to the Abba Paulos. He might be able to help us send Alicia back home."

Arthur was imagining Caroline trying to climb the rickety ladder. "Yes, a good plan. Shall we?"

There was no line, but an attendant was at the tent flap entrance. He was ancient and dressed in a blue suit with a bow tie. He merely held out his hand as a gesture for them to enter. He smiled and showed his missing teeth.

They entered, mesmerized by the giant whale, and passed the giant frog, two little girls, the hunger artist, and then there she was, Alicia, balled up in a cage as if in shock. The engine that serviced the whale puttered and clanked. Reece examined the strange locking device on the cage and determined that it took several moves to open, like unknotting a thin necklace. There was no one about, and all of the little girls in their cages sat unmoving, staring.

"Alicia," said Reece. "Alicia. Psst!" He was trying to untangle the lock. Suddenly, the solution came to him, the data fur no doubt.

Alicia uncurled and sat up, rubbing her eyes. "Mr. Reece! Please help me. I'm so hungry. Hurry before the men come."

"I've got this," said Reece. "Almost," and he slipped the metal loop sideways. The door to the cage opened with a loud squeak.

The little girl in the next cage had taken an interest and stood, stooped over. "Help me, too, mister."

Reece nodded at her, his heart breaking. Alicia left the cage and hugged Reece, then Arthur.

"Hey!" It was the man with yellow hair and bad teeth, and behind him came the man with a broad chest.

"Take her!" said Reece.

"Come!" said Arthur. He grabbed Alicia's small hand and pulled her as he did his best to run. Caroline just stood there.

"Caroline, go!"

The men were upon them, and one pushed past. The man with yellow hair grabbed Reece and flung him aside. Reece fell and grabbed his legs. The man fell, cursing. Caroline was in a near faint. Reece jumped up and pushed her. "Run!"

Caroline had never once run in her life, but she managed a sprint. The man with yellow hair was up and running after her with Reece on his tail. Reece leaped and dragged the man to the ground. He took his elbow and ground it into the man's windpipe, choking him. He jumped up and ran outside. He could see Arthur running with Alicia, toward the edge of town, going the wrong way. He watched Caroline trip and fall, but Arthur and Alicia had crossed into town with the broad-chested man coming up short, stopped as if by an invisible barrier. Reece caught up with Caroline and dragged her after him. The man with yellow hair was behind them, panting and gasping for air. Reece and Caroline passed the magic barrier and looked back.

"You fools!" said the broad-chested man. He shook his fist at them. The man with yellow hair glared, and they both turned back to the tent.

"I'm afraid I can't run any farther." Caroline collapsed in a heap, her dress blowsing around her.

"Yes, we must rest," said Arthur. He was leaning over, taking deep breaths.

Reece grinned. "We got her. You okay, Alicia?"

Alicia looked forlorn but managed a smile. "Thank you for coming back. I'm so hungry."

"Let's get her some buster, and then try for the Abba's place. They evidently can't follow us into town," said Reece.

Now four, they walked to the nearest buster establishment. Inside was a live camel, wandering among the tables. They endured abuse from the staff, fed Alicia, and then headed outside and gathered at the edge of town, plotting their next move.

"We have to pass along to the left here and then down below the cliff line. The way looks clear. Ready?" asked Reece.

"I am ready," said Arthur. "Come with us, little one."

"What about me?" asked Caroline. She had regained her color, but her dress was covered in dust.

"And you as well," said Arthur.

They crossed the town's edge and made their way to a now familiar path, following it for half an hour. Caroline complained, but kept up even though her dress snagged on thorns every few feet. By the time they arrived at the ladder, her dress looked like hell, and she was weepy and tired.

"Who's first? Arthur?" asked Reece.

Arthur grabbed the ladder, which bowed under his weight, and began the climb. Next was Alicia. Reece decided he should go last.

"Up you go," said Reece. "I'll avert my eyes."

"I'm afraid this is too much. My dress."

"Your dress will be fine. Just press into the ladder and

take your time. Arthur will help you at the top. Otherwise, you'll have to climb the rocks."

At that, Caroline whimpered and put her fancy shoe on the lowest rung. She climbed rung by rung, holding on for dear life, crying out more than once. At the top, she looked for Arthur, and he held out a hand. She was afraid to release the ladder and stared into his sweaty face.

"Come now, Fraulein," said Arthur. "Take my hand." He refrained from saying "My dearest bitch."

With a little yelp, she let go and grabbed his hand. He pulled her up, grunting. Reece followed, and soon they stood together, a sad-looking little group.

"You two will kill me, I'm sure," said Caroline. The taffeta beneath her dress showed through the tears and holes. She seemed on the verge of weeping.

"You're okay, lady," said Alicia.

"Thank you, little girl. You are kinder than these brutes."

Arthur rolled his eyes. "Brutes? I think we are saving your life."

"My apologies," said Caroline. "Men are just so rough." She managed a small laugh.

Reece could hear the sound of metal on rock. "Okay, let's go see the Abba," and he led the way, passing the Abba's small house.

"Such a crude structure," said Caroline. She was once again walking with what she deemed grace and only wished for a parasol. She had lost her fan on the jeep ride. The large sun above shone through wispy clouds shaped like daggers.

Reece was first to the green door in the rock. He shouted, "Hallo!" and looked in, seeing the golden Ark on its pedestal. The pick on rock ceased.

"Abet!" came the reply of the Abba. He came outside and marveled at the collection of strange ferenji. He stood there, waiting.

"Umm," said Reece. He wanted to ask the Abba if it was possible to transport Alicia back to 2003, the universe of Alicia's dad, Freddie. He stumbled for words. "Umm," and he pointed to Alicia. He bent down and wrote 2003 in the dirt. "Umm, father, ubati."

The Abba Paulos gazed at the numbers in the dirt and looked stymied.

Reece remembered the holy book from the Abba's house. He erased the numbers with his foot and drew a Cylinder that was pinched in the middle. He pointed from one side and then to the other, and then pointed at Alicia. The Abba's eyes lit up.

"I do think he understands," said Arthur, "although I do not."

"I want my daddy and mommy," said Alicia.

The Abba stood there smiling.

"Perhaps he needs some money for this favor," said Arthur.

"Yeah, right," said Reece. He fished ten birr from his pocket, from the money that Terry had given him. He turned both of his pockets inside out to indicate that was all he had.

The Abba took the money, frowned, and looked at Arthur.

Arthur followed suit and turned out his pockets. "My dear lady," said Arthur. "Would you happen to have any money?"

Caroline thought. "Yes, but you must turn away." She turned away and reached into her bosom, pulling out a silk purse. Inside were coins of silver. She emptied the coins into her hand. "Here. It's all I have. But I still do not understand why we are here. For what will he use the money?"

"To send Alicia home," said Reece. "Show him the coins."

Caroline held out her hand. The Abba peered at the coins and took one, biting it. He held it up to the sky and gazed at it.

"Ishi," said the Abba. He took the five coins and proceeded to his hut for the jewel-studded raiment. Back, he motioned for Alicia to come with him inside the cave.

"What's he going to do?" asked Alicia. "I'm scared."

"He's going to send you back to Freddie, your father," said Reece. "You have to trust me that you'll be okay. Just go with him and do what he says, okay?"

Alicia looked at her feet and then at the Abba's outstretched hand. "Okay, but you have to wait here. Okay?"

"Don't worry," said Reece.

"You promise?"

"I promise," said Reece

"Mr. Arthur, do you promise?"

Arthur looked touched. "Yes, dear lass, we will go no farther."

Alicia took the Abba's hand and followed him into the church carved from rock.

Laura placed the electrodes on Reece's scalp. Markush felt that Reece would be making a breakthrough soon and watched the hurricane waves on the screen in the nurses' station. Markush had called Kristin to check on her, and she hadn't suggested that he visit her. While he was on the unit, he decided to check on Grayson. He had re-emerged from his grand mal seizure and was awake, spitting fire as usual. Markush walked into three and locked eyes with him.

"Goddammit," said Grayson. "I was there! I was there!"

"Where were you?" asked Markush. "There's a cold beer with your name on it in the fridge."

Grayson groaned. Despite his confusion, the mention of a cold beer caught his attention. "You better not be shitting me, Doc."

"It's my promise. Heineken, your favorite. I bought it myself." Markush pulled the chair next to the bed and sat.

"I was there when it happened. Dahlia was there too, everywhere. I could taste her sweet cunt, the bitch."

Markush nodded. "Go on."

"For Christ's sake. I was there, at the beginning. The beginning of the beginning."

Markush thought. "Do you mean the Big Bang?"

Grayson laughed. "That's *new*. I'm talking about the beginning, the beginning of everything. I heard the music and Dahlia didn't, the cooze."

"What's at the beginning?" asked Markush. "What did you see?" Prickles ran down his spine.

"Riddle me this, good doctor." He strained against his restraint. "What is there when there is nothing?"

"Nothing?" asked Markush.

"Ha, you wish. How could there ever be nothing? There's always been something, always and forever always." He laughed. "And I saw it, or rather I heard it, its music."

"I don't know the answer," said Markush. "You'll have to help me out. I'm here to help, but we have to work together."

"Together as one! Yeah right. Now give me that beer."

"But you haven't told me what you saw." He lifted his eyebrows and darted his hand through his long gray hair.

"That's all one beer will get you, Doc."

Markush considered his options. Maybe he would talk more after the beer. "Okay, be right back."

He waited at the door, and Lars buzzed him in.

"Progress in three?" asked Lars. He glanced at the monitor.

"It could be the biggest breakthrough yet. I'm bribing him with beer." Markush retrieved a cold bottle of Heineken. He popped the lid. He looked for a straw. He opened three drawers and found one. Back in three, he held up the bottle. "Just as I promised. The only thing missing is a sandy beach."

"Screw the fucking beach, just give me some suds."

Markush put the straw in the bottle and maneuvered it to Grayson's mouth. He sucked long and hard, swallowing mouthfuls. The straw slipped out, and Grayson belched.

"Damn, that's good. Tastes like good old pussy." Grayson laughed deep and hard.

"More?" asked Markush.

"What the fuck do you think? This is big, really big."

He slipped the straw back into Grayson's mouth and watched him drain the bottle, sucking for the last drops.

"You're a good man, Charlie Brown. Now, where was I? Oh yeah. I was there and it was awesome. I saw everything. I saw Lila there." Saying his daughter's name, he went sullen and seemed choked up.

"She's still alive? Lila? That's great. Fantastic. What was the setting? Where were you? What did you see? You promised, remember?"

Grayson relaxed into the bed, clenching his fists. The color that had returned to his face drained. "I don't think you would understand," said Grayson. "You can't hear the music, or can you? Are you one of us?"

"Mr. Grayson, I would give anything to be like you, to be discovering things like you do. I'm just an intermediary. You are the important one here. If you could stay as calm as you are right now, we might take off the restraint."

"You don't trust me, do you?"

"We have to consider safety. Often, you're a danger to yourself and the nurses. You're a big man, and you could do some serious damage. We just have to consider that."

"Yeah, well, one Heineken got you this far. But I've got the crown jewel. Do you like Scotch? I do. You have any of that Laphroaig? Am I pronouncing it right? That would sure hit the spot and might even get me to talking more. You want information? You have to pay for it. I've got you behind the eight ball, and you know it."

Markush laughed, thinking about a Thurber short story. "You've got me by the balls. Yeah, I'll admit it. You do.

I tell you what. I'll get that Laphroaig, bring it tomorrow, maybe a twenty-year, and maybe you'll share more with me, right?"

"Damn straight, Markush. You've got my word. But what I tell you goes no further. Understand? There are prying eyes and ears out there who want to destroy me, who want to keep Lila hidden. You might be one of them for all I know, but you've got me strapped to a bed, like a spider in a web, like a grapefruit in a bongo drum. I have to give you the benefit of the doubt, right, Markush?"

"Like I said, it's for everyone's safety, including yours. I'm on your side. Just keep that in mind. And that Laphroaig is yours. I promise. I'll even bring a glass tumbler. You like it with water or ice?"

"Hell no, straight up, like a warrior fudge popsicle." He laughed a loud and deep laugh and strained against the restraint, popping his neck veins.

Markush was careful to stay away from his hands, which poked through the full-body restraint. "Okay then, sweet dreams until tomorrow," and he left the room, forgetting to wash his hands. He made the rounds, peering into rooms. Freddie was awake, sitting on his bed, and they chatted for a few minutes. Freddie was counting on Reece to return his daughter. If they could travel together, they would meet in Ethiopia 3981.

Markush moved on and settled by Emma's side in six. She was blinking and squeezing his hand on command. She turned her eyes his way, and he swore that her mouth moved. "I think you're trying to speak," said Markush. "Are you? Squeeze my hand if you are." She squeezed his hand. "Great, fantastic. Just in case you forgot, you're in a secure hospital called Organon. I'm Dr. Markush. Are you traveling when you seize? You know you're having seizures. It's possible that you seem to be back in, perhaps, Ethiopia. Am I right? Blink twice if I'm right." She blinked twice. "Wow, super. I'll let you rest now. Sheldon is your nurse, and he'll be by to check on you, okay?" He patted her hand.

He walked into seven and gazed at Reece. Reece trembled, every muscle from his head to his toes quivering. He decided to try to call him back. It seemed as if Kristin's presence earlier had somehow brought him back, as if he could hear her across the void.

"Reece? Mr. Myers?" he said in a loud voice. He touched Reece's shoulder. "Reece?" He gazed at the EEG, watching spikes appear when he spoke. "Reece?" A polyspike. "It's Markush." A polyspike. He wondered if it was the music of his voice that Reece could hear, if there were a million Reece's listening to him speak, all looking for a Mia. He looked away as the guard Amanda passed. She was plump and cute and divorced. He turned back to Reece.

Reece's eyes fluttered, and his mouth made a Q. His shoulders and arms writhed as if he were slipping through a pipe filled with thick mud. Markush watched, fascinated. "Reece?"

Reece's eyes opened, and he convulsed once, coughing. After a moment, his lips moved, but nothing came out. He was between there and here, coming full circle. He spoke. "Oh God. No. I need...to go back. The Abba. The Abba was trying to send Alicia back, back to here. He was chanting, and there was a blue light." He spoke to the ceiling.

"What, you're kidding. I'm sorry. It's my fault. I called

you. Maybe close your eyes and concentrate. I'll leave the room and come back in five minutes." Markush left the room and jogged to the nursing station to watch the EEG from there. Lars buzzed him in.

"Looks like Myers is back. He went from gamma to alpha."

"Yeah," said Markush. "He's trying to go back, to will himself back." Markush watched the alpha waves slow, and then a series of spikes ensued. The EEG scrambled, and then there were the gamma waves. "He must be back. Good. I'm going to transcribe some notes in my office, but let me know if he comes back."

"Yes sir," said Lars.

Markush left and waited as Lars buzzed him into the hallway.

Reece, outside the rock chamber, sprawled on his side, dirt in his mouth. Arthur was shaking him and calling his name, Caroline looking bored. Reece sat up and fell back. He was near the green door in the rock. *Alicia?*

"Reece, dear God, what a terrible time to have been traveling. She's gone, the little girl has disappeared. There was a tremendous light."

Reece sat up. "Gone. That's good, right? Where's the Abba?" He slurred his words and spat. Arthur was helping him to stand. Caroline was there wringing her hands.

"I'm not sure. Let us look in the chamber." Arthur peered inside. The smell was that of a lightning storm.

Reece stepped in. The Ark was gone, the pedestal empty. Behind it, the Abba lay on the ground, moaning. Reece rushed over and checked his carotid pulse, which was very slow and bounding. "Abba? Abba Paulos?"

"What a frightful experience," said Arthur.

Reece helped the Abba to sit up. "Fetch some water from his house, from the clay jug."

"I will do it," said Caroline. "It's good to be useful at such a time."

Reece sat with the Abba who was speaking in Ge'ez, his eyes shocked and wide open.

Caroline returned with a yellow cup and handed it to Reece. Reece splashed water onto his hand and then onto the Abba's face. "Abba?" He put the cup to the Abba's lips.

"Poor man, he's wounded," said Caroline. "I've never been so frightened in my life."

The Abba took a few sips of water and gazed around. Reece helped him to stand. The Abba's legs quivered, and he sank. Arthur grabbed his other arm, and they walked him outside into the bright sunshine.

"To his house," said Reece.

Inside the warm house, the tin roof creaking, they put the Abba on the stool in front of his crude table. The ancient book lay there opened to the drawing of the pinched Cylinder. It took a few minutes, but soon it seemed that he had regained his faculties, and he pointed at the image surrounded by figures of angels. He touched the black angel. "Dahlia," he said. "Dahlia." The jeweled vest seemed to glow.

"Holy cow," said Reece. "Maybe he saw Dahlia. I'll bet this sort of thing makes Dahlia furious, if I understand."

"What a terrible person this Dahlia must be," said Caroline. "I don't quite understand. This lovely vest he is wearing is quite intriguing. Are they real gems?"

"I am sure of it," said Arthur.

"They must be," said Reece. "But never mind...Dahlia sent Alicia here and put the impostor in her place. She was hiding her, studying her here, and now she's gone, hopefully back home. I hope so for Freddie's sake." Reece felt faint and sat on the Abba's neatly made bed, a Mennonite quilt on top with a small leather pillow embroidered with an Orthodox cross.

"How will you know where Alicia has gone?" asked Arthur. He stood behind the Abba, his hand on his shoulder.

"I suppose she will just show up, hopefully in the right place, maybe even back at her house. The only way to find out is to travel back. I have to tell Markush to look for her.

She could wind up in the wrong hands."

"Poor little girl," said Caroline. She took a small broom, sweeping the floor.

They stayed with the Abba for another half hour, gesturing to him, but letting him recover his strength. It was as if he had mightily tried and nearly been defeated. Hungry and exhausted, the three said farewell and descended the ladder, walking back through the brush. Reece was worried that the town they had left would not be there, but soon the edge of the town came into view. First, they had to cross an expanse of six hundred feet past the circus tent. All seemed quiet, and they hurried by to escape among the nondescript buildings of Gadam.

Caroline spotted the buster bar and led the way inside. It was the last place they had been, the one with the camel. The beast stood near the bar, chewing its cud.

"Back so soon," said the bartender. His name was Chico, and he was dressed in a sheet with holes for the arms. "I thought maybe you guys would still be fucking each other in the mouth." He was drawing down three heavy bowls of buster for them.

"Such language," said Caroline. "I'll have you know that we are on a holy mission, and your remarks are not needed."

"Yeah, put the dust cover back on your pussy hole, you old wench." Chico smiled like an old friend.

"Well—"

Reece chimed in. "Looks like you've been sucking your own dick. Why don't you bend over and shit cum into your mouth?" Reece took his bowl and passed bowls to Arthur and Caroline.

"Well said," said Arthur.

Chico looked taken aback, but regained his smile.

They took a table as far away from the camel as possible and then devoured their buster.

Reece said, "Why don't we find the room, the one we cleaned up, the one with Carl. You guys can get some rest, and I'll try to travel back to let Markush know what's going on."

"I am so weary," said Caroline. "I would like to sleep for a week."

Arthur agreed, but wished for more buster, and in a jiffy, Chico appeared with a tray of bowls. Everyone steeled themselves for rebuke, but none was forthcoming. "Enjoy" is all that he said.

"I think that young Reece here is adept at handling these ruffians," said Caroline.

Arthur smirked. "Perhaps, but I do believe that I'm learning their tricks of speech."

"If you say so."

"Yes, I say so."

Reece laughed. "No need to bicker. Maybe it's because I'm just as base as they are. I suppose I should be ashamed of myself."

"Not in defense of a lady," said Caroline. She was pinning her hair back in place, but it still looked like a bird's nest. "Perhaps Reece has never found occasion to push a lady down the stairs. Hmmph."

"Perhaps he has never had a wild tiger yowling in his salon," said Arthur. "I do wish to be left alone, now as then."

"Okay, settle down," said Reece. "We have to work together. We might not have rescued Alicia if Caroline hadn't been here."

Arthur sighed and drained his buster.

They bickered for a moment more, but Reece stood, calling for them to come and find their room. A new room was out of the question, he reasoned, thinking that a life would have to be taken to make space for them. They would know the place by the presence of the affable Carl.

Arthur felt that he knew the way, and they walked through the middle of town, soon turning left down a lane that looked like all the others. Arthur hesitated at an intersection, looking for a blue star on the left.

"Just ahead," said Reece. "Here we go. Let's keep our fingers crossed."

Arthur held the door for them, and Caroline entered first, thanking Arthur. Ahead, Reece could see Carl in his chair, reading a magazine.

Carl gazed at them sideways. "Well, well, look what the cats drug in, three dead mice. And the little girl has turned into a pumpkin. Ha!"

"We, sir, are here to occupy our room. We are exhausted, as you can probably see." Arthur smoothed out his wrinkled sleeves.

"What! You never said you were coming back." He bit a fingernail and spat it on the smooth floor. "Just trouble and more trouble."

Reece frowned. "Someone else is in our room?"

"Yeah, do I got to draw you a picture?" asked Carl. "But if you give the word. Finders keepers."

"Um, is this person in the room?" asked Reece.

"Of course he's in the room, probably wearing a diaper and peeing himself."

Reece looked at the magazine Carl was holding. A copy of the *Black Warrior Review*. Where had he seen that before?

"Well, as a lady, I request that we be allowed this—"

"No!" said Reece.

"Too late," said Carl. "The room's yours. It's already in the fur." He went back to reading.

"Which room is it?" asked Caroline.

Arthur glanced at Reece and grimaced.

"This way," said Reece, and he counted three doors down on the left. He took a deep breath and pushed the door open. All was silent. He walked in as if on glass and peeked at the beds. He opened the bathroom door. "Shit."

"Another body?" asked Arthur. He looked in, saw the bloody arm protruding from the bath. "Dear God."

"Who are these people?" asked Reece. "I don't get it."

"What could it be?" Caroline put her hand to her mouth and ran to sit on the large, soft chair of marigold.

"Let's get a sheet from the bed," said Reece.

Arthur stripped off a sheet and returned. Together they lifted the body from the tub onto the sheet and quickly covered the face, a smooth face, a boyish face with horrible bruises. Huffing, they dragged the body through the door and into the hall. Caroline had fainted into the chair.

"Here they come," said Carl. "I guess you want to interrupt my reading and have me open the goddamn door. Jesus Christ, Jiminy Crickets." He went to the door and held it open.

As before, Reece and Arthur dragged the body outside and laid it next to the building. Silent, they returned to the room.

Reece checked on Caroline, who was limpid in the chair, but she opened her eyes to slits.

"Is it over? Is it gone? I'm afraid, so afraid." She waved herself with her hand, wishing to have again her Japanese fan.

"We're good," said Reece. "Unless someone wants this room. But we might as well stay, to avoid further carnage." He put his hands in his pockets. "So, you guys, uh, guy and lady, take the beds. I'll take the chair. I'm going to try and go back to Organon, home sweet home."

They agreed, falling onto the beds in their clothes. Within minutes, Caroline was snoring louder than Arthur. Against his better judgment, Reece used the bathroom and washed his face and hands. He turned the shower on hot and let the water splash into the bloody tub...

Lars kept a close eye on Reece for the rest of his shift. Reece was still traveling. It was at shift change that Claire noticed a reversion to alpha waves. As instructed, she put in a call to Markush to let him know. Her date the night before had gone badly, the guy getting blind drunk. She'd had to take a taxi home from the bar.

In seven, Reece roused, opening his eyes. He felt that he'd traveled a zillion miles, and he had. He pushed a button and raised the head of his bed, feeling terrible about the young man who had died for them. He was back just in time for breakfast and said thank you to the young woman who brought his tray. He removed the lid and saw eggs, sausage, and a fluffy biscuit. He uncapped the coffee, warm, and drank it down, followed by the cup of orange juice. He wondered what month it was, and it was June. Mia would have been on summer break. They would have gone to the beach to stay with friends on St. George Island. He imagined sitting beneath a large yellow umbrella, sipping a cool, sweaty beer, Mia splashing in the waves, Kristin waving at her, taking pictures with a disposable camera. He shook his head and focused on the eggs.

He ate every bite, and Debbie offered to order another tray, but he only wanted more fluids, lots of juice. He told her about the room, about the murder, but she only nodded, not quite sure what to make of it, plus she had five others to look after. It was eight before Markush came, but he was all ears.

"Hey," said Reece. "Lots to report." He chewed some ice.

"Is Kristin still here?"

Markush looked sad. "She's leaving this morning, taking a limo. She didn't care for the helicopter."

"Oh," said Reece.

"What happened with Alicia? You were with the Abba." He poised his pen.

"When I got back, the Abba was on the floor and Alicia was gone, just like that. You have to look for her. She must be here somewhere. Not in here, but somewhere, maybe where she lived. Freddie's from Utah, right? He told me."

"That's fascinating," said Markush. "His wife still lives in the same house. Do you mind if I go ahead and put in a call to her? This could be critical."

"Yeah, my thoughts exactly," said Reece.

Markush dashed out of the room, headed for the nursing station, bumping into Debbie. Claire buzzed him in. How would he explain this to Freddie's wife, Gloria? He grabbed Freddie's chart and turned to the contacts page and dialed. The phone rang. It rang eight times.

"Hello," came a sleepy voice. It was only six in Cedar City, Utah.

Markush almost forgot how to speak. "Hello, Mrs. Mentone?"

"Yes? Who's this?"

"It's me. Dr. Markush. From Organon. I have something urgent for you."

"God, don't tell me that Freddie's made up another lie. Look, it's awfully early—"

"No, wait. Just be patient. This will sound crazy to you, but...you need to check the house for your daughter. Check the neighborhood. We've had a breakthrough. Are you there? Shit." He dialed again and got the answering machine. "Mrs. Mentone, please, just do as I ask. Check her room. Check the entire house. Please call me back at this number." He ended the call, wondering how fast he could get to Cedar City. "Claire, if someone calls for me, let me know. I'll be in seven."

"Sure," said Claire. She'd never seen him so excited. She brushed back her black bangs and scanned the monitors, wishing that she were a blonde.

Markush stepped into the hall, paused at Freddie's room, but headed to Reece's. "Hey, I called his wife. I asked her to check the house, the neighborhood. She hung up on me. I don't know if she went back to sleep or went to check. Damn. This is killing me."

"Wow," said Reece. "Now I really know that you believe me. I've never seen you so alive. I swear on my bones that she's back. You may have to go there yourself. What if the mom finds her and whisks her away? She might be afraid that she'll go missing again."

"I thought of that," said Markush. "Damn. Dammit to hell. Why did she hang up? Look, don't say anything to Freddie, okay? Not just yet."

"Yeah, okay," said Reece. "You gonna go?"

"I'll give her an hour to call back. If necessary, I have military transport at my fingertips." He swooped back his gray hair. "High five, Reece."

Reece laughed and slapped Markush's palm. "This could be the beginning of bringing Mia home. The Abba is the key, the Ark. The Abba chanted, and the Ark came to life, and *poof*, Alicia was gone. I didn't see it, but Arthur said so. The Abba was a wreck, though. I can see why he wants to be paid. God, I hope nothing happens to him."

"Yeah, me too. You need a translator to talk with the Abba, to find out more about what he knows. I need some coffee. Let me grab some brew and I'll be back."

The room intercom buzzed.

"Yes!" said Markush.

It was Claire. "Scocpol in ten is in a grand mal. Richard's with her. No phone calls yet."

"Shit," said Markush. He hurried out and headed to ten. Timera Scocpol convulsed in the bed, eyes rolled back, feet flexed, hands turned inward, the bed shaking. Her EEG was a mess, like a 9.0 on the Richter scale. Epileptiform waves scrawled up and down asynchronously. "How long?" asked Markush.

"Less than a minute." Richard looked clean-cut as usual, his beard neatly trimmed. He maneuvered a rubber stick between Scocpol's teeth, and she almost bit him.

"Go ahead and get some Dilantin ready," said Markush. "Whatever's happening, she's in crisis."

Markush took over the bite stick. "Mrs. Scocpol, we're with you. This is Dr. Markush. Got some medicine coming to help you." He spoke louder than he needed.

Richard was back with a syringe and a bag of normal saline.

"Let's push twenty-five milligrams slow and then a hundred in the bag. Run it in over six hours."

"Got it," and he swabbed the IV port with alcohol, clamped the tube, and injected the Dilantin over a minute, holding tightly to her arm. He prepped the IV bag of saline and piggybacked it into her main IV, adjusting the drip rate.

"Great," said Markush. "Thanks." He watched the EEG, and the spiky waves began to gain width and lose height. She jerked once more and then went quiet, her EEG showing shallow, wide waves, a post-epileptic fugue. Scocpol exhaled loudly, and her eyes twitched. "Okay, she's done. Damn, I want to talk to her when she wakes up. Let me know, okay?"

"Right," said Richard. He was prepping a cool washcloth to wash her face, which had gone from contorted to relaxed with a few tics. "You're okay, Timera." He spoke close to her ear. "We got you covered. Seizure's over with, okay?" He patted her on the shoulder. "That was rough."

Markush checked his watch. He would wait thirty minutes before making arrangements to fly to Utah. Back in seven, he asked Reece about any further information he had from his recent travels.

Reece thought, and then a light went on. He hadn't told him about Caroline Marquet, the old nemesis of Arthur. He went into great detail, recounting the story of Arthur pushing her down the stairs in Berlin all those years ago.

"You've got to be kidding," said Markush. "Bizarre."

"It's fun to watch her with Arthur. We're hoping she'll somehow be able to help, although she's rather helpless herself."

"You might need a lady's touch. I wonder why she arrived there, how, for what reason?"

"She just popped up in Alem Ketema. You should have seen her on top of the jeep. She was hysterical. But she performed well at the circus. I think the men watching the cages were caught off guard. What I last remember is her snoring on the bed." He then told Markush of finding the body in the bathtub.

Markush scribbled as fast as he could, checking his watch. He paused. "I wonder. You don't think this Caroline could be some iteration of Dahlia, do you?"

Reece pondered that. "I hadn't considered it. I doubt it. Dahlia always takes the form of a young girl."

"Yeah, right," said Markush. He remembered Grayson and his evasive talk of witnessing the beginning of everything. He had to go to the liquor store and buy the Scotch.

The intercom buzzed. It was Laura. "Hey, Markush, a woman on the phone for you. It's Freddie's wife. She sounds desperate."

"Gotta go," and Markush ran to the nursing station. He pushed in and hurried to the blinking phone. "Markush here." His heart beat wildly.

"She's in bed! She was in bed! Alicia is in bed! How? Why? I tried to wake her up, but she wouldn't open her eyes. Should I call nine-one-one? What do I do? Oh God. I need to get back up there. I'm afraid she'll be gone again."

Markush had jumped from his chair. "That's super, great news. Go back and stay with her. Don't let her out of your sight. If she's breathing okay, do not call anyone. I'm going to schedule a flight there asap. You have my cell phone number, right?"

"Somewhere," said Gloria. "Give it to me again. This is a miracle." She wrote the number on the back of an envelope. "Let me go. I've gotta go."

Markush held the phone to his ear for a few seconds and then placed the receiver in its cradle. "I can't believe it. I just can't believe it."

Debbie had been listening. "What do you need me to

do, anything?" She guessed at what Markush had been told, but it sounded too far-fetched to be true.

"No, not that I can think of. I'm going to fly out today to Utah. You've got my cell phone number. Call with any new information." He dialed Godman Airfield and arranged for an urgent flight, final destination Cedar City, Utah. To save time, he withdrew the contact sheet from Freddie's chart and pushed it into his jacket pocket. "Okay, gotta go," and he rushed from the unit.

Claire looked at Debbie and shrugged her shoulders. "What was that all about?"

"Well," said Debbie. "I think he found Freddie's daughter." She shook her head.

"Holy moly," said Claire. She glanced at the monitors and saw that Reece was traveling again.

To the sound of snores, Reece opened his eyes. He slumped on the big soft chair, his neck bent and hurting. Caroline and Arthur lay asleep on the beds. He let himself slowly come around, remembering Markush bolting from his room. It could have meant only one thing, he hoped. Like waking from a shot of morphine, he gathered himself into a sitting position, fighting the dizziness. He was thirsty and headed to the bathroom.

He drank three glasses of water and belched. The water was still running in the shower, and he turned it off. Blood remained on the walls and the rim of the tub. *What's next?* Alicia had been taken care of for now. He had to focus on finding Mia. Should they go back to the Abba right away? Was there a need to recheck the circus? It was pointless to just wander around town drinking buster. Or was it? He wondered about Freddie saying that he traveled to Addis Ababa in the same world. Maybe Mia was in the big city. Maybe Freddie would know where to look. He splashed water on his face and hair, a big cowlick in back. He went dizzy and felt for the wall.

He walked back into the room, watching Arthur and Caroline dead asleep. He decided to wake Arthur and see what he thought. How many hours had passed? He had no idea.

"Arthur? Herr Schopenhauer?" He shook Arthur by the arm.

Arthur snorted, and his eyes opened. He yawned and stretched. "Dear God, how long have I been sleeping?"

"I think a few hours."

Arthur glanced over at Caroline, sprawled on her back, her scaffolded dress pushed into the air. "Yes, it is real. I thought perhaps that I had been dreaming. She sounds like a cow giving birth."

Reece laughed. "While you were sleeping, I seized. I saw Markush, and I think maybe that Alicia is back home. I won't know for sure until I go back." He moved to the foot of the narrow bed as Arthur struggled to sit up.

"That is capital," said Arthur. "A veritable miracle, if it is true."

"You thirsty? Your skin looks dry."

"Yes, very." He smoothed back his white hair.

"There's a faucet and glass in the bathroom."

Arthur grunted and stood, holding his lower back. "Thank you," and he went that way.

Reece decided that it was now or never. "Caroline? Frau Marquet?"

Her snoring hiccoughed, and she made chewing motions.

Reece shook her by the shoulder. "Caroline?"

"What? What? I am afraid...I am sleeping." She opened one eye and then the other, gazing up at Reece. "Well, hello, young man." She tried to push her dress down, but it rose again.

Arthur returned. "Ah, the madame wakes, but how she snores!"

At that, Caroline sat up, swallowed in her dress. A ringlet of hair sprang across her eyebrow. "That is no way to speak to a lady, I dare say."

"My apologies," said Arthur, and he bowed at the waist.

"Young Reece has some news. The little one, Alicia, has possibly returned home."

"That would be grand news. She was a common little thing but lovable, nonetheless. I was imagining making her a dress. No need to stare." She threw her legs and dress over the side of the bed. "How I need the salon. My hair is frightful."

"Are you thirsty?" asked Reece. "There's water in the bathroom. Everyone needs to be hydrated before we head out into the sun."

"That hideous room where the murder occurred? I cannot go in there. I will surely faint. Can you bring me some water, dear boy?"

Reece said, "Sure," and returned with a glass of water.

Caroline drank and requested another, which Reece fetched for her. He realized that he was beginning to treat them like his beloved grandparents. His grandmother Dora was ten years the junior of Horace. Reece was sure that they would visit him at Organon if they were allowed. He would discuss it with Markush when he went back.

"Merci beaucoup," said Caroline, and she stood.

"Arthur, do you think we should visit the circus again? Just in case? They have one empty cage now. Maybe on the way to see the Abba. We have to see him as soon as possible."

"Hmm," said Arthur. "I think not, as we might wind up in the cages beside that monstrous whale."

"Okay. But if we have no luck with the Abba, we could sneak in for a look on the way back, or at least I could."

"Perhaps." Arthur paced with his hands behind his back. "There is the matter of eating. Perhaps some buster and then we'll be on our way?"

"That would be lovely. I'm utterly famished," said Caroline.

"Yeah, okay," said Reece. "But let's not forget to tell Carl that we'll be back."

After Caroline had primped and fastened her hair with pins, the three entered the hall for their encounter with Carl. He was at his station, twiddling his thumbs, a stack of magazines beside him. He looked happy to see them.

"Well, lookie here. Here come the cornholers."

"We're going out," said Reece. "And we'll be back. You'll save the room for us, right?"

"You got my word. Getcha some of that tender cherry pie last night?" Carl crossed his legs, looked at the ceiling, and grabbed his crotch. He was wearing a yellow bandanna with a golf visor.

"We will be going along now," said Arthur, and he ushered Caroline in front of him. She wasn't quite sure what had been said, but the data fur made it plain, and she sniffed.

Outside, the hot tiny sun beat down on Gadam. A lone raven flew in circles. They walked toward the center of town and passed through a mist door into a buster bar. Reece recognized the giant faucet that seemed suspended in the air, water pouring from its mouth. Leonora, with the tattoo of a vine on her arm, was working the taps. Her flattened face gave her a feline appearance.

"What'll it be?" Leonora seemed deflated. "How about a glass of antifreeze for the lady?"

Reece laughed. "Just buster. Let's sit at the bar," and they did.

Leonora placed their bowls on the counter, and they drank and had another bowl, everyone now having to pee.

"Is there a restroom?" asked Reece.

"What, you been drinking water?" asked Leonora. She pointed to the far corner, a dark hallway.

"Yeah, water," said Reece.

There was only one restroom, and they took turns, then ventured back outside. Reece led the way until the edge of town. The circus was gone, the field empty.

"That settles that," said Reece, and he continued, pushing through the brush and thorns as the others followed.

Caroline held them up, her bushy black dress catching on the scrub, but they arrived at the ladder and ascended, Caroline nearly swooning at the top. Reece saw the Abba's small house and listened for the tap of the pick, but heard nothing. Reece knocked on the door. He knocked again and decided to open it. The Abba was on his bed, lying on his side. They stooped and entered.

"Abba?" asked Reece.

The Abba pushed up on an elbow, his arm shaking. The encounter with the Ark had left him nearly lifeless. He spoke in a low voice. Reece understood the word. *Dahlia.*

"He seems utterly exhausted," said Arthur. He approached the Abba's bed with a plaintive look. Caroline fanned herself in the stuffy room that reeked of sweat.

Reece tried his best again to explain what they wanted, saying "daughter" and pointing at the ancient book lying on the table. The Abba sat up and spoke as if that would be impossible. He scratched at the small sores on his neck.

"Damn," said Reece. "I don't want to kill him, but we

need him. Maybe if we had more money." He turned to Caroline. "Is there anything you have that we could pay with?"

"I gave of my coins, and I have no more," said Caroline.

"Perhaps he would take my shoes," said Arthur. He pointed at his shoes and then at the Abba, but got no reaction other than a blank stare.

"My pockets are empty," said Reece.

"I do have one thing, but I do hate to part with it." She fished the silk purse from her bosom and opened it. From it, she took a gold cross encrusted with small rubies and diamonds. "This was given to me in payment for a wedding dress that I made for a duchess."

Reece took the intricate cross and showed it to the Abba. He sat up and gazed at the object. He took it from Reece and looked at it for a long minute, and then, with a grunt, his legs were over the side of the bed. He put the cross into the folds of his yellow robe and groaned, as if in pain. Reece lent him a hand and helped him to stand. Sweat beaded on the Abba's forehead, and he looked as if he had a fever.

"Wuha," said the Abba, and he pointed at the clay pot with the yellow cup over its mouth.

"He wants water," said Reece. He tilted the jug and brought the cup to the Abba, who drank in slow gulps.

"He has my precious dainty," said Caroline. "I do hope we reap the rewards."

Arthur scowled at her.

The Abba walked to the book and opened it to the page of the pinched Cylinder. He pointed at Reece.

"Um, Mia, set lidj, my daughter," said Reece.

"Yellum, Mia," and he pointed again at Reece. He turned the page to the two circles, each with the same image of a human dressed in colorful clothes inside. He pointed to the first circle and then at Reece, and did the same for the second circle. "Dahlia."

"What does it mean?" asked Arthur. "He obviously wants you. Perhaps you can aid him in some way."

"Perhaps," said Reece. "I think he wants to send me to Dahlia." A thrill shot through him, and a symphony of music filled his head.

The Abba shuffled to the chest against the wall that held the sacred vest, and he lifted the vest with difficulty. The cloth was thick, the jewels heavy. There was an opening for his head, and he put it on, seeming to suffer from the added weight.

"Nah," and he beckoned for Reece to follow him. He would need to recall the Ark, it seemed, and Reece must be with him.

In silence, they followed the Abba to the green door in the rock. The Abba motioned for Reece to come inside and held up his hand, disallowing Arthur and Caroline.

"In boca lupo," said Arthur, wishing him good luck. He backed away as the Abba closed the door.

Inside, the Abba lit a candle and placed it on the floor. He motioned for Reece to kneel near the wall and mimed that he should cover his head. Reece knelt and put his head as close to his knees as he could, the cool of the room sending a chill through him. He wondered what would happen. Would he meet Dahlia? Would he die? Would he ever see Mia again?

The Abba took his position behind the resting place

of the Ark and began a guttural exposition in Ge'ez, the ancient language of Ethiopia. As he spoke, his strength seemed to gather, and his voice grew bold. Reece opened his eyes, sensing a great calamity in the making, and he shrank down as tight as he could go. There was a dull roar, followed by the blue light, soft at first but gradually intensifying. Reece shut his eyes and gripped his head. The dull roar became the sound of a thousand men marching on metal, and the blue light penetrated his eyelids. He muttered a prayer, the first in a long while.

The room filled with blinding light, the Abba holding forth his hands, the gems on his vest shining like lasers. The marching elevated to the scream of a jet, and Reece nearly fainted. What seemed like hours took only seconds, and all was quiet, as if the jet had crashed into a great wad of foam. Reece opened his eyes and listened, hearing only the labored breathing of the Abba. He looked, and the Ark was there, the Abba kneeling behind it on his knees. He waited for a minute and then went to the Abba and tried to rouse him. He seemed to be in a deep trance and only muttered. Reece feared looking at the Ark, and from the corner of his eye could see the cherubim's wings above the gold edifice.

"Abba Paulos?" He shook the Abba, who raised his head, his eyes looking dead. "Abba? What next? Mendeno?"

"Take from me this vestment," said the Abba.

Reece understood him and wondered. He lifted the jewel-encrusted vest from the Abba's limpid shoulders. Should he lay it on the ground? "Abba, tell me what to do next."

The Abba sat up straighter. "You must go to Dahlia. She is waiting. Stand in front of the holy Ark."

Reece, shaking from head to toe, did as he was told, soon standing in front of the gold-plated Ark. He waited and watched the Abba stand and waver, looking for something to hold onto, but there was only the Ark, and he seemed afraid to touch it.

"Prepare to meet thy maker, for ye shall be standing in her presence shortly." The Abba stumbled but caught himself. At first, he spoke in whispers and then again in Ge'ez, his voice rising.

Reece trembled, feeling sick, and stared at the space between the wings of the cherubim, feeling a great presence fill the room. The Abba's voice grew louder, and there appeared an arc of fire between the wings, which blinded Reece. He struggled to remain standing and opened his eyes to see a white vapor between the wings, which tempered the arc of fire. The Abba's voice had risen to a boom...

Markush was on his way to catch a jet to Cedar City, Utah. It was day shift, and the patients were being particularly noisy, especially Scocpol in ten and Grayson in three. Freddie was in the dayroom, smoking a cigarette beneath a ventilation hood. Debbie and Richard hustled from room to room, attending to their patients. Every thirty minutes, Shark and Gumbo switched hallways and checked the rooms. "Suck me." "Eat dog food and die."

Timera Scocpol had been comatose for an hour after her grand mal but had come around and was shouting for someone to help her. Her bald head made her face look very large, and with the EEG leads, like an alien.

"Timera, relax," said Richard. "You're back at Organon. Tell me what happened. What do you remember?"

"Lacie, my Lacie," said Timera. "She's in the tunnel. Dahlia put her there. I smoked a lot of dope and found her."

"Are you still in Shashamane with the Rastas?"

"Yes, with the Rastas in Shashamane. Haile Selassie is helping me. We went to Mikael Church. There was a priest. We gave him birr and ganja." Timera's eyes darted to and fro. "She's in the Cylinder."

"Tell me about the Cylinder," said Richard. "Like a tunnel?"

"Like a tunnel through time pinched in the middle. It's black and as big as the universe."

"Hmm," said Richard. "You saw Lacie, but you couldn't touch her?"

"No, no, the Ark showed me. The angels' wings. I saw her face, and she told me she was in the Cylinder."

"Can you go to the Cylinder?"

Timera squeezed her eyes shut. "I can try, I can try, but I don't really know. Dahlia put her there with the others."

"Who are the others?"

"The other childrens, too many to count."

Richard wrote down what she was saying. She looked desperate. "Okay, I think you need to rest for now, okay?" She was loosely restrained.

"I need to get back to see about the priest again. The Ras told me that the priest could bring her back from the tunnel, but he called it a Cylinder."

"Who's the Ras again?" asked Richard.

"Haile Selassie, Ras Tefari, his real name."

"Why did Dahlia put her in the tunnel?"

"To see what her music would do. She has the music." Timera pulled on her restraints. "Can you untie my hands? Just for a little?"

"I'm not supposed to, but you seem pretty stable now. Just don't get out of bed, okay? If you want to sit in the chair, I'll need to help you."

"I need to get out of this damned diaper."

"You're wet? Yeah, let's take care of that. You want to go a while without it? We can do that. I'll put a pad under you, though, just in case, okay?" He pulled the sheet down, unfastened the diaper, and turned her on her side. He pulled out the wet diaper and ran a blue pad beneath her. He took a warm, wet washcloth and wiped down her backside. "There, that should be better. If you're still stable by this afternoon, we'll get you a shower, okay?"

"Yes sir," said Timera. She raised the head of her bed. "She's in the Cylinder. Did I say that? Yeah, I said that."

"Yep, in the Cylinder. Okay, the TV remote is right there, and so is the call button. Just holler if you need something, okay?"

"Yes sir." She pulled the sheet down to her waist and took a few deep breaths.

Richard hurried out and went to check on Clark Peters in five. He passed eight and saw Debbie with Reece in seven. Peters was up in the chair, his hands wiggling at his mouth as if they were feelers. He looked creepy, like a giant cockroach.

"Hey, Mr. Peters." Richard washed his hands.

"Hello," said Peters. His voice was flat and monotone, like a robot. He'd been taking Thorazine for years but had recently been switched to a new antipsychotic. The years of Thorazine and Haldol had left him with the telltale shuffling gait and a variety of tics, his muscles always tense. He spoke garbled words.

It was lunch, and Richard took Peters' tray from the dietary assistant. "Thanks. Got your lunch here. You ready to eat?"

"Ready to eat," Peters said in a low growl. He flapped his hands like a dolphin's flippers. "Eating with Dah-lia." His eyes widened.

"Do you see Dahlia?" Richard looked around the room.

"Ye-es." He pointed to the foot of the bed and closed his eyes.

Richard nodded and put the overbed table with the tray in front of him. "Okay, as long as she behaves, right? Do you want her to be here?" He uncovered the entrée,

Salisbury steak with gravy.

Peters let out a low moan and opened his eyes.

"Okay, let's eat." He unwrapped the plastic fork and handed it to Peters, who took it upside down. Richard repositioned the fork. "Here, let me cut up your steak." He took the plastic knife and carved the soft brown steak into pieces.

"Urrr," said Peters. He glanced at the ceiling and held up the fork as if to ward off a demon.

Richard saw that he would need to feed him and took back the fork. He speared a piece of steak and held it to Peters' mouth. Peters' eyes darted, and he opened his mouth and chewed slow like a cow. Richard gave him some corn, which he spat out like little rocks. It took ten minutes, but he got most of the food into Peters and put his hand to the small of his back, aching from leaning over.

"No!" said Peters. He covered his head with his hands and whimpered, looking up.

"Oh Lord," said Richard.

In three, Debbie was with Grayson, trying to feed him and listen at the same time. He took a mouthful of the Salisbury steak and licked his lips. "Good?" asked Debbie.

"Yeah, and you look good enough to eat as well, pretty thing." He strained against the blanket restraint, his large fingers wiggling, seeking something to grab.

"No need to get fresh," said Debbie. "You have a wife, remember?"

"Oh hell, that bitch is gone. She gave me the boot." He took the spoon of corn and then a spoon of mashed potatoes. "Prison food. Just to keep me alive."

"It's better than most hospital food. Tell me more about

your last seizure. What did you see?"

"You'd like to know, wouldn't you? Maybe then Markush would fuck you, like a treat."

"God," said Debbie. She raised his bed so that she wouldn't have to lean so far. "We're gonna give you a bath later." It would take the two guards plus her to do the job. He hadn't had a bath in two days because it was so much trouble.

"I love the feel of your hand on my balls. You gonna put some baby powder on there, make it nice and slippery?"

"Whatever you like," said Debbie. She put the last piece of steak in his mouth, and he swallowed without chewing.

"I saw the beginning," he said. "Did Markush tell you? He wanted to know what there was at the beginning. He's going to bring me some Scotch, Laphroaig, twenty-year. Gotta make sure I'm properly reimbursed for my information. As far as I know, I'm the only one besides Dahlia who has been there."

"I'm afraid he had to leave suddenly. Probably won't be back for a couple days, an emergency." She was glad she hadn't said that before feeding him.

"What? The bastard! He promised. Goddamn Indian giver. Did you know that Gandhi was an Indian giver? Did you know that John the Baptist gave head? I've met them both, not bad guys, very helpful in the right ways. Jesus wiped." He made a loud sound, as if downshifting from fifth to first at high speed.

"Yeah, you said that Gandhi was helping you out to find your daughter."

"Damn straight. He's a puny little thing, but he's in touch, if you know what I mean."

"Take all the help you can, right?"

"You like the word sidelong? I pronounce it sid-a-long." He laughed. "I scare you, don't I?"

"No room here to be afraid. We're just taking care of you." Debbie pulled the overbed table away.

"Whatever, baby. I'll give you the riddle. What is there when there is nothing?"

Debbie paused at the sliding glass door. "What?"

Grayson frowned. "You're supposed to guess…" and he relaxed, his eyes closing, his EEG registering a confusion of spikes followed by gamma waves.

"Tell Gandhi, hey," said Debbie, and she was on to her next task.

Markush flew from Fort Knox on a six-seat Lear Jet C21A, headed directly to Cedar City, landing in under three hours. At the airport was an armored Lincoln Continental driven up from Las Vegas. The man with the placard that simply read "Markush" looked like a Navy SEAL. He wore black slacks and a thin, tight, short-sleeve shirt over his massive chest. Without speaking, they headed through the tiny airport to the taxi drop-off. High stratus clouds daubed the hot sun.

The swarthy man held the door for Markush, closed it, and hopped in the front seat beside the driver, a fortyish male with a buzz cut.

"You have the address?" asked Markush.

"Yes sir," said the driver. He leaned back to shake hands. "Call me Dot." The other guy turned as well. "Colonel Masters."

Markush shook their hands. "What do you know?"

"We know what you know, as far as this mission is concerned," said Masters. "A little girl. I take it, sir, that we're not acquiring her, just finding her."

Markush was taken aback. "Yeah, just to find her. There may be a chance that we get her and her mom to fly back to Fort Knox for debriefing. That's it for now. Afterward, I'll need to grab some chow."

They accessed Veteran's Memorial Highway heading north to East Nichols Canyon Road.

It took about ten minutes, and they entered the neighborhood, nice, neat houses with small green lawns.

"Nine-o-five, nine-o-seven, target is just ahead," said Masters. There was an American flag flying over the front porch, a silver Honda Odyssey in the driveway. Markush felt the blood rushing to his head, dizzy. He needed a tall drink of water, a stiff martini. Dot backed the car into the driveway and then parked on the street facing the way they had come. He would remain in the car with engine running. He and Masters tested their two-way radios.

Markush stepped into the heat. He was about to meet a little girl who had been abducted by Dahlia, or was he? He loosened the knot in his tie and wished that he'd dressed more casual.

"You follow me," said Masters. "I'll knock." He gazed at the house as if memorizing it. Before he could knock, the door opened, and he stepped back. "Gloria Mentone?"

"Yes, yes." She motioned them inside the cold house. Stairs led up to the second floor. Gloria was a plump woman with an underbite, wearing stretch pants and a loose top with green stripes. "Get in, get in."

Markush entered as if he were entering a church. He almost touched his head to see if he was wearing a hat. The spacious living room opened to their right, furnished with a pair of leather couches facing one another. Markush listened for the sound of a little girl.

"God, I'm so glad you're here. I just don't know what to do. You told me not to talk to anyone, and I haven't. I mean, what will the neighbors think? How will I explain it to the police?" She paced between the couches. "Let me go check on her, really quick. I'm so afraid she'll be gone again." She trotted up the stairs. Markush took a seat on the couch, and Masters patrolled the dining area, looking into the kitchen with its modern appliances. He pulled back the curtain on the door and looked into a small backyard made of gravel, seeing a wall made of rose-colored stone.

Markush wanted to sit on his hands. He could barely contain himself and suddenly needed to pee like a racehorse, but Gloria was descending the stairs, her black hair a mess.

"She's there, still sleeping. She's exhausted and even snoring. I've never heard her snore before."

Markush stood. "That's super. That's great. May I use your restroom?"

She pointed out the door, and he disappeared for a minute and then returned. Masters was sitting on the couch facing the large living room window. Markush sat, but Gloria remained standing as if on pins and needles.

"You called, and I thought it was a joke. I hung up, but I had to go look. She was on top of the bedspread, just lying there. I tried to wake her, but she was so sleepy."

"It's a miracle," said Markush. "There's so much to explain, what I know, but I also need to find out what you know, what Alicia knows. Would you be willing to fly to Fort Knox? I really need to talk with Alicia about what she has experienced."

Gloria sat on the edge of the couch. "Goodness, I haven't thought about anything except her waking up. It's too soon. She needs rest. But my baby is back. How, how did it happen? I mean, Freddie was right all along. I feel like a dunce."

"It's perfectly understandable. Everyone thought what you thought. This is the kind of situation that defies logic."

"It defies everything. I mean. I saw him...kill her. He was in a rage, just hitting her over and over. I tried to stop him, but he's so strong. He's a mechanic, you know."

"And you're not alone," said Markush. "There are others like her, others that seemed to have been killed, but they're impostors...sent by Dahlia."

Gloria frowned. "This talk of Dahlia. I can't get my head around it. Who is Dahlia? Why would she want to kidnap my daughter and then allow such a terrible thing to happen?"

Markush explained his basic concept, that Dahlia was an alien entity, that Dahlia seemed to have the power of spanning universes, that there was something Dahlia was trying to understand. "Your daughter, Alicia, she was sensitive to music?"

"Yes, obsessed with it. Not everyday music, but the music in things like trees and food and even people."

"Well," said Markush, "I think that's what attracted Dahlia to Alicia, her ability to hear this music. It's just an educated guess. Freddie has the gift as well. That's how he knew it wasn't Alicia when he killed the impostor."

"It still doesn't make any sense. How did she wind up back in her bed? That's just so ridiculous. Did Dahlia bring her back?"

Masters listened with one ear, his other ear plugged with the two-way radio.

"It gets even crazier," said Markush. "We have another patient with Freddie. He found Alicia. Like Freddie, he has seizures and travels to other places and times. There was a monk. Have you heard of the Ark, the Ark of the Covenant?"

Gloria sighed. "Well, we're Lutheran. Of course, I've heard of the Ark in the Old Testament."

"From what I know, the Ark, the original Ark, is in Ethiopia. It has powers that we don't understand. The priest used the Ark to send back Alicia."

Gloria shook her head. "How she got back probably doesn't matter to me, at least not just yet. I guess I just have to believe you. I thought you were as crazy as Freddie. I'm sorry for giving you such a hard time."

"No need for that," said Markush. "I can't imagine being in your shoes. I would have thought I was crazy as well."

"That makes me feel better." She stood. "I have to check on her again." She hurried up the wooden stairs stained a rich caramel.

"It's a strange world," said Masters. "Do you think she'll let you see the girl?"

"I think so. I hope so."

Gloria descended. "Still there." She sounded like a happy child, but worried beyond reason.

"Do you think I could see her?" asked Markush. "I promise not to wake her. I mean, if she wakes up, I'd like to talk with her, but I'm just as amazed as you are."

Gloria thought. "You're not here to take her away, are you?"

"No, no," said Markush. "She's your daughter. You're in control. But I strongly recommend bringing her to see us at Fort Knox. This could have implications for national and global security."

"I'll have to think about it. But you can see her if you like. Just a peek. And your friend will stay down here?"

"Not a problem, ma'am," said Masters. He was getting

bored.

"Okay, come on."

Markush followed her up the stairs and saw a bathroom. He followed Gloria to the end of the hall. The door was open. He looked in and saw a little girl with black hair lying on the bed, a Winnie the Pooh blanket covering her legs. He stared, absorbing the experience. He watched Gloria tiptoe on the carpet and adjust the blanket. What could he say? It was her. *Alicia.* He had photos of her at his office. He had a photo from the funeral of the impostor who was buried nearby.

Gloria turned and pointed at the stairs. "That's enough for now," she said in a quiet voice.

Markush nodded and turned, looking over his shoulder.

The green door had flown open, and a smell of molten steel lingered in the air. Arthur peeked into the rock-hewn chamber and saw nothing at first.

"What's happened?" asked Caroline.

Arthur called out. "Reece? Abba Paulos?" He stepped down. The Ark was not there. Reece was gone. He peered over the edge of the wooden pedestal and saw the Abba collapsed on the floor. He went to his side and struggled to kneel. His old bones creaked. "Dear God, Abba?" He shook his arm. He couldn't tell if the Abba was breathing.

"Madame!" he said. "Come and help." He still couldn't bear to say her name.

Caroline lingered at the door, afraid to enter.

"Damn, Caroline! Come!"

Caroline entered, hesitant. "Is he dead? What a fright."

Arthur shook the Abba, and the Abba raised an arm. Arthur let him be for a minute until his eyes opened. "Dear Abba, we will take you to your bed. Come, Madame, and assist. We shall each take an arm," but he was very heavy with the holy vest, and Arthur removed it carefully and placed it against the wall.

Together, and with great effort from both, they lifted the Abba. He dragged between them as his sandaled feet scuffed the rock floor. He was mumbling. They had to lift the slight Abba up the two steps. They rested at the doorway and walked him to his small house. Inside, Arthur took over, placing the Abba on his bed. The Abba opened his eyes and thanked him, asking for water, wuha, which

Arthur discerned. He ordered Caroline to prepare the Abba a cup of water, and she complied, but said, "No need to be so stern with your commands, your majesty."

Arthur grumbled and helped the Abba to lift his head and drink. Within seconds, the Abba's eyes closed, and he entered a deep slumber. Arthur felt lost without Reece and looked about the small room, his eyes falling on the ancient book.

"What about that vest the Abba was wearing?" asked Caroline. "I would so like to see the stitching and those rare stones."

"It is better to let sleeping dogs lie," said Arthur. "It could prove harmful, having some great power, which we do not understand."

"Perhaps," said Caroline, "but I should like to see it."

"At your own peril, my lady," said Arthur. He turned to the book, skipping pages of Ge'ez script, looking at the illustrations. One page showed a man sitting inside a circle of fire and flying, surrounded by angels and demons. He found the page with the drawing of the Cylinder that narrowed at its center. The Abba had pointed out the most distant figure, a black angel, as Dahlia. Her flowing dress was black, her hair golden, and her skin brown. She seemed to hold a staff with a burst of lightning coming from its end. The other figures in white and bright colors with blank faces seemed to be lesser beings, perhaps minor demons. He turned, and Caroline was gone.

Caroline stopped at the green door, listening for some unheard noise, some unseen being. She descended to the rough stone floor, letting her eyes adjust to the gloom, and searched for the holy raiment, finding it lying against the wall, the twelve jewels glinting. The cloth was a weave of textured linen and wool, filtered with gold threads. She could not tell how the stones were attached, seeming to float on the intricate pattern of whorls. She looked for stitching in the dim light, but it appeared to be seamless. As if her hand was another's, she hesitated and touched the stiff cloth. She felt a small thrill, but she was still alive. There was no burst of light. She recalled the chanting of the Abba, thinking it was required to enliven the vest. She let her fingers run across the jewels and wondered at their size and value. She would be able to buy the finest house in Berlin. She reached and then picked up the garment, which was very heavy. There was a neck opening and two embroidered holes with which to attach, perhaps, some other larger garment.

Against her better judgment, she struggled and lifted the raiment and slipped it over her head. She felt dizzy with its weight and couldn't resist standing behind the wooden bier on which the Ark had rested. Perhaps she would be imbued with some lasting power? She tried in vain to quote some remote scripture, realizing her lack of knowledge, and frowned. "Make me rich!" she said to the cave-like room, but nothing happened. Perhaps if she called on this Dahlia? She called out the name, and a weird light appeared, frightening her, cementing her in place. The light hovered over the table and grew in brightness, blinding her, and she sank to her knees.

In the light there appeared a young girl, perfect in every way, skin brown, eyes blue, and golden hair. Caroline sensed she was being watched, sensed a great heaviness in the room, and opened her eyes, amazed at the sight. She wanted to shut her eyes, but could not. Her scalp tingled, and she remembered seeing this little girl as a child, the one who visited her at night, the one who had covered her head with what seemed like a mask. She had screamed, and her mother, who was also a seamstress, had come running.

"Please," said Caroline, her voice cracking.

Dahlia spoke, but it was a voice of many voices, and Caroline did not understand. A powerful music inundated the room, one that Caroline found ugly and repulsive. She covered her ears, but the noise continued, and her scalp felt electric, on fire. She said, "No! Stop!" and pulled the vest from her neck and fell backward, shutting her eyes.

All was quiet. Caroline waited, as she did when she was a child, listening, hoping that the apparition was gone. She lifted her head and, seeing nothing, removed the vest with its jewels and hurried from the chamber into the dazzling sunlight, holding her prize. She wanted to run, to be back in Berlin, to know the safety of her own small rooms above that of a baker called Jurgenson.

She returned to the Abba's humble home, Arthur still perusing the ancient book. He turned and started. "Caroline, put that vest away! You'll bring down harm on us all. It is a holy object that belongs to the Abba." He looked very old.

"But what need of it does he have? We can use the jewels to pay for our return home. I can't bear this place any longer."

Arthur closed the book. "Madame, the only one who may be able to send us home lies on that bed. Will you sell him what belongs to him?" He wanted to grab the vest from her, but feared touching it again. Why was it not harming her? "Place it in the chest. We will find money by other means."

The Abba slept, his eyes twitching beneath his lids.

Caroline sighed and carried the holy object to the chest, placing it there and closing the lid. "When he wakes, he must send me home, as he did with the little girl. I can't suffer you another minute, I'm afraid."

"Dear God," said Arthur, "do you think I value your presence? Certainly not, but I have taken you on. You may prove valuable yet. I am here, as far as I can tell, to help young Reece find his daughter, and we will remain until such time." He hit the table for emphasis.

"You old bore." She glanced at the chest and the Abba.

"He must rest. I fear that we will kill him with our asking of favors." He stood. "For now, we should go back to the room. Reece has left us, and there is nothing more we can do for now."

Caroline changed her tack. "I saw Dahlia in the cave. I called her...and she came."

"What?" said Arthur. "Dear God, you lunatic! Did you wear the vest?"

"Yes, it's very finely made, a real wonder. I would like to study it further. Perhaps I can call for this lost daughter, and she will appear. Perhaps I am the key and not this slumbering priest." She looked confident in her speech.

"And you saw Dahlia? How did you know it was she?"

"I just did. She visited me as a child. I had almost forgotten until now."

"How did she appear?" asked Arthur.

Caroline described her, the skin, the eyes, the hair.

Arthur sat and rubbed his head. "Then it's true, it must be. I was also visited as a child by the same being, although I did not know her name. You must be very careful, Caroline. No more wearing of the vest, only the Abba. It will be the death of you otherwise, I'm sure."

Having survived the encounter had emboldened Caroline. "We'll see about that, old man. You and that dusty book disgust me. I shall never forgive you for pushing me down the stairs."

"Ha!" said Arthur. "I pushed you through the door, and then you lay at the bottom of the steps, saying that you had fallen, that I had pushed you down the stairs. You are a liar, Madame."

"And you're an old grouch," said Caroline.

The Abba was snoring, oblivious.

"I suppose we're bound to help one another, dear...Caroline, so let's be on our way before we lose our room."

Arthur pushed through the door, and Caroline followed, brushing off her ragged dress. They made their way back to Gadam, wandered as if lost, and stopped for a bowl of buster at the establishment with the giant fishhook. The old man with the shaved head was there. He drew down two bowls and placed them on the counter.

"I'll bet he's a swell fuck," said the bartender to Caroline. "Does he put his pinky in your wrong hole?"

Caroline was drinking and coughed. "You are a delinquent, sir. A shame to those of us who may be human."

Arthur smiled. "You, my dear fellow, have the face of an old dog."

"Thanks," said the old man. He took a soft cloth and rubbed the fishhook, which was ten feet high.

They drank in silence and, within half an hour of bumbling about, found the building with their room. Carl was there, staring at an electronic device.

"Well, hello, ladies and gents, back for a quickie?"

"Yes, hello to you as well," said Arthur. He pushed Caroline in front of him and down the hall to their room.

"No need to be so rough," said Caroline.

"No need to dawdle with that ruffian," said Arthur. He opened the door and hurried in. There was someone in the room. "Yes?" asked Arthur. Caroline had closed the door and gasped.

"Hello! I heard there was a vacancy, so here I am." He was dark brown and as tall as Arthur. His hair was red, but his beard was black. The beard reached his chest. "I'm glad you dog fuckers lost that loser. Anyway, I've got the soft chair, or so the data fur tells me. By the way, I'm Clem."

Arthur pondered their options and came up blank.

Reece felt that his eyes were closed, but when he opened them, they were already open. He seemed not to be breathing, but he did not feel breathless. He was in a vast colorless room inundated by a fierce blue light that should have hurt his eyes but did not. He was sitting on a chair that seemed more air than chair. There was no particular sound, other than a hum that skipped a beat here and there, as if searching for the perfect pitch. He heard a distant giggle, and there in the distance was a speck that grew larger, taking on the shape of a human, and then that of a little girl. His heart leaped. *Mia!* But he couldn't form the word. He wanted to stand but felt compelled to sit.

The little girl drew closer, and it wasn't Mia, but those eyes, the eyes of all those little girls that bedeviled Mia. The blue eyes shot with infinite depth or perhaps jest. She was smiling and singing a little song about birds and flowers. Her voice was sweet and off-key, just a bit too loud. She skipped, as little girls do, and soon was within a body's length. She looked at Reece, as if pondering his soul, turning her head sideways, smiling.

Reece tried to remember the sequence of events required for speaking. The word came out dull and forced. "Hello?"

"Hello. Did you come for your daughter?" It seemed as if this question were routine.

"Yes," said Reece. "Mia, my daughter. What's your name?"

"I'm Dahlia, but you already know that." She wore a yellow shift that touched the tops of her bare feet. Her golden hair glowed in the blue light. "Mia was jealous of me, and that made me sad." She took on a pouty look, turning down the corners of her mouth.

Reece was stymied. He'd always been rude to these little girls, waiting and watching for them to hurt Mia. The little girl in Richmond, what was her name?

"Her name was Charlotte," said Dahlia.

"Right," said Reece. "She was trying to hurt Mia, to harness her for you, to salvage everything that Mia knows about music, the music of...nothing."

"I didn't mean to hurt Mia. I wanted to help her. She has a secret."

"And you want her secret?" asked Reece. He took a breath even though it didn't seem he needed to.

"Of course. I want to know. I have to know. I never had a mommy." She made a sad face again, turning down the corners of her mouth.

Reece wondered what that meant. "Do you mean you've always been around? That you didn't have a mother in that sense?"

"You're pretty smart," said Dahlia. She spoke like an adult.

"What is this big secret that Mia has? Is she here?" He looked in the four directions at the endless space, the electric blue light.

"I can tell by your music that you know, but you haven't thought of it yet. Mia knows, though. She won't tell me. That's why I get mad at her. She's not nice to me."

Reece felt chilled. "Give me a clue. What do you want to know? What will it change?"

"Well, then it will be like I have a mommy. I'll know where I came from. Mia knows."

Reece thought. "But you've always been here? How is that?"

"There was something before me, but I don't know what it was. Now everything is infinite. It didn't used to be that way. I have too many places to go to find the answer. I'll never find my mommy if Mia doesn't help me."

"Does it have to be Mia?"

"No. There's lots of Mias. I just have to choose them one at a time. And lots of Alicia's. And lots of Violets. And lots of Janitas. And Jills. And Betties."

"What about me? Lots of Reeces? Why did you visit me? Why did you map my head with that mask?"

"You had a daughter later on, right? I had to get you when you were little. Maybe Mia would tell you the secret, and then I would know. I don't really like boys, though. They're mean sometimes."

Reece laughed. "You remind me so much of Charlotte. Is there just one of you?"

"You can only see one, but I'm pretty much everywhere all the time. I live at the center of the Cylinder, at the Pinch, the one you saw in the book. I like the Abba, but I didn't give him permission to send you here. You know you can't go back."

"I'm not dreaming? This is a real place?"

"No, you're not dreaming. What's a real place? I don't understand. You're here, right?"

"I mean, is this some sort of universe different from the one I came from? Is this just one big room?" asked Reece.

"You're in the middle of it all. There are others like you.

They live over there." She pointed. "I call it Dogtown. You'll just be here, is all."

"Dogtown? What will I do here?" asked Reece. The novelty of the situation was wearing off. He was getting worried. "But I have to find Mia. Bring her home."

"Not anymore. Just pretend that I'm Mia." She smiled, showing her perfect white teeth. "You can be my daddy." Her brown skin glowed in the blue light. All she needed was a pair of golden wings.

"Look, just tell me where she is. Even if I can't go there, I need to know. I need to know that she's alive, that she's okay."

"She's okay. She's in Gadam 3976. You missed her by a few years. But a whole other universe, too. She has a pet monkey that she takes care of. She named it Marvin."

"Marvin the monkey," said Reece. "Emma had a monkey named Marvin."

"Yep," said Dahlia. "Mia remembers you talking about it."

"Is anyone taking care of her? I mean, the people in Gadam 3981 are very strange, and there's no children there." Reece touched his face to make sure he was real, and he was.

"Yep, I sent someone to take care of her. You heard of Helen Keller? She's from Alabama, too. I sent Helen. They live together. I sent Arthur to be your friend in Gadam. He's a nice old man. He didn't really push that lady down the stairs like she said. Plus, she was making a lot of racket."

Reece's jaw hung open. "Helen Keller? Why her? I guess I understand why Arthur."

"No reason. It just seemed like they'd get along. I mapped Helen when she was little, right before she learned to talk. There's lots of Helens, though." She frowned again, as if her life was just too much.

Reece thought of a Helen Keller joke.

"Don't make fun of her. That's what I mean about boys," said Dahlia. "I just want my mommy."

"What if I could help you find your mommy? If you send me to Mia, I'll ask her what the secret is, and then you'll know. Or maybe you can bring her here." He was desperate.

"No, you can't leave, and someone would have to send her here. I could hide her in the Pinch, but that would be that."

Reece leaned back in the pliable chair. "Can I touch you? Are you real?"

"I'm here, but I don't want you to touch me." She did a pretend hopscotch on the smooth, translucent floor.

Reece had a thousand questions. "What about my body, my body at Organon? I suppose I'm having some kind of epic seizure there."

"I'm sorry. That body will probably die. I can't help it, though."

"Oh," said Reece. "So, I'll just hang out in Dogtown for the rest of my days."

"There are no more days, just you, here."

"But I have to find Mia. You put an impostor in her place. There has to be a way for me to go back. Are you saying that you won't let me find Mia, that I'm forbidden to find her?"

"I need Mia more than you do, Mr. Reece. You think

you need her, but you don't. There's lots of Mias out there you can have, just not this one. I'm learning from her."

"Look, this is crazy. I can help you. When I find Mia, I'll make sure she helps you. I promise." Reece stood, and the floor was electric smooth. "It could even be that I can will myself back to Organon, back to Gadam. I made myself seize and travel at Organon. I know I did."

"Seizures don't work here. You'll like Dogtown. You'll make friends. Would you like to visit?"

"I need to leave this place, but maybe someone here can help me."

"No, I'm afraid not," said Dahlia. "They can't leave either."

"How many are there in Dogtown?"

"Oh, billions and billions. It goes on forever."

"But I don't see anyone else around. Why is it empty here?"

"Because this place is infinite. I don't really know how, but it is. I may never see you again. That's usually what happens."

"God, it just gets worse. Okay, I'll just wander off that way and I'll be in Dogtown and I'll meet other people?"

"You're funny, Mr. Reece. I need to go. I'm always learning and learning. I have to find my mommy. Okay? Bye bye." She turned and walked away.

Reece watched her diminish in the distance. "Hey!" But she was soon just a speck, and then he decided to follow her.

Before leaving Utah and Alicia, Markush arranged for a military attaché to take up residence in the Mentone's residence. It would be his job to represent Gloria as she began the process of reintroducing her daughter into the community and of reversing the murder charges against Freddie. In addition, a guard was assigned for security, much to Gloria's relief. There would be no official attempt at trying to explain the reappearance of Alicia, but a campaign to characterize the whole affair as a hoax was in progress.

Markush arrived back at Fort Knox the day after he had left. Gloria had allowed him to see Alicia one last time and had reluctantly allowed him to draw a sample of blood as she continued to sleep and take a baby tooth that Alicia had lost a year earlier. Back home, he took a forty-five-minute power nap and then rejoined the crew at Organon. It was two in the afternoon, and his first task was to have the blood sample and tooth sent to CODIS, the FBI agency responsible for maintaining and analyzing a national DNA database. The samples were taken by a junior officer associated with base security to be hand-delivered in Washington, D.C.

No one had called him from Organon during his absence, which was a good sign. Claire buzzed him onto the unit, and Freddie Mentone met him in the hall. He'd been waiting for him to return. Shark stood from his chair, just in case Freddie had bad intentions. He wasn't supposed to hang out in the hall. Markush put his hand out, and

Freddie shook it.

"Hey, I know you've been away. Debbie told me that maybe there was a new development with Alicia. I don't think she was supposed to tell me, but she did. And that guy Reece has been seizing now for two days. I was hoping he would come around and have some news."

"Freddie, I can't say anything just yet. Let me check in with the nurses and the other patients, and then we'll talk. There have been developments. Will that work?"

"Yeah, but have you found her? Is that what your trip was about? I need to know." His eyes looked desperate, and Shark was moving his way.

"Listen to the doctor," said Shark. "Give him some space."

"It's okay," said Markush. "He has a right to be concerned. Just give me ten minutes to get caught up. We'll talk, I promise. It's been a hectic couple of days." He turned and knocked on the nursing station door. Claire buzzed him in.

"What's up?" asked Markush.

Claire's face registered relief. She got bored watching the monitors. "Well, lots of activity since you've been gone. Grayson in three had another grand mal, but he's back."

"Damn, I promised him some Scotch. Shit. I'll have to go off base. How's Scocpol doing?"

"She had the grand mal but has been stable since," said Claire.

Debbie was knocking, and Claire buzzed her in.

"Hey there, good to see you," said Debbie.

"How's Reece doing?" Markush glanced at the monitor and grimaced. "Shit, what's that?" The tracing showed long, slow waves with a shallow amplitude.

"You got me," said Debbie. "He's been out for the past two days, but his vitals are stable. I put the feeding tube back in, per the standing order."

"Do his pupils react to light?" asked Markush.

"Yeah, but sluggish, pinpoint almost. I didn't call since he was stable. Not much we can do, right?" She sat down to chart. "How was your trip?"

"Groundbreaking, but I can't talk about it just yet." He stared at Reece's EEG. "Damn, almost comatose."

"It's like he's slipped away," said Debbie.

Markush went to the small bank of lockers and opened his. He took two small magnets that fit his hand. "I'll be right back."

He walked to seven and gazed at Reece lying on his side, propped with a foam wedge. His eyes were open to slits. Markush placed the magnets on either side of Reece's head, the temples, and watched the EEG. There were a few spikes, but as soon as he removed the magnets, the long, slow waves reappeared, uninterrupted. He tried it again with the same result and held them there for a full minute. "Damn." He listened to the slow thud of Reece's heart and checked his pupils, pinpoint like Debbie said.

He saw Richard passing in the hall and followed him to Grayson's room. Freddie was in the dayroom waiting for him, and Markush held up a finger. "So, how's the big guy?"

Richard stroked his neat goatee. "Traveling off and on. He's gone now. He keeps talking about Dahlia, though, in riddles."

"He's onto something but won't tell me," said Markush.

"Yeah, he wants that Scotch," said Richard.

"Right," said Markush. "Let me know when he comes around. I'll have to jaunt to the liquor store."

"Will do."

Markush decided he should speak to Freddie and went to the dayroom. Freddie was smoking.

"Have a seat. Tell me what you know."

Markush thought. The information was classified. "This is not to leave this unit. We've found Alicia. She's back in Utah—"

"The fuck," said Freddie. He put his head in his hands. "No way. How? Why? When?"

"Day before yesterday. Reece had something to do with it. Alicia was in the same place he travels to, as he told you. A monk helped him and sent her back. I saw her. It was her. Your wife is overjoyed, but paranoid that she'll disappear again." Markush was already chiding himself for breaking the news, but how could he not?

"Wow, how do I thank you? I mean, I don't believe it. Are you sure? You were there? You flew there?"

"Yep, out and back. We're arranging to reintroduce her, to paint the whole thing as a hoax. It's the only way. The news will have a field day, but that's okay. We have personnel on site, though, to keep her and Gloria safe."

"What about me? I'm not a murderer anymore? Can I just leave? I need to see her for myself."

Markush cleared his throat. "You'll need to be patient. It's not an overnight thing. Plus, you still travel. Or at least I think you do. You can still help us find the others."

"Yeah, but I can't stay here. I've got to see her."

"It may be that you no longer travel, now that you don't

need to. Let's give ourselves a week to let this situation pan out, okay?"

Freddie grimaced. "Goddamn, how am I supposed to just sit in this place?"

"I know it's hard," said Markush. "Just work with us for another week, okay? I'll bring you a gift from the liquor store, a way to celebrate. What would you like?"

"Shit," said Freddie. "A six-pack of cold brew would be nice. Nothing fancy, a lager of some sort. Yeah, celebrate is the word for it. Hot damn, I can't believe it."

"Neither can I," said Markush. "Okay, let me go. I want to be ready when Grayson is back. I promised him some Scotch."

"Yeah, right, Doc. This is fantastic. So can I tell Debbie?"

"She's sworn to secrecy, but if you could hold off, that would be great, just for now." Markush stood.

"Thanks. This is probably the best day of my life." Freddie laughed.

"Could be mine too," and he left the unit, headed to the liquor store.

He slid into his Volvo and drove to the gate, toward Radcliff. He pondered the events. What did it mean that one of the abducted girls was back? He thought about Reece and Mia. How would this affect them, and where was Reece? He was desperate to know what had transpired, desperate for information about Dahlia. A car horn blew, "Shit," and Markush jerked his car back into his lane. Grayson had teased him with a riddle. More or less had said that he knew what Dahlia was looking for. The key would be to crack open Dahlia, right? He soon reached the liquor store, a hole in the wall, but they had a great selection of Scotch. Out of his Volvo, he felt for his wallet, and it wasn't there. "Damn!"

Caroline hid behind Arthur. "We can't share a room with a stranger! It's bad enough that we have to share between us."

Arthur grunted and pushed her away.

"Nice to meet you as well," said Clem. "Which one of you smells like piss? I'm up from Addis Ababa, taking a little tour." He lay across the big chair, his legs dangling over the side, his beard resting on his chest. His red hair was a bit wild.

Caroline folded her arms across her chest, a look of utter dismay on her face.

"It seems to be a custom of this place, this sharing of rooms, so we welcome you, Clem." Arthur sat on the bed closest to him. "It is in the data fur that our young friend Reece has departed but no more. Are you experienced with this data fur? It is all very much overwhelming for me."

"Hey, I'm out from the big city, getting away from information. The last thing I need is some heavy data fur. That's all people do, sit around and troll for useless information. One thing leads to another. It's endless. Bad for the brain. Goddammit, you're from Berlin. You pushed Caroline down the stairs, or did you? See, there it goes. Oh Lord, some egghead has discovered the X-ray. Stop!"

"It seems that you have a natural affinity for this data fur, but that you are weary of processing the information? Still, you could be of some use to us. We only require one bit of data."

"What is it that we require?" asked Caroline. "I forgot."

"You want to find this Mia, for God's sake," said Clem. "No, no, no! I won't even try. You guys are just ruining my vacation."

Arthur stood back. "No need to overreact, sir. The little girl's location is critical to us. Our only other hope is the Abba Paulos, but he requires money for his services, of which we have none, plus we nearly killed him with our last task, the sending away of young Reece." He spoke with his hands behind his back.

"Yes, as he says," said Caroline. She fanned herself, excused herself to the restroom, resigned to the residual blood there.

"Would you take credits for your information?" asked Arthur. "You could use them at the local whorehouse, the purple stars."

"Yeah, I see your five hundred. I could use a good fuck. I'll do a bit of trolling, five hundred credits, because it's my goddamn vacation. Otherwise, I might spot you some info. Let me check the prices at the brothel. Hmm, double penetration is six hundred credits, that's no good. A straight fuck is four-fifty. So, we're good, done deal."

Arthur noted that his credits were now fifty. "This data fur is quite handy for finances."

Caroline returned and sat on the bed as if ready for a picnic. "Have we located the little girl? I do wish we could rid ourselves of this task. It seems never-ending, and I should like to return home."

"He's going to process the data fur for us, to locate Mia," said Arthur. "Clem, what is your livelihood? You are rather helpful in a way that most have proven futile."

"I make buster. Yeah, you like it, don't you? Want the recipe, don't you? I'm a no talkie, though." Clem laughed.

"I suppose the recipe is in the fur."

"One would think," said Clem. He stroked his beard and patted his belly. "So, let's get on with it. Your credits are hot off the griddle. Let me give her a look-see. You damn vacation upsetters."

Arthur smiled, but then looked grim as Clem leaned back in the chair, closing his eyes. Caroline dabbed at the corner of her mouth with a bit of tissue from the bathroom. "He seems to be sleeping. Is he amusing us?"

"Madame, no interrupting. Your voice is least needed at the moment." The words "Don't get your panties in a wad" came to him.

Clem made a humming noise. "She's not in the circus... something about time, something about the pinched Cylinder, whatever that is. Uh oh, Dahlia coming in loud and clear. Uh oh, Dahlia latching onto my feed." His face reddened, and he gasped. He choked and coughed. "Gadam, thirty-nine-seventy-six. Marvin...the Monkey... Helen... Keller!" He arched and let out a gasp." He seemed a bit woozy, his eyes watering. "Damn, I didn't expect that. Almost got drawn in, to the fur that is. So, you happy?"

"Gadam, thirty-nine-seventy-six," said Arthur. "Just a few years back. Are you sure? Is there a guarantee? How do I know you're telling the truth?"

"Indeed," said Caroline. She yawned, thinking of her encounter with the holy vest.

Clem relaxed and took a deep breath. "That's gracious. Calling me a liar? Even with Dahlia on the feed. That alone should clue you in. But it could be a trap. A nasty trap."

"No, not a liar, sir, just a precaution," said Arthur. "If we engage the Abba to somehow place us there, we need to be absolutely certain. I'm sure you understand."

Clem lay back as if weary. "I get you, old man. We're done here. This is my vacation after all, and you've nearly ruined it. I hope I can get it up. I'd say I've done a bang-up job for you. But Dahlia's onto you, on the wavelength if you know what I mean."

Caroline's smile drooped. "This talk of Dahlia makes me tired. I've spoken with her. I wore the vest. I'm sure she's reasonable, being a jeune fille, just a little girl."

"Ha, I suppose you're the expert," said Arthur. "Why don't you lead the way, my dear, and conquer all with your wanton curiosity? If I didn't know better, I'd say your mind works as does that of a little girl."

"Say, I like your style," said Clem to Caroline. "You take credits? I could put some juice into that dry cunt of yours. Next, you'll be saying you invented the data fur or that you know the recipe for buster."

Arthur laughed.

Caroline had turned red, visibly shaken. "You, sir, are a scoundrel. I wish to not speak with you and your vulgar language." She harrumphed.

"Simmer down, Grandma Moses, whoever that is. But maybe you do think like a little girl, and that could prove useful. Dahlia and all."

Arthur nodded. "Perhaps you are useful after all, my dear. But we should not stand here bickering; we have business to care for, five years to traverse. The Abba is not fit to help us, plus we have no money. It may be that you could facilitate our transfer with the holy raiment. I hate to admit it, and I must excuse myself."

He went to the bathroom and saw the yellow urine in the bowl. The data fur kicked in, and he found the silver button, sending the waste gurgling away, then adding his own, wondering at such a device. He splashed water on his face and drank from the glass, returning somewhat refreshed.

"Yes, it will take a lady's touch, I'm afraid," said Caroline. "I do feel the burden of my necessity in this...quest."

"Why don't you two skedaddle and let old Clem here get some shut eye before he digs into a big juicy pussy. Ah, this is the life. Vacation."

Arthur rubbed his hands together. "Madame, shall we? Shall we put your prowess to the test?"

Caroline examined the holes in her poofy dress. "Perhaps I can change there, in this thirty-nine-seventy-six. There seems to be no trade in clothes here. I do miss my fitting room and sewing tools. I look a veritable shambles." She looked lost in reverie and stood.

"Come," said Arthur. "Young Reece is dependent upon our work. And, Clem, sir, please make sure that this room remains taken, should we fail. No need for more bloodshed."

"Will do, dingleberry. This will make for great water cooler talk at the factory. Mind if I stretch out on the bed there?"

"Yes, I mean no," said Arthur, and he led Caroline into the hall. They walked past Carl, who was on his electronic device. He hocked a big one and swallowed it as they passed.

"Careful of the worm holes," said Carl.

"Of course," said Arthur, hurrying past.

"And good day to you," said Caroline.

They exited. A spherical object coursing along paused and scanned them. Caroline shooed it away. "Go, go!" To steel themselves, they stopped in a bar, a red star, the one with the polar bear mural. Lura waved at them as if they were old friends.

"Perhaps some Ketel would suit our purposes," said Arthur.

Lura raised her arms and shook her breasts at Caroline. "You like? Two copper kettles coming right up."

Caroline looked away, eager for a drink. "Perhaps it is really a foolish errand. I am beginning to doubt my skills in this matter. What if I kill us both, or just me?" She took the intricate glass from Lura and smiled a bittersweet smile.

"Anything is possible, but we do seem rather indestructible. At this juncture, it is our duty. Perhaps the act will release us back to Berlin, and you can drop your charges against me."

Caroline laughed. "But I need the income, dear Arthur." She drank half her drink and coughed.

Arthur was not amused and downed his drink. Soon, they gave leave to Lura and headed into the bright sunshine. It seemed a summer day, like all the other days lorded over by the tiny furnace in the sky.

Arthur knew the path to the church in the rock very well and picked their way through the scrub and thorns with confidence until they reached the rickety ladder. Up went Caroline, slowly, but without complaint, followed by Arthur, who grunted as he reached the safety of level rocky ground. Inside the Abba's house, the warm air sat sullen as the Abba lay still, a bundle of yellow cloth on the bed. If he noticed them, he did not show it and breathed ponderously like an enchanted Rumpelstiltskin.

"Abba?" said Arthur, and he leaned down for a reply, but received none. "Poor fellow." He reverted to the task at hand. "Now, my dear, you retrieve the vest. We know it does you no harm." He rubbed his hands together.

"Yes," said Caroline. "I shall." She opened the chest, and the sparkle of the gems dazzled her.

"Take it," said Arthur.

She reached and touched the thick embroidery, pulling back her hand as if bitten, then with some effort drew the vest into her arms. "I feel as if it belongs to me."

"No such thoughts, my lady," said Arthur, and he led the way out and to the green door in the rock.

Inside, the coolness felt welcome, the smell of the rock like an old friend. Arthur watched Caroline draw the vest over her head with some difficulty and walk with pomp to a place behind the low pedestal of hard and ancient wood. She stood there like a priestess but seemed at a loss for words.

Arthur stood in front of the wooden structure. "What words shall you use?"

She remembered uttering Dahlia's name. "What was the date again?"

"Thirty-nine-seventy-six," said Arthur.

"Three thousand nine hundred and seventy-six!" said Caroline. She held her breath, but nothing happened. She prepared herself to utter Dahlia's name. "I am frightened."

"On with it, woman," said Arthur.

Caroline took a deep breath, her lips in place. "Dahlia?"

A flicker of light, and the room grew more quiet than quiet. From all corners, the light coalesced, and an image of Dahlia appeared, her golden hair glowing. "Hello," said Dahlia. The voice seemed to coat the walls.

Arthur cringed, looking from one corner to the next. He felt full of springs.

"Yes, young lady," said Caroline. "Thirty-nine...seventy-six."

The room seemed dissolved in froth and pudding, blue light, an utter roaring silence. Arthur moaned and went to his knees, closing his eyes. He remained stiff for what seemed an eternity. The room wavered and bent, Arthur swaying side to side. There was a notion of what seemed to be seaweed, a darkening depth.

Reece wandered toward the speck that was Dahlia, but the speck disappeared. He couldn't tell if he was walking in a straight line. He turned to look behind and saw nothing, except the electric light, like being inside a sunlit glacier of blue ice. He seemed to be wearing clothes made of paper. He walked, without tiring, and walked and walked. He wondered if he was walking in circles. He stopped to try his voice and heard himself say, "Hello?" but no one answered. Was the floor moving beneath him, or was he moving across the floor? He walked on.

After what seemed hours, he veered left and continued walking, and seeing something in the distance, he quickened his pace. Perhaps another hour passed, and what had seemed a black dot became a human figure, walking away from him. He broke into a run but seemed to be gaining little ground.

"Hey! Here!" He dropped into a slow jog, wondering that he did not need to breathe. The figure stopped and turned, and soon they were facing one another. "Hello," said Reece.

"What do you want?" asked the man. He was a big man with unruly brown hair and beefy hands. He had a wild look in his eye. "You just get here?"

"I think so," said Reece. "This is Dogtown, right? Dahlia told me that this is Dogtown."

The man laughed. "Yeah, that little cunt. She's a pistol. But I've got her number."

"I'm Reece, Reece Myers. I'm looking for my daughter,

Mia."

"Good to meet you, Rice. My daughter's Lila. Just call me Helmut, Helmut Grayson. He had an aggressive voice and wore a blue paper gown.

The name sounded familiar. "Your daughter, she's missing as well?"

"Yep, that goddamned Dahlia."

Reece noticed another dot, seeming to grow larger, coming toward them. "Dahlia says there's no way out of here. Is it true? I need to get the fuck out of Dodge."

Helmut laughed. "I've got her number. She thinks she knows everything."

The figure of a heavyset woman approached, walking methodically as if to an office get-together. Helmut turned and greeted her.

"Well, hey there, Scocpol. Join the party."

The name sounded familiar?

"Hey," said Timera. "What's going on? Anything new?"

"This guy Rice is new."

"Lord, looking for your daughter. The same old story. My daughter's name is Lacie. Lacie Scocpol. You at Organon too?"

"Organon? You guys are at Organon? My daughter is Mia. So that's where I know your names from. I'm in room seven."

"Three for me," said Helmut. "Got me tied to the goddamn bed."

Timera laughed, then looked sad. "I'm in ten."

"Huh, Dahlia told me I couldn't leave. But you guys go back and forth?" asked Reece.

"She's not the most truthful little girl," said Helmut.

"Some can and some can't. I suppose it's a matter of how you got here."

"A monk, a priest sent me, the Abba Paulos. You come across him?"

"I know me some priests, but not that one," said Timera.

"Nope," said Helmut. "But I know Gandhi. Cute little fellow. Got a mustache."

Reece laughed. "Gandhi? The Gandhi?"

"Yep, Gandhi in the flesh. He's helping me out," said Helmut.

"Who's helping you?" asked Reece.

"Well, the Ras Tefari. Haile Selassie. He found me wandering around," said Timera.

"So, how do you guys get here? What do you do here?"

Helmut sat cross-legged on the shiny floor. "Through the seizures, the big ones. Grand mal is what Markush calls them."

Timera nodded. "It's not pleasant. I just walk around looking for Dahlia. She makes herself scarce. She knows where my Lacie is. The little bitch."

"You can get intel here," said Helmut. "I've been to the middle, the Pinch. Nearly killed me, but I saw some things there. I've got Dahlia behind the eight ball. She lets me come, thinking I'll spill the beans, but not till I get my Lila back."

"The Pinch? What's that?" Reece sat beside him.

"The middle of things, the center of it all. You can see way back, all the way to the beginning of everything."

Timera chuckled. "Not me, no sir, unless I have to. Some folks go and don't come back."

"What did you find?" asked Reece.

"I can't say. Dahlia, you know. Let's just say that it's where the music starts, what Dahlia wants to know. Did she give you that shit about missing her mommy?"

Reece thought about that. "Yeah, she did. Sounds interesting. Maybe I should go there. Is the Pinch going to help you find your Lila?"

"Not sure," said Helmut. "It can't hurt."

"Pretty sure you can't leave, though," said Timera. "Priest sending you." She walked in circles around them.

"Heck, you could try it," said Helmut. "You can go anywhere from the Pinch, if you know where you want to go. Just don't die is all."

"What do you mean die?" asked Reece.

"Don't let your body die, the one at Organon. Met one guy here who died. He's stuck for sure, poor fella. He depresses me. He's around here somewhere. Dahlia teases him, shows him where his daughter is."

"Really?" asked Reece. "She is a little girl, mischievous, I suppose. How does one get to the Pinch? I'd like to give it a try."

"You just have to start walking," said Helmut. "That's when I saw the beginning. It could be near or far away. Hard to tell. You'll know by the blue light. It gets brighter. At some point, you have to close your eyes, but then it goes black as night."

"Sounds like a nightmare," said Timera. She wasn't breathing.

"When you get back, can you guys tell Markush that I'm okay, not to let...my body go?"

"Sure thing, pal," said Helmut. Timera nodded.

"Great," said Reece. "It's now or never. I guess I'll start walking. Maybe see you around. Thanks for the info." He stood and stretched, smiling.

"Good luck," they said.

"Thanks," and Reece was on his way.

He took a straight line, walking, alternating with jogging. There was no breeze. It was neither hot nor cold. In the distance, he saw a speck and then specks. The specks soon assumed the shapes of people. As he got closer, he could distinguish faces. They seemed to be hanging out together like a school of fish, not talking. He came to the edge of the group, and one or two looked his way.

"Hey, I'm Reece."

No one spoke at first.

"Hey," said a thin woman wearing the paper gown. She was attractive with long blonde hair and a sad face. Everyone had a sad face.

"What's going on?" asked Reece.

"Nothing," said the woman. "Just waiting is all."

The group of men and women, fifteen in all, gradually turned and shifted their attention, all in the blue paper gowns. They looked like crazy people on a psych ward, subdued with chemicals, the life washed out of them.

"Everybody looking for their daughters?" asked Reece.

"Yep," said a blocky man with slicked-back hair. "Waiting to head back out, whenever that might be."

"Um, I'm headed for the Pinch." Reece remembered the drawing in the Abba's book and suddenly understood. "The Pinch in the Cylinder, right?"

"Oh Lord, the Pinch," said the woman. "Yeah, you might try just going straight. You'll find it sooner or later."

"Thanks," said Reece. He gazed at the disinterested faces. "I'll be on my way," and he skirted the group, heading off. One or two grunted.

Reece walked, jogged, walked, and even ran. Every hour or so, he came across a small group, just milling in silence. At first, he stopped to speak, but after the third group, he just kept going. The brilliant blue light extended in all directions. He walked.

He imagined that he'd been walking for hours and hours, perhaps a day, but nothing had changed. There was a moment, perhaps a full minute, when he became dizzy and slowed, losing his sight to blackness. It soon cleared, though, and on he continued. He shifted course slightly right, for no reason, and continued. His mind was a blank filled with an occasional image of Mia, of Arthur, of the mugs of buster, but he felt no hunger.

He walked for days, never tiring, walking with his eyes closed, his eyes open. He wasn't wearing shoes, but his feet didn't hurt. He remembered Kristin and wondered what she was doing back in their homey house in Richmond. Fleeting images of Charlotte, of his students, of his parents lying dead inside Luby's. He gave himself mental tasks, rewinding a day in his life at the lake with his grandparents. For perhaps an hour in his mind, he swept the driveway and the roof clean of pine straw. He imagined Emma working in the clinic, handing out vitamins, worm pills, and famine biscuits. The Icelanders appeared: Svana, Eydis, and Gudmunder. The evening he was shot. The tornado that had ravaged the hospital and nearly sucked him from his bed. Debbie Dee with the cold sores in the corners of her mouth.

He had slowed and lost sight of the horizon in the distance, not noticing that the blue light was coalescing there, and on he walked. But then he noticed and stopped. He seemed to hear a whir and stepped his walk back up to a jog. He remembered Caroline and laughed, imagining sharing stories about her and her nemesis Arthur. The light grew brighter, and a feeling of accomplishment filled him. As if finished plowing, he was ready to plant the seeds. What would Markush think of all of this? The light grew brighter and spread before him, casting a shadow behind him an infinite distance.

He paused, wondering what to do. *Just keep walking, toward the center?* There was something on the floor in the distance. It was a body. He stooped and checked the pulse, but there was none, and then the body moved. Surprised, he stood and stared at the young man, perhaps thirty, and wondered if he too was at Organon. God, he wanted to talk with Markush, to share everything that he was seeing. The man formed his mouth into an O or perhaps an A and then lay his head back down. Reece continued, now seeming to have the light at his sides as well as in front of him.

In the middle, the blue light took on a glaring white, and Reece had to look down as he walked, nearly blind. For several more hours, he walked, drawing deeper into the light, feeling it against his skin, the hum growing louder, its music becoming clearer and clearer.

A liter of Scotch in a paper bag and a six-pack of Miller High Life, Markush passed through the reception area, through the first door, and then paused to be buzzed into the secure unit. He nodded at Gumbo, glancing into three at Helmut Grayson. Grayson seemed to be awake but not fully. It had not been long since his grand mal seizure. Claire buzzed Markush into the nursing station.

"Claire, what's up with Reece?" He walked to the bank of monitors.

"Still comatose, it seems," said Claire.

Markush examined the slow, wavy lines. "How about Scocpol and Grayson?"

"Grayson has been back for about half an hour. Looks like he's quiet. Scocpol is back from the grand mal, but she's traveling again, gamma waves."

"Anything else?"

"No," said Claire. "That's about it. Debbie and Richard are just staying busy. Freddie's been in and out of the day-room."

"Okay, good, no emergencies, although I'm worried about Reece. There's been some disconnect. Let me go check on Helmut." He exited the station. Grayson lay in bed, his head up to forty-five degrees, his eyes open to slits. He grunted when he saw Markush and tried to speak, but was still disoriented from his seizure.

Markush went to his side, careful to avoid his big hands poking through the blanket restraint. "Mr. Grayson?"

Grayson spoke, but his speech was garbled.

"Hey, just so you know, I have the Scotch. Let me go for a few minutes, and I'll come back. We'll have a drink."

Grayson seemed to smile.

Markush headed to six, peeked his head in at Debbie, winked, and stepped into seven. Reece's breathing was very shallow and slow. Markush felt his carotids, and they were slow as well. He took his penlight and checked his pupils, pinpoint and sluggish. He took his knuckle and ground it into Reece's sternum, looking for a response, but there was nothing.

"Reece, it's me, Markush. Checking on you, good buddy. Hang in there, okay? We'll get you back one way or the other." He gripped Reece's hand.

Debbie stepped into the room. "Anything?"

"Nope," said Markush, washing his hands. "Just keep an eye on him. How's Emma?"

"Hasn't been traveling. She's opening her eyes and moving her hands. She's in there for sure, slowly coming around."

"Great," said Markush. "Keep an eye on her, too. If she could only talk."

"True," said Debbie.

Markush, with his Scotch, walked around the unit, peeking in at the patients. He said hey to Richard, paused at Scocpol's room, and stepped inside. Her body trembled, and he spoke a few encouraging words to her. Back in three, Helmut Grayson was a bit more animated.

"Hey, I'm back, just like I promised," said Markush. "How about that Scotch? You up for it?"

Grayson grinned. "Hey...Doc. Ready if you are."

Markush uncorked the bottle of Laphroaig, smelling

the smoke of the peat, the sea salt of the alcohol. "Twenty-year." He looked around for a glass. "Maybe sit you up a bit more." He raised the head of the bed to sixty degrees. "I know I promised you a real glass. Be right back." He went back to the unit and could only find a clean coffee mug.

He poured two fingers for Grayson. "Ready?"

"Damn, don't rush a good thing, Doc."

"Sorry." He held the mug to Grayson's lips and tilted. Grayson slurped in a mouthful and grimaced, swallowing. He coughed. "Whooee!" He coughed some more. "Trying to drown me?"

"Sorry about that," said Markush. He waited while Grayson got his breath back. "Just tell me when."

"How come you're not having any?"

"Yeah, right, just a taste, though." He poured a finger into a plastic cup and sipped. He winced. "Smoky."

"Okay, now, just a sip this time. Got it? Or I'll wring your goddamn neck." Grayson laughed a loud laugh.

"Watch the remarks, Mr. Grayson. Remember, we're working together."

"Whatever," said Grayson. "If you'd untie me, I promise to be a good boy. Okay, I'm ready."

Markush held the mug to his lips, being careful this time. A sip went in.

"Ahh," said Grayson. "Good times. Good times." He sang a line from "Radar Love" and ran his tongue over his yellowed teeth. "The niceties of life. If we could get Debbie topless, I'd have it made in the shade in the shade in the shade."

"So," said Markush. "You had some information to share about Dahlia, right? This whole bottle is for you, my friend." He took a little swig and wiped his mouth on his sleeve.

"Oh yeah, got your curiosity up, huh? Like I was telling that fellow Reece—"

"You talked with Reece? Reece Myers? How?"

"Forgot about that. He said not to let him die. He's headed for a little adventure at the Pinch. Saw him and that Timera lady in Dogtown."

"Really, what did he say? This Dogtown puzzles me. I know it seems to be where Dahlia lives or visits."

"Yep, in the Cylinder. He saw Dahlia, he said. He can't leave, though, because he was sent by some priest. Or so Dahlia says." He nodded toward the mug.

"That's bad news. So, tell me more about the Pinch, in the Cylinder." He held the mug to Grayson's lips.

"Oh, the mighty Pinch, where everything gets squeezed down to nothing. Nearly killed me. Well, anyway, he's looking for his daughter, Mia, just like my Lila. It's a special place, all right." He took a sip and twisted his lips.

"Will he be able to find her there, the Pinch?" Markush's green eyes were wide.

"I don't know. Didn't help me, but I was overwhelmed, wasn't prepared. But that's where I saw it, the beginning of everything."

"Tell me, what you saw..."

"Can you get Debbie to sit on my face?"

"No," said Markush.

"That's a bummer. Maybe you should just wait for Reece to come tumbling back, if he can."

"Look, any information you can provide will help us find Lila. I'm sure of it. We have to help each other here.

What was it you saw?"

"I saw black. It's more or less what I felt and heard. The music. There can only be one thing when there is nothing."

Markush was on his toes, waiting for the reveal. "And?"

"Another sip first."

Markush looked in the mug and then took the bottle and poured another finger. Grayson slurped in a sip, coughed.

"No guesses?" asked Grayson.

"No guesses," said Markush.

"My friend, you ready for this? The answer is time. That's what we're made of. That's what there was when there was nothing. You see, time collected and collected until the weight of it all, boom! Like buckshot, universes scattering, collapsing, expanding. There's not really time anymore, just the idea of time. All time is simultaneous. There, satisfied."

Markush thought. "But you can't have time without matter, right?"

"Nope," said Grayson. "You're wrong. Dahlia wants to go there, to the beginning. She is time itself, but she doesn't know it. She thinks she has a mommy, but she doesn't, or does she? Time is her goddamn mommy. And there, the secret's out."

Markush wondered how this information would help. "Okay, I'll go with it. So, there was never a time when there was nothing. There has always been time?"

"I think you got it," said Grayson. "Hey, I'm feeling a little buzz. Let's keep it coming."

Markush let him drain the rest of the cup. "We'll have

to slow down a bit. Can't have you drunk."

"Ha ha, you're a good fucker."

"Okay, thanks, Mr. Grayson. I appreciate it. I feel like you've uncovered something, but I'm not exactly sure what it is. I'm going to go for now, okay? Just push the button if you need anything." He put the call button within his reach.

"Ha, got your dope and gonna run, huh? I just need to get back, keep on looking with Mr. Gandhi." He sighed. "Thanks for the drinks."

"You're welcome," said Markush, and he left, entering the nursing station. "Claire, we need to keep a close watch on Reece. He may be headed into some trouble."

"Yeah, sure. Still comatose, though." She sat up straight. "No, wait, polyspikes, Jesus, look at them."

Markush gripped the edge of the counter, watching Reece's EEG go haywire.

On his knees, Arthur stared at the rough rock floor. He looked around the dim chamber. The pedestal was gone, and so was Caroline. He struggled to his feet, tearing a hole in the knee of his pants.

"Curses!"

He walked toward the door, which seemed smaller than before. The rickety wheelbarrow was there, a pick leaning against the wall. He stepped into the bright, hot sunshine and squinted against the light. To his right was the Abba's house. He walked that way, steadying himself twice against falling. He heard the sound of a small voice coming from inside and knocked on the corrugated steel door.

The voice stopped. Another voice. "Abet?"

Arthur stood back as the door opened. It was the Abba Paulos, but five years younger, looking spiffy in his gold robe and matching hat. He peered into Arthur's eyes and gazed at him up and down.

"Umm, tenesteling?" asked Arthur. He could see a little girl, sitting on a stool, eating from a yellowed bowl. She looked prim and proper, with golden brown hair, almost red, and freckles. He pointed to the little girl. "Mia?"

The Abba looked even more surprised and stood aside to let Arthur into the small room, fitted with a bed, a stool, a chair, and the table on which lay the ancient book, and then a small charcoal stove with a metal pot on it. The chest that held the holy vest with the gemstones was there as well.

"Hello," said Mia. "How did you know my name, sir?"

"My goodness, it is you! Your father is looking for you, dear girl. You are here."

"Yes, my father is lost. He is looking for me, though. Do you know him?"

"Yes, we have been...living together, in another place, another time, rather. How did you get here?" He nodded and smiled at the Abba.

"I don't really know. Dahlia probably put me here. She's studying me, trying to hear my music. She's silly." She was eating boiled sorghum with a wooden spoon.

Arthur drew closer and touched her shoulder to see if she was real. "Your father will be overjoyed, no doubt."

"Is he here? Where is my father?"

"Well, young lass, he travels to and fro, looking for you. He's not here. I somehow need to notify him of your location. Are you doing well for food? Do you sleep here?"

"Yes, the Abba lets me sleep on his bed. I just love what he cooks for me. But I can't understand him. We speak different languages."

"Yes, true," said Arthur. "Is there a town nearby? Have you been there?"

"A town, nearby?"

"Perhaps we should go and look. Would you like to go to the town?" Arthur made encouraging gestures for the Abba, who looked concerned.

"I don't know, maybe. The Abba keeps me safe. He digs in the cave all day, though."

Arthur looked at the Abba. "Gadam?" And he pointed toward where the town should be.

"Ow, Gadam," and the Abba pointed but frowned. He

pushed his way between Arthur and Mia.

Arthur took a step back. "Perhaps I should go and explore, to make sure the town is there, to find a room. They should have food for you there, perhaps better than the Abba's gruel?"

"Kind sir, I guess that would be fine," said Mia.

"Yes, well, dear girl, I shall return." He turned and bowed to the Abba. The Abba bowed.

Arthur descended the rough ladder and followed the scruffy path, huffing and puffing. He followed the cliff line and came to the end of the open field, where the circus had been, and then there was the town, much as it was in Gadam 3981. Thirsty and hungry, he made for the first green star, a buster bar. He entered the brown building through a mist door. Inside was dim. On a tiny dance floor behind the bar, six young ladies grooved in miniskirts. Lights over them changed colors as they gyrated to traditional Amharic music.

Arthur took a barstool and sighed, waiting to be served, watching the girls dance, and they were quite attractive with their shaved legs.

One of the girls stopped dancing and came down. She was thin with wide hips and an ample bosom. She had a mole on her cheek. "Hey there, gramps. Got the clap? What'll it be, today's special?"

"Yes, the day's special?"

"Well, you bend over..." She laughed.

"What may I call you?"

"You may call me Anise." She slapped her behind and made a sizzle sound.

"Anise, I will have the buster. I assume it's nourishing

as always."

Anise turned, the bottoms of her butt cheeks showing. "Order up!" She slid the bowl to Arthur, spilling just a bit.

Arthur drank it down in one fell swoop. On the off chance that perhaps Reece was somehow in Gadam 3976, he said, "My dear, have you knowledge of a Reece Myers?"

"Not in the fur," said Anise. She drafted him another bowl. "I'm done with you, old man. I gotta dance." She remounted the stage, switching her hips.

Arthur drank and belched, watching the ladies shimmy and shake in cotton miniskirts. Why had he come to town? He had found Mia. He somehow had to let Reece know, but where was he? Perhaps the Abba could call him, but how would he explain, plus he would want money. He remembered making the circus disappear.

A man sitting in back came forward. A puff of chest hair pushed from his shirt. He jumped over the bar and ascended to the stage. He had two bills and slipped them into a garter worn by one of the young ladies. She rubbed him on the head, and he danced with her for a moment. The same song continued to play, an accordion and a masinqo, perhaps a tambourine. The lyrics of the male singer vibrated and rose and fell.

Arthur noticed that all of the young ladies had bills in garters attached to their thighs. He knew that it was a custom to tip dancing girls back in the bars of Berlin. He decided to try his luck in obtaining some of the bills. Rather than climbing over the bar, he lifted a section of the metal counter and passed through. The stairs were narrow and steep, the stage very small, and he squeezed in among them, much to their delight, and they began to dance with him as he shuffled his feet and snapped his fingers to the rhythm. He pulled up his pants legs, revealing his calves and dingy black socks. He was much taller than the ladies and looked down at his feet to keep from falling.

"Get your stink on, grandpa," said Anise. She pressed against him, and the music changed to a loud and grating tune, "Highway to Hell" by AC/DC. Arthur wondered if the music system was dysfunctional and marveled at the man's gravelly voice. Anise took one of her bills, licked it, and stuck it to his forehead. Arthur provided her with a gracious smile and grabbed the bill, stuffing it in his pocket.

Now the girls were pressing him, and a small crowd had gathered at the bar, nodding their heads to the heavy guitar. Arthur imitated them, high-stepping like a soldier, careful not to bounce anyone from the stage. His heart beat faster and he broke into a sweat. Another bill was pasted to his forehead, but it fell, and he stooped to retrieve it. The small crowd was shouting his name, "Arthur! Arthur!" He increased the tempo of his footsteps and feared lapsing into a frenzy. Wadded bills and coins were being thrown to the stage, and he kept his eye on them, pleased with himself. He wondered what Caroline would think and had a brief moment of regret at having left her.

The song ended, but another took its place. It was "The Metal" by Tenacious D. The man was talking, seeming to orate. Arthur didn't understand the lyrics, but kept dancing, increasing his tempo even more. He lost his balance and fell at the edge of the stage, sliding off, feeling a pull in his groin. He grunted and pulled a few of the bills from beneath the dancing feet, pushing them into his pockets.

The crowd was booing him, and he felt it best to continue dancing and did so behind the bar, twirling in circles. The faces of the small mob registered dissatisfaction, and Arthur took note as they pounded the bar. Thinking they might attack him, he pulled himself onto the bar and stood, kicking his buster bowl onto the floor where it broke to much applause.

A steady stream of people entered the bar, gathering at the front, pushing and shoving. It was Norwegian death metal, the man's voice like a demon, the music louder than ever, the crowd chanting and pushing fists into the air. Arthur stamped his feet, caught up in the moment. He'd never had such a powerful feeling before. He threw his head back and screamed, losing his balance, whirling, and fell on top of the crowd. Instead of hitting the floor, they held him aloft, passing him back and forth.

Arthur was spent. He stared at the ribbed ceiling, wondering what sort of animal craze he had fallen into. The music cut and resumed into a peaceful melody of Middle Eastern yodeling. The crowd went limp, and Arthur tumbled to the floor, drenched in sweat. Someone stepped on his hand, and he groaned, making his best effort to stand, the pain still in his groin. The crowd filtered away, many leaving the bar as if the show was over. On stage, the girls had lapsed into a mellow dance, their faces drawn blanks. Arthur took the bills from his pocket and counted them. He had to get back to the Abba and bring Reece here.

Reece succumbed to the light and went to his knees. Loud music beat steadily with flairs of melody. He crawled forward, feeling heavier and heavier. He focused on his heart thudding, slower and slower. He remembered the Ford Ranger plowing through the glass at Luby's, the driver, George Hennard, coming out of the cab with guns blazing. The life of Hennard passed before him, and he felt sick, nauseated, and on he crawled for what seemed days. All around him, he heard the laugh of a little girl embedded in the music. *Dahlia.*

"Can I come with you?" asked Dahlia, her voice echoing as if in a vast chamber. "I want to meet my mommy."

Reece opened his eyes for a flash, but there was only the blinding light, and he squeezed them shut. He tried to speak, but nothing would come. He willed Dahlia to be gone, but what could be lost by letting Dahlia follow him?

"I've been there before," said Dahlia. "Don't worry."

He could feel her around him, all of them, as if he were swimming in a school of minnows. The hum had become a roar, and he struggled to stay conscious, to keep his thoughts going. He focused on a photo of Mia from preschool. The teacher had gathered her hair on top into a whale spout with a hair tie. She was smiling with apple-red cheeks, just woken from a nap. The image seared into his brain, into the backs of his eyelids, glowing red.

"You're such a good daddy," said Dahlia. "We're almost there."

Reece put one hand forward, then one knee forward,

and repeated the motion over and over. He didn't feel tired but felt that he might die, that he would implode into a dot of human tissue.

/a poodle brandishing a fork/red birthday cake/
/a poodle brandishing a fork/red birthday cake/
/a poodle brandishing a fork/red birthday cake/

Reece lay on his belly, inching forward. He sensed that there would be a lip of something to grab onto, to pull him over the edge. He remembered the house at 47 Asterion Lane. The little girl Charlotte, who visited almost every day. She was there, pressing against him, seeking his knowledge. The noise of the music crushed him, flattening him to the floor. He felt his eyes would explode, and then his hand felt nothing. He strained against what could be a mighty wind, pulling on the nothing. His arms were through, and then his head. He screamed inside and fell, falling it seemed, or was it floating? All was quiet except for the tinny noise of a music box. He recognized the tune as one of Mia's music boxes, which she had adored. He dared to open his eyes and saw black, nothing, but racing with images that flew past him at the speed of light.

Hairs on toes that hurt. Buster. Emma. Kristin. The Abba, his neck inflamed with pustules. The night Dahlia mapped him. The thin mask filtering into his scalp, into his skull. And then the images faded, as if the entire history of everything had passed before him in less than a split second.

He decided he was floating and felt about, but there was nothing. He let his mind relax and remembered Dahlia telling him that Mia was in Gadam 3976 and realized that it was a lie. She was here, in the ether of blackness, and he called out to her. "Mia!" The void reverberated with the name as if there were walls.

"She's not here," said Dahlia. "I would know. Arthur is with her. You should go there and see her. She misses you."

"Dahlia," said Reece. "Do you hear the music box?"

"The music box..."

"You can't hear it."

"Don't be silly," said Dahlia. "My mommy is here. Do you see her?"

Reece tried to grab onto something, anything, but there was nothing except the music box, plinking out its simple tune as if it would never quit.

"You'll never understand," said Reece. "You can't hear the music. Is the music your mommy?"

Dahlia sighed. "If you want to leave, you have to tell me."

Reece paused for what seemed an eternity, letting the music cleanse him, wash over him, through him. An image of Mia unfolded. *The Abba. The Icelanders.* Mia was with the Icelanders and Emma.

"You funny boy," said Dahlia. Her voice swirled around him.

"She's in Gwar, 1987," said Reece. He suddenly understood what there was when there could be nothing.

"Oh, that's silly," said Dahlia.

Reece tried to block her voice from his mind. "Gadam, 3976, another impostor," he said. "You're putting Arthur in danger."

Dahlia laughed. "You're a smart cookie. But you're wrong. That's where Mia is."

Reece felt as if he were tumbling in a dryer and tried to steady himself. "You're a liar, and you know it."

"No, don't go. You're my daddy, and I want my mommy."

"The world is my will and my representation," said Reece.

"No!" said Dahlia, but the Pinch began to swirl, leaks of light infiltrating the nothingness.

Reece felt a tremendous pressure, as if he would be crushed. He clenched his eyes and balled himself, tumbling and tumbling, Dahlia's long cry chasing after him.

Debbie and Richard had just ended their shift, reporting off to Laura and Sheldon. Claire signed off with Lars, who took her place. Claire, against her better judgment, was going out again with the guy who had made her pay for her dinner on their second date.

An alarm alerted Lars that Reece's ECG had gone flat. "What the fuck?" He hit the code button and yelled into the speaker to check on seven.

Laura arrived first, followed by Sheldon with the crash cart. Reece had no pulse, wasn't breathing, and was a deathly shade of yellow. She knocked down the bed rail and began chest compressions as Sheldon manned the Ambu bag, giving Reece two respirations for every ten chest compressions.

"Dammit," said Laura. She counted off ten. Lars squeezed the bag. "Need some epi, stat."

Sheldon opened the top drawer of the crash cart and threw her the injection. Debbie had started an IV on the previous shift, anticipating giving Reece Dilantin. Laura pushed in the epi and checked for a pulse. Nothing. She went back to compressions as Sheldon manned the Ambu bag.

"Need to shock him," said Sheldon. In a flash, he hit the power button of the defibrillator and turned it up to 160 joules. As he worked, Laura gave Reece mouth-to-mouth between compressions.

"Clear!" and Reece's torso jumped. Nothing. Both his EEG and ECG were flat lines.

Markush ran onto the unit, having been alerted in his office. He entered seven. "Has he had epi?"

"Yeah, one bolus."

Reece looked dead.

"Another!" He grabbed an epi syringe, uncapped it, and pushed it into the IV hep lock. He waited, hearing the grind of bone as Laura compressed. Nothing.

Markush held the defib paddles. "Clear!" Laura and Sheldon stood back from the bed. Reece flounced but with less vigor. Markush waited two minutes, but Reece was gone. "Fuck. Dammit to hell. He's done. No more." He reached up to silence the ECG alarm and gazed at Reece, his arms sprawled, his eyes partially open. "Fuck and shit. What the hell happened?"

"He just went flat line," said Laura.

Sheldon picked up litter from the floor. Laura folded Reece's arms over his body. Reece was the second to die on the unit, and it came as quite a shock to them all.

"Damn," said Markush. He paced in the room, but could do nothing further. "This will entail an investigation, I'm sure, definitely an autopsy. I'll call Kristin and let her know." He left the room, pushing past the night guards who had been watching. Lars buzzed him into the station.

"Sorry, sir," said Lars. "It's like a light switch went off."

"Something drastic happened on the other end. He's as healthy as a horse otherwise, despite the seizures."

First, Markush called Washington to report the death to his superior there. The phone call took ten minutes, and then he called Kristin. She was beside herself and cursed, asking him if he was sure. After a long silence, she broke, crying. Markush comforted her and offered to drive down and visit with her and figure out what was next. She wavered at first, but then said okay, that the next day would be fine.

Freddie had been up when Reece coded and was worried that it would somehow compromise the safety of Alicia back in Utah. His wife, Gloria, had agreed to visit Fort Knox with Alicia before the publicity campaign to reintroduce her to society took place.

In seven, Sheldon helped Laura prep Reece's body. She closed his eyes and taped them. She then tied his hands at the wrist with a roll of gauze. Organon had anticipated such an occurrence, and there was a morgue just for Organon patients. Reece's body would be flown to Bethesda, Maryland, to Walter Reed for the autopsy. Laura placed a clean gown over his body as Sheldon retrieved a stretcher from the nursing station.

Using the bottom sheet, they pulled him onto the stretcher and covered his body with a clean sheet. Debbie was to copy his chart and place the original with him in the morgue inside a plastic bag. As with all things Organon, the transfer of the body would be covert and handled by the military.

"Hey fuckers!" said Grayson as they passed his room. "Got'cha a cold one, huh!"

Reece hurtled from nothing into a great smear of orange and green. He felt that he hit the earth as a meteorite, blowing open a crater half a kilometer wide. He lay there for nearly an hour, gradually uncurling from his fetal position, stiff and bewildered. A few children had drawn near, staring, waiting to see if he had any candy. He was in what had been the old Polish airfield, where the circus had been. He sat up, and the children scattered with worried looks, then laughing.

"Ferenj!"

Reece gripped small rocks, steadying himself as he sat up. Where had he been? *Dogtown. The Pinch.* Dahlia had been there, trying to get him to return to Gadam 3975. He had seen Arthur there in the stream of images. It was a trap, a detour to throw him off the true location of Mia, which he now understood to be Gwar 1987. Now to find her. Should he venture into the village or head directly to the Abba Paulos? Would she be here in this version of Godo? She had to be, and he stood, his vision blurring. He felt drunk and staggered.

Soon, small huts appeared, and from memory, he stumbled forward, alarming all he met. Young women covered their mouths, and a group of children followed at a safe distance. A man took off his hat and bowed slightly. Reece tried to smile, but wasn't sure if he did or not. He passed through the market square and veered at Afewerki's house. He paused but moved forward, headed to the old Baptist compound. This place was called Gwar, and it was 1987.

He soon came to the walled compound and knocked on the gate.

"Abet!" The voice belonged to Ketow, and he opened the gate a crack, peering at Reece. "Mendeno?" He looked puzzled and glanced back into the compound at the group sitting around the fire. He said, "Eiyee!" and retreated.

Reece pushed through the gate. Mia was there. He glanced at the group and broke into a run. "Mia!" He fell.

The Icelanders stood, their mouths open. Reece stood, watching himself trip through the green grass. "The fuck," he said.

Mia jumped up and ran to Reece, the Reece that was her father. "Daddy!"

"What in hell?" asked Emma. She looked from the seated Reece to the Reece kneeling in the grass, clutching Mia, weeping.

"Mia, I've found you. I've found you," said Reece. His tears blurred his vision.

"Daddy, daddy!" said Mia. "I missed you and mommy so much!"

Reece gained control of his emotions and stood, gazing at the group that was staring at him. He noticed the thin young man who looked like him. He deduced that the others were the Icelandic team, and he knew right away who Emma was. Something was not right, though, something in the air. He glanced around the compound. He saw Ketow whispering to Zenebek and Misrak in the cook house, as if he had seen a snake.

Emma was the first to speak. "Reece?"

"Emma," said Reece. He lifted Mia and held her in his

arms.

"It seems we have two Reeces," said Gudmunder.

"I am not believing this," said Eydis.

Reece let go of Mia, afraid that she would disappear, gripping her hand. "I'm Reece Myers. I've come to take Mia home."

"Is he your brother, your twin?" asked Svana.

"I don't know," said Reece. He approached Reece and held out his hand to see if this person who looked like him was real.

They shook hands and spoke at the same time. "Hello."

"I know this is crazy," said Reece. "I'm basically from another time and place. I used to work here. I was shot."

"Oh Lord," said Emma. "But that guy died. How could you be him?"

"Another time and place. That wasn't me. I lived. But you, Emma, you have to be careful. I know an Emma who worked here, well, it was called Godo, who was also shot. I'm afraid this is not a safe place with the Donkey, or the Hyena, the Snake, whatever he is here."

Gudmunder ushered him to a chair, where Reece sat, holding Mia in his lap. Gudmunder yelled for Ketow to bring another stool from the cook house, and he did with a terrified look on his face. The news was spreading through Gwar. Reece explained how he had been traveling through seizures and the Ark. How he had met Dahlia, and how she was behind everything. No one asked questions and just let him talk, Reece watching Reece. The newly arrived Reece was wearing ragged shorts and a t-shirt, the other jeans and a scrub top.

There was no fire in the fire ring, and the ashes seemed

to call out, searching for a spark of understanding. All eyes were there, and there was a knock on the gate and a loud voice. It was the Snake and Ketow opened the gate. The Snake was holding a little girl's hand, and she had golden hair and blue eyes. He walked inside, bright-eyed. The little girl was holding a knife. And then behind him came another little girl and another.

"Dahlia," said Reece. "They're coming for Mia." He grabbed Mia and pushed her toward the dining hut. "Stay here. Don't come out. Promise me."

"I'm scared, Daddy."

"Inside, just for now." He pushed her through the flap, and there were five little girls all with knives, and they kept pouring in, two and three at a time, forming a group, a small army. Everyone was standing now, with looks of fear and bewilderment.

"What is this?" asked Gudmunder. "I don't understand."

"You have a pistol in your tent. We need it."

The battalion of little girls grew larger, pushing toward them, singing off-key, a children's song, "The Itsy Bitsy Spider."

The Snake had backed himself against the fence, chewing qat leaves, his eyes wide and laughing.

A chill ran down Reece's spine, and he went to Gudmunder's tent. He knew where the gun was and pulled it from beneath the pillow. He ran and stood in front of the dining hut. "They're impostors! All of them! You can't be afraid to hurt them. Otherwise, they'll kill us!" The group stared at him as if he were a madman, and he was, waving the pistol.

"But they are little girls," said Eydis. "We cannot hurt

them."

"They're angels of death," said Reece above the eerie song, lacking in melody and spirit as if a tape player was losing battery power. "Get back. Can't you see? They have knives. They want Mia."

Emma tried to speak, transfixed by the burgeoning crowd of little girls, the song getting louder, the girls in front inching their way forward as more crowded from behind. But her words were lost in the song. The Snake had felt his way along the fence and now stood behind them, shielding himself, holding his AK-47 at the ready.

Someone was climbing over the fence from the government clinic. It was Afewerki, and he too ran to the group. "What?" he said to no one. He stared at the little girls and lost his voice.

"Move back," said Reece. He pointed the pistol from side to side, choosing a target and then another. The little bodies fell with smiles on their faces. And still they pushed in, at least a hundred and growing in number, singing that sickly sweet song. "And washed the spider out!" starting again like a recording. The group was now gathered in front of the dining hut with nowhere left to go but back, but Reece held his ground. The Icelanders had run for the fence.

A semicircle of little Dahlia's began to form around the dining hut, soon cutting off any means of escape, spreading from one side of the compound to the other, enveloping Emma's house. The noise of the song grew louder and then stopped for a few seconds as they took up "Jesus Loves the Little Children."

"Red and yellow, black and white, they are precious in

his sight!"

The group flowed around the dining hut, Reece gesturing with the gun. The Snake was terrified, pointing his rifle at the slow onslaught of little girls. They continued to press in, soon backing the Icelanders and the Snake into the far left corner. Inside the cook house, Zenebek and Misrak screamed for their lives.

The forward wall of little girls pressed in. There were only a few feet left between them and the group. Reece fired into the crowd, and the song jerked as if it were a record, but continued.

"Jesus loves the little children, all the children of the world!"

The Snake was panting, his eyes wide, and he couldn't take it a minute longer and opened fire, spraying the little army with bullets, and little bodies slunk to the ground, but still more came.

Eydis and Svana screamed, backpedaling with their Reece.

"Come! Over the fence!" said Gudmunder. Eydis was stepping into his hand, and he heaved her up. She grabbed at the sharp sticks of the fence and threw herself over, ripping her scrub top. Gudmunder was helping Svana, the Snake screaming for his life. Over went Svana. Over went one Reece. Gudmunder shouted at the Snake and then managed to pull his own bulk to the top of the fence. From there, he watched as the little girls descended on the Snake, hacking into him with their knives.

Reece, Emma, and Afewerki stood their ground with Mia inside the dining hut, panting like dogs.

With his dance over and limping with a pulled groin, Arthur bade the dancing girls goodbye and headed back to see the Abba and Mia, his pockets stuffed with coins and bills, Ethiopian birr. He had to bring Reece there. What came after that, he was not sure. How would he find his way again once Mia had been returned? He imagined living his life in Gadam and hurried even faster, breathing deeply as he trotted, nearly in a run.

Pushing through the thorn trees and brambles, his pants and shirt were rife with tears as he ascended the ladder, being careful of his groin. He knocked at the door, and Mia said, "Come in." The Abba was not there, having returned to the rock chamber. Mia was looking at the ancient book, opened to the page with the pinched Cylinder.

"My dear Mia, we have to bring your father here. He is desperate to find you. Oh, how happy he will be."

"Sir, can you explain this picture?" asked Mia.

Arthur looked surprised. He examined again the colorful illustration, drawn perhaps a thousand years ago. The cherubs, one black at the edge of the page.

"Your father seemed to take some happiness from it, but I'm afraid I have not a clue. It has to do with traveling through time, I think. But your father..."

"Yes, father will be happy to see me, and I need to see him. Can you bring him now?" asked Mia.

"It will require the talents of the Abba Paulos. I shall return." He stopped to catch his breath and hurried toward the green door. From inside was the sound of pick on rock, a steady knock. He stepped down into the dim light. "Abba Paulos?"

The Abba leaned his pick against the wall and brushed dust from his yellow robe. He met Arthur near the entrance, his eyes questioning.

"I know you don't understand, but we need to bring Herr Myers here. Reece Myers. To see his daughter Mia." He pulled the bills from his pocket and held them out, over two hundred birr in all. He then produced the coins.

The Abba nodded his head as if he understood and took the bills and coins. "Ato Reece, abat," meaning father. He held up his finger, meaning that he would need to retrieve the holy vest. He pointed at the empty pedestal.

"Ah, yes," said Arthur. "I understand." He folded his hands behind his back, the urgency of the matter weighing on him, pacing back and forth through the shaft of light.

The Abba returned within minutes, draped in the holy raiment. Arthur marveled at the size of the twelve gemstones. The Abba led him by the elbow in front of the Ark's pedestal and motioned for him to stay there. Arthur was confused. He wanted the Abba to bring Reece, not to be sent to him. He considered that he had no way of telling the Abba this. He would go, and they would return together. It seemed to be the only way. He took a deep breath.

The Abba mumbled to himself and lifted his arms. He would soon know where Reece was as he explored data fur from multiple universes. He began his chant in ancient Ge'ez, and the air began to circulate. He chanted louder, the stones on his vest blazing. His face took on a glow as he found the information for which he was searching. He went to his knees as if drained but stood again, touching each of the stones as his voice grew louder, his countenance glowing. Arthur felt a tremendous surge in his bones, as if they were flooded with lead. His vision blanked, and he was hurtling through blackness, his arms flailing, seeking something firm.

"Arthur!" said Reece. Dahlia had circled the hut. Knife blades thudded on the walls made of poles.

Arthur pulled back the flap and swayed and nearly swooned at the sight of hundreds of little girls, all with the same brown skin and bright golden hair. "Dear God!" A children's song defeated his voice. The voices in unison, out of tune. The ABC song.

"Back!" said Reece. He grabbed Arthur. "Inside!"

Arthur hit his head and fell to his knees. Mia was there, and he marveled. "Mia!"

There was nowhere left to go, and the pistol held only six shots.

"H, I, J, K....!" The sound was deafening.

Reece fired at little hands pulling back the flap, his eyes glazed, drool in the corners of his mouth. Mia hugged his leg, her voice drowned. Arthur knocked over the table. Emma was screaming, Afewerki mute. Dahlia was coming through the flap in the tent, knives raised.

"The world is my will and representation!" said Reece, but he couldn't hear his own voice. He yelled the phrase once more, feeling that his vocal cords would rip...

Reece was face down in grass, snow on his nose. He opened his eyes and lifted his head. "Mia!" She was curled into a ball. He scrambled over the body of Arthur to reach her. "Mia!"

Reece cradled his daughter's head in his arms. She was breathing. The sun was shining. There was the wooden rail of his neighbor's fence, and behind him the house at 47 Asterion Lane. "Oh, Mia." He looked into her face, and her eyes opened.

"Daddy," she said, and he knew that he was finally home.

Reece helped her to sit up and turned his attention to Arthur. He shook his large body, clothed in tattered pants and a shirt. "Arthur!"

Arthur stirred, moving his legs. He opened his eyes, gazing sideways at the ground. He couldn't speak yet and sat up with great effort.

"Arthur, we did it. We're home. Mia is here."

"Daddy," said Mia. "Daddy."

Just down the hill, lying atop one another were Emma and Afewerki. The other Reece was missing.

Reece heard the familiar sound of a sliding glass door and footsteps on the deck, stained cedar red. He turned and saw Kristin, a shocked look on her face.

"Reece? Mia! Oh my God." She tripped and fell, stood, and hurried into the yard, standing there clutching herself.

"Mommy!" said Mia, and she jumped up.

Kristin ran and kneeled beside them, glancing at the figure of Arthur.

"Mommy, Daddy," said Mia.

And in the air there seemed to be a song, a children's song, in perfect tune.